6/6

P9-CDA-724

· LORD BYRON'S NOVEL ·

The Evening Land

ALSO BY JOHN CROWLEY

Otherwise: Three Novels
Beasts
The Deep
Engine Summer

Little, Big

Ægypt

Love & Sleep

Dæmonomania

The Translator

WILLIAM MORROW

An Imprint of HarperCollins*Publishers*

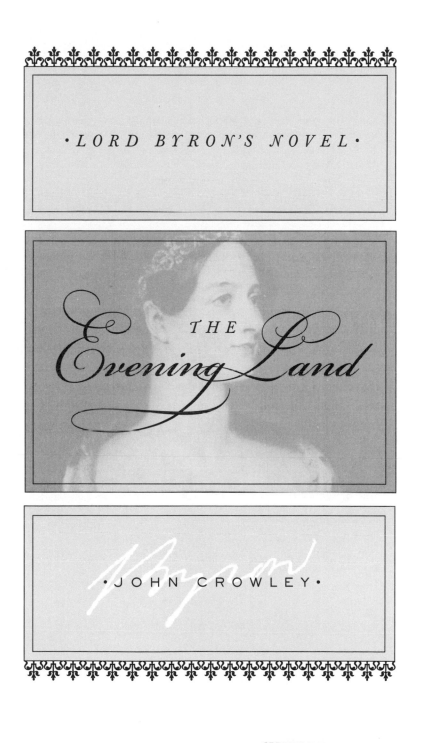

· LORD BYRON'S NOVEL ·

THE
Evening Land

· JOHN CROWLEY ·

LORD BYRON'S NOVEL. Copyright © 2005 by John Crowley. All rights reserved. Printed in the United States of America. No part of this book may be used or reproduced in any manner whatsoever without written permission except in the case of brief quotations embodied in critical articles and reviews. For information address HarperCollins Publishers, 10 East 53rd Street, New York, NY 10022.

HarperCollins books may be purchased for educational, business, or sales promotional use. For information please write: Special Markets Department, HarperCollins Publishers, 10 East 53rd Street, New York, NY 10022.

FIRST EDITION

Designed by Judith Stagnitto Abbate/Abbate Design

Printed on acid-free paper

Library of Congress Cataloging-in-Publication Data

Crowley, John, 1942–
    Lord Byron's novel: the evening land / John Crowley.—1st ed.
        p. cm.
    ISBN 0-06-055658-7
    1. Byron, George Gordon Byron, Baron, 1788–1824—Fiction. 2. Lovelace, Ada King, Countess of, 1815–1852—Fiction. 3. Manuscripts—Collectors and collecting—Fiction. 4. Fiction—Authorship—Fiction. 5. Fathers and daughters—Fiction. 6. Literary historians—Fiction. 7. Poets—Fiction. I. Title: Evening land. II. Title.

PS3553.R597L67 2005
813'.54—dc22
                                                                        2004063575

05 06 07 08 09 WBC/RRD 10 9 8 7 6 5 4 3 2 1

I began a comedy, and burnt it because the scene ran into reality—*a novel, for the same reason. In rhyme, I can keep more away from facts; but the thought always runs through, through . . . yes, yes, through.*

· BYRON, *JOURNAL,* NOVEMBER 17, 1813 ·

· LORD BYRON'S NOVEL ·

The Evening Land

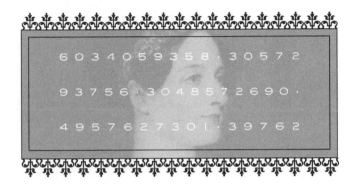

6 0 3 4 0 5 9 3 5 8 · 3 0 5 7 2

9 3 7 5 6 · 3 0 4 8 5 7 2 6 9 0 ·

4 9 5 7 6 2 7 3 0 1 · 3 9 7 6 2

2. British Women of Science

Ada Byron, Countess of Lovelace
Dec. 10, 1815–Nov. 27, 1852
First Computer Program, 1842–1843

Ada Byron was the daughter of the Romantic poet George Gordon, Lord Byron, and Anne Isabella Milbanke, who separated from Byron just a month after Ada was born. Four months later, Byron left England forever. Ada was raised by her mother, Lady Byron, and had no further contact with her father (who died in Greece in 1824).

Lady Byron had a penchant for mathematics, and saw to it that Ada was tutored in mathematics, science, and other topics rather than in literature and poetry, to counter any tendencies she might have inherited from her father, who was famous for being "mad, bad, and dangerous to know." Ada built her imagination on science, from electricity to biology to neuroscience. She earned fame in scientific circles. An anonymous Victorian best-seller about evolution (*Vestiges of the Natural History of Creation*) was widely believed to be hers, though it wasn't.

In 1835, Ada married William King, ten years her senior, and became Countess of Lovelace in 1838. Ada had three children; her younger son was named Byron, and later became Viscount Ockham.

Ada's friend of many years was Charles Babbage, a professor of mathematics at Cambridge and the inventor of the Difference Engine. This large machine, which took years to design and build, was actually more of a calculator than a computer, using the "method of finite   >>

differences" to cast logarithm tables and make other calculations. Ada met Babbage in 1833, when she was just 17.

Babbage had made plans in 1834 for a new kind of calculating machine, an Analytical Engine, which (as Ada perceived) truly was a forerunner of the modern computer—it could be programmed to produce (and print out!) results of many kinds. Ada noted that the Analytical Engine could weave algebraic patterns just as a Jacquard loom could weave birds and flowers. (Jacquard's loom wove patterns determined by a sequence of punch cards.) In 1842, an Italian mathematician, Louis Menebrea, published a memoir in French on the subject of the Analytical Engine. Babbage asked Ada to translate the memoir, and she added a set of Notes longer than the memoir, which expounded the vast possibilities of such a machine, and included a small program of step-by-step instructions that the proposed machine could follow to solve a particular problem. However brief and primitive, this is the first workable computer program—an instruction set that a machine can follow to reach a result.

Ada died of cancer in 1852, at the age of 36, and was buried beside the father she never knew. [AN]

[NOTE: *Page still under construction*]

| Home | Next | Previous | About Strong Woman Story | Search |

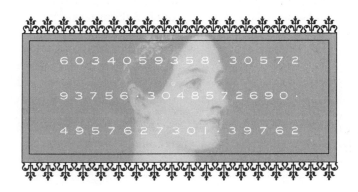

ONE

In which a Man is baited by a

Bear, and of the precedents of this

OBSERVE—BUT NO! No one may observe, save the unfeeling Moon, who sails without progress through the clouds—a young Lord, who on the ramparts of his half-ruined habitation keeps a late watch. Wrapt in a Scotch mantle little different from that worn in all times by his ancestors—and not on the Scotch side alone—he has a light sword buckled on, a curved and bejewelled one not of this northern land's manufacture. He has two pocket pistols as well, made by Mantons—for this is a year in the present century, tho' what the youth may see in the moon's light is much as it has been for these past seven or eight. There is the old battlement that faces to the North, whereon he stands, whose stones he rests his hand upon. Beyond, he sees the stony cliff, bearded in gorse and heather, that builds toward the mountains, and—for his eye is preternaturally sharp—the thread of a track that for aye has ascended it. Black against the tumbled sky is the top of a farther watchtower, reached by that selfsame track. Farther on, in the darkness, lie a thousand acres of Caledonian wilds and habitations: to which this outwatching youth is heir. His name, the reader will perhaps not expect to hear, is Ali.

Against what enemy does he go armed? In truth he knows of none—not his servants asleep in the hall below—not bandits, or rivals of his clan and the Laird his father, such as might once have threatened from the dark.

1   The Laird his father! The reader will remember the man, if the reader be one who listens to tales in London theatre-boxes, or frequents race-courses, or hells; if he have haunted Supper-clubs, or places with less euphuistical names; known Courts, or Law-courts. John Porteous—who inherited, on the death of his own amazed and helpless sire, the singularly inappropriate title Lord Sane—was a catalogue of sins, not only the lesser ones of Lust and Gluttony but the greater ones of Pride, Anger and Envy. He wasted his own substance, and when it was gone wasted that of his wife and tenants, and then borrowed, or coerced, more from his terrified acquaintanceship, who knew well enough that the Lord would stint at nothing in revealing their own indiscretions, to which often as not *he* had tempted them in decades past. 'Black-mail' was a word he professed to shudder at: he never, he said, employed the mails. What he spent these gains upon, however got, seemed less of interest to him than the expenditure itself; he was always ready to tear down what he contrived to possess, just in the moment of possession. It was just such an outrageous act of destruction that had earned him the sobriquet, in a time that liked to bestow such, of 'Satan'. He was a wicked man, and he took a devilish delight in it—when he was not in his rage, or maddened by some obstacle to his desire; indeed a fine fellow, in his way, and of a large circle. He had travelled extensively, seen the Porte, walked beneath the Pyramids, sired (it was said without proof) litters of dark-skinned pups in various corners of the South and East.

2   Of late 'Satan' Porteous has kept much to his wife's Scotch

estates, which he has improved and despoiled in equal measure. Onto the ancient towers and battlements and the ruined chapel a former Laird added a Palladian wing of great size and bleak aspect, ruining himself in the process; there the present Laird kept Lady Sane, well out of the fashionable world and indeed out of the world entire. She is rumoured to have gone mad, and as far as Lord Sane's heir knew of her, she is not all of sound mind. The lady's fortune 'Satan' ran through long before—then when he had need of funds, he squeezed his tenants, and sold the timber on his parks and grounds to be cut, which increased the melancholy sense of ruination there far more than did the windowless chapel open to the owl and the fox. The trees grew a hundred years; the money's already spent. He keeps a tame bear, and an American lynx, and he stands them by him when he calls his son before him.

Yes, it is he, his father, Lord Sane, of whom Ali is afraid, though the man is this night nowhere nearby—with his own eyes Ali saw his Lordship's coach depart for the South, four blacks pulling with all their strength as the coachman lashed them. Yet he is afraid, as afraid as he is brave; his very being seems to him but a candle-flame, and as easily put out.

The Moon was past midheaven when, shivering tho' not from cold, Ali retired. His great Newfoundland dog Warden lay by his bed, so fast asleep he hardly roused at his master's familiar tread. Oldest, and only true, friend! Ali pressed for a moment his face into the dog's neck. He then drank the last of a cup of wine, into which a minim of Kendals drops were dropt. Nevertheless he did not undress—only wrapt his mantle close about him, his pistols within reach—propped his watchful head upon cold pillows—and—believing he would not sleep—he slept.　3　4

In deep darkness he woke, feeling upon him a heavy hand. He was one quick to wake, and might have leapt up, taking up the pistol near at hand—but he did not—he lay as motionless as though still asleep, for the face that looked into his, tho' known to him, was not a man's. A black face, the eyes small and yellow, and the little light shone upon teeth as long as daggers. It was *his father's tame bear,*　5 the hand upon him its hand!

Having ascertained that Ali was awake, the black beast turned away and trotted across the chamber floor. At the door, which stood ajar, it looked back at Ali, and what it would convey in its looking back was evident: it meant Ali to follow it.

The young Lord arose. What had become of his dog Warden? How came the door to be unbolted? The questions appeared in his mind and then vanished, unanswered, like bubbles. He took up his curved sword, tossed back his tartan cloak, and the bear—as soon as it saw that Ali intended to follow—stood to a man's height, pushed open the door, fell again upon its four feet, and went ahead down the dark stair. It seemed odd that no one else in the house had roused, but this thought vanished too as soon as thought. Ever and again the bear turned back its great head to see that the young Lord followed after, and went on. Tho' he may stand on two legs to startle and amaze his enemies or reach the fruit on a high branch, the black bear goes on four legs like a dog for preference; and tho' his claws and teeth rival the lion's, he is a mild gentleman, and prefers a meatless mess.

Thinking this—and nothing else of all the things he might be thinking, on such an errand—Ali went out through the blasted park and across the arch of a narrow bridge flung in a former time over a tumbling flood, then away from the road and up the white clay track which, before, his eye had traced in the moonlight, toward the watchtower. And—mysterious—the Moon had made no further progress across the sky, but shone as and where it had, and the wind blew coldly, come across the Atlantic, and the Irish isles, and America—this Ali pondered, who had not ever seen those places—and he walked along behind the inkblot of his ursine guide as though a little afloat on the way, as though no effort were asked of him to mount.

The watchtower stood ahead, and the bear lifted itself again to stand as a man does, and with a curved yellow nail indicated it. The door at its base was long fallen away, and a light could be seen, dull and guttering, within.

'I may not go farther,' said the bear, and Ali took note of its speech without wonder. 'What lies in yonder tower is for thee alone to find. Do not mourn; for sure I shall not, for he has been as cruel to me, nay to all dumb things whatever, as to thee. Farewell! If ever thou shall see me after, think that thy time is come, and a different journey is to go on.'

Ali was of a mind to seize the beast, beg or demand to be told more, but it was already faded, as it were, upon the dark air, only its words remaining. Ali turned toward the tower and its light.

Thereupon the world and the night gave a sort of shudder, as a shudder may pass over a calm sea, or a horse's flank; and like a building fallen around him in an earthquake, the Night fell away in pieces, his Sleep shattered, and he awoke. He had slept, and *dreamt!* And yet—most strange—still he found himself on the track to the watchtower, which stood ahead—more far off than in his vision, and a deal more solidly made of stone and mortar, but the same— the earth and the air likewise—and his own Self. He had no knowl- edge that such somnambulations—as they are termed—could be;—knew not how it could be that in a dream he could have armed himself, gone out his House, climbed a Hill, and not tum- bled down and broke his neck. A species of wonder flew over him like an icy draught—and *dread* too, as icy but contracting to his heart, for he could see, even from where he stood, that there was, as in his dream, a small light within the tower.

Now the Moon was almost down. He felt, as much as per- ceived, the way ahead. Not once did he think to turn back, and later would consider why he had not:—because he had been told to go on—because it lay ahead—because he could do no other.

Not only the door but all the floors within this ancient pile were decayed and fallen away, no trace left of them, the tower hollow as a whitened marrow bone, the top open and a few stars visible. Oth- erwise blackness, and the single light, a lantern that burned its last drop of oil as though gasping for breath. He must turn, Ali must, to see what thing the lantern's shuttered beam fell upon—was *aimed* upon, certainly of a purpose!—and he finds, some three feet in the air, a form like a man's—face black, eyes starting from their sockets as they stare upon him, black tongue thrust out as in mockery. The strong rope from which this form depends is strung from the upper floor's stone brackets, and winds about him like a spider's thread. It is no devil from Hell, caught in his own toils—and yet, it is all we know of such in this our earthly life—and his name is Legion. The man in the ropes is 'Satan' Porteous, Ali's father, Lord Sane, DEAD!

OW A YOUTH bearing the name of the Prophet's son-in-law, a youth whose skin was bronze and whose eyes were onyx, came to reside in a far land nearby to Thule, where blue-eyed boys with hair of tow or straw sprout palely beneath the low-lying sun, may not be beyond conjecture—ships and carriages care not whom they transport, nor from where to where else, and many a London house can boast a blackamoor at the gate, or a turbanned Hindoo at table-side. But that such an one should not only be resident in a Scotch Thane's house but its Heir—that, as it seemed by the ghastly sight that transfixed him there in the tower, he was now in very truth the successor to the bound and strangulated Lord who seemed to stare back at him, and possessor of all his titles and his fiefdoms—*that* may be thought to merit explication.

In spite of his being brought thence at an early age—or perhaps because of it, for the Heart obeys its own logic and no other in respect of the workings of Memory—Ali retained an unclouded vision of his childhood land. For sure he knew not, when he was a child, what mother had borne him, nor what his father was, or had been—he was accounted an Orphan, and had always lived with an aged guardian in a simple cot, or *han,* in the mountains of the province of Ochrida in high Albania—amid scenes which, if ever as a child he pondered the question, he would have believed began with himself, at the beginning of Time: and surely of these mountains it can be said, as of few human habitations, that they have persisted unchanged since Adam's day, or at least Abraham's.

He tended flocks, as his forebears always had: his goats provided his milk and his meat, his wide Albanian belt, and his sandals—when he put on such, which was not often. They demanded little enough tending, for in that country the goats are left daylong to their own devices, which are many; you may come upon them in the deepest wood, or see them hanging on the high rocks' highest point, like the goats in Virgil, and only when they are gathered in the evening, and the children with their sticks drive them within the walls, do they appear to be at all domesticated. In the Winter Ali and his fellows took them to the mountains, and in Summer drove them again to the warmer plains; and, the harvest being done and the vintage taken in, the goats were let out upon the vineyards, where they ate and contended and disported themselves—with Bacchus' blessing—in the expected manner, to their masters' increase. All the ancestry that our Thane-to-be knew of, was that old man—a Shepherd, rapidly going blind from the open fires within his *han,* whose smoke exited, or more often did *not* exit, from a hole in the roof. Few Albanians can reach a very advanced age without suffering to some degree the effects. Tenderly Ali saw to his needs—and brought him his flat-bread, his bowl of coffee, his *chibouque* to smoke in the evening. The touch of this old blind man—as rough and plain as though he were only the eldest of the goats they tended—was much of what Ali knew of love: though not *all.*

For there was another child who was also given into the old man's care—a girl, whose name was Iman, not more than a year older than Ali, orphaned like himself—or so they believed and said, what time they spoke of it, which was not often—for as children do, they thought not to ask the world why and wherefore they had come to be as they were, content to know themselves, and one another, as they knew the heat of the sun, and the taste of the mountain's water-springs. Her hair was as the raven's wing, but her eyes—as is not uncommon in that land—were *blue,* not the blue of our Anglo-Saxon blondes but the blue of the deep Sea—and into those frank and wide orbs, so seldom cast down, Ali fell entirely. Poets talk of maidens' *eyes,* and divagate endlessly upon them, and we are to understand that by those liquid spheres they mean to indicate all the beloved object's parts and attractions—which we are free to speculate upon. Yet Ali was hardly conscious of what other charms his little goddess possessed—in her eyes he did indeed drown, and could not, when she looked upon him, look away.

In another, colder clime, Ali forgot progressively that language he had first lisped in, and grown up to speak; but he never forgot what *she* said to him, or what he answered; the words were not as other words, they seemed as though minted in gold, and even long after to speak them over to himself was to enter a little treasure-house where they alone were kept. Of what did they two speak? Of everything—of nothing; they were silent, or she spoke, and he answered not; or he boasted wildly, his eyes upon hers, to see if his tale would *keep* her—and she listened. 'Iman, go thou the long way—these flints will cut thy feet.'—'Ali—Take this bread of mine, I have enough for two.'—'What do you see in that cloud? I see a hawk with a great beak.'—'I see a fool who makes hawks out of clouds.'—'I must go for water. Come with me—I sha'n't be long— Take my hand and come!'

They two were the only souls in that land—each the only object of the other's thought. As two swans take their turns to lift their wide wings and thresh the air, and walk upon the water for each other's delight—*what* they spoke of was of no matter—so that their intercourse continued, and was repeated. She—imperious as a queen, bare-foot though she was—could cause and *did* cause suffering when she chose—perhaps only to test her power, as one might test a stick against a hapless blossom; soon enough she was sorry, and they again compounded, with many caresses and offerings of kindness.

It may be averred that a passion of such degree is not possible in one so young—for Ali had hardly reached his second decade— and it is perfectly logical for them to think so *who have never felt it*— such ones we may not persuade, and so do not address:—whoever has known such a feeling in earliest youth has known a singular power, and will keep a memory of it in his inmost heart, which— though against it no other and later may be *measured*—yet it will be the Touchstone against which all others will be struck, to see if they be true gold, or counterfeit.

Throughout that time it was seen that Ali—though in truth the lad took no particular notice of it—was marked in an especial way; favours and gifts came upon him from sources unclear—a delicacy of victuals—a bright scarf for his head—a look of approval or of interest from his elders. On his reaching a particular anniversary—though *which* year in his short life it was, he did not know, for an uncertainty surrounded his birth-date as it did his true ancestry—he received, from the same font of benefactions, an old pistol, which he was proud to stick in his belt, only sorry that it must reside there all alone, where all men of the least standing carried two at a minimum and a dagger or short sword beside. He never had occasion to discharge this piece, having no powder given him along with it—and this was likely to have been a lucky thing, as in that country such old weapons—though finely worked upon the stock in silver—were often neglected in their barrels, and locks—and commonly burst—or burned the hand that used them.

Thus armed in manly wise, and having a firm compact with his Iman, he went to the *han* to seek out the old shepherd, who was in his eyes the rule and wisdom of his world, and finding him among the men around the common fire, told him that it was his intention to have the girl for his wife.

'That you cannot,' said the old one, responding as gravely as he had been demanded of. 'For she is your sister.'

'How is it she can be my sister?' Ali responded. 'My father is unknown, and who my mother was, that matters not.' Indeed it mattered much—to *him*—who that lady might have been—and in his throat there came a catch when he made this bold dismissal—he must rest his hand upon his weapon, and set his feet apart, and lift his chin, so it would not be noticed; but in the *legal* sense he was correct, and the old man acknowledged it with a nodding of his head: no inheritance comes through the mother alone.

'And yet she is your own clan and kin,' said he to Ali. 'She is your sister still.' For among those clans of Albania's mountains, *brother* and *sister* can name any blood relation in the same generation, and a connexion in the tenth or even the twelfth degree is forbidden. And now round the fire those who sat on the men's side—and those on the other side spinning their distaves—had taken notice of Ali's suit, and he heard laughter.

'I will have no other, I say, and so says she,' he said in a big voice, at which the laughers laughed the more, and nodded and puffed their pipes, as though delighted that one so young should kick against the pricks,—or because they thought it a great jest that such a claim should be *asserted,* which never could be made good. Ali thereupon—knowing himself for the first time mocked because he knew not the world's ways—which were not *his own*—looked upon them all in anger, and—lest he weep—turned on his heel, and went out, pursued by further and louder cackles of glee; and for a time he would speak to no one, and answer naught when spoken to: even if it were Iman herself.

A little later he received a mark of distinction different in kind from those he bore already. On a certain night he was taken among the women, and the eldest beldame laid bare the boy's arm, and with her best and sharpest needle—the old shepherd guiding her hand with his words—she punctured repeatedly the skin of Ali's right arm. The blood welled darkly at each small wound, and yet the boy grit his teeth—and would *not* cry out—and at length was formed there a rayed circle, and within it a serpentine mark that might be seen to be a *sigma*—tho' for sure not by those unlettered folk. The old woman, humming and clacking with her tongue to soothe the boy, daubed the place now and again with a clout of lamb's-wool, and studied her work as any craftsman might, and here deepened and there enlarged—till Ali nearly fainted—though no complaint had yet escaped his lips. Then finally his tormentor took a pinch of gunpowder, and rubbed it in the pin-holes she made—let whoso has had gunpowder by any chance touch an open sore bethink him what Ali felt then, as the beldame's thumb pressed the stuff in, and rubbed it well, and mingled it so with flesh and blood as to color it forever. Then—as we see on the limbs of the sailors of all nations, not excepting our own most *civilised* one—there was impressed upon Ali's right arm a mark that (supposing the arm remained attached to the body, a thing not to be regarded as certain in that land, or among those people) could never be erased. A common thing it is indeed in those mountains, and any man might show one or two such—but the mark upon Ali was of a new design, and all who saw it knew it.

Upon his release from this cruel *typographer,* Ali sought out the company of his little love, and they two walked alone, and it may be that with her he permitted himself to shed a tear from pain, or perhaps he was brave Ali still. Surely she comforted him—and gazed with wonder upon the new mark—and fain would touch it— and he suffered her—for sharp and deep and lasting as it was, there was another and a deeper, in a place that could not be *seen*—he knew, but could not say!

I N THE LAST DECADE of that century, the Empress of Russia, infamous Catherine, advanced, with her ministers, a scheme—one of many such, which persist among the Czars her heirs to this day—to overcome Constantinople and dissolve the Porte; and to advance this scheme, she compounded with the mountain peoples of Suli, and of Illyricum, and Albania, promising them freedom and the rule of their nations when the Turk their oppressor was defeated. They rose at her promise—who were accustomed to rise without any such—though now with greater fury, and in larger numbers. Not long afterwards, Great Catherine changed her mind—for she was, however Imperial, however Great, a *woman*— and the campaign against the Sultan was abandoned—and a treaty signed—and many marks of eternal peace and amity exchanged. The fighters of the Highlands were thereupon abandoned by their Russian allies, and the Sultan's vengeance upon them was simply this, that he withdrew from their lands his own Governors and Generals, and gave rein to the freebooters and brigand chieftains, who had no longer any constraints upon their activities—which consisted only of robbing, murdering, slave-taking, extortion of tribute, and otherwise of contesting with one another, the best man to win. In this way the Sultan's retribution was exacted for him, and he needed merely to watch and see which of the rivals would defeat the others, and pile their skulls upon the plain—on him the Sublime, the Merciful, could then bestow the title of Pacha.

The tyger who ate all the other tygers bore the same name as our young hero, and would come to rule over wide lands, with his seat at Jannina—a *pachalick* greater than any forged there before him, and an army so large that the Sultan in Constantinople was pleased to call him vassal, without daring to demand much in the way of further duty from him. His fame spread widely, in the Gazettes and the foreign newspapers he was now and then called the *Buonaparte of the East,* he had even commendation from the *other* Buonaparte, whom he actually equalled in deeds, given that he had smaller compass—*proportionally* as many of heads removed, life-blood spilled, Widows and Orphans made, eyes put out, villages razed and livestock and vintage despoiled—though no more than the *European's* were his wars and his arms able to dry a single tear, or cure the least sorrow: and so much for Greatness, in the little or in the large.

8   This Pacha was preparing his armies to fall upon the lands that our Ali's clan inhabited—for those stern people had refused allegiance to him, and to his titular overlord of the Porte. They had cut the throats of his messengers—this being the common response among those peoples when a request is to be declined—and the Pacha had grown impatient. He had a grandson, too, a pretty boy-Pacha, as bedight with jewels and daubed with paint as a Mayfair hostess—for the mighty of the East love so to adorn their cherished Sons, and it does not spoil their characters—at least this one's was not spoiled, for he desired lands as fiercely as Papa did, and heads to chop off ditto, and enemies to spit and roast. The Cohorts were now readied, the turbanned soldiers gathered by the hundreds within and without the great courtyard of the palace at Tepelene, the kettle-drums were beat, the ululations were sounding from the Minaret, when a visitor, a Bey from the northern lands the Pacha had earlier conquered, appeared and begged for an audience—for he had a *boon* to ask—and a story to tell—and when, in an upper room the pipes had been called for and lit, and the lengthy compliments paid, and the coffee drunk—he told it.

A dozen years before, this Bey related, he was traversing those lands which (as everyone well knew) the Pacha now intended to subdue and attach to his *pachalick*. His purpose in journeying there had been that he might shoot, if he could find one, a son of a family in that region, with whom his own family was *in blood*—engaged in a blood feud whose beginning the eldest of their families could not remember, and whose end might come never, for when the brave and desperate men of one family despatched a son or cousin in the first or the tenth degree of the other—with a single shot, commonly, for they take careful aim; or perhaps with the edge of an *ataghan* suddenly cold against the throat; at night by the lonely path, or in the public market at the blaze of noon—then it became the duty of the other to renew the vengeance.

(As in other matters, the Albanians are by us accounted 'lawless' for their incessant feuds, in which blood must answer blood; yet they are in fact bound, like the Greeks of Æschylus, by the sternest of Laws, from which there is no appeal. Of murder they have a horror no different from that of other peoples, and for the taker of life there is ample and swift punishment—when the murderer can be found—but still the higher law of Honour knows no exceptions, and to fail to fulfill it is universal and inexpungible shame. *Our* laws—when we choose to obey them at all—lie far more lightly upon us.)

Thus, the Bey explained, he had done the deed of vengeance expected of him, and cleansed his Honour, and thereupon had fled into the hills, hotly pursued by his victim's relatives, who were intent on taking their turn in the game, and removing an opposing man from the board. His horse having stumbled and been lamed, he was on foot—suffering severely from thirst and hunger—and growing delirious. He sought a Cave into which he might creep, knowing his enemies were near, but was unable to go further—he heard the sound of their horses drawing nigh, and their voices crying upon him—and he readied himself for a brief defence, and likely death. Then there came another noise—the sound of another troop of horse, coming from another direction—and as he watched, this new company appeared before him, interposing themselves between him and his pursuers. The Captain of this troop was an Englishman, though such were at that time so rare in the fastnesses of Albania that the frightened Bey did not recognize this—his scarlet tunic frogged in gold, his high boots and white gloves, were outlandish indeed though dusty and soiled and out at heel, and his followers a mixed party of hired Suliote warriors, a few men in red like their leader though not so splendid, and a Turkish sipahi. What caused them to take the embattled Bey's side in his quarrel, the Bey himself did not know, but their numbers—and the Suliote guns—and the British soldiers—all persuaded the pursuing band to slink away. The grateful Bey, making deep obeisance before the Englishman, felt himself taken up and looked upon with a Gaze neither warm nor cool—neither reassuring nor alarming—the indifferent gaze of a beast, or a head carved in stone: at which the Bey felt his heart turn cold within him. Nevertheless he made it known to his saviour that all he had was now his, his Life and Goods were his to command, and that he desired nothing more than to offer his oath of Brotherhood in perpetuity—which the Englishman was seemingly disposed to accept. That evening, then, the much-restored Bey and the great Englishman became Brothers, in the usual fashion—that is, they pricked each a forefinger, and dropt a few drops of blood—the Bey pleased to observe that the other's was as red as his own, and thus that he was a man and not a *Jinn*—into a cup of wine, of which they both drank.

'Now,' the Bey asked of his new relation (for the ritual they had partaken of made them as truly kin as if they had been sired by the same Father), 'tell me, if you will, why you have come into this country, and where you go.'—'That I shall not,' said the Englishman (he spoke through the Turk, who alone was fluent in both tongues), 'for the reasons are not such as would bring honour to you to know. Where I go, I know not, for I confess to you that at this moment I know not where I *am*.'—'As to that,' said the Bey, 'I can instruct you; and now my house, which is not two days' travel away, is yours; go there, give to my steward this ring, and you shall receive all that you require. For myself, I must avoid the place, as my enemies will wait upon me in that neighbourhood; but when they have been disappointed in their aim, and gone away, then you and I will meet there again.'—'Done,' said the Englishman; and in the dawn they parted ways.

Some time later, when the Bey felt it safe to return to his house, he found it not as he had left it. The Englishman and all his troop had gone, after making free, as it seemed, with the Bey's stores and his stable. His Wife—the youngest of his three, the best-beloved, the most beautiful, the blue-eyed—hid from him, in fear—or shame—or both, and the reason became clear enough in time: whether by force or suasion, the great *Redcoat* had helped himself to the one thing belonging to his Brother that he might not, and there would be fruit of his transgression.

The unhappy Bey, out of respect for the brotherhood he still and irrevocably held with the Englishman, would not slay this wife on the *spot,* as another man might, and as he had every right to do—and here the Pacha nodded in entire agreement—but instead contained his anger, and waited, till the child was born, a goodly lad, and well-made—after which the poor woman was unprotected, and shortly suffer'd the long-postponed wrath of her husband. Her child he soon sent away to the far limits of that country, with an old Shepherd for his only protector: to this old man the Bey communicated a certain sign, with which, if the boy lived, he desired him to be marked.

Now the years had passed—the Bey's own sons had fallen to the horrid exigencies of feud, and one by one been murdered by the sons and grandsons of the men their father and their uncles and grandsires had long ago murdered; and the Bey repented of his stern rigor in that time—he better remembered his beloved wife, so like a gazelle, and his love for her. Therefore he asked that he be allowed to accompany, or *precede,* the Pasha's forces into that land, and seek out the boy—whom he would know by the mark he bore, which the Bey now drew in the dust of the floor for the Pacha to study—and whom he intended to restore to his House, and take for his own. And should any of the Pacha's soldiers come first upon him, if he be in arms, the Bey begged that the boy's life be spared, and that he be remanded to him.

The Pacha heard his supplicant out—and ply'd him subtly with further questions—and fell to thinking, and to tugging at his wonderful beard, and stroking it and smelling of it, as though wisdom might come to him of itself out of it; and he clapped his hands for his servants to fill his guest's pipe and cup, and intimated that what he asked might be done, *if it were possible*—the Bey would have his answer in time—and he then went on to speak of other matters.

The honest Bey took his leave of the Pacha, and set out upon his road. Immediately the Pacha sent certain men after him—and if that Bey ever reached his home and his *haram* again, those men sent in pursuit of him would not afterward dare to be seen as far as the Pacha's power reached, which was to the ends of the earth as they conceived it. Soon thereafter the Pacha's horde fell upon the lands where Ali's adopted clan had for lifetimes lived and herded, to bring their Chiefs into subjection, and their tribute into his Coffers.

There is that in human hearts—and not only in hearts that have learned from written Histories, or the orations of Statesmen—which loves Liberty above Life; and which greater oppression only enlarges—for 'like the chamomile, the more it is trodden upon, the faster it grows'—which may well be true, of *chamomile,* though I cannot say so of my own experience; of *Liberty,* I know that the Suliote women who, pursued by the Pacha's troops in an earlier time, and seeing all lost, threw themselves with their babes in their arms from the height of the Zalongue rocks rather than surrender, acknowledged no higher good; and were not persuaded to prefer Tyranny above even the direst and last alternative.

The Ochridans, freedom-loving like the Suliotes, but not so famed for fierceness, ran before the wind of the Pacha's forces—among which were now many hired Suliote warriors, be it said—bearing what goods they could upon their backs or in their wooden carts, and leaving their simple cots to burn behind them. Ali and Iman, driving their complaining goats before, hurried through the valleys to the North, but their flight was as vain as a coracle's, that rows beneath the storm-wave's fall; before they could see the foe that came upon them they could *feel* the hoofbeats in their own bare feet. The men of their clan—holding a high point, and resisting the onrush with cries and gunfire (more cries than gunfire, for they were but poor in arms as in much else) only to win time for their women and children to escape—vain hope!—are soon ridden over; Ali turns in his flight to see a great Stallion bear down upon him and Iman, the man upon its back lifting a glittering curved sword on high, and the wind lifting in turn his capote around him, his teeth bared like a wolf's as though he meant to employ them too in vastation. Ali draws his weapon, charged with the single ball and jot of powder he has been able to appropriate; he stands before his Lady, and aims—none who has not withstood a charging Suliote horseman will know his courage!—and fires, or rather misfires—yet the rider pulls up, so violently as almost to bring down horse and self alike. His wolvish teeth now displayed in a gladsome smile, he takes hold of Ali's arm, that still bears the useless pistol; he sees the mark upon it—laughs in delight, for the Pacha has announced a prize, and he has won it!—and with a single mighty swinge he lifts the boy (who will always be slight, though strong and well-formed) upon his horse's crupper. Iman, seeing this, shrinks not, flees not, hesitates for not a moment before she attacks the horseman with her little fists, a tyger—and for a moment it seems the roaring warrior may lose his prize, having both to keep the boy astride and the furious girl away—what madness has the Devil visited upon the two, that they will not part?—but at length he kicks his steed, and Ali is borne away too swiftly to free himself. Iman races after him calling his name, and Ali's own free hand (the other being clasped in the strong grip of the warrior) still reaches out toward her as though it might somehow cross the widening gap between them—as his heart, his soul, *does* cross it, borne on the cry he makes, leaving his breast as though for ever, to remain with her. The grievous cries of children, endlessly multiplied! Surely they must storm Heaven, surely to them the ears of even the hardiest of brigands must attend, and their hearts be softened—and indeed they do attend, sometimes, but not very often—only a little more often, perhaps, than does Heaven.

Ali's captor now turned back, against the swell of battle, if battle it could be named, and kicked harder his horse's flank; and Ali, who had before tried with all his might to leap from his bounding perch upon the beast's rump, now in fear clung to the rider, lest he be flung from that height down upon the stones, or under the hooves. When some leagues had been put between the two of them and the Pacha's still-advancing forces, the warrior slowed his pace; and Ali—already farther from home and familiar scenes than he had ever been—had no choice but to keep his seat, and bounce along into what might come. No word had yet passed between him and the rider—perhaps they would not have understood each other's *dialect*—and indeed there was nothing to say—for Ali knew not what to ask, and the other would not have answered. When the day was at length drowned in green evening, they made their camp, and the brigand gave food to his captive, and, smiling upon him as before, bade him with many gestures to eat his fill; but when they retired—upon the ground, beneath the blanket of their capotes, and the black tester of the infinite spangled night—he tied Ali's wrists to his own wrist by a thong of leather. Then did Ali beg to know what was to become of him, and why he alone had been rapt from the catastrophe of his people and his beloved; whereupon—whether he understood, or did not—the fellow ceased to grin, and waggled at Ali a long and dirty finger, expressive of Prohibition and Silence, and turned to sleep. Ali at his side wept, when he thought he would not be heard: wept, for Iman—for his old Mentor—for his goats, whose familiar names he spoke in silent syllables—for the life of slavery he had reason to be certain was all that was to come.

But instead—and one who has read the tale thus far will not be astonished to learn it—he was brought after many stages to the Pacha's house in Tepelene, the largest and finest he had ever seen, not as a slave but as an honoured Guest. He was brought before the Pacha himself, who smiled upon him, and caressed his dark curls— took his hands in his own, and look'd gloatingly upon the mark he bore—placed him on his silken Sopha at his right hand, and gave him sugared nuts, and sweetmeats, while his own grandson look'd on shocked and affronted. When we know nothing at all of the world beyond a single valley and its slopes and vineyards, then we are perhaps not so amazed at the things that befall when we are suddenly and swiftly transported beyond it, having no means to form expectations. Ali took no exception to his treatment by the smiling old tyrant, and was moved neither to gratitude nor devotion; he put on without question the rich apparel that was given him, consisting of a long white kilt of softest wool, a gold-worked cloak, an embroidered vest heavy as a breastplate, great belt, and a scarf for his head of as many colors as Joseph's coat. Only the sword that the Pacha himself put in his hands, curved and brilliant like the Devil's smile and meant as much for hurt, moved him, and caused him to speak—he vowed that *he would not ever after be parted from it:* nor would he, till years had passed, and a stern magistrate demanded its surrender—but all that was long to come, in a far land he yet knew naught of. How he went thither, and what then befell him, all remains to be told; however, having proffered more than sufficient matter for a Chapter, I shall here break my page, and rest my pen.

9

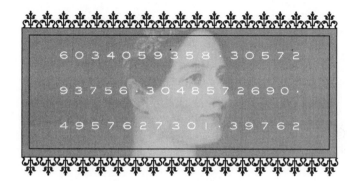

From: "Smith" <anovak@strongwomanstory.org>
To: "Thea" <thea.spann133@ggm.edu>
Subject: Hey

Sweetie—
Here I am, here I really am. God what a trip that is. I know you said
so but jeez. I think that pill you gave me was the wrong one—it was
sposed to be a valium right—well I took it somewhere out over the
Atlantic and had a mini-bottle of wine and slept 20 minutes and then
I was AWAKE from then on, and jittery and anxious—are you sure it
wasn't some kind of upper? And then you get to London and it's
dawn of the next day, though it should be like two in the morning,
and you can't get in your hotel till noon—what do you do? Well I put
my stuff in the Left Luggage at the train station and went walking.
In the RAIN. I had my raincoat but I needed an umbrella. I went to
the Lost Property Office—remember Frankie told us that was such
a great place? And I wrote down the address? Well it is great—
and they had hundreds of umbrellas people had left on trains—and
briefcases and hats and PRAMS (?what happened to the babies?)
and books and bundles. The little guy there was so cute—with sus-
penders (I mean braces) and a tie tucked in his shirt and a little
toothbrush moustache. He showed me umbrellas. I got a Swain
Adeney. The absolute best. He said so. It's got a big thick handle of
some kind of bamboo. "You can use it as a cosh," the guy said, and
showed me.

So now anyway I'm in Bloomsbury and the room Georgiana got me is nice and I don't know how I can still be awake, I feel like any second I'm just going to pitch forward onto the keyboard. It's still too early to call you. I get to meet Georgiana at five. For TEA and talk about what to do next. I am a little nervous. I've never seen a picture of her even, but I know just what she's going to look like. Do you ever have this thing where you set out on some trip that seemed like a good idea and suddenly it feels like you jumped off a cliff, or contracted a disease you'll never shake, and all you want is to be home. O that my love were in my arms and I in my bed again. The small rain down can rain. Write me. I love you.

Smith

———————————

From: "Thea" <thea.spann133@ggm.edu>
To: "Smith" <anovak@strongwomanstory.org>
Subject: RE:Hey

babe so good to get the note and find youre not in the
drink   maybe having a drink tho thats good
listen you know thats the first time you ever wrote that   i l y   you
did say it a couple of times   thats important   or maybe it isnt
but listen heres something   i went to dinner with barb and some
of the craftspeople   those people she knows   they were nice but
sometimes I dont have much to say to them   you know   about
yarn or wood or whatever   but they were asking about me   getting the biz on me   and I talked about you and I said the woman
whos my partner   thats the first time Ive said that   partner   it
just came out   then i worried   is it okay

anyway i l y 2

me

———————————

From: "Smith" <anovak@strongwomanstory.org>
To: "Thea" <thea.spann133@ggm.edu>
Subject: RE:Re:Hey

Howdy, podner—

Tea with Georgiana was *not* just what I thought. She lives in St. John's Wood, which isn't a wood, just a part of town, a nice part; an old messy apartment, and she's not an ancient dame in lace, she's a skinny stringy woman who looks a little like Jessica's mother, that sort of worn Waspy type, of course they're *all* Waspy here, and she was wearing jeans and a sweater. But nice really. Her apartment is so full of books and papers and journals that it's hard to find a place to sit; she showed me her bedroom, which was so full you can't get to the bed, she sleeps in another room, a little den. Every room has a fireplace with this little fake coal fire in it, electric. "The electric fire" she says. It's so funny. She insists on calling me Alexandra. Her head sort of bobbles when she talks, like those silly dogs people put in the back of their cars. I like her a lot.

We ate the tea (it's a meal, you know, not just a drink) which was a little primitive, cookies out of a box and some bread and butter, though she took a long time with the tea and it was strong and nice. Then I was sitting on her couch and she went off to answer the phone and she talked a long time, this little droney English voice, and I tried to overhear, and then suddenly I opened my eyes and she's looking down at me smiling. I fell asleep. For like ten minutes she said. Embarra*seeeen* as Rocky says. I said I was all right but she put me in a taxi. Oh well.

So now it's 2 AM and I'm full of pep. Write me again, and again

S

———————

From: "Smith" <anovak@strongwomanstory.org>
To: "Thea" <thea.spann133@ggm.edu>
Subject: Georgiana

10 AM. Back to Georgiana's. She said she wanted the site shut down while it was redesigned, and I said that I thought that was a bad idea. She hates the pop-ups and the ads. She said it was like trying to read an encyclopedia article in the middle of Piccadilly Circus, "you'd say Times Square." She won't talk about how much money it would take to redo the whole site and relieve it of advertisers, but she certainly has big ideas. Of course I really don't get to say *Okay hey, show me the money,* and what do I care anyway? Let the Sondra (Lilith) Mackays of the world worry about that, I just do my job. Anyway it seems now I'm working for her. So we hovered over the site and talked.

I learned that a long time ago she wanted to get a degree in math (she says "maths") from a US university but her family talked her out of it. So there's the primal scene. And now *she's* the head of the family and can do what she wants. She didn't say that.

WOW. I'm exhausted. I'm going to be here a month at least, and do Mary Somerville, Charlotte Angas Scott, Rosamund Franklin, and Ada Lovelace, and a couple of others I never heard of. See me rubbing my hands together? That's glee, not the chill. (It's weird: the "electric fire" is *all the heat there is,* and if you get out of range of it—like on your way to the *bathroom*—it's cold as hell.)

World's longest email. Write me again and again.

S

———————————

Mom—Don't you love these lilacs—they're at Kew Gardens—remember, "Come down to Kew in lilac time," I haven't been there yet but the postcards are everywhere

No lilacs yet though. I'm here doing research for the Web site. I don't have a real address yet—I'll call you soon to let you know.

Love Alex PS Hi to Marc

————————

From: "Smith" <anovak@strongwomanstory.org>
To: "Thea" <thea.spann133@ggm.edu>
Subject: Amazing

So guess what, one day after I get here to look at letters and papers of Ada Byron King, Countess of Lovelace. An amazing thing. One of those *things* that happen to me, that come after me to happen. Those where I tell you: ah, the world isn't what we think it is. And you just roll your eyes up, mathematician.

Somebody got in touch with Georgiana yesterday with an offer. Some papers have turned up and this person (Georgiana isn't even saying a name) wants to sell them to Georgiana because she's like a collector and the person knows she'd be interested because the papers are Ada's! Georgiana says she wasn't told exactly what they were but the person told her they were "extensive" or anyway there was one big something. They were found in a trunk that's claimed to have been the property of Ada's son. Whose name was Byron. (His first name. Ada's father was George Gordon, Lord Byron, the poet.) The son was also a lord, Lord Ockham. So Georgiana is going to go and look at them, and she wants me to come. She's not really sure what's up here and this is all a little odd to say the least (she said) but she asked me wouldn't it be such fun to see them. Well sure. I'm ready.

So see? Amazing things gather around your lover & podner. Don't tell me it's all random. Some things are Meant To Be.

Smith

————————

From: "Thea" <thea.spann133@ggm.edu>
To: "Smith" <anovak@strongwomanstory.org>
Subject: Not amazing

gosh weird   good luck with this woman   better you than me

just because its important or interesting doesnt mean its not
random   things wouldnt be random if they were uniform   if they
are truly random you have to expect crazy runs of luck   you dont
get more than anybody   you just notice it more   or maybe you
do get more because some people would have to randomly get
more   but who gets more is randomly distributed   have to think
about that one   but anyway theyre only amazing to you because
they have to do with you

like meeting you was amazing to me   amazing luck   but not not-
random   just amazing   and it still is

t

─────────────────

From: "Smith" <anovak@strongwomanstory.org>
To: "Thea" <thea.spann133@ggm.edu>
Subject: RE:Not amazing

Thea—I know—coincidences are only important if they're important to *me*—or to *you*—frinstance—but I'm a historian (sort of,
anyway) and history's made of coincidences—you hate history
and you don't think it's important because after all people in the
past were wrong about science and that's that.

Ada and Byron and me and these papers and Georgiana and now:
that's what I mean.

S

─────────────────

From: "Thea" <thea.spann133@ggm.edu>
To: "Smith" <anovak@strongwomanstory.org>
Subject: RE:Re:Not amazing

okay i dont get it   i never read byron and im not going to start now   all i know about ada is whats on the site and what i have heard   like the first computer program which i always wondered about   you think i hate history and think its unimportant for science   because science is only one way   but no   not math   math is partly about the history of math   i just never thought ada was a real part of it   so explain to me what all this is and who byron is and adas son is   dont write too much and i will try to remember

t

—————————

From: "Smith" <anovak@strongwomanstory.org>
To: "Thea" <thea.spann133@ggm.edu>
Subject: Story

Thea

Here's the story as I know it, which isn't very well, not yet, but I feel I'm going to have to learn it lots better.

Byron (1788–1824, I just looked it up for you, no trouble) was a famous poet and a broke lord when he married Annabella Milbanke. He was 24, she was 18. He was like a rock star, like Mick Jagger: in the sense of being somebody who made women faint, and in the sense of being an innovator, making up something that seemed completely new, and in the sense of his poetry being about his own hot self. He was also bi. He was *demonic,* sort of—they say—and one of his lovers said he was "mad, bad, and dangerous to know." That's the famous phrase. Annabella was kind of uptight, a sheltered single child, high-minded, with zero sense of humor. She had studied math, which Byron thought was unladylike and sort of comical. They were a hopeless couple, and I don't know why they chose each other. When they had Ada they'd been married two years, a tough two years, and the marriage fell apart. He was a disaster as a husband—taking opium, drinking, making nightlong scenes, having affairs with actresses. *And* she found out he was having an affair with his half sister Augusta. *Or* she found that out *and* that he had had affairs with boys when he was in Greece; *or* those things plus he tried something on her in bed that was a sin, and a crime too, you guess what. He was drunk the night that Ada was being born, and came in after it was over and said *Is it dead?*

So Lady B. stood this for another month, and then she ran off with the baby, and demanded a separation, which she got, and he left England forever, and never saw Ada again. Her mother (always called Lady Byron) never told Ada much about him, and she was always afraid Ada might inherit his criminal mad tendencies. (Remind you of anybody? Yeah, me too.) Then he died in Greece in 1824 when Ada was 9. She didn't encounter him again until a ship brought his body home—pickled in a barrel of alcohol. "Papa's ship," she said. The mourning for Byron was huge, it was like Princess Di: a bishop said he couldn't be buried in Westminster Abbey (too wicked, I guess), so his remains went by carriage to his home village in the North, accompanied all the way by vast crowds bringing flowers, tributes, tears, etc. Ada would never forget.

So Ada grew up and married another lord, William King, Lord Lovelace, and got to be friends with Charles Babbage, see Web site, you lazy podner. She wrote the notes describing his calculating machine, see Web site, which included the first thing that was sort of a computer program, s.w.; and she died of cancer at the age of 36. And her mother lived on. And saved every letter she got, and all of Ada's papers, and half the letters she *sent,* because she made copies, or demanded them back from people. All those papers are in the Bodleian Library at Oxford, all catalogued. Room 132. People go there and pore over them. But nobody's ever seen *this* stuff. I'm going to see things nobody's seen since they were written and hidden away.

So what most do you want from here? Besides my body back.

I could go visit Diana's grave, speaking of her, and bring you a flower. I remember how you cried. I wish you were here, or I was there.

S

———————————

From: "Thea" <thea.spann133@ggm.edu>
To: "Smith" <anovak@strongwomanstory.org>
Subject: Di

hoo yeah i did cry but i remember too when they got married the big wedding we watched on tv i was a kid and rocky was my friend then and we said we were going to stay up all night and watch and rocky yelled yay up chuck and di we said it all night up chuck and di and fell asleep on the couch together me and rocky i remember that was way before you way before rocky n me even r you jealous now i hope

cable guy came today so now i can watch bad tv all night

t

———————————

From: "Smith" <anovak@strongwomanstory.org>
To: "Thea" <thea.spann133@ggm.edu>
Subject: The Dead

Thea—

We got the stuff.

We had to go to this big new hotel on the other side of the river. There are a lot of new buildings over there. It looks like Cleveland or somewhere not old. My heart was beating so fast, don't ask me why, and Georgiana took my hand in the cab, not like a move or anything but to calm me down, like she sensed I was weirded out. Maybe I already was. The hotel was like a Hilton, all glass and marble and fake gold; he was registered under the name of Welch (Roony J. Welch) which doesn't even sound like a real name. Anyway his room (suite, actually) was way up high and you could see London all around, the BBC tower and St. Paul's and all the church spires.

I don't know what to say, what's important. First of all he was American! Maybe New England or maybe not. He was a small guy with a gray longish crew cut and a short gray beard. He was about sixty, anyway he looked the same age as Derek or your dad, sort of. Why do I think you need to know this. He had a little gold ring in one ear. He had on his overcoat, a long black one, and he never took it off the whole time we were there. The thing was on this glass and gold coffee table in the suite. So strange that everything around was new and it was so old, like an exhibit in a new museum.

A sea chest, he called it. Sailors kept their stuff in them. It was about the size of a backpack lying down, maybe bigger, a baby's coffin (I've never seen a baby's coffin) or a case of wine, okay? Just hold your hands this way and that way the size of a case of wine, about. I am so tired and weirded out. It had a rounded top and was made of leather or covered in leather, and was rotting in that way that leather does, turning to powder at the edges and flaking up like psoriasis and had that dry sweet smell. And he sort of circled around it without opening it and told us about how he'd come to have it, and it all sounded like a lie to me, and he wanted us not to tell anybody else the whole story—it was a *condition* so I'm not going to, not even you, because I can't screw this up for Georgiana.

Then he opened it up.

He'd put all the stuff back in that he'd found inside, I guess so he could re-create the moment of discovery for us. He talked and talked, and lifted out this and that. There were seaman's papers and some letters that proved the trunk belonged to Lord Ockham, Byron's grandson. Some other papers in a folder tied up with ribbon. And a huge pile of other papers, not in a folder but wrapped up in a kind of shiny or greasy heavy paper; he took them out and opened the wrapping, and it was—well I don't know what. Somebody had taken a bunch of sheets printed with numbered lines, and filled in other numbers on the printed lines. Hundreds of pages. Beautiful old handwritten numbers. They looked like forms filled out, or test papers, or accounts of some kind. So many.

Something happens to me when I see and touch old papers that people who are dead now used and handled and wrote on, and folded and put away, and took out and opened again, and folded back up. I feel like I have proved that a person who is dead now was really and truly alive once, and to prove that is to find out that the dead live. Georgiana was trembling. Maybe just the cold, I don't know, or nerves: but I think it was the dead, finding out again that the dead live. Does it feel like finding a proof in math? I don't know.

Smith

————————

From: "Thea" <thea.spann133@ggm.edu>
To: "Smith" <anovak@strongwomanstory.org>
Subject: RE:The Dead

thank you for your letter   you did not even say if this person sold you the stuff   or how much it cost   or what the hell it was   if anything   i will await further whatever

t

————————

From: "Smith" <anovak@strongwomanstory.org>
To: "Thea" <thea.spann133@ggm.edu>
Subject: RE:Re:The Dead

Thea—
He didn't know what they were. He said that (I guess this part's okay to tell) they'd been found in an old building in Bristol that he

bought, which used to be a bank long ago—they "came to light" he said when they were doing renovations, in an old vault nobody knew was there. But he was sure they were this Lord Ockham's. He didn't know what the papers of numbers were, but the papers tied up in ribbon were apparently something written by Ada. There was a miniature too, in a case, that looked like Ada, and a lock of hair inside the case. He passed it around. It was cold. Georgiana said she would like to have the papers assessed and their authenticity established, and he started getting a little strange. He said that this would be the only chance for the papers to remain in Britain, because he was going back to America very soon, like tomorrow, and would not return. He said that he didn't want to haggle, that the money wasn't even all that important, which yeah right. Then Georgiana looked at me—she looked so brave and scared, she had a cigarette held up before her like she was protecting herself with it—and she asked dear, did I mind stepping into the bedroom while she talked to him. That was when the money thing happened. I stayed in the bedroom and I could hear their voices but not what they said. I felt like looking in his suitcases or his closet or his pants pockets but the room seemed to be empty. Huge and empty. I thought of lying on the bed too. Like Goldilocks. I thought about you. Then Georgiana called me in, and she was already putting her coat on, and he was standing by the window so he was hard to see, but I think he was smiling; and she said *Thank you, shall I see you tomorrow,* and he said *Not me, and thank you too.* And we left. The stuff is going to be delivered to Georgiana's and she'll trade it for a check, or a cheque.

I think she cried in the cab. This little snuffle. I didn't dare take her hand or ask why.

Smith

───────────────

From: "Smith" <anovak@strongwomanstory.org>
To: "Thea" <thea.spann133@ggm.edu>
Subject: Touched them

Thea, I got to go over the things today, and I even touched them. It was so pathetic and strange. They smell of paper and dust, it's a very particular smell that's sad and cold and sweet at once, the smell of a cemetery except cemeteries don't smell. All harm and hope and life gone out, but something still left. Ghosts would be like that: they might rage for vengeance or justice but their rage would be just like old papers, old papers. The biggest thing is the mathematical work, that got Georgiana very excited: the handwriting might be Ada's though it's hard to tell because it's all numbers. What is it all and why did Ada have it? And why did *he* have it? Lord Ockham I mean, her son. Why did he keep it in this box or trunk? We don't know.

The story of Byron—I mean this Byron, Ada's son, Lord Ockham— is strange. I didn't know it. He apparently hated being a lord. All his life he tried to get out of it. When he was a kid he liked hanging with the workmen on the estate, pitching in with tools. His father put him in the Navy (at 14!!) to straighten him out, but he soon ran away and signed on a ship as just a regular seaman. And later he became a dockworker and shipbuilder, and called himself John Oakey or something, and just lived and died on the docks. He was pretty young when he died. And I guess he never came back for the box, which he'd put in a bank, just like a lord would do. And this was what he had in it, that he cared enough about to save it: this stuff of Ada's, her writings and her work if it is her work, and the things of his like his seaman's papers, and something else. Something really puzzling.

Oops battery's running out, I knew it would, cord's back in hotel. I'll send this so I don't lose it. God bless wifi

S

From: "Thea" <thea.spann133@ggm.edu>
To: "Smith" <anovak@strongwomanstory.org>
Subject: RE:Touched them

what   puzzling
i did not know you were going to get off on this tangent   how
longs this going to take   i get mizzable alone you know   not that
i want to lay a trip on you   you didnt when i went to stanford   i
will always be grateful   but god   last night i went to this dyke
comedy show   i asked barb to go but she was too depressed   well
i shouldnt go by myself to things   it was funny really   but u can
get a little tired of tampon jokes   anyway i think theres something
about being in a big crowd and laughing a lot that makes people
horny   maybe its the pheromones   maybe its me   im putting out
some heavy chemicals   im going to get hit on by some kid with
wristlets and a chain for a belt   crosseyed with lust   dont be surprised if i dont turn her down   lol

trixie (yeah shes back   yo)

————————————————

From: "Smith" <anovak@strongwomanstory.org>
To: "Thea" <thea.spann133@ggm.edu>
Subject: Yo

Thea (oh I mean Trixie)—
I didn't think you liked those metal butches. I thought you liked
the raggedy angry-waif type. Was I wrong? Ooh I'm scared now.
Puzzling: The long Ada manuscript (50 pages) in the trunk seems
to be about a novel that Lord Byron (the father, the poet) wrote. It,
the novel, was lost or stolen, and then turned up, and Ada had it,
she says. She wrote these pages about how she learned about it
before anybody else and got hold of it. And then there are some
pages of sort of rambling notes that I guess are supposed to be
about it. It's all in pencil and it's faint and hard to read. I'm working on it.

Then there's another page. It's not written by her and it's in ink. One page. On the other side is some printed notice in Italian, which I happen not to be able to read, because I'm not a phd like some people. The handwriting's even worse. You'd have to be this person's wife or lover to read this handwriting. I say wife or lover because I think I get what it might be. Georgiana hates to see me touching it so I can't work with it too much. We're like people in those movies who find a million dollars of stolen money, along with a dead body, and they can't tell anybody or think about anything else, and it ruins their lives at least till the last scenes.

I forget—is lol lots of love or laugh out loud

S

————————————

From: "Thea" <thea.spann133@ggm.edu>
To: "Smith" <anovak@strongwomanstory.org>
Subject: RE:Yo

i did not say she wd be my type   but i might be hers   lol   laugh out loud

what is the math stuff   can you tell

t

————————————

From: "Smith" <anovak@strongwomanstory.org>
To: "lilith" <smackay@strongwomanstory.org>
Subject: Georgiana

Lilith:
Just a quick report on how it's going with Georgiana. Like I said on the phone, amazing woman. I can see why you thought this was important. She really does want to entirely remake the site and

make it the best on the Web for women's science history. We sat a long time looking at things like the Jewish Women's Archive and the other sites we get so jealous about, and she kept saying no prob. Well she doesn't say that, she says things in the English way, like *How delightful* and *Won't it be such fun,* and she says *Of course* a lot, meaning I don't know exactly what. I'll say *What we need to do in the engineering is this,* and she says *Of course,* like she already thought of that and it's in the works.

I told you I'm not going to talk to her about money, right? I told you. She keeps trying to and I keep putting her off. It would be great if you could drop her a note and say the money is your end. But wow just to have to fight off the bucks being offered is a strange new feeling, huh? Should we be worried? Are we being secretly taken over by a Daddy Warbucks or something? A stalking horse, or a Trojan horse, or whatever?

Meantime she's very passionate about me staying here and doing some research and assembling materials and looking at stuff, even before decisions get made about changes at the site, and it's okay with me if it's okay with you. I might be moving into her apartment, flat as she says, to save money. (See it's not bottomless pockets just deep ones.) She's cleaning out a room. Which is not so nice but okay.

So I'll keep you posted. Say hello to everybody and tell them I've got union jack tea towels and queen dolls for everybody.

See ya

Smith

———————————

From: "Smith" <anovak@strongwomanstory.org>
To: "Thea" <thea.spann133@ggm.edu>
Subject: Difference Engine

Thea—

The one page was written by Byron, the poet. I thought it was. You can tell easily if you look at some of his writing reproduced in books. I can't really read all of it, or even most of it. Remember how long it took me to read those Royal Society letters, and then when I could, you didn't know how I could, it just looked like scribble to you—well that's what this looks like to me, scribble. But I know it's written by him. Why one page, what is it, why is it here.

I don't know what the math stuff is. Like I said it's a lot of printed pages, just a page number in the upper right and then blocks of numbered lines in four columns, fifty lines to a column. The lines are for writing in, like a form, I guess; and what's written is strings of numbers. Could they be mathematical tables? I know that the Difference Engine, that Ada worked on with Babbage, was designed to print out tables of logarithms—that was supposed to be its main job, calculating them and printing them, but as I remember the printing part never got completed. What if this had something to do with the Difference Engine? Wouldn't that be something?

There's a museum here that actually has a copy, a newly made reproduction rather, of the Difference Engine. Maybe I'll go ask them. Subtly.

S

————————

From: "Thea" <thea.spann133@ggm.edu>
To: "Smith" <anovak@strongwomanstory.org>
Subject: Movie

log tables would be easy to recognize   i could tell you   just send me a page or two know what i watched late last night on tv the history channel youre surprised huh they had that movie about the movie company in wherever it was baruchistan or faroukistan or wherever it was in the 1920s grass you remember thats your dads movie right it was weird i fell asleep before it ended

t

———————————

From: "Smith" <anovak@strongwomanstory.org>
To: "Thea" <thea.spann133@ggm.edu>
Subject: RE:Movie

T—

Yeah that was his first film. *Grass.* He wrote that one before I was born. The story is that he discovered this whole old movie, well not whole but hours of film shot in the 1920s in Baluchistan, wherever, by the same filmmakers who made *King Kong;* their film was supposed to be called *Grass.* He wrote a script about the filmmakers making that film, and then used their old footage in it. A big romance story. I never saw it, was it good. Some people seem to know all about it, I meet them. A cult film, somebody told me. Better than the others when he got famous.

I haven't thought about him in a while. Hm.

I'm going to the Science Museum tomorrow if I can get away from Georgiana. I don't think she can be cool, I feel so disloyal saying it, but she just sort of beclouds things. It's raining but I've got my Swain Adeney.

Smith

———————————

From: "Thea" <thea.spann133@ggm.edu>
To: "Smith" <anovak@strongwomanstory.org>
Subject: him

what   you havent ever checked his website   i mean the produc-
tion company website   i would if i were you   even if I was scared
actually today i did   you never told me hes so good looking   but
he looks like he knows it   that whole david bowie thing going on
but with the farseeing eyes   man   he might be a phony tho   i
know hes awful   i hate him but he does good things   did you
know hes making a film now about east timor   recreating an awful
massacre when east timor wanted freedom   well   i bet you know

anyway hes not coming back

t

————————————

From: "Smith" <anovak@strongwomanstory.org>
To: "Thea" <thea.spann133@ggm.edu>
Subject: RE:him

That's him. The pervert. I do look. I just don't tell you.

The Difference Engine is the most amazing thing. It weighs tons,
really tons. You can't stand in front of it without thinking about
how intense they were in the past, to have thought up and designed and then *built* a thing so heavy and so perfect, I mean so
finely made that you can make the whole mechanism move with
one hand. The guy showed me. You set these wheels etched with
beautiful little numbers, and then you turn the handle, and the
columns of numbers turn, and these arms turn other columns as
they carry numbers over and add them (all this whole thing does is
add!) and it makes this slick sound that grips your head or your
heart or some part of you—if you like the sound of slick machines
turning their parts.

But of course Babbage *didn't* build it—these guys at the science museum built it—Babbage never finished it, he dropped it and went on to design an even better machine, the Analytical Engine, that could be programmed, with punch cards, like an old computer. You know all this, I'm just thinking out loud, okay? So what would a long program of punch cards look like, I asked him. If somebody had written one out, back then. And he didn't really know, or he thought it could look like a lot of things, that the whole process had never reached that stage.

He was pretty snippy about Ada as a mathematician—he says she really contributed nothing much to the thinking about the Analytical Engine—but he *did* say that it was *she* and not Babbage who saw the possibilities, that the Engine could be a manipulator of symbols, and not just of numbers—a "generalized algebra machine," this guy said. That's the importance of her insight that the Analytical Engine could weave algebraic patterns just like a Jacquard loom could weave birds and flowers. (Jacquard's loom wove patterns determined by a sequence of punch cards—that's where Babbage got the cards idea.) It all depended on the instructions. And that's really the concept of a computer.

See what I'm wondering? Georgiana's rushing ahead, she's not wondering, she's sure we have a computer program written by Ada Augusta, Countess of Lovelace. But what if she's right.

I'm faxing you a couple of pages of the math. Tell me what you think.

S

──────────────

From: "Thea" <thea.spann133@ggm.edu>
To: "Smith" <anovak@strongwomanstory.org>
Subject: Log

okay   I got the fax   no its not a log table   guess again   anyway
why are we sure its hers

t

──────────────

From: "Smith" <anovak@strongwomanstory.org>
To: "Thea" <thea.spann133@ggm.edu>
Subject: RE:Log

What do you mean guess again? *You* guess again, you're the numbers guy. If it isn't logs what is it? And does it have something to
do with the Analytical Engine? If you go to the Web site there's a
link to Ada's description of the Analytical Engine, and the little
tiny sample set of instructions you might give it—"the first computer program," we say.

I *don't* know this thing is hers. I just think it is and hope it is.
I hope, I hope this is something. The Ada written stuff from the
trunk, if *that's* hers, is very faint and hard to read. Dead person
talking: you have to listen hard, and be quiet.

S

──────────────

From: "Lilith" <smackay@strongwomanstory.org>
To: "Smith" <anovak@strongwomanstory.org>
Subject: 'Sup

Smith:

Wow, glad you're there and that everything is going so well! Great
to hear your voice! Isn't Georgiana *great*? I really hope you guys
get along. I knew you were the one to do this, I just had the feeling,
you know how I get the feeling? Well I had the feeling. But now

listen. She tends to get a little vague. When she was here and it all started she used to wander a little. Like she had a lot of stories she thought were real important but they tended to sort of flow, you know? So one led to another before the first one ended. All I'm saying is she took a *lot* of listening to. I really trust you to be able to bring this off with her but you know there's all the regular stuff too to do on the site that nobody can do but you, we all run around like chickens with our heads cut off, and we want you *back*. But no pressure, just do this with her. I love you babe.

Lilith

————————————

From: "Smith" <anovak@strongwomanstory.org>
To: "Thea" <thea.spann133@ggm.edu>
Subject: Chicken

Thea—Did you ever think about this—people use comparisons that don't mean anything to them because they've never seen the thing they're using to compare with. I mean: People say *we're running around like chickens with our heads cut off* but they've never seen a chicken with its head cut off. It's like what they really need is a comparison to show what a chicken with its head cut off is like. *That chicken with its head cut off ran around like Sondra (Lilith) Mackay after a double espresso and a bad phone call.* See what I mean?

S

————————————

From: "Thea" <thea.spann133@ggm.edu>
To: "Smith" <anovak@strongwomanstory.org>
Subject: RE:Chicken

yeah   like i heard on tv   somebody said somebody else was mad as a wet hen   i have never seen a wet hen   i can sort of imagine it

like my mom   you know   hey thats funny that wet hen looked as
mad as my mom when a cop stopped her the 2nd time in a day
we shd make a list
btw my mom called the other night   couldnt get a lot out of her
boy i hate hanging up on her   when theres nobody here

t

——————————

From: "Smith" <anovak@strongwomanstory.org>
To: "Thea" <thea.spann133@ggm.edu>
Subject: Coming

Okay here's what I'm going to do. I'm floundering here and Georgiana is like very confused. She still doesn't want to take any of
this to any experts. I'm starting to think maybe she is profoundly
weird, no matter how together and bright she seems. I need to
know what the hell this stuff is. I'm going to scan the mathematical stuff and put it on a CD and send it to you; you tell me what
it is.

And I'm going to write to my father and ask him to help. After all
he was a college professor once and this was his field, what he
knew about. So I'm going to.

S

——————————

From: "Thea" <thea.spann133@ggm.edu>
To: "Smith" <anovak@strongwomanstory.org>
Subject: RE:Coming

SMITH   DONT WRITE TO THAT BASTARD   I MEAN IT   ITS
LIKE CHECKING INTO HELL JUST TO GET KURT COBAINS
AUTOGRAPH OR SOMETHING WHAT ABOUT ALL THAT
THERAPY   ITS NOT WORTH IT EVEN IF HES SO SMART THAT

HE CAN TELL YOU SOMETHING   WHICH HE PROBABLY ISNT
EVEN   YOU   NEVER   WROTE   HIM   BEFORE   WHEN   THINGS
MATTERED A LOT MORE THAN THIS   SO DONT NOW

I LOVE YOU

T

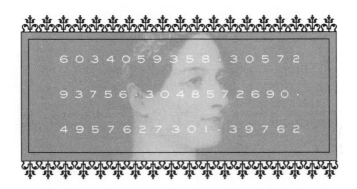

TO THE READER

Inasmuch as the world has long evinced the greatest interest in every scrap of writing associated with my father's name, an interest that has not diminished appreciably in the twenty years that have now passed since his death; and since every person, who ever had occasion to converse with him or to overhear his remarks, has eagerly rushed his remembrance into print, no matter how slight the acquaintance, or trivial the matter, it may seem wonderful that a large number of pages from his hand could have survived until now without notice—and, in consequence, doubts as to their authenticity, or at the very least, a justifiable curiosity as to their provenance, may arise. Therefore I deem it my duty to give a brief account of how the following tale came into my hands, and why it only now comes before the reader—and if such a reader does indeed one day come to exist, and his eyes do indeed now fall upon my words, and upon *his,* he may trust that, whatever my interest in this matter has been, it is not pecuniary, or to seek celebrity for myself; for if ever his words and mine see the light of day, I shall be dead.

It may indeed be questioned, whether such a Work as this one is, containing passages—nay, entire ranges of subject—which can neither redound to the Author's credit, nor without offence be put into the hands of a general readership, be worth preserving. In the present instance there is the additional question of the Work's bearing upon the Author's own history, therefore upon the vexed and much-bruited questions of his culpability at a certain crossroads of his life, one to which I was myself a blissfully ignorant witness. It should be remembered that certain parties deeply concerned in that history, including Lady Byron his wife, assembled together upon the Author's death, and jointly agreed to put into the fire the Memoirs he had written, containing his own version of events as well as stories of his foreign adventures, which, though he had willingly committed them to paper, cannot but have harmed his memory, as well as injuring those others intimately concerned. Ought not the partial and unpolished Work now in my hands meet a similar fate? I can only answer that perhaps it ought, but that I myself cannot so consign it, as I could not myself have given his Memoirs to the flames; those of stronger fibre than myself have done, and must in future do, that service for Lord Byron, if service it be.

To my story:

In the years before and after the upheavals of 1848 I was privileged to know, through the good offices of my honoured friend Charles Babbage, several of the men in the circle around the sacred figure of Mazzini. Mr Babbage was always a friend of Liberty and the advancement of Man, and he delighted in the company of these men of Italy, who, exiled from their native land only for having its best interests at heart, were at times suspected and annoyed by the government of this land as well. Signor Silvio Pellico, Count Carlo Pepoli, and a man who became my special friend, Signor Fortunato Prandi: in the company of such men I heard of the regard in which my father was and still is held in their native land, and what he undertook in behalf of Italy, when he was residing in that country. It was from one of this number—I will not name him even posthumously, not because he requires a cloak of anonymity for any dishonourable action, but simply because from the beginning a secrecy was enjoined upon me in this endeavour that I will not now break—that I first learned of the existence of a manuscript, purported to be the work of Lord Byron, though in prose not verse, of which no other copy exists. According to the tale I was told—the truth or falsity of which I cannot now adequately examine—an Italian occasionally in the company of Lord Byron in the period of his residence in Ravenna acquired this manuscript, either by gift or other means; at some later time he consigned it to another, and this second possessor had recently revealed its existence to the gentleman who now told me of it. I asked if his acquaintance possessed the papers still. He did. I further asked if this gentleman had considered depositing them with Lord Byron's executors, with the firm of John Murray, his publishers, or otherwise delivering them up to his heirs and assigns. The man had so considered, he said, and might have done, but for a number of difficulties. The chain of events that had led to his possession of the manuscript could be interpreted as the reception of stolen property, an imputation that could only be strengthened by the length of time he had held it without informing anyone. Moreover the possessor believed (my informant said) that the manuscript was of such value that it could be traded for money, of which the Republican cause was badly in need, and therefore he was loath to bring it to the attention of those who might claim it by right, without compensation. It was this obstacle which my interlocutor put before me. He would, he said, by any means he might, acquire this relict of my father, which by the laws of men and of Heaven belonged to me and to my children, and ask nothing in return, for himself or any other party or cause, no matter how worthy; but he begged me before enlisting his aid in this action to think first of the commotion that would immediately ensue upon any attempt to wrest the manuscript—containing who knew what—from the present possessor.

I did indeed bethink myself. What, for instance, would such a manuscript be worth? My father regarded his own manuscripts with a cavalier lack of interest, and often (after ensuring that a fair copy had been made) bestowed the originals on whomever stood by. Though the *present* age considers the remains of our famous authors to be worth having—certain collectors even paying goodly sums for such things—the amounts are in most cases but inconsiderable. How much good could the likely asking price do in the struggle for Italian freedom? Perhaps, I thought, it was not the provenance so much as the contents of the manuscript that in the possessor's eyes made it worth acquiring; but of that I could know nothing without personal perusal. How, furthermore, could I be confident—it seemed impossible to be *certain*—that the monies demanded would actually benefit the cause to which my friends were devoted? If I received assurance on that score, then the acquisition of the manuscript might be considered as simply a means to an end desired in itself, even if the sum were incommensurate with the value of the thing bought. These calculations—and they arose as the operations of a mind stringently *logical* in its operations, as I may aver few minds are—were akin to those that devotees of the turf are accustomed to make when pondering the imponderables of a race card.

Having come to a conclusion in which I could have confidence, I implored my friends' assistance. I wished, I said, even if it were unwise for me to negotiate for the papers in my own person, to have at least a look at the present possessor of them; and my informant said that this might be arranged—I could observe, if I liked, an examination of the aforesaid manuscripts in a public place, where I might remain anonymous. The funds wherewith to purchase the papers I could supply from my own resources, and after negotiations to which I was not a party, a sum was named to me, to which I agreed. The meeting-place settled upon, where a first examination would take place, was the Crystal Palace exhibition halls, specifically the Dome of Discovery where Dr. Merryweather's Tempest Prognosticator was then displayed, an engine which I had in any case a curiosity to see. Accompanied by my trustworthy acquaintance, and a female companion who was uninformed of our intentions, veiled and inconspicuous, I went to the gallery above named at the hour specified. I cannot now say with any certainty what I may have learned of Dr. Merryweather's interesting device, for all my attention was upon the meeting, at a little distance from where my companion and I stood, of the gentleman engaged for me and the possessor of the manuscripts. The latter was an unprepossessing fellow, grey of hair and slight of frame, a gold ring in his left ear the only mark of the adventurer about him. I can say nothing more about this personage, who after passing to my friend a shabby portmanteau, the contents of which he permitted to be but briefly examined, rose from his seat, and disappeared into the throng. I have never seen him more, nor heard further of his fate.

When I had been assured of the nature of the manuscripts, insofar as my friend was able to ascertain it, I agreed to the payment; and under circumstances dictated by the possessor—again involving a public place, and anonymity—that portmanteau or carpet-bag was acquired on my behalf. I am assured that the sum which that day changed hands was put to the promised uses, but of that also I can furnish no further details. When the bag was later delivered to me, I found inside, wrapped in oiled parchment, the novel upon which you, gentle Reader, in whose existence I shall continue to believe, may now embark, as I did then—I hope with less difficulty than I at first encountered. Many of the pages were foxed and faded, some were out of order, and Lord Byron's hand was never an easy one for me (I had as a child never been given any of the letters he had written to me, or to my mother; indeed I had never seen his handwriting until Mr John Murray presented me with the manuscript of his poem *Beppo,* when I was a married lady whose morals it was presumed would not be harmed by the poem). At the head of the first page was the title—as I assumed—though it seemed, as I began my first perusal, an odd one indeed, and I wondered—I looked again, and determined that the words were written in a different ink, by a different pen, perhaps at a different time, which caused me to wonder the more.

I told not spouse nor parent what I had, and certainly not the world; and that for reasons which students of my unfortunate family (of whom there is an army, and new recruits daily) will understand. What my father had written was, for that time, mine alone. I set about making a fair copy, even as I learned to read the hand. I shall not describe with what emotions I did so.

I had at that time reached what I may call an epoch in my feelings about my paternal ancestors. Not long before, my husband William, Lord Lovelace, and I had accepted an invitation to visit Newstead, the ancestral seat of the Byrons in Nottinghamshire, now in the possession of Colonel Wildman, once Lord Byron's schoolfellow at Harrow. There—amid scenes where the father I never knew was wont to roam and to make merry; where his forebears worthy and profligate had lived, and whose incomes they had wasted, in former ages; where nearby stands the little parish church, in whose crypt my father lies with his people—I know not how, but all that I seemed once to have known concerning that troubled and tempestuous spirit, all that I had been taught to think about him—and to hold him guilty of—all vanished, or lifted as cloud; and I knew myself to be, with all my own faults, a *Byron* too, as was *he,* with *his:* and if I could not love him, without charges upon his soul, I could not love myself, or his grandchildren that were my children. In a letter that is quoted in the Life written by Mr Thomas Moore, Lord Byron stated his belief that a woman cannot love a man *for himself* who does not love him *for his crimes.* No other love, says he, is worthy the name. Whether or not my own soul is capable of so august an ideal of love, I hold it to be applicable as well to a daughter as to a spouse; and none may hinder me now from aspiring to it.

AS I HAVE HEREIN met the need for an Introduction or Prolegomenon, I have had in addition the temerity to provide a number of notes, illuminating where I can the matter of this curious tale, and connecting its accounts to the scenes of my father's life, of which, I am obliged to admit, I have often little personal knowledge. It has however been to me a source of diversion, even of delight and solace in difficult and painful times, to have thus laboured over those connexions which I was able to discover, and to expound; and I beg those readers who find my glosses presumptuous or otiose simply to pass over them, as they might the troublesome informations of a guide to a cathedral or castle, who has only his passion and his devotion to sustain him.

NOTES FOR THE 1ST CHAPTER

1. *The Laird his father:* The wickedness of Byrons past has become legendary, and as such contains a great admixture of un-
   truth. Ld. B. himself delighted, it is reported, in shocking his
   friends with tales of his ancestor, William, the fifth Lord, who
   despoiled his estates and murdered a man in an irregular duel;
   Ld. B.'s own father, 'Mad Jack', went through the estate of his
   first and then of his second wife (Ld. B.'s mother) in an astonishingly short time. He fled to the Continent to avoid his
   debtors when his son was but two years old, and never saw
   him again, for he died abroad at the age of thirty-four, penni-
   less, perhaps by his own hand. When I was two years old, my
   father left England forever; he died in Greece at the age of
   thirty-six.

2. *his wife's Scotch estates:* Ld. B. is pleased to set his story in a
   habitation like his own Newstead Abbey in Nottinghamshire,
   but transported to the land he liked to consider himself to have
   sprung from; indeed he talked of 'we Scots', &c., often enough.
   His mother, Catherine Gordon, was indeed Scottish, and

possessed estates at Gight—those that her husband sold for debt—and from his infancy to the age of ten he lived in Aberdeen, and swam in the Dee. His mother, he said, was inordinately proud of her descent from the Stuarts, and looked down upon the 'Southron' Byrons.

3. *Kendals drops:* Lord Byron at the end of his time in England was known to use laudanum—in a combination with stimulants such as claret or brandy. It is a palliative known to many with afflictions both physical and mental, though now-a-days *morphine* is preferred to the old-fashioned black drops. My own physicians recommend a regimen of *alternating* opiates with stimulants, which has proved beneficial at times, though the prospect of deliberately *lowering* a mental exaltation by the use of a narcotic is at times repellent even to one who knows the consequences of too high, and too rapid, a flight.

4. *his pistols within reach:* Lord Byron was an excellent shot with the pistol, though he said himself that his hand shook, and he had to train himself specially to squeeze the trigger at the right moment. When I was a child it was thought possible that my father would send agents to my mother's house to abduct me; possibly he would himself return to England for that purpose. My grandmother, Lady Noel, kept loaded pistols by her bedside to foil such attempts; the thought of that kindly and gentle lady actually employing them seems as amusing now to me as her conviction of sinister plots afoot.

5. *his father's tame bear:* Byron kept a bear when he was at Cambridge, and for a time it was resident at Newstead Abbey, where it amused his friends. Ld. B. was always surrounded by animals in whatever household he established—dogs in particular were favourites, but the poet Shelley remembered coming upon a crane, a goat, a monkey, and cats as well as dogs at his house in Pisa. A love and *respect* for animals is a trait that I discovered in myself long before I learned that I shared it with my father. The

beasts that Descartes regarded as *automata* without more feeling than a clock-work will one day be shewn to be more like ourselves—or, ourselves to be more like them—than we can now conceive.

6. *somnambulations:* Lord Byron could not have known of the speculations of Dr Elliotson and others concerning what that physician calls 'diseased sleep', a state, like that a poet or saint may fall into, in which the most vivid visions are imparted, as visions of palaces and damsels were to Coleridge at Nether Stowey, till he was awakened by a person from Porlock come calling. (Those regions, so poetical in themselves, are well known to me. Coleridge's visions were excited as well by the use of opium.) Dr Elliotson's remarkable successes in the use of those techniques of special sleep once called Mesmeric—but which I prefer to term Hypnotic—are well known. The light and fantastical treatment of the subject in the later pages of this work proceed from the author's understandable ignorance of the astonishing development of this science in our time; nevertheless, as poets can, he saw far into its possibilities.

7. *Albania:* Lord Byron's journey in youth to Albania, told of in *Childe Harold's Pilgrimage,* a journey undertaken at a time when few Englishmen had ever ventured there, was a signal part of his fame, or notoriety. He had indeed a love of movement, an imperviousness to discomfort, and what Dr Johnson calls 'a willingness to be pleased' which is the sign of a good traveller. Whether his descriptions of the land, the people, their customs, &c., be accurate, and whence he derived them if not from his own experience, which was after all quite brief—none of this I know very certainly, but my researches continue.

8. *Pacha:* Ali Pasha (1741–1822, as near as I can determine), whom Byron visited at his capital Tepelene, on his journey to Albania. In his letters to his mother Byron describes this figure, and his painted grandsons, much as they are here described.

9. *a long white kilt of softest wool,* &c.: This describes exactly the
    Albanian dress my father purchased for himself when he was
    in that country, and dressed in which he was painted by Phillips.
    That picture hung over the mantel at my grandmother's house,
    Kirkby Mallory, where, for some time after I was born, my
    mother and I dwelt with her mother. The picture was covered
    with a cloth of green baize, and I was not allowed to look upon
    it—for what baleful influences might flow from thence into my
    young being? Such a shrine—with its cloth drawn before the
    holy of holies, as the curtain is drawn before the scroll of Scrip-
    ture in a Jewish temple—ought to have fascinated, rather than
    discouraging; tempted, rather than saving; and perhaps it
    did—but in actual fact I do not remember it there at all, and
    only when the picture itself was given to me after my marriage
    was the story told me of its concealment. Strange are the ways
    of the zealous & careful parent.

In which a Father and a Son are

joined, and of the consequences

HOW ALI PASSED the next months in the Pacha's court—how he learned the arts of war, and of horsemanship; how he accompanied the patrols on their less dangerous rounds—for his precious skin was not to be unduly risked, as he came to understand; how he came to recognize the envious or resentful glances of certain of his fellows among the Pacha's Guard, and how he won over his enemies by his modesty, and his open heart, and his generosity; how he filled his days with activity such as any lad would delight in, and his nights with wakings, and dreams, and griefs that none else were to know of—all that need not be recounted at length. There came a day when Ali, while in the hills practicing with his fellows at pistol-shooting, a sport at which he excelled over even some of the eldest and most experienced of them, was summoned to appear before the Pacha, and a guest who ardently desired to meet him.

The guest's equipage and suite were in evidence in the court-yard of the Pacha's house when Ali entered there—horses in strange harness, men in foreign clothes, including a Turk or two with high turbans and trowsers amazingly wide. Above in his room of state the Pacha sat in his accustomed place upon the sopha—and his hawk-like Vizier stood up behind him—and beside him in the place of honour was a man Ali knew not—the sight of whom sent through his being a flash of dread or horror. To what might this be attributed? The man was huge, indeed—even folded up as he was upon the low seat this was evident—but Ali had known larger fight-ers; and his head-cloth was done up in the Turkish fashion—but the Vizier's was too; and beneath his capote the brass buttons of his red tunic might be seen—but the capote itself was not so different from that which Ali himself wore. Then was it a presentiment of all that lay ahead, that he was to do, and to bear, because of the man? No—it was simply that the stranger's *face was clean-shaven*. He was the first grown man without moustaches that Ali had ever seen, and Albanians have a horror of such—the Bogey in the tales their grand-dames tell to children, who comes to eat them up, has just such a white and hairless face as Ali now looked upon—as looked upon *him* with interested eye.

The man was John Porteous, Lord Sane, it need not be said—his the eye, and the interest—and it is appropriate, or at least conve-nient, here to describe in greater detail the appearance of one who was to affect so singularly the youth who now stood unmoving within his fixing gaze. Those characters cruel or haughty who pro-ceed through the pages of our romances (and the *poets'* pages, too, be it admitted!) and do deeds of dreadful note are often as not painted as though to persuade Mr Kean to portray them upon the stage—the tense and braided muscle, the great eyes that flash darkly, quivering visage, nose like a hawk's beak, red mouth cru-elly cut, at once sneering and sensual, &c., &c. The face of 'Satan' Porteous was not so: it was, to speak truly, as round and bland as a pudding, and his eyes small and shrouded by pale lids, wherein but a crumb of glitter could be seen—the which made them the more horrid to look upon—for the eyes had a cold alertness like a sleepy reptile's, when they slid in one's direction; they chilled without thrilling, and induced a horrid lassitude in those—a large class—upon whom their possessor had some design.

The Pacha summoned the frozen lad, and bade him sit upon the divan between himself and the wondrous beardless monster, who put upon Ali's shoulder a hand heavy as though it were a leaden statue's, and spoke words to him and to the Pacha that Ali could not interpret. The Pacha smiled, and nodded, and hummed, pleased at the scene; he took the man's right hand, and placed Ali's within it, and closed them both in his own. 'My brave Ali!' said he. 'There has come a wonderful providence into thy life, by the will of Allah. Behold here beside thee thy father!'

So startled was Ali that he snatched his hand from within the others', as though it had been nearly caught in a rat-trap. This occasioned laughter from the older men, who were not *just then* in a mood to be offended, and were as well delighted with the boy's discomfiture. When their glee was past, Ali was told that he was indeed the Englishman's son—the Sigma indited upon his arm was identical to that on a Seal-ring the Englishman wore, in indication of the name he had inherited. Moreover and more wonderfully—the Pacha smiling said—the Englishman had decided to take Ali back with him to the land of Britain, which was a small grey island far away, but one with many ships and guns; and there he would be the Englishman's son and heir, and have wealth and honours beyond telling, and was not this a fine thing, and were not the dispositions of Allah to be praised?

Ali in horrified amazement leapt up from his place upon the Pacha's sopha—dropt to his knees before the old sinner, and lifted his hands in supplication. 'But *thou alone* art my father!' quoth he. 'I am thy son, if love and devotion have power to make me such. Send me not from thy presence—for have I not been faithful, and put away all old loyalties whatever, and pledged to thee my arm and my soul?'

Yet the word of the Pacha was not to be challenged, nor would

Ali have dreamed of challenging it—better to believe that a tomcat was his father, if the Pacha pronounced it so, than to say the word *No* to that long-bearded face!

What bargain the old warrior had struck with the English adventurer—by what means he had first learned of the man's return to these dominions, and of the object of his coming there—what advantage to himself or hurt to his adversaries he expected by fulfilling his wish—I cannot say—nor whether the Milord he fawned upon had the powers to bring about those Results which he intimated to the Pacha he might. Certain it is, however, that such bargains had been made, and were not to be unmade. And as in this land the filial bond is the strongest that any man can know—the duty owed to Fathers the one least and last to be shaken off by any man of honour or common sense—Ali was left without grounds on which to protest; he must at last bend the knee before this spectre, his Father, and kiss his hands, and offer his Duty.

'Come,' then said Lord Sane—speaking to Ali as though the boy could understand him,—'You are flesh of my flesh, and from here, where there is nothing, I shall take you to where you shall have much. And now let us have no more talk. We leave today for the coast. You need bring nothing: all will be provided.'

And thus suddenly it was done. In the courtyard of the Pacha's palace there was a great stir, as with a clashing of bells, ornament, and weaponry Lord Sane's Suliote guards mounted, screamed out their ululations, fired their guns in air. A lad brought forth a mount for Ali—the most beautiful he had ever seen, its trappings and harness gorgeous. The Englishman showed by a wave of his hand that the horse was his, and the lad as well—who thereupon helped Ali to mount—which help Ali hardly knew how to accept. At the same time a groom also led a huge Arabian stallion from the stable, a steed glowing black as the desert night, haughty and enraged—so it appeared by his rolling eye, and bared teeth—and every horse in that enclosure trembled, shook head, started and reared, as though in the presence of a Lion rather than one of their own kind. Lord Sane called its name as harshly as though he pronounced a curse—struck its face to still its tossing—took its reins—and threw himself upon its back; and though the beast reared and twisted, the Lord subdued it. With a raised hand he summoned his train and his guard, the gates were opened, and he went out.

This black charger was the first of Lord Sane's beasts that Ali would associate with his father—beasts wild—fierce—unyielding—mad & dangerous. Such beings alone his father could love simply, without hypocrisy or design—who responded only to force, whose spirits were as huge & contrary as his own, whom he could contest with, and break. The horse was hardly still a moment beneath him, and if ever he became so, Sane would challenge him the more, and dig into his shining flanks the little roundels Ali saw at his heels, sharp and hurtful: Ali supposed—for he had never seen their like before, as they are not used in that country—that his father had conceived and made them himself, for the torment they inflicted.

As they passed downward from the stony heights, Lord Sane was silent; or contrariwise, he talked long to his son in a low grating voice without inflection, talked and talked as though he could compel his son to learn to comprehend the tongue of his father and his father's fathers merely by the force of his speaking: which Ali could not do, and so listened merely to the *tone*—which was compelling enough—the *matter* he would not gather for many weeks and months to come. Once on a time, said the Lord, he had come to these lands for adventure, and by reason of tales told in the South of Gold, for which men will undergo the harshest of privations, and do deeds of the greatest and most dreadful courage, ever heedless that not one El Dorado in a thousand yields up a shilling's worth of gold, whereas the bones of countless seekers whiten in the deserts and forests of the world. No gold—his comrades (if such they may be named) dead around him, or deserted—himself cashiered upon return to his regiment for absence without leave, and for the string of lies he had left behind (what may we not admit to, if our hearer knows nothing of our tongue? What sins our dogs and horses are privy to, if they could but reckon them!)—and so he came again into his homeland, where there were many who thought they had seen the last of him, and who did not rejoice to greet him again.

Not for gold was he now come back into these mountains,

though. No! It was an *heir* that Lord Sane had returned to find, having no issue of his marriage, and no longer expecting any—for a wound in his thigh, suffered in a duel, would not permit him to engender further—which made it also superfluous for him to divorce, as he had for some time planned to do, his wife—broken in health herself—whose lands and fortunes he had despoiled, and take a fertile maid to wed. Therefore—though he knew not if the child he had so rudely spawned in these parts had lived, or was *male*—knew not the fate of Mother or Husband—was only driven to press on with his design, however mad the world would surely have deemed it, had the world known of it—he had come again to the coast of Epirus, and mounted his expedition. The one emotion perhaps creditable to the giant Lord was this, that he would not see his line extinguished; and who can say that he did not, in his cinder of a heart, feel remorse at least for this—that, had he not *acted as he had* in time gone by, a legitimate Heir might now be waiting to succeed him.

A day and a night passed in the telling of this tale, in all its parts, some more dreadful than any here recounted, though the consequences of those untold deeds may yet figure in the present account; and at its end Ali was not wiser than he had been. Upon the following day, Lord Sane, by forcing his mount down a way that the horse considered too steep, the rock-strewn path too loose, caused the animal by his cruel goading to slip, and fall upon its delicate cannons, and twist a leg at the hock. When Lord Sane's fury at his horse's *betrayal*—as he considered it—was past, his groom was commanded to care for the horse, whose wound was considered by those horsemen as likely to heal with proper care, and to follow on after—by no means was he to *mount* the animal, but only to lead it. Lord Sane took another horse, and the party went on. When they had come to a town large enough to support so large a number as they were, they stopt, and with only the showing of the Firman he had obtained from the Pacha's Vizier, Lord Sane and his son and his aides-de-camp were offered the upper storey of a large fortified house. The accommodating Landlord, who seemed to hope for something more than the approbation of Allah for his hospitality—though whether his hopes were realized Ali never knew—went, with his wives in closed chairs, to another house in the wooded hills. The Suliotes built their own cookfires in the courtyard, and set up to sleep on the ground floor with the beasts— yet till late at night they did not sleep, but passed the Wineskin, and sang their harsh balladry, and danced—man with man, at first stepping delicately and gravely as in a minuet, but by degrees growing wilder, and whirling faster, as the music of the drums and stringed gourds sped—let no mere *waltzer* of our lands attempt it! First among the dancers—a head higher than any of them, like Beelzebub amid his cohort—was the English Lord, his scarlet coat pulled open, and his handkerchief—as is the custom in that *gallopade*— aflutter in his right hand.

At eve the next day there came into the courtyard two of the guard, who had gone ranging, and with them that groom into whose care Lord Sane's admired black charger had been given. They had come upon the hapless fellow, on his way far elsewhere, it seemed, and *astride* the horse—though the poor animal's wound, and its stagger, were much the worse, indeed now beyond repair. The man was brought before his employer—trembling in justified terror, and begging, indeed *singing* in a heart-rending shriek for understanding, exculpation, mercy—Sane silent, and looking down upon him—then upon his quick word or two—which words compelled the miscreant to louder shrieks—the man was bound and carried to the stables, and prepared for the *bastinado:* which fearful *1* process no one there present, perhaps not excepting even the one who was to undergo it, would have denied the foreign Lord the right to impose upon his servant for his dereliction. When all was in readiness, Lord Sane settled himself at a distance upon a stool brought for him. Ali—for he was specially commanded to be present, at his father's side—stood behind. The Lord called for his pipe, which was quickly brought him, and a coal to light it with; and when it burned to his liking, he signalled—by a gesture as small as it was unmistakable—that the punishment should begin.

Man's ingenuity in the devices of torture and pain is endless— for it must have taken a deal of patient experiment to learn that the blows of a slim cane upon the bottoms of the feet, though not violent, are, when continued sufficiently, unbearable—the strongest man may not help crying out, and this groom was not of the strongest—no doubt he had seen others undergo what he now faced—and his wailing increased in pitch and volume before the first blow was struck. Lord Sane without expression went on smoking his pipe as the groom was beaten, unmoved even when it became apparent that the man's bowels had loosened in his agony. It was in that hour that Ali learned that he hated cruelty—knew that from that time forward he would never, if he could with honour avoid it, inflict or cause to be inflicted such acts as this he witness'd upon any being unable to resist, be it human or animal. As all men do who live in society, he learned to *abide* cruelty, when he could not *prevent* it—which largely he could not, the world being at all times over-full of it—he learned even to jest at it, speak lightly of it, in the world's way—but he would find himself unable to *witness* it with equanimity, and be compelled to stop it, when he could: as on that day he could not.

When the punishment was done, Lord Sane gave over his pipe to his boy, and left the stables, where the groom still sang out his pain and shame—went to the courtyard, where the once-proud stallion hung its head—took a pistol from his belt, primed and cocked it, and shot dead the poor beast himself without a word.

They went down from the mountains to the sea, through country almost without roads—though they passed a company in the process of repairing one of the few—a company of *women,* for in that land, in contrast to the homelands of the Turk, women are not put out of the world but do all the work that men do—nay, more—they are often driven like beasts, and not highly regarded. One among these women breaking stone—the youngest and loveliest of them— raised her blue eyes to see the strange party pass, and Ali as though stabbed to the heart believed for a moment that his Iman had somehow come to be transported here; the illusion quickly passed, and yet he still felt—for the first time in all its awful strangeness and *permanency*—that he had left his home, and all that he knew and loved he might never see again.

But the sea then appeared, its blue prinked with diamond sparkles, at first glimpsed between the peaks, then the great plain of it reveal'd, which Ali could not at first conceive to be truly *made of water,* as the more travelled among the band assured him—laughing—that it was; and Ali in terror and delight rode down to where the small waves fell, but drew his horse away from the curdled foam that crept up the sands toward him, just as a maiden draws her skirts away from stain. Lord Sane, coming up after, commanded him—with many an imperious gesture—to enter into the water, which Ali would not do—perhaps not believing that his sire truly intended such a thing. 'Go on, Sir!' cried Lord Sane in his own tongue—and the meaning of *this* at least was clear enough to Ali—'Go on, I say!'—'The boy cannot swim, my Lord,' said his chief of soldiery, in Romaic, and Lord Sane replied, 'Of course he can n't! But the *horse* can!' And with that he struck with his crop the flanks of Ali's horse, and struck again when it shied. Ali then—turning to face his tormentor, and to save his horse—glared upon his father—who seemed at once enraged and delighted with his son's resistance, and pointed again to the sea. The bedeviled boy for a moment paused, as though at a choice, whether he would confront his father, or the Deep; then he pulled hard at the reins, turned his horse, kicked his heels into its side—and the horse raced across the strand and willingly enough into the waves! Ali gasped for the cold—though that sea is as warm to an Englishman's limbs as a society hostess' dish of tea—and for the reaching of the surf upon his clothes, as though it meant to seize and pull him down—but still he urged on his steed, possessed by a nameless rage and uncaring now if he drown, or ride to the other shore—if there be one! The brave horse swam well and steadily till all four of its feet were off the bottom (for indeed it could swim, as every mammal can, from cat to elephant, if it but *choose* to, or *have a need*). Spray dashed in Ali's face, and he tasted *salt*—impossible!—and felt himself slip from the horse's wetted back—but he kept his seat—and knew a strange exaltation! When a great ninth wave (for as is well known, or at least commonly believed, each ninth wave of the sea is greater than its fellows) came near to swamping the

3

horse despite its courage, Ali, barely clinging to his seat, turned it
again to shore. Emerging thence—like Theseus' bull—he was surprized to find that he now stood some fifty yards from where he
had plunged in—the reader will understand by what action he
had been carried, but Ali did not. Down the strand toward him
raced the Suliotes, who in delight at Ali's courage had drawn and
now discharged their weapons—it is their common means of expressing any strong emotion. Lord Sane remained where he stood,
and Ali, for the salt spray that burned his eyes, could not see
clearly his father's expression, nor read what it portended—of satisfaction, or scorn, or the contemplation of further exactions—he
knew not.

They went down the coast to Salora, the port of Arta on the
Ambracian Gulph, to take ship for the greater port of Patras, where
Lord Sane had intelligence of a British brig-of-war soon starting for
Malta, thence by stages to the Isle of Albion, Ali's new, as it was his
ancestral, home. Yet there was a stretch of sea to cross between Salora and Patras, and Lord Sane sate a day in the pleasant garden of
an inn in Salora, where captains were wont to refresh themselves
and gather news; he fed his son on a pilaw, flavoured with a lemon
he pluckt from the tree that overhung their table, and a pair of
grilled eight-legged fish called *octopodes,* which he would not suffer
his son to send away. Successful—as it then seemed—in his negotiations, he next day took his son and the captain of his soldiers aboard
a little Greek Saick, forty men and four guns. The weather being fair
and the winds light, they were away from the harbour by noon.

Greek ships famously cling fast to well-known shores, and
Greek sailors, though skilled, are uneasy when out of sight of
land—it may be that those who sailed the long ships to Ilion felt the
same—and thus our passengers were able to pass close to the ruins
of Nicopolis, and later to behold the white Moon in the blue sky
over the Bay of Actium—there where the Ancient World was won,
and lost—where Cleopatra show'd herself no Admiral, however
otherwise *admirable* she was—events of which Ali was wholly ignorant, and to which his father was as wholly indifferent. As night
came on the wind arose, and the sea turned chopping; in such a

wind—soon amounting, the Crew by a sort of *democratic* assent decided, to a gale to be feared—they were of a mind to take in sail, put up the helm, and give themselves to the whims of Æolus, till softer weather obtained; but Lord Sane overmastered them, and, the gale blowing fiercer, ordered them to run before it. The Captain of the vessel, finding himself unable to refuse, ordered the Europeans below, and enjoined them to *pray*—which the Crew, in their several languages, had already commenced to do. Ali, who had never sailed a ship in any weather, supposed he was now to die—a common assumption of new travellers, in this instance shared by several of the Crew, who might be thought to know better; but though for a time he rocked and tossed in his stifling cabin below, could finally bear it no more, and climbed to the deck. There— where the seas came over the gunwales to polish the decks, and the helmsman was lashed to his Wheel—there sat Lord Sane, wrapt in his great black cloak, resting his back against the Mast, a fixed stare and a smile upon his face, as delighted in the uproars of Poseidon as though he had caused them himself.

At Patras, which they achieved almost too late, they were piped aboard the British brig-of-war even as it swung away from the harbour, and out to sea—past Missologi and thro' the doorposts of the two high Capes, of Araxos and Scrophia, bearing the noble Lord, and his plunder—a Son—as Lord Elgin bore away the marble children of that fair, unhappy land. Hail, Hellas, hail and hail again! *All* that has been stolen from thee—thy *Liberty,* the works of thy Genius—surely it will be returned to thee in the ripeness of Time— and *sooner* than thine Oppressor imagines!

Aboard this brig, that now passes into the open sea, there was another English passenger—a scholar and a linguist, with all the mild intelligence of the best of that species. He was a small and *circular* fellow—his head a circle, and his stomach, his round eyes, and his spectacles—and Lord Sane contracted with this gentleman to instruct Ali in the English Tongue, for as long as the voyage lasted—'Lessons to be continued at the bottom of the sea, should we arrive there,' quoth the merry Lord. Ali, proving an apt pupil, with a natural gift for languages that surely would have lain

5

unused had he not been thus transplanted, was soon able to understand something of his father's speech to him over his port, and as well some of the cruel sport he made of the circular linguist—as, 'Sir, your general *design* so resembles a *bladder* that I hold it as certain, were you to fall by evil chance into the sea, you would surely float beautifully—I propose to test this *theory*—how say you, Sir? Would you not chuse to advance Science by such an experiment? We shall write a letter to the Royal Society, *whether we succeed or no,*' and much more of the same character, and the small man bowed—and smiled—and *sweated*—as well he might, if he knew aught of his Lordship's jests on other occasions.

So it went, until deep blue sea turned at last to green, and the ghostly cliffs of Dover appeared before Ali's wondering eyes. Not only had he reached the end of the Earth—and how much farther was it than he had thought!—but a year, he supposed, had magically fled away in the passage, for surely now it was Winter, as witness these rolling clouds nearly close enough to touch, and this damp chill, and this fog; yet it was not so, as his Tutor exclaimed, it was still high Summer—only let Ali wait and see what Winter would bring! He suffered himself to be put into the ship's boat—there was no choice!—and was brought to Plymouth, where Lord Sane's Valet and *major-domo* awaited them.

The man was the right and proper guide, Ali perceived, to the land where he had come, for he was as lean as a desiccated Corpse, white as Bone, and silent as the Grave. In the low Inn to which he conducted them—Ali in his Albanian dress the object of every loiterer's eye—he found that this Valet, who shall hereafter be called Factotum, had laid out upon a bed a suit of clothes for Ali, which included boots, stockings, and breetches, a linen shirt, a buff waistcoat, and a coat of bottle green—to put on all which correctly, Ali must in profound shame ask the lean man's aid. There was no time though for a proper toilet, even had Ali known the finer points of such—no time either for refreshment, or rest, for a hired coach was already at the door, and Lord Sane in furious haste had his impedimenta piled upon it, and thrust his Company within. No doubt he had reason to be gone, which reason may have been connected to the arrangements he had made with the Captain of the Brig—who was proceeding to the same Inn even as Lord Sane's equipage was lashed out of town and abroad into the grey land of England. Poor Ali, in his tight carapace of English wool and leather, foist between father and corpse-like Factotum—both of whom to the boy's astonishment fell quickly to sleep despite the vehicle's juddering career—could but consider his situation as northward they flew.

'Now am I become the ghost of myself,' thought he. 'I have no land, but this of mist and cloud; no dress but the dress of my father's people, which is not my own. The only creature on earth who truly knows me and my heart, and loves me, is sundered from me by a limitless ocean; my tongue, with all that it alone could name, is shriven from me, and another's put in its place, like dust in my mouth. Am I not truly dead, and in the land of the dead?'

BUT IN ALL THIS TIME, as we have examined his Pedigree, and his fore-history, the man himself (yet hardly more than a boy) has sat in the old Scotch tower before the horrid mystery of his father's murder—sat, for his legs would not hold him upright! What colloquy he holds, while there he sits, with that Being strung up and staring without life or meaning at him, cannot be told—for there are things that words can but betray, by being *words,* and the stuff of conscious thought—of which the young Ali was then incapable.

When he has somewhat recovered himself, he stands, takes from his side the sharp *ataghan* that was the gift of his godfather the Pacha, as recounted, and cuts away at the ropes that, like a spider's web wound round its prey, have wrapt the body of his father. He grapples to him the horrid bundle in a filial embrace—or the picture of one—so that the great corse might not tumble down upon the floor; and he lowers it with what care he can to recline upon the stones—and he is attempting to free the dead man further—not knowing why he does these things, only that he is compelled to do *something*—when he hears, and sees too, on the path, a band coming upward toward him.

It is the Watch—two Officers, the only two that the Royal and Ancient Burgh within which the house and tower stand affords; and others too, tenants of the Laird, bearing torches of pitch-pine, to light the way. Ali considers not how this band has gathered—how apprised that there was matter here requiring their attention—he knows nothing—for a long moment is unable to recognize his neighbours among the crowd, or even to believe with certainty that they are men.

The leading Officer—the elder and graver—was a long man mounted on a very small galloway white with age; he wore a tricorn hat, the same; his progress would have been quicker had he gone on foot, but he perhaps thought this a diminishment of his dignity. He had dirk and broadsword; his smaller and dismounted fellow had a mousquet and brace. At the door of the tower they paused, and the long officer dismounted—took from a Citizen the flambeau he carried—and thrust it within the tower to illuminate Ali, who with his own sword in his hand was bent over the corse of his father.

The Laird! The cry goes up. *'Tis the Laird! 'Tis the Turkish boy! 'Tis he!*—Groans and cries of horror and rage mingle as these news are passed from front to back. As though he stands upon a stage, 'discovered' by the torches to this audience, Ali for the moment remains frozen. When he rises and steps toward the Officers, there is a general cry of alarm, and the tall one takes hold of his weapon.

'How do you come to be here?' Ali asks, for the curious aptness of the Watch's arrival at this drear place, and in expectation of trouble, now dawns upon him.

'We have had, Sir, *intelligence,*' says the Watch very solemnly.

'Intelligence! Why, what intelligence had you?'

'We had that, Sir, that brought us hither. But too late, too late.'

'Well, then,' Ali says. 'Come quick. You must not stand like stocks. We must find the one, or ones, who have done this deed.' The wide eyes before him, and their stillness—as of stocks indeed, or stock *fish*—inform him that they see no need to go a-hunting, or to search any farther than this place.

'I know nothing of this,' Ali says—to which the Officer makes no reply—seeing no better a one than the scene before him. 'Sir,' says he, 'you maun give up your *weepon*. I command you in the name of the Law.' Only at that moment does Ali grow conscious of the sword in his hand, the gift of the Pacha. He knows a wild impulse to resist, to strike at the foolish faces that regard him. And yet he does not—though to say *he thinks better of it* were false, for indeed he thinks of nothing, as though he still walked asleep—and turns the handle of his sword to the Officer, who takes it gravely from him. 'Now ye maun come along, young sair,' says he then. 'Offer no resistance, that it go not hard wi' ye!'

Injustice! Can there be a terror like it, to know that we are innocent, and yet found guilty—nay, *proven* guilty, our guilt clearly demonstrated, so irrefutable it can almost convince ourselves, however we know ourselves to be inculpable? And how much more so if the crime be one that a thousand times we have committed in our dreams, nay in our waking thoughts, in the dark haunts of our hearts?

Ali permitted himself to be taken—he offered no resistance. His head was high, tho' his face was deathly pale. With painful care the tricorn remounted his little nag; his fellow directed some six or eight of the company to take up the corse—which with much reluctance they did, tying it like a shot roe-deer to a pole, and carrying it over their shoulders: and so they went from that place of death, a solemn *cortege,* the Laird bound in his ropes, the son bound in his, and by torchlight they wound their way downward. At the end of the path from the tower they parted, some to carry the great relict to lie in his Hall, there to be duly examined—mourned too, it may be, by his dogs at the least; others to go with the son to the town on the harbour below, where he would be clapped—he was let to know—in irons. When, after a walk of some length—the Moon now low over the black sea—they achieved the Town, it appeared that some had hurried on ahead, to wake the Magistrate: for that personage was at the doors to the Tolbooth—as the Scotch denominate their guardhouse, which here was the courthouse too.

The doors were opened at the Magistrate's command, and Ali

was brought in; lights were lit that did not dispel the ancient gloom, and the Magistrate, taking from a serviceable and homely hook a shabby robe, which he donned, mounted the Bench, and looking with an air solemn and charged with grave responsibility upon all those gathered before him, demanded of the Officer his evidence. It was brief enough; that gentleman recounted how he had received *intelligence* of something afoot upon the hill; how he had gathered a force about him sufficient, as he calculated, to the occasion; how they had mounted the track, &c., &c., and there was the Laird laid by the feet, and the young Laird above him, armed. All eyes turned upon Ali.

'You had intelligence?' quoth the Magistrate.

'I did, please your Honour. That a *crame* of dreadfullest wickedness was in process at that moment in the place denominated the Old Watchtower upon the hill of the forest.'

'And your intelligence, as you judged it, was good?'

'It was as good as gold, your Honour.'

'I would beg to know,' Ali now said—and the Magistrate, and the generality who looked in at the doors, stood shocked, as though they had not known him capable of human speech—'I would beg to know, of your worships and honours, how it could be that I could conceive to perpetrate this deed, and at the same time, to send this—this—*intelligence* of it—to these Officers.'

'Make not light of this matter, Sir!' retorted the Magistrate. 'You are here charged with a horrid parricide! It may be, Sir, that in the lands from which you have sprung, this amounts to no more than a misdemeanour—it may, for aught I know, be common—yet in this land it is very unnatural indeed—and will be treated with all due severity—I warrant you!—and punished to the full extent of the law!'

'I have done nothing,' Ali said, 'and it shall be proven so.' Thus spake he—and yet his voice trembled to say so.

'Fifteen good men and true, and the King's Bench, shall be the arbiter of that,' said the Magistrate—for a Scotch jury is fifteen men, though south of the Cheviots it is thought that twelve suffice, being the number of the Apostles and not therefore to be exceeded; in the North, the more the merrier. The Magistrate lifted the curved ataghan which Ali had delivered up to his captors. 'And if this not be a case *prima facie* I know not what may be.'

'I would beg the return of my property,' said Ali, and stood with as great a dignity as his bound arms would allow.

'No, Sir, your weapon was material in a high crime, and thus will become a deodand to the King. *Prove your innocence,* and you may apply to *him* for it again.' He let fall the sword, and summoned the officers. 'Make fast the prisoner!' he said. 'Lock him up in yonder cell, and see that shackles be put upon his legs!'

The two minions of the Law, the small and the tall, put hands upon him. 'Wait,' said Ali. 'If there is to be a trial, I ask to be granted liberty till then.'

'Liberty,' pronounced the Magistrate, as though unfamiliar with the word, and considering what it might signify. 'And into whose recognizance do you ask that this court release you?'

'Why, into my own,' Ali said. 'You shall have my word of honour.'

The Magistrate's face betrayed what he thought of this offer, and after chewing on it for a moment as though he liked not the taste of it, he asked what other surety the accused could provide; to which Ali responded that his word ought certainly to be sufficient, but if it were not, he would provide what surety the court liked, in lands or bonds. Upon hearing this the Magistrate squeezed the podium from which he spoke, and glared down upon the hapless young man who stood unbowed before him. 'If,' said he, 'this crime be proved upon ye, as I have nae *doot* it will be, then all your lands and goods will be forfeit, forasmuch as ye may not profit by a murder—the Law, I say, is clear upon the point. And thus if ever these lands and goods was truly yours, or you had any certain claim upon them—the which permit me to question—ye hae none such now to pledge.

'And so bear him awa',' he concluded, 'and let him think upon his deed, and upon the Law's Majesty!'

For the Law has undoubted Majesty—and that Majesty is not diminished when we observe the Law's wig askew, or its waistcoat misbuttoned; nor in that we have seen the Law drunk at the Fair, or

upon the public road; nor by our knowledge that the Law has profited, in a small way, from the traffic in Contraband so prevalent
upon those rocky coasts: *not* diminished, when it has the power
absolute, our guilt or its absence notwithstanding, to close an iron-
bound door upon us, and turn the key, and pocket it!

NOTES FOR THE 2ND CHAPTER

1. *bastinado:* In response to my inquiry, Mr John Cam Hobhouse, now Lord Broughton, who accompanied Byron on his
   youthful journeys, informed me that Byron's account of this re-
   volting and unlikely practice is indeed quite accurate, and re-
   flects in detail a scene witnessed by himself and Lord Byron
   when in Turkey.

2. *a company of women:* Mr Thomas Moore in his Life of the poet,
   prints a letter of Byron's to his mother from Albania, in which
   he reports exactly this sight, of women breaking stone upon the
   public highway, treated as beasts of burden, and made to
   labour while their men enjoyed war & the chase. As but a very
   young man, he could censure it, but was unconscious enough
   then of injustice to note that this 'is no great hardship in so delightful a climate', a sentiment which the women themselves
   might be imagined to answer, and the author himself later to
   regret.

3. *indeed it could swim:* Lord Byron is correct that horses can swim
   well, and will sometimes do so merely for delight. I know this

of my own experience. After a long childhood illness which prevented me from riding, indeed from walking except with aids, when well again I became a passionate and perhaps even a reckless equestrienne, and more than once rode my favourite mount into the sea, to its evident enjoyment.

4. *Theseus' bull:* Reference is to the vengeful bull from the sea, summoned by the incest of Phædra with her adopted son. It is of course the son, Hippolytus, who is destroyed by the bull, and not Theseus—a rare slip for Ld. B., who was well versed in classical reference. I note it because I am not myself well versed, and am glad to have noticed this.

5. *Missologi:* The Greek town of *Missolonghi* was where Lord Byron breathed his last, a martyr to the cause of Greek freedom. It is strange that he in his fiction should place his characters so close to this fateful place. There is a mystery in coincidence that, in centuries hence, may be reduced, by tools we as yet know not of, to mathematical description.

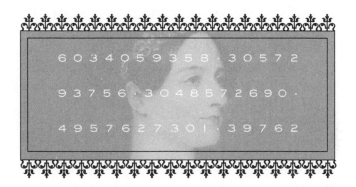

From: "Smith" <anovak@strongwomanstory.org>
To: lnovak@metrognome.net.au
Subject: Question

Hi. It's Alexandra (your daughter).
I have a question that I can't think of anybody else to ask—I mean anybody else who might be able to answer. So is this you?

PS I know it's been a long time.

From: lnovak@metrognome.net.au
To: "Smith" <anovak@strongwomanstory.org>
Subject: RE:Question

Alexandra—

How wonderful, how really wonderful to hear from you, after so long.
People usually say "after so long" in order to reproach their correspondent; but I know that it's me and not you who's been so long in writing. I could give the usual excuses—that I didn't know your address—that I'm goddamned busy so much of the time, and so far away from everything, etc. But of course I could have

found your address—after all you found mine; I could even have asked your mother for it, though that would have meant first finding hers, which since you turned eighteen and my legal relations with her pretty much ceased, I haven't kept track of; and of course I'm never too busy, not too busy to do what I want. Anyway now that I've begun again I'll go on. That's a promise.

So yes this is me. Now what's your question? And how are you, and how have you been?
Love
Lee

PS What is strongwomanstory.org? I suppose I should know how to look for it on the Web, but so much time spent in places that often didn't have phones or typewriters let alone computers and Internet connections has made me both shy and arrogant in the face of the World Wide anything.

————————————

From: "Smith" <anovak@strongwomanstory.org>
To: lnovak@metrognome.net.au
Subject: RE:Re:Question

Okay—

I know you're very busy, and I don't want to take up a lot of your time. The question is this. Did Lord Byron ever write a novel? I went online and to the library and it was hard to find out for sure. Like if he didn't it would be proving a negative, or something. I mean it obviously wasn't a big part of his work, or I would see it listed, right? I'll explain why I need to know when I know. That sounds snotty, huh?

To see the site I work for just put the URL—that's strongwoman story.org—into the SEARCH box on Google or whatever you use. Or just in the address box up top and press ENTER. You don't have to use *http://* and all that. Then just CLICK on stuff; you won't get hurt, or get sick; the worst that could happen is you'll get lost, or bored.

Alexandra

──────────────

From: lnovak@metrognome.net.au
To: "Smith" <anovak@strongwomanstory.org>
Subject: RE:RE:Re:Question

Alexandra:

Well—that worked—eventually. Congratulations, I think. You are the editor, I see by the credits; I don't think I know what that means in Web terms. More like a film editor or more like a text editor? I looked at some of the pages. I admit I hadn't ever heard of most of the women, which I guess is the point. The facsimiles of autograph writings were the best part. I couldn't tell if looking at it all made me feel closer to you, or farther away.

To your question. It's actually been a long time since I've thought about Byron. I don't have any reference works with me here. Pretty soon I'll be heading on from this very isolated place with the rest of the crew for some R&R in Tokyo; there they have plenty of reference works in English (their libraries are full of them—as many as in the best American university libraries). But off the top of my head I cannot imagine what you're referring to. Lord Byron never wrote a novel. He never even completed any stories in prose. His sometime friend Edward Trelawney urged him to write a novel, and Byron said that well he would have if Walter Scott hadn't already written his, and that in any case a man shouldn't write a novel until he was 40—an age which as you may know he never reached.

On the other hand, he did of course begin one. It's one of the most famous scenes in English literature. It was at the Villa Diodati that Byron rented in Geneva. Shelley, Mary Shelley, and Byron all sitting around on a dark and stormy night and Mary speaks up and says *Let's each write a ghost story!* And they do. And Mary's is *Frankenstein*. Shelley never got far with his, and the few pages that Byron began of a vampire novel he later handed to the other member of the party, a certain Dr. Polidori—who without Byron's knowledge expanded the pages into a huge novel of his own—one of the first vampire novels in English—and published it anonymously, while letting everybody think it was by Byron. Polidori also named his main character, the vampire, after the main character in a spite novel by Caroline Lamb, who was one of Byron's old lovers; the hero of *her* novel is a monster of wickedness who is recognizably based on Byron—you getting all this?—which nettled Byron no end—I mean Polidori's behavior and Caroline's too. *Not* no end, though, really: except for real slights to his honor, or real betrayals, Byron couldn't hold a grudge; he ended by laughing it all off.

I'm amazed that you've wandered into this old territory of mine. I remember that your mother's first words to me—very nearly—were *I never liked him*. I'd just broken the ice with her at a faculty party—god how many years since I've entered one of those—and mentioned my Byron studies. I said *Well, of course you don't like him. You don't know him.* I may need to say the same to you—no?

So I'd love to hear more, about why this question has come up—I'm guessing it has something to do with Ada—and more about you too, and I promise to answer any questions promptly, or send them on to a person who can, if I can actually remember who those people were—I keep up very few of the old academic contacts.

I love you, Alex.

Lee

————————

From: "Smith" <anovak@strongwomanstory.org>
To: lnovak@metrognome.net.au
Subject: Secret

I don't know if what I do should even be called "editor." I got into this because I (almost) got a degree in History of Science, and I used to work on a project to publish all the correspondence of a scientific society of the 18th c., and so I learned to read a lot of old handwriting on bad photocopies. The people who funded the Strong Woman site in the first place aren't really historians of science, or historians at all, and one of the ideas they had was instead of just taking letters and documents out of books, they'd go back to the originals in the archives, and retranscribe them—in case there had been errors, or *suppressions,* you know—and put up facsimiles, which was unnecessary really of course but actually in the end kind of cool, because you get to see the writings, and diagrams and equations and stuff they actually put down, and sometimes crossed out—I love when they cross things out—and crammed into margins, and some of them are obsessively neat and some of them are wild and messy.

So I'm the one who finds and reads these letters and things, and I also learned the Web basics, and so I put it up too, and other stuff, and I write some of the commentaries. But there's a team.

Yes it's something to do with Ada. I'm in England and I'm doing research on her for the site, to upgrade the biography and include some new things. Some new documents have been uncovered, and we are thinking about what they might be. One of the things is some pages of notes, by Ada, and the story of how she acquired the manuscript of a novel he wrote; she says she's going to write notes for this novel too, and there they are. There's no manuscript of a novel though—but there's one page that might be from it. Only one page. If you take a phrase out of it and go search the online Byron texts you don't find it (I've tried). So what is it and where did it go, if it was really an "it" at all. Any thoughts? I'm attaching the one page of text that's turned up. I scanned it so you can look at it. It's hard to read, but you can.

The papers came to the site privately, and nobody wants publicity yet. So.

Alexandra

<u>Attached: Onepage.doc</u>

*man—no matter—I am myself just as ignorant of those
vast lands in many ways, an ignorance I delight in, for I
have done with the world I am not ignorant of. Perhaps
we shall go to the undiscovered West, and down the Mississippi, as Lord Edward Fitzgerald did—the only pure
hero I have ever known, or known of—and like him look
even farther, to the South, to Darien, the Brazils, the
Orinoco—I know not.*

*And so farewell. I am not so foolish as to think Amer-
ica is a Physician, or a Priest—I know that all diseases are
not cured there, nor all sins forgiven. And yet on this
morning I feel as one who has nightlong in a dream struggled with an enemy, and has waked at last, to find his
arms are empty*

———————————

From: lnovak@metrognome.au
To: "Smith" <anovak@strongwomanstory.org>
Subject: Page

Alex—

This is certainly striking, and I'm not really the one to ask, but you
certainly ought to be wondering if it's a forgery, especially considering the mysterious provenance you mention; discoveries like
this usually are trumpeted to the world, and the subsequent
publicity drives the price up—like the million-dollar trunkful of
Melville letters and papers that was discovered in an old barn in
the Berkshires or somewhere a few years ago. So the first thing to
do is get it authenticated, and I'm certainly not the man for that.
Certainly it seems impossible that the MS. of a Byron novel has
been lying in an archive somewhere unnoticed.

It is strange though. America. In the last years of his life,
before the Greek adventure was decided on, Byron talked often of

going to America: South America most often—he didn't make a big distinction—and start a new life as a planter. George Washington was one of the few historical figures he admired without irony; but another was the Fitzgerald this page mentions.

Could I get a look at the notes Ada wrote, if you scan them too? It doesn't damage them to do that, does it? These are highly valuable papers, as I'm sure you're aware, if they are what they seem to be. What if they really are? Well then wow. Are you going to go to the Lovelace archives and see if you can find out about this? It seems impossible that there's an entire novel by Byron lying around somewhere in her papers that's been overlooked, but we can hope.

Now I have two (immediate) questions for you. One is: Why did you think of me when you needed this question answered? There are a lot more knowledgeable people around than me. The other question is why you call yourself "Smith" in the address line of your letters—is that just some Internet thing?

Lee

————————————

From: "Smith" <anovak@strongwomanstory.org>
To: lnovak@metrognome.net.au
Subject: Smith, etc.

I guess the reason I wrote to you was because it was a secret. I couldn't think of how to ask anybody else without giving it away. That's all. I'm not a scholar or a historian really. I'll send you the Ada note pages when I scan them. It doesn't hurt them. I wear these little white gloves.

Almost everybody I know calls me Smith. Partly it's because of the college. A long while after I dropped out of my first school I went there on a special program to get an MA (the *Ada* Comstock program, how do you like that). And also partly 'cause I once joked that I wanted a last name for a first name, like all those cool movie stars and so on with names like Parker and Drew and Reese. Why not Smith, said I. So it, you know, stuck.

I hate thinking the papers are fake. I'm going to start looking. Thanks and I'll let you know.

Alexandra

———————————

From: lnovak@metrognome.net.au
To: "Smith" <anovak@strongwomanstory.org>
Subject: RE:Smith, etc.

You know for the last six months of your prenatal life you were going to be named Haidée, for a girl in Byron's *Don Juan*. Your mother was okay with that, but then changed her mind. I couldn't fight her. Smith is fine. You were never really Alexandra to me. Alexandra is a cold regal beauty. Alex is butch. Sandy is a cute kid with pigtails (and a dog named Annie . . .). I don't know why your mother liked it.

I should point out that no one is really a historian, all the way through, just as no one is really a writer, or really a saint. Those things can only be what you do, not what you are: you write, or you conduct historical investigations, or you do good, etc. Let other people call you the big words—Robert Frost says "poet" is a term only other people can apply to you. Believe me you can go through life unsure if any such a title truly applies to you, the you inside. Poet. Star. Genius. Criminal.

Lee

———————————

From: "Smith" <anovak@strongwomanstory.org>
To: "Thea" <thea.spann133@ggm.edu>
Subject: Hey

Thea

I've scanned the mathematical tables and I've sent them to you on a CD FedEx, it would take 4ever in download time, it took me all day and night to scan and copy them so you could even see them. I think it's crazy we can't ask somebody here to look at them but Georgiana is so spooked about anybody finding out about the stuff till we can make a big announcement. She thinks too much in my opinion—I don't think people care as much as she thinks. She even worried a little about you but I told her you were my bondage love slave and so it's safe.

Lee wrote. I wrote back. Okay so far. Well it's weird but somehow not weird the way you expect. That's what's weird. I guess we'll have to really say something sometime. It would be weirdest of all if we didn't.

————————————

From: "Thea" <thea.spann133@ggm.edu>
To: "Smith" <anovak@strongwomanstory.org>
Subject: RE:Hey

you will   believe me   and then we will see   i do not approve of this but I will not send the fbi his email address   they have it any-way or they dont care   i dont care either   about him   i just want you not to be hurt

spring break at the college and so the THEMS have gone home or to fla   and here i am alone at night with only my v   aw shucks

t

————————————

From: "Smith" <anovak@strongwomanstory.org>
To: "Thea" <thea.spann133@ggm.edu>
Subject: v

I'll bring you a new v, love. The Sporty Spice Special.

I'm going to go look at the Ada papers at Oxford. Georgiana wanted to come too—we'd motor down together, dear—but then she had a family thing. I'm not sorry. But I'm a little afraid to go alone. Oxford. I feel like a Country Mouse, only without a City Mouse to show me all the goodies, and the dangers too. Like I might get eaten alive. I had a dream last night about that: going in someplace huge and dark and angry (like places can be in dreams) and not finding a way out, and nobody telling me or caring at all. I think they must come from childhood, those dreams, where adults pay you no attention and you can't say why you're afraid.

Write me. Tell me I'm brave, and I will be.

Smith

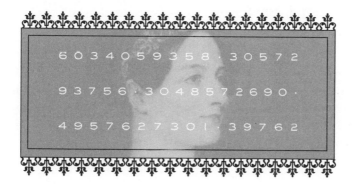

THREE

Of Ali's Education, in

several subjects

BY THE SOUTH-WESTERN coast of Scotland, between the ocean and the mountains, the ruins *1* of an Abbey stand, join'd incongruously to a house of the last century, and fronted by a Park where once noble trees consorted, and deer cropped grass and ate apples. A small lake, bounded by granite works, the plaything of a former Lord who liked to float miniature fleets upon it, and engage them in mock battles, no longer spouts from its centre the glittering pillar of water it was wont to show. This pretty piece of water was the smallest of a linked series of *2* lakes, where Waterfowl congregated in their season, set in a wide oakland that once sheltered game and fed pigs even-handedly. The woods being cut down, the lakes overflowed their bounds and spread into a marshland, of barren aspect and forbidding.

To this house, after a month's travel from the South, came Lord Sane and his son Ali—now his son by *English law* as well as by Nature's; for Sane had taken care to sojourn a time in London and there have all necessary writs of adoption prepared, and other papers, with their seals and witnesses, their Whereases and their Subjunctions in proper form, duly signed and registered. Thus was a flaw in his marriage to the Lady of this manor healed—as Sane himself perceived it. For, drunk as he had often been during the brief Courtship by which he had won that Lady's hand, he had not fully understood her estates to be entail'd upon her heirs—that, absent an Heir of Lord Sane's own getting, all would revert, upon the Lady's death, to distant Cousins still in their infancy, her husband to retain but a portion (already borrowed against and spent) of the Lady's money. Lord Sane, having more soberly and with the aid of solicitors examined all the encumbrances upon the estate, had determined that the heir of the family being the *legal child* of the Lady, it need not be *the child of her body;* and thus by his papers and his writs his own son became heir to his adoptive Mother's lands, albeit with the same entailments. How often we entangle ourselves in our own dark futures, merely as a consequence of not reading with care what our agents and our solicitors have sent us, and explained to us, and begged us to attend to! Life—our life—is in them, as plots are in novels; we reach our last page in peril, if we have skipped over them!

A further obstacle to Lord Sane's ability to do exactly as he pleased was harder to remedy: not all the lands and titles in question together produced sufficient income for the ancient manor's upkeep, especially when diminished by Lord Sane's early debts, and the interest upon them, and the Jews and middlemen (and middle-*women,* worse than any of these) who held his bonds, and who had granted him Annuities, which he was still obliged to pay tho' the income obtained was long gone. Thus Lord Sane when not engaged in profligacy, was perforce engaged in the raising of money wherewith to pay its costs, and the race was not always equal. He could not sell the ancient seat—but he could sell all that it contained, and had for some years been doing so. In former times

the rooms had held gilt mirrors and feather beds, book-desks and
their books, firearms in cases, china-ware from China as well as
from France—Lord Sane could see no difference in a Cup, or cared
to see none, but Messrs Christie did, who also sold the house's
Reynoldses, its Canalettos, and its Knellers, tho' they scorned the
rest. At last, having sold all those *un*necessaries, he proceeded to sell
the brass locks from the doors, the lead from the window-panes, the
chimney-pieces from the chimneys, the tattered rugs from beneath
the sleeping dogs.

3

When Ali came to the house, it was thus spoliated and de-
nuded: but the youth could not truly perceive this, who had never
lived amid fine things—even his godfather the Pacha had had, except for his carpets and his weapons, nothing of display or munifi-
cence about him or his habitations, where he lived as in the tents of
his Ancestors, ready to move at any moment—of pictures that gentleman had had none, and the Koran forbade the representation of
his forebears, had he known who those worthies were. What Ali
felt then, when the great doors were thrown open, and those few
servants still attached to the estate came forth to greet their Laird,
and by them he was escorted within the Great Hall where once an
hundred Monks had broke their fast together, was a species of
awe—which emotion, reflected in his features, was evident to his
sire, and not displeasing to him.

Lord Sane took his son through the empty galleries and the un-
inhabited cloisters—the cells where once those holy men had
prayed, or had *not*—their ancient kitchen, now but ruination, its
fireplace as large as many a cot in Albania. He bore him downward,
into close passages of mouldered brick, vaults once broken into by
the Laird in search of buried treasure, which as everyone knows
only the *good* will be directed by Heaven to find. No treasure therefore having been found, the breached walls were left in that condition, the tools abandoned. In the roofless chapel, vegetation sprang
from high cornice and ogee, and fallen stones, some of them the
faces and limbs of saints and angels, impeded the foot. All these
sights—taken as the sun set, and darkness swept over the ancient
demesne, and an owl was heard from its place in the crannied

stone—which might in an English breast have started the most *Gothic* shudders, and emotions of sublimity and dread—affected the young Albanian only with curiosity, and wonder, and a sort of *vacancy,* that he knew not whether he stood here, or not, or what *he* might be, if he be a *he* at all, and not a mere wisp of spirit lost.

'Now,' said Lord Sane, when the two had refreshed themselves with a Scotch woodcock (that is, a dish of eggs, all that the kitchen afforded) and the contents of an exceptional bottle of Claret—for the cellar, of all that house, was left undespoiled—'now, you will please me, if you will go and pay your respects to your lady mother, in her apartments above. My man will conduct you thither.'

'The lady is not my mother,' said Ali.

'What do you say, Sir?' asked his father, surprised, for he had not been crossed by the youth before: all that Ali had endured, he had endured silently—not till now had he found it impossible *not* to speak.

'The lady is not my mother,' Ali repeated. 'I am happy to pay my respects, but not as to a mother; for I had a mother.'

'Dead,' said Sane. 'Well dead.'

'I shall honour her memory,' said Ali, 'and not call another by that name I must reserve for her alone.'

'You are too nice,' said Lord Sane, colouring. 'Her death being the condition of your coming to be, and of your coming to be *here,* she has done what she might; you had best look to another for more.'

'How do you mean,' Ali said, 'the *condition* of my coming to be?'

'Why, in that your engendering was counted a capital crime by her people,' his father said, and struck the board. 'As soon as ever *you* were known about, her death was certain; the sky should have fallen, rather than such a blot on the escutcheon remain. I should be dead too, save for the chance of my being, by your people's determination, blood-brother to your mother's husband, and therefore unassailable.'

Ali—who, if his young soul had still a childish fault, it was a slowness to believe evil of those among whom he found himself, and therefore to draw the right, that is to say the *worst,* conclusions from their actions—only now saw clearly what his case was, and what his mother's had been. 'You knew, then,' he said, 'that you condemned her to death.'

'Ah! Who can know to what any adventure may lead? Let us have enough of this old business.'

'Knew that you had so shamed her husband, that he must take her life—she who but for your ravishment might be alive today!'

'Your regrets are misplaced,' said Lord Sane. 'It mattered not to them. Women are as cattle among your people; if the woman had not died so, she would have been worked to death soon enough— a life of toil was all she did not live to see.' He drained his glass, and then added: 'If the story I had from the Pacha be true, my *brother* drew the knife across her throat himself.'

Ali now, as by an involuntary spasm, reached for the Pacha's sword, which he had belted at his side—his father himself had in-sisted he wear it, on the long Northward highway where brigands still roamed—and gripped its handle, his eyes flashing.

'Do you draw on me, Sir?' said Lord Sane, arising, in a voice where fury and *contentment* strove incongruously. 'Do you? Then draw! You see I have but a stick, but I will strike you down if you offer me offence!'

For a long, an endless moment, the two men stood on either side of the table, the great frame of the Lord, the slight one of the son, and neither moved, nor took his eyes from the other's—nor did the footman move, nor the Valet, nor the serving-girl in the doorway.

What now would he do, our youth? Seeing clearly his condition—engendered in Sin and Murder, abstracted from his home, friended only by the man before him, who seemed as willing to slay him as he had been to bring him hither—what *could* he do? Without a further word, but unbowed, he took his hand from his weapon; he stood down from his posture of opposition. He would do as he was asked, or commanded, because he had for *now* no choice: but never again would he acknowledge any *duty* to the man before him.

'Permit me to point out the hour,' said Sane, in all conscious-ness of his triumph over the youth. 'Her Ladyship is early to bed, and late to rise. It were best if you go now. She will be expecting you.' And with a nod he set in motion his Valet, who came gravely to take Ali away. 'You may bring her my compliments,' said Lord Sane, 'but do not promise, nor *suggest,* that I shall visit her. Not this night, nor on the morrow either.'

So Ali followed the spectral Factotum from the hall, and through the door and chamber, and up stairs. The Valet paused to light a candle-stick at a lamp that burned on a landing, and then pro-ceeded upward till a painted door was reached, and there he turned to Ali, and seemed upon the point of speaking—for his lip curled, and his fish's eye lit dimly—but then he only knocked, and hearing something from within that Ali could not, he opened the doors, and announced Ali in a dusty whisper.

It seemed to Ali as he entered that the room was empty. It was more fully finished than other chambers and halls through which he had passed—its drapes had not been pulled down, its paper'd walls were not so stained with water, the carpets upon the floor were whole, and a great bed retained its tester and its clothes. From within this bed Ali now heard a small voice, and at the same time the doors behind him were closed.

'Art thou the boy?' repeated the dim voice of a personage unseen—and Ali, stepping farther into the dimness of the chamber, now perceived through the bed-hangings a large figure, in white, as pale nearly as the sheets—a figure who now lifted a hand, in wel-come, or in weak defence—Ali could hardly tell.

'Madam,' said he, and inclined his head, as he had seen his father do.

'Lord Sane has sent thee to me,' said the Lady—for it was she, or her great ghost, lifting itself from the pillows. 'That I might give thee my blessing.'

'I should be glad of it,' said Ali.

'Come closer,' said she, 'that I may see what son I have been given. Come.'

Ali came as he was bidden, and approached the bedside of Lady Sane, who now closer to him, was revealed to be, though pale and somewhat *indeterminate,* a cheerful personage, with a kindly smile, and a mass of curls that escaped from beneath her snood. 'What is thy name?' she asked.

'Ali.'

'Ali! Did he not give thee a Christian name, then?'

'No, Madam, he did not, though his advisors thought he ought, and urged him to have me christened, as it is called. Lord Sane thought not so. It amused him—he said so—that his son bear always the name he was given at birth.'

'And has he been kind to thee?' asked the Dame, as though she had reason to think quite otherwise. 'Has he given thee what thou art in want of, at the least?'

'Madam,' said Ali, 'he has given me all that I asked of him.'

At that she fell silent for a time, perhaps understanding what Ali had said, as he *meant* it. Then, seeming more to marvel at, than to object to it, she said—'So I now have a son who is a Turk.'

'No, Madam,' Ali said again—and for the first time his strange career seemed to him comical, and his situation fit for laughter:— 'No, I am no Turk. I am half an Englishman, if my father's tale be true, and half a man of the Ochridan people, who have among them killed many a Turk. Indeed I am nothing, or a part of something and a part of something else. Yet I do not think I am parts—I think I am whole—or may be whole—and all one.'

As he spoke, the bedclothes about the figure of Lady Sane were stirred, as frothy ocean-pools are stirred by waves inpouring. Her head she lifted from its pillows, and her eyes—gentle and young as a faun's, which Ali thought remarkable—widened, and took him in. 'Why, indeed you are, dear child,' said she. 'You are but one, and all one. And yet'—here Lady Sane touched her chin thought-fully—'if you are no Turk,' said she, 'and have no Christian name—are you then a Christian?'

'I am not,' said Ali. 'I have just begun to make myself under-stood in English, and to wear English clothes—I have no other En-glish qualities about me.'

'Well,' Lady Sane reply'd, 'I have not thought it an English quality to be Christian—and you are not now among that nation— and you have a soul, have you not?'

Ali knew not what answer to return to this question; he believed it to mean that he had that within him which was not his flesh, yet was the true self, the *one* he was, or might be. 'I think I may have,' he said.

'Then it may be saved,' she said, and so saying she took from the table at her bed-side a black-bound book that any among us this side of the Middle Sea would know at once. She held it out to him—not as a thing for him to take, but only to *behold*—for, as many do who hold that Book in the greatest reverence, she seemed to think its virtue flowed as strongly from it when closed, as *open*—indeed perhaps more strongly, or simply. 'Come to me,' she said, 'and together we shall read.'

'Madam,' he said, 'I cannot read.'

'Then you shall learn,' said the lady, rising in her bed, 'for who cannot read or hear, cannot be saved.'

'Saved?' Ali inquired, at the reiteration of this word, which is so pregnant with meaning—or *meanings*—indeed, with a varied and contrary offspring. The lady touched a place on the broad bed, indicating that there he should sit by her, and when he had with care and some trepidation taken that seat, she regarded him the more closely with her melting eyes. 'I see you are in want of a friend,' she said, 'and so am I; let us pledge to each other, that we will be each the other's support, and protection.'

'If you wish it,' Ali said in all gentleness. Indeed he knew not how this lady might protect him—nor how he would repay that service in turn—as it seemed she might well require of him: and yet for sure he stood in need of such a one, and no other champion had appeared, or seemed likely to—none but his own *soul,* upon which he dared not wholly lean. And so he made a soft answer, and took her hand fat as a pluck'd quail, and as cold; and pitied her, as he would not deign to pity himself. And soon the lady sent him away, with a promise, *when she felt stronger,* to send for him again.

———————

THUS WAS ALI PUT to school with Lady Sane, to learn the meaning of those signs and symbols he had at first begun to recognize in the company of the Circular Tutor aboard the Navy brig that brought him at first to Albion. Lord Sane was not entirely pleased to learn that his son had been invited to spend much time in his wife's company, and look'd upon Ali with his *reptilian* consideration—and yet said nothing to forbid it—and soon enough he was gone from home, if that humble but dear name be applicable to the House he occupied. He had spent but a month there—feeding and teasing his Menagerie—by day riding at breakneck speed over the fields of his hard-press'd Tenantry, or disputing with his Steward—at night drinking his own hock and Claret, knocking the heads off the bottles with a poker, the drawing of corks being too mean a labour for him, and the summoning of his *man* too *tough a job.* 'Enough!'—then cried he—and called for his Coach, and his brutish Coachman, large as a Patagonian, and the four matched blacks which that Coachman alone could control—and he betook himself South to the Fleshpots, and the companions he delighted in.

Each morning Ali mounted the stairs that led from the ancient Abbey where Lord Sane presided—even in *absence*—to the modern house, where Lady Sane was in residence—tho' seemingly not always *present,* for her thoughts turned often from the books and the papers upon which Ali indited his crude letters, to dwell on past times, or in dreams, or in Heaven, to which she meant to lead the son of her husband. But often, in going about in that far realm, her imagination lit upon Heaven's *opposite,* and she trembled at a thing she could not say—a tale she would not tell—and seemed to fear. When Ali, alarmed, asked her what was the matter, and what it was she feared, she answered only, 'Why, to be *damn'd,* and suffer for aye!'—and would not say, upon what grounds the divine Judge might make such a disposition. Ali, not disposed to consider his *own* after-fate, no matter how Lady Sane pressed the matter upon him, could not but ponder, and grieve for that gentle lady's suffering.

Of the other souls who haunted that palace in Limbo, there

were housemaids, who shied from him like deer, as they had learned to fear the attentions of the Master of the house, and thus whoever might stand in his stead—and a Cook, and scullery-maids and footmen, a sullen one or two—and a lady's maid nearly as ghostly as her Lady was. Ali, who had no knowledge of the right manner of treating with servants, alarmed them sometimes by sitting silently among them in their kitchens and shops—where he learned much that, when he began at school, he would be required to *unlearn,* though he would not *forget*—and unwittingly affronted them by not suffering them to wait upon him, but rather doing for himself what was needful. Happier was he alone and abroad, with

4   no company but a black Newfoundland dog, chosen by him from a litter out of his father's favourite bitch. This animal would come to seem a part of himself—his own best self, ready to stand and run and sleep beside him, ever loyal, without *motive,* without reservation, with all his strong heart. *Thy warden,* Lady Sane called this companion of her son's when Ali brought him even to her chamber; and when Ali had ascertained the right meaning of the word, it became the beast's name, as it was his nature. With him Ali strode for leagues over the naked hills and through the new-sprung woods; oft he was observed far from the Abbey, careless of the weather, without occupation and—for a time, a day, a blessed Hour!—without *thought,* save for the ache in his joints, and the air in his lungs, until he truly seemed to have returned to the hills of Albania (which to his eyes these of Scotland resembled, except in respect of *moisture*) and was again following his goats, with his people, and his beloved.

Iman! She could not fade from his heart, but her image—undimm'd—could not alter, either, nor grow, nor change: she became a painted picture—a single mood—a gesture—or but a few—her voice, the same, still heard, but like the voice of one who walked away, and looked not back. In the Park, not far from the Abbey,

5   there grew an Elm with a double trunk—two *sundered* limbs that had sprung from a single root, and had grown year by year farther apart. Upon the two uplifted arms, Ali, with the point of the sword he had brought from the land of their birth, carved his own name, and *hers*—in the letters of *this* land—the only he would ever learn.

One other among that house's inhabitants showed him kindness, and bent his mind to make him welcome. 'Old Jock', as this ancient was known, was formerly a retainer of the 'auld Laird', Lady Sane's father—indeed, he seemed to carry with him, in the bright roses of his cheeks, his ready smile, and the frost upon his curling hair and whiskers, the spirit of a merrier age, and a happier house. The smoke of his long pipe, and the touch of his rough hands, reminded Ali of the old goatherd who had raised him, and predisposed him to love the man. With him Ali learned the making of bullets, and the cleaning and care of pistols and guns, and when at length he left the old Abbey and its guardian spirit, he had learned to put out a candle with a pistol-shot at forty paces. By Old Jock's fire, seated upon a 'creepie', or Scotch stool, Ali listened to tales that reached back to the Covenanters, and in the repeated hearing of them added a Scotch burr to his English that not all his later schooling would rub off. From Old Jock he learned of the wayward lords and the noble ones who, though he shared no blood with them, stood now in a row behind him like the parade of Banquo's sons in the witch's mirror, he being the heir of the house.

'There is nae other *naw*,' said he. 'And naw will never be, none but thee; for a curse fell upon the house long ago, that it would be barren, and produce none.'

'A curse?'

'There was but a single child born to my Lady,' said Old Jock, and his voice had sunk to a whisper, as though someone—someone he need not name—might overhear. 'The birth was not easy, and the child was soon dead. And after that time, my Lady shut herself up, out of the world—or was *put* awa'—it mak's nae *muckle* difference, how 'tis said.'

'This amounts to no curse. Many a one is born to die.'

'Ah,' said Old Jock. 'Ah, young Sair. We *make* a curse of what befalls us, if we are certain 'tis meant to be. The old Laird, blessings be upon him: on his own death-bed, he was heard to say, that his only daughter's marriage would bring about the downfall of his house.'

'It still stands,' said Ali.

'And here art thou, as well,' said Old Jock, and the glitter in his eye was kind, and yet too wise for kindness. 'Aye, aye: *here art thou!*'

Yet it is not sufficient to make an English gentleman, that he learn his letters at a pious Dame's side, and the crafts of life from a Countryman. There came a time when Ali must go to school—he was already superannuated. Lord Sane and his wife were of different minds on the subject—for Lady Sane wanted to have the boy *near,* and Lord Sane cared nothing for that, so his situation be an *approved* one, where his fellows would bring him out, and *polish* him, as though he were a gem found by the wayside. The school chosen for him (Lady Sane in feeble opposition notwithstanding) was far to the South, nearly as far as London.

7   Ida—so she shall here be named—was then the first, or it may be the second, Academy where those too old to learn from their Parents and too young to learn from the World were ensconced, to learn from Masters wise (or contrariwise), and much *more*—not all of it *lofty*—from their Fellows. Here Ali arrived, in the summer of his fourteenth year, late and ill-prepared for what might now become of him—for his protector Lady Sane could not, and his father had not cared to, describe it to him. The crowd of boys in their tall hats and tail-coats at once drew him in among them, and at the same time made clear to him his absolute difference from them, in experience and knowledge; he was tarred for being *young* and for being *too old,* for being *too tall* and too delicate, for being ignorant of things he could not have learned elsewhere. He was shocked to discover that as a junior scholar he would be the dependent, nay the *servant* of others, who might demand of him anything. Only a touchy and implacable combativeness—whereby he often bled, as much as he caused others to bleed—kept him from the worst indignities, as being too much trouble for his seniors to inflict. They found it easier, and found that it caused pain as great, to *mock* him, though not always to his face—they soon grew wary of that—and material suited for such teases was easily come by.

'They have called me Turk, and what is more, Bastard,' he wrote to his father, 'which I am none—and I would rather they threaten my life than my honour. I will not appeal to the Masters, as those who have insulted me have all more influence with them than I, who have but newly come here, and am looked upon with suspicion, as a kind of Monster, tho' I am able to answer to them in classes, and in examinations, well enough to show I am but a Man like them. I wish you to defend me, as you have not so far done, and inform those Masters, who have done nothing to sustain me in the face of these enemies, of the Insults I have borne, and to demand of them what Remedies they may apply. I am also in want of Moncy, whereby to buy small presents for those who may be of my party—it is the common thing—I want nothing for myself, but I am given gifts, and am not able to *give* any, which is to my shame.'

To this his father, not quickly, responded. 'What!' he wrote. 'Do they call thee Turk, and contemn thy halting speech? Well all that is but the case—and naught truly wounds us but what *is* the case—and therefore, be wounded, as it suits thee—or give back as you have been given, with the Truth if truth be at hand, or what is *like* the truth if the truth suit not your purpose—and if none of this win for you the redress you seek, or inflict wounds painful enough to cause your tormentors to withdraw—then something more *sharp* may do so, and this you have brought from the land of your birth. That is the sum of my advice to you; ask me for no more till all these be tried. As for Money, I have swept all mine out of doors—you must apply to Lady Sane if she have any—or do without—or steal.'

Ali wrote again, after he had read (and torn to pieces) this communication of his father's: 'My Lord—If I am to be insulted and mocked *for what I cannot help* nor change, even if I would, which I *would not*—very well—I shall take the Help you offer—tho' it be but *words*—and ask not for other. It matters not much. Others have begun with nothing and ended greatly. I will carve myself a way to greatness, but never with Dishonour.—I am, my Lord, your Lordship's affectionate & obedient Son—ALI.'

So said he: and the Lord his father was not to know that, while in sunlight he braved his Fellows well enough, and even rallied them and won some hearts among them for his courage, and for his cheek too, and for how he spoke up to his Masters, whether

gravely or in jest—yet in the dark alone he wept, and no one comforted him. He had never known a mother's dear caresses, he
hardly knew to ask Heaven for what he most desired, a Friend! His
being was as tender and easily hurt as a snail's soft seeking horn,
and—for the snail's selfsame reason—he built around himself a
stony carapace. Oft would he slip away from his fellows and their
occupations, to retire alone to a famous and ancient Church-yard—
not to commune there with the dead (for Youth but rarely ponders
its own mortality, and, even when gloomily asserting it, does not
truly believe in it)—but to lay down there the burden of his impos-
ture, as he saw it to be, of heedlessness and temerity—as a knight
doffs his heavy armor in his tent, where no one sees.

Silence and old stones are good company for the solitary, but
there came a time when Ali, slipping away to be with his granite
companions, found another, as alive as himself, already in posses-
8   sion there, and reclining upon *his* favoured gravestone. He was
known to Ali—and saluted Ali cheerily—and made room for him
there upon the commodious breast of him interred below. But Ali
in response only demanded what he did there—to which the boy
answered with the same question turned round again—and for a
moment Ali looked away, to the long view over field and valley,
which he had also come to regard as his *own*.

'Come,' he heard the other say. 'There is room for two.'

'I prefer the company I chose,' Ali said, not deigning to turn.
'That is, my *own*.'

'Oh, *stuff*,' said the lad—and when Ali in fury turned upon
him, he saw that the newcomer was smiling lightly, and that his jibe
was meant only to win Ali away from rigid Solemnity—and tho' he
desired still to keep the face he had chosen, he found he could
not—and instead came to sit where, with laughter, the other invited
him, and accept his hand, and an arm put round his shoulder.

9   Lord Corydon—so shall we name this child—was scion of an
impoverished House, already in possession of his title tho' far from
his majority (his father having recently died in a fall from a horse).
Younger than Ali—as most of his fellows were—he had been but little noticed by the older student, except that in chapel he sang, and

exquisitely, seeming transfigured by his own soul, which, exiting from him (as the ancients supposed it could do) in the form of song, entered into his rapt listeners, none more rapt than Ali. True it was that Ali's first—his *only*—joy had been to be *alone*—but there are other joys—rarer and less reliable—but by so much the greater! From that day the two marked the beginning of a true and deep Friendship, that they were sure would never cease.

How shall their youthful intercourse, intense as it was slight, be here recorded? The jests they made lived only in the moment of their being spoken, and are now long faded—their boasts and challenges vanished upon the air—the Scholars and Masters they spoke of in ardent admiration or scorn are dispersed, and all changed— for the boys are no longer *boys,* and some are dead. Ali—the reader *10* will have gathered this—was one who felt wrongs intensely, for the which he had surely ample reason—yet his heart was sound and clear, and nothing of bitterness had so far shadowed it; he was jealous of his *honour,* by which he meant his embattled self, always seemingly on the point of *evanescence,* and hardly to be chained within his flesh but by constant vigilance. Lord Corydon was his opposite, or *complement,* in colour as in all other things—for he was as much fairer than his fellows as Ali was darker, and his eyes of palest sapphire as light as Ali's were deep; he was as poor as Ali, yet cheerful and uncaring; stood never upon ceremony, or precedence, over which Ali fretted overmuch, as he well knew; slow to take offence, quick to forgive, and yet careless of his Affections too, as Ali—whose heart once given was given for aye—would sometimes feel, to his pain.

Still it was very nice, for sure, to have someone to comfort you in such a place as Ida was, and nurse you in afflictions; to *protect* you, or to *be protected by* you; to undress with you and together take Ida's cold bath, and after to share a warm bed (for a bed of one's own cost the more, and neither could afford it); and hand in hand with whom to laugh, and outface the world!

At end of term, the friends would not be parted, and the younger invited the elder to his own house, to stop as long as he liked. He laughed, indeed, at the hospitality Ali would there see.

'It is nothing like an *abbey* or a *castle*,' said he, 'and there is no enter-tainment to be had—nothing but climbing hills, and singing part-songs, and looking out the window—now I have done my honest duty, and warned you!' Yet he had *not* done *all* his duty, nor told all that there was to tell about his house and family, which Ali divined from the laughter in his eyes—though he asked no further ques-tion, only wrote to Lady Sane to say that the long journey to Scot-land & back again was inconvenient in so short a time, and that he would be well provided for—he had Lord Corydon subscribe a compliment, and a reassurance—and then they tumbled West-ward on a public conveyance, with hardly a shilling left over to share be-tween them—and Ali in wonder thought that never in his life be-fore had he ever embarked on a journey, with none but good hopes, and happy expectations!

NOTES FOR THE 3RD CHAPTER

1. *the ruins of an Abbey:*   Lord Byron's portrait in these pages is of his ancestral home in Nottinghamshire, Newstead Abbey, sold by him for debt in his youth and ever afterward regretted (so I believe). It was not often in its history a happy place. The fortune that might have allowed the Byrons to preserve their seat was seized by Cromwell's auditors, and never afterward restored; Lord Byron's ancestor, the Fifth Lord, tho' known to the world as 'Wicked' Byron, may not be entirely blamed for the damage done to the estate, the selling off of its furnishings, &c., &c., as that gloomy Peer had in fact no other resources to maintain a property that he could not sell, and one that, no matter how much my father loved it, he could not himself keep.

   I have myself only recently returned from visiting the place, which I had never seen before, and to which my husband and I were most kindly invited by the present owner—Colonel Wildman, least wild of men—, a gracious host, a *devotee* of my father and his memory, who in restoring the house to something exceeding its glory in any former time, has also been most careful to preserve every relic of my father's life there. I admit that at first I walked the fine halls and inspected the new-planted grounds with something approaching a depression of spirit—it seemed the Mausoleum of my race, where history lay entombed, not to be *touched* by living hand or mind. I felt that I myself was turning to stone. At the same time I could not shake the feeling that *this should have been MINE:* a feeling not of delight, far less of envy, but of a profound melancholy, as of a chance missed, or a duty overlooked, that now can never be performed.

Yet the following day, leaving the house early, like the youth Ali I walked alone in the so-named 'Devil's Wood', where the 'Wicked' Fifth Lord had liked to put up stone figures of fauns and satyrs, as though in bacchanal—now so mossy and overgrown as to give no offence. There Colonel Wildman found me—that gentleman having conceived that I was in some distress—and we talked long, of the Byrons, of his love for his old schoolmate, of *myself*—to which he listened with the greatest kindness and patience. What had clung to me—or what I in error clung to—seemed then and there to fall, or fly, away. I knew myself to be the *child* of a race that had left to me what is more than lands and stones—a *nature,* that I had lived within as within a mansion of many rooms, some timeworn and fallen, or refurbished by others for their use, but not all explored—no, not even yet.

2. *a linked series of lakes:* Dark and deep and very cold the remaining lake is still, and the wild birds do still sleep upon it.

3. *Canalettos,* &c.: It is of interest to compare Ld. B.'s picture of this devastated and abused Abbey with the picture he paints of 'Norman Abbey' in the last extant cantos of *Don Juan.* In that poem, his own Newstead is reimagined as he might have wished it to be—filled with comforts and fine things, including portraits of ancestors, and crowded with guests of rank and achievement—its ancient woods still uncut. That picture is as much better than his own house's state, as this is worse. So are tales made from the facts of life.

4. *black Newfoundland dog:* Lord Byron's dog, beloved in his youth, was named Boatswain, though I cannot determine why. He expired in a fit of madness, and Ld. B. cared for him most solicitously in his last agony, wiping the slaver from the dog's lips with his own hand.

5. *an Elm:* This great tree still stands, grown only older, in the Park at Newstead. The names inscribed upon it are those of my father and his half-sister, the Hon. Augusta Leigh. I bear her name as part of my own, and that is not all. The lady is very recently deceased, and I never had that intercourse with her that would allow me to speak to her character. *De mortuis nil nisi bonum.*

6. *'Old Jock':* Lord Byron was devoted to an elderly servant at Newstead called Joe Murray. In a portrait that hangs at Newstead today, he has the rosy cheek, the kind smile, and the long clay pipe here ascribed to a Scottish counterpart. Byron never knew his father, and perhaps in Old Joe Murray, and later in others, he found some part of the lack fulfilled.

7. *Ida:* Lord Byron attended Harrow School from 1801 till 1805, and said that he hated it in his first years but came in his last year to love it. Dr Joseph Drury, the Headmaster against whom he would battle at first and come later to admire and love, recorded his impression that a 'Wild mountain colt' had been given into his care. The fact of his *lameness* was a source of troubles, not only in the sports and games from which it kept him taking part, but in the taunts and cruelties of other boys; he had always to prove himself as strong and as bold as any of them. His own sharp sense of *amour-propre* led him to contest with all, including Masters, whom he conceived to have offended him, and at times he had to be removed from amongst his fellows and given room in a Master's house. It takes little effort to translate the young Lord Byron's deformity of body into the alienated nature of his imagined creation.

Harrow School, which I have visited upon one occasion, and now and then passed at a distance, remains a tall and plain place on a hill that has ever instilled in me a feeling of desolation and loneliness, I know not why.

8. *his favoured gravestone:*   There is in the church-yard of Harrow-on-the-Hill, by the church where once the young scholars attended divine service, a flat stone that commands a view over the valley. It is called 'the Peachey stone', no doubt for the one supposed to lie beneath it. It is now pointed out to visitors as the place where the young poet loved to retire, and where he first turned his thoughts to verse. In the common way of such sights, it has also come to be misunderstood, and is sometimes called 'Byron's grave', which certainly it is not: that is in the parish church of Hucknall Torkard, in his own county of Nottinghamshire, with his ancestors—for the which, see below.

9. *Lord Corydon:*   This figure combines the characters of Lord Clare, with whom Byron became the closest of friends at Harrow, and John Edelston, a chorister at Cambridge, who was but fifteen when Byron developed a profound affection for him. Of Lord Clare, he said in a late letter to Moore that he 'always loved him (since I was thirteen, at Harrow) better than any (*male*) thing in the world'. Edelston was poor, and thus in his picture Byron perhaps contrived to blend in one the two youths he most loved.

10. *some are dead:*   John Wingfield, who was with Byron at Harrow, later died in battle. He too, and Byron's grief for him, must form part of the story he tells of Lord Corydon and his fate.

FOUR

A vision of Love, with its result,

Marriage; and of Money,

with the same

THE HALL OF THE CORYDONS was not as that of the Sanes. Its oaks still stood, and spread their shade over a rose-red house and its towers, a jumble of them—and arches, and windows, and chimney-pots, and parterres, and colonnades, added and subtracted and added again since the days of Good Queen Bess. The late Lord, an *optimist* of the most ardent, not to say blindest, sort, had taken much of his birthright upon 'Change, and there had seen it inflate magnificently, till he was rich 'beyond the dreams of avarice'—at least until the following week, when new news swept the market, and what had expanded so miraculously, just as miraculously went down (*miraculous* indeed it seemed, to those who were not among the select few puffing away at the empty bladder of it). It soon vanished utterly away, so that—most miraculous of all!—even the original investment, solid Pounds Sterling and golden Guineas though it had been, was nowhere to be found. The unhappy Lord bethought him of the suffering his ruin must bring upon his beloved wife and children, and considered putting a bullet through his breast—but his optimism had not entirely vanished with his Money, and he went home instead, where he was comforted, and all his kin agreed with him that something would surely *turn up*—and the next afternoon, following his hounds (they have since been sold), the optimistic gentleman was flung headlong from his horse, and knew no more of Chance, or Price, or Possibility.

Still the bereft Hall smiled, or seemed to, upon visitors, or sons returning, who came down through the 'chequered shade' to the door. The Lady of the house, having been apprised, who knows how, of her son's approach, had already come forth, and now nearly *leapt* from the steps to embrace him—her smile was as the Sun. Lord Corydon brought forward his friend—who had desired not to interrupt Corydon's home-coming, but rather to observe it, as a thing new to him, and deserving of study. Lady C. then advanced upon him, her arms open as an Angel's, and she made him welcome with all her heart. Behind her there came tumbling from the open doors the youngest children of the house, a boy with a hoop, and another with a bow-and-arrow—both fair, both golden— and then, after them, as though conjured by the armed and laughing Cupid who called to her, a Form clad in white and in all the radiance of sixteen years.

'May I present my sister Susanna,' said Corydon, as though he spoke of a matter of no particular importance, while knowing better. 'Susanna, I am pleased to introduce Ali, my friend, the son of Lord Sane.'

'Welcome,' said she to Ali, in that low voice that is 'an excellent thing in woman'. 'I am very pleased to meet the friend I have often read about.'

The gentle pressure of her hand upon his, the glance her sapphire eyes paid him, the commonplace greeting to which he found he could not return even a commonplace reply—what Ali felt need not be *named,* for even those who have not felt it can name it, its name is ever on the world's tongue. But Ali's confusion was due to more than the sweet common cause—for Susanna so resembled her brother that the eye was baffled to look upon them both. Her brother came and linked his arm in hers, and kissed her cheek, and they both smiled upon Ali. They were Eros and Anteros, or more simply the twinned boy & girl in a comedy—a very Viola and Sebastian, interchangeable. It was their sport—as Ali would come to realize—to pretend that they hardly understood their resemblance, and that there was nothing remarkable about them—and yet they delighted in Ali's bemusement, even as they would not acknowledge it.

    'Come in, come in,' cried Lady Corydon, 'come in, and refresh yourselves!' And that admirable Dame swept them all before like goslings before their goose-girl, and even before they had entered in, she had begun upon a *gazette* of the family's doings since her beloved Son's last return.

    That the house was much impoverished did not diminish its warmth, nor its cheer—for Lady Corydon, tho' it shock'd her neighbours, would not remain in mourning, which she thought did not suit her—nor would she draw her drapes, and shut out the healing Sun—and no diminution of her Income would keep her from filling her house with fruits and sweetmeats in profusion—and lights, good waxen candles—and Music, by means of a Pianoforte, and her children's voices. Susanna played, and her brother beside her sang, and Ali sat beside Susanna and turned the pages at her nod (for the marks upon them were all a mystery to him) and wished the piece endless—that he might remain always near, yet be under no obligation to *speak*—which he did not think he could creditably do. 'If Music be the food of Love, play on,' as saith that Comedy aforementioned; and if it be so, then they two, Corydon and Susanna, were the true purveyors, indeed the grocers in general—and if it be *not* so, then what sweets Love *does* feed upon need not be listed—no, they need not.

    True it was that the house provided little other amusement—but what to one *alone* might result in *ennui* and irritation, did not in

1

company—for circumstances change cases—and in the days Ali spent with the inhabitants of Corydon Hall he found an intire and blissful satisfaction. They walked the hills and woods, hand in hand—they look'd out the window, as promised, but since they looked *together,* cheek by cheek, what they saw was of endless interest. They even enjoy'd Angling, that most witless of pastimes, and with rod and line and net sate by a stream to await, for an hour or two or *three* by the clock, the approach of some inedible being dull enough to be fooled by their gins—who often as not still escaped unharmed, to swim another day.

Susanna wish'd to know—as there they waited—what Ali's story might be, and how he had come among Englishmen, and the scholars of Ida; and she asked so gently, and without prejudice as to an answer, that he told all that he could—for the first time since coming to this Isle—of himself, and his life among the Albanian hills, and his becoming a soldier of the Pacha—leaving aside only tales of such horrid and bloody character as he supposed might cause so fine a being as this to draw away from him. Even so 'she loved him for the dangers he had passed', at which she marvelled, and grieved too; and 'he loved her that she did pity him'. Her brother, of a heart not less tender but always willing to let present happiness annul—nay, to make sport of—distant sorrow, would not by his laughter permit the two to persist long in *sentiment.*

'You are no Turk, nor Albanian,' said Corydon, 'and no foreigner neither, for I perceive you are, as a result of your adventures, nothing at all—neither good nor bad—fish nor fowl—but a *blank slate* upon which any name may be written—and once written, sponged off again. I would it were my own case!'

Ali knew not if the gay young man's thought were true, but a strange new hope dawned in his own heart, as homeward they wended. Thought he: 'If I am nothing in myself—since all that I might naturally have been was taken from me—then let me be any thing. Let me be *what I choose*—and *change* what I choose when I choose to do so!'

Well might he vow this, in the clear sight of Youthfulness— which indeed sees clearly, though chiefly its *own self* as it *might someday be.* Yet the rest of the world would still assign to him but *one* character—though permitting no outward sign of it, in dress or manner, and truly knowing nothing of it but the Name—and that name was *Turk.*

THE SCHOLARS SOON returned to school, with their fellow-blackbirds. Lord Corydon was grateful to be again from home, but Ali cast backward his look, as one expelled from Eden, an Eden whose existence he had not suspected—whose Eve as well he left behind. Did he think not, then, of Iman far away, and was he not reminded, in the sharpness of his present feelings, of that child? No, indeed he was not—except in how he *marvelled* that he was not—for the knowledge had not yet dawned upon him, that even the most singular of hearts can possess *two* such fair beings within its compass (the more so, if one be *near,* & the other far). Moreover, he had for constant companion her Brother, Corydon— and it was as though Ali had two roll'd into One, so much could he see Susanna in her Brother, and hear her in his voice, and feel, in the pressure of his hand, her own.

Ida absorbed the young men again into its pleasures and its occupations—its strife and struggles too. When again term ended, Ali purposed to avoid his own house, whether his Father were in residence or not—there where he had only the gentle *heap* of his nominal Mother for a protector—and to walk instead upon the hills of his friends' pleasant shire. It was during his preparations for this visit, while listening to Lord Corydon's listing of the sports and feasts they would enjoy there (for it was Christmas, and a pudding and a Goose were not at all unlikely, even in their reduced circumstances, and skating, and a Yule fire), when a Master came for Ali, and took him away to his own study, there to tell him in private certain news—which to his credit, he did with all careful kindness: that his Mother after her long years' illness had at last given up the ghost, and passed from this vale of tears. Ali found he could make no reply to the Master, who puzzled over what seemed a strange hardness of heart, and bethought him what it showed concerning Ali's *nature* and *temperament*—tho' he said nothing in words, but only offered all assistance he could, to see that the lad, as were his Father's instructions, at once started for Scotland and the Abbey, where, as he said, 'All love and comfort might be found in this his affliction and grief': and Ali, unable to respond still, departed.

2   When the coach Lord Sane had sent brought him to the Abbey at length, it was not his father who greeted him but Old Jock, who with tears in his eyes conveyed to the lad the tale of Lady Sane's last days—her prayers for Ali—her fears and sufferings, too, at the approach of Death, for such a one as Old Jock would see no use or good in disguising such mortal facts. Indeed, all that levels distinctions between Laird and Dependent, those common things that all men share, are freely admitted there: where in the South, a *gentleman's* griefs, or his mortality, or his boils and his catarrhs for the matter of that, are of a different and superior kind, and not to be mourned or deplored in the same breath as his servant's, or his sweep's.

Leaving Old Jock's fire-side, Ali sought out his father, who was dressed for a Journey, and seemed to have little time to entertain his son's questions concerning the woman who had so long been shut up in the upper rooms of the Abbey where now he reigned alone. 'May I not,' Ali asked of him, 'visit the place where she is laid? I cannot think it is too much to ask. She was, after all, *my Mother.*'

His father regarded him for a moment, as though he would discern if he were mocked or not. 'I have pressing business far from here,' he then said, 'and may not linger. But if you insist upon the point, I shall accompany you to the vault where she lies, comfortably enough, with her ancestors. Let us be quick, however; the dead, you know, do not resent a brief Obsequy—no, nor nothing else, as I perceive the matter. Ha! *Quick, dead:* I see I have the makings of an amusing quibble here.'

He ordered mounts to be saddled, and soon was leading Ali across stubbled fields and over hedges at a dash, as if to cause him to lose heart, or seat—though Ali did neither—till at eve they came

to a small and ancient church, so small and ancient as to seem at 3
first but a pile of flints agglomerated by chance, though 'twas in
truth the work of pious hands in ages past, and there was a Chan-
cel, and an arched window, and a stair to the vault below. No sex-
ton met them; alone the two went down into the dark, where—it
was a trait passed from Father to Son, as few others had been—the
acuity of their eyesight made out the forms of Lady Sane's ancestors, and her own casket, newly squeezed in among the others. Not
long indeed did they linger there—they did not pray—they did not
speak—though to his eyes and throat Ali felt tears arise, that he had
not expected—for her kindness to him, and also at the thought of
her long seclusion, bereft of all she loved, and her dim Candle now
blown out. Was life no more than this? Did it at death begin again
elsewhere, in a sphere where all was light, and activity, and force,
and love? *She* had thought so; he wished, *for her,* it might be so.

When they stood once again in the frosty sunlight, Lord Sane
regarded the fields before them, his gloved hands clasped behind
him and the crop he held twitching like the tail he did not possess.
'Do not suppose, by the bye,' said he, 'that you have gained materi-
ally in this Lady's death. You are indeed the titular heir to her
lands, unimproved as she has left them, but you no more than I,
have the power to dispose of them. Indeed you may incur greater
expense in preserving them to the next Generation, than you will
profit by them.'

'I understand that,' Ali said, 'and have no wish to dispute the
conditions.'

'I shall be frank with you,' said his Sire, 'as I have been in all
things. The *title* you shall inherit from me when I lie down in that or
in another vault, an eventuality I intend to avoid in any case, is
nude of any property—all gone. You are without a shilling, and the 4
rents and monies due you from your mother's estate, which will
begin to come to you upon your reaching your majority, will not be
sufficient to repay even your present debts. You have mortgaged
your future to pay for present needs, never wise, and now face swift
ruin. I see no help for it but that you gird up your loins, travel to
the populous and fashionable centres of the land, and find yourself

5   a golden Dolly, marriage to whom will at a stroke recoup our family fortunes.'

'I know not what you mean by a golden Dolly,' said Ali.

'Why, a marriageable woman with two or three thousand a year,' said Lord Sane. 'I do not deceive myself that you shall have the easiest shooting in that field, for no doubt all but the least eligible of the golden race will, at a minimum, prefer an Englishman for a husband, or at least a man of some more familiar nation than yours. Nevertheless there is game there that the nimble and the clever may garner. When I am returned, I shall set before you a List, and you may begin to consider where first to make your strike.'

With that his Lordship took his horse's bridle, and from the stone at the church-door he mounted at a leap—he was away without farewell, and without waiting upon his son—who took no *particular* offence at it—as he had expected no more.

Ali had not spoken, upon that occasion, nor contradicted his parent, though he had no intention of going fortune-hunting. Insofar as he was capable of considering such a step as marriage—and to him it rather resembled in likelihood a voyage to the Moon, or an exchange of heads—he would consider but one object only, and that was Susanna. Yet he did not picture himself standing before an Altar—or negotiating for a dowry—or securing one—tho' he knew well enough that all these things are commonly done. He knew that Nations strike Treaties, too, and Kings abdicate, and Navies engage—and these had as little to do with him, or his beloved friends. He did not know—could not have supposed!—that the gentle girl he thought upon so often could easily contemplate what *he* could not—though she did not presume to advance the business by any word or act. She knew as certainly as did Lord Sane what price her self and parts might command in the market, and she knew how little a bond with her might advance Ali's fortunes, whose state she knew too (for they *can* make such calculations, even the purest of those souls, as well as they may play a sonata of Scarlatti's or sing a song of Moore's—it is very commonly among their *attainments*). Her brother might make a joke of their inseparability,

and talk of an *exchange of rings* imminent, and a long married life—
breakfast taken every morn amid the clamour of their *graduated*
offspring, &c., but Ali and Susanna dismissed his drolleries, and
together walk'd on, 'in maiden meditation', though perhaps not   6
'fancy free'. Ali did not wish for time to stop, that this Eden might
endure, as no Eden may: for he did not yet truly know, in his soul,
that Time rolls on, and *over* our most precious possessions. He had
no reason to suppose his state would change, for he did not desire
it to change. In this is Youth eternal, the still garden from which all
streams spring—and thus we remember it to be, when we are far
down river of it.

So his sands ran—to alter the figure, from water to earth—and
he did not count them. He grew tall—slim as a wand—forgetting   7
his supper, when it was not put before him, or he led to it. At Ida
he learned games that his fellows had played since infancy, and
excelled too, in one or another. He learned to *swim,* and thought   8
that he was perhaps the first of the Ochridan race to do so, and in
the cold waters of the stream that flows past Ida's base he outdid
even Corydon, who was the fleetest formerly of them all. One by
one he completed his school terms, and on a certain 6th of June he
performed for the last time before his fellows and the Masters and
Guests foregathered—his choice a speech of Edmund the Bastard's
out of *King Lear,* done in the best manner of the Young Roscius,   9
who was then triumphing on the boards in London. 'Now Gods,
Stand up for bastards!' sang he, and all the rest of that ringing
declaration—the planned undoing of his *legitimate* double, the taking of his brother's lands, and the capturing of the exclusive *love of
his Father.*

It happened that, upon that very day, Ali's own real, or *physical,*
Father was in retreat from London, in consequence of a scheme
gone wrong.

It has been noted that there was little, or nothing, that 'Satan'
Porteus would stop at in pursuit of the objects of his desires—and
yet his soul was such that, had he spent however long on the evolv-
ing of some scheme of crime or extortion, he was well able in a moment of rage or pride to spoil it. The tale was told in the City (Ali

would later hear it, and not once only, or from one informant) how he had once raised up an impecunious adventurer to impersonate the lost heir to a fortune—drilled and schooled the fellow in his part for months—busied himself in the laying down of the necessary forgeries and evidences—then, just as the scheme is about to succeed—he falls into a passion with his creature over some trivial matter—an impertinence perceiv'd—the turn of a card, or of a *drab*—and, forthwith, they draw, and Sane slays the fellow where he stands, knowing full well the fortune's lost to him: and yet those who were present marked the horrid delight that rose then in his eyes to do this deed—it chilled their blood so that it would not warm thereafter—as though he delighted as much in the wreckage of his *own* prospects as in the wreckage of others'—as though nothing delighted him so much as wreckage itself. Here, said his henchmen to one another—even as they laboured, at his command, to conceal the crime—here was Satan himself, Nay-sayer absolute!

Whatever well- or ill-laid plans had, in the present instance, failed to mature, Lord Sane was now on progress to the distant North, to his lair. But first his coach arrived at Ida, there to bring away his son. He found him among the Scholars, who were still attired as the characters whom they had portrayed in the day's festivities, and distributed about the green lawns like immortals in Elysium—a strange sight, which yet seemed entirely unseen by the Lord. There stood his son, in his costume as Edmund, and with him Lord Corydon, who had taken no part that day, and Susanna—and upon them in the bright day fell the long shadow of Lord Sane. To him Ali with strange reluctance introduced his friends, who made response without any sign of the darkness Ali felt had come upon them—and Sane in turn took their hands with a merry interest that Ali felt to be all the more chilling. 'Let us be gone,' said he then to his son. 'Doff these mummeries, and put on clothes for a journey. We have much to discuss along the way.'

———————————

*T*HOUGH HE HAD evinced but slight interest in Ali's companions when introduced to them, it was not long after his coach was upon the North-ward road that Sane inquired musingly about the family.

'Lord Corydon has not yet reached his majority,' said Ali. 'His sister Susanna is but seventeen.' Susanna! To speak her name, here beside his father, seemed to Ali to risk much, though *what* he could not say.

'Corydon,' said Sane then, with an air of one drawing from a deep well. 'His father was the fifth Lord.'

'I know not his number,' said Ali.

'I partly knew the man. He had money in the Funds, and in Irish mortgages, quite safely; but he took bad advice, and put his fortune—nearly the whole of it—in West Indian shares, and was quickly ruined. He died by mischance not long since. Is this he?'

'I am ignorant of his business dealings,' said Ali, 'but yes, this was he.'

'Why, the house is declined almost to nothing,' said Sane. 'They are poor as church-mice; the girl will have not a shilling. No, it is absurd. I have expressed to you plainly that she upon whom you turn your attention must bring in some considerable Fortune, or else you must look elsewhere. I need not repeat myself upon the subject.'

'Forgive me,' said Ali in a low tone. 'But there is no point in pursuing these considerations. I will have none of them. I will make no choice from your *List*.'

Lord Sane inquired, in as low a tone as his son's, 'Why he should be so certain of this, and had he a choice of his own?' Ali professed that he did not, and turned his gaze upon the passing scene. He could not dispute the plain truth his father stated— Susanna would bring no fortune to his house—but she would bring what was worth more—she would bring light, and gaiety, and goodness, enough even to sweep away the heaviness that brooded over the Abbey and its grounds and messuages—to shake out, as from a dusty rug, the gloom that the centuries had there accumulated.

Sane now wished to know what the young Corydon, whom he termed, with an air of cold amusement, *the present Lord,* intended now to do. Would he go up to University? Ali thought he would not—that his ambitions had turned to the Army, where several of his family had made their careers, and where his prospects were good. Sane thereupon said nothing more, until Ali thought him fallen asleep where he sat—and was startled then to hear him ask, 'Whether Ali had himself had made a choice of University, between the two?' Ali said he had given it no thought, for he had not supposed it to be his father's wish that he go up—indeed, it seemed to him quite otherwise, and that he too would be sent to the Army, as his father had been, and his father's father too, who had earned credit by his service that his son had not entirely squandered away.

'Ah no,' said the Lord. 'When the expected profit is great, we do not spare expense. A sound education is an Investment. A better one than shares upon 'Change. Take a Degree, and it will improve your prospects in many ways.' With this it seemed he smiled upon his son, though in the case of 'Satan' Porteus that commonest of all human expressions had a cast *unlike* the common, and had not the common effect upon those toward whom it was directed. Nevertheless he said no more, and closed his great hands upon his waistcoat, and slept indeed.

NOTES FOR THE 4TH CHAPTER

1. *Viola and Sebastian:*   In Shake-speare's comedy *Twelfth Night,* the brother and sister shipwrecked on the sea-coast of Illyria, which is oddly a part of Albania, though surely the Bard knew nothing of that. Ld. B.'s knowledge of Shake-speare was wide if not deep, and his habit of quoting (or *partly* quoting) his lines was persistent in his letters, though it may seem a fault in his fiction.

2. *Lady Sane's last days:*   To prove that the present manuscript represents an initial draft, it is sufficient to point out that this lady, whose death is here reported, is described on the first page of the story as alive, though sequestered and mad, on the night of her husband's murder. Ld. B. is commonly conceived as a rapid and even as a careless writer, but a mere glance back at his initial pages would have shown him this glaring solecism— and therefore it would seem he did *not* look back. Yet he *did* write thoughtfully, however quickly. The many corrections, markings-out, interpolations &c. in the original MS have not been preserved in my fair copy—but I have otherwise altered nothing, not even his *grammar* when it is wrong.

3. *a small and ancient church:* The Byrons are laid in the vault of
Hucknall church, nearby to Newstead. Ld. B. here exaggerates
it to describe it as an agglomeration of flints, but the church is
indeed in bad repair and without much to recommend it. I de-
scended as Ld. B.'s hero did, to see his ancestors *and mine* laid
cheek by jowl in dimness. I put my hand upon him, or the con-
tainer of his earthly part. I have never feared death, nor did *he.*

4. *nude of any property:* It is an unfortunate thing—Ld. B. was not
the only who felt it to be so—to receive an ancient title, without
the means to keep it up. The present Lord Byron, Admiral and
Lord-in-Waiting to her Majesty, received nothing from my father's estate, all of which went to my mother and to his half-
sister Mrs Leigh; and all the property was gone long before. As
a young girl I was grateful for the present Lord's hospitality;
my mother, in her frequent illnesses, could not always attend to
my needs, and he was one who gave generously of his time and
solicitude. He exhibits no trace of his ancestors' characters—
neither of his cousin, my father, nor of my father's father, 'Mad
Jack' Byron.

5. *a golden Dolly:* It is generally believed that my father attempted
to repair his fortunes and settle his affairs, which were in a bad
state, by a *coldly calculated* marriage with my mother, who was
in possession of a small fortune, and had prospects. However,
if my own investigations into the matter be reliable, I should
rather state that Ld. B. believed himself the richer of the pair,
for he thought he would sell Newstead Abbey for a hundred
thousand pounds or more, and bring a considerable sum to his
marriage with the then Miss Milbanke. Only later, when the
Newstead sale disappointed, and inheritances from Lady Byron's mother upon that lady's death were divided between
them, did Ld. B. see a great advance in his situation from his
marriage. His reasons for making that marriage were otherwise—
though I am at a loss to explain what they were.

6. *maiden meditation:* Shake-speare's *A Midsummer Night's Dream.* See the note above on the subject. It is possible that the presence of other of the Bard's lines has escaped me, and still others are so familiar as to seem not worth annotating.

7. *slim as a wand:* Lord Byron, it is related by several who knew him well, had a tendency to fat, and a horror of it too, and used by strenuous fasting and abnegation to combat his natural condition—salads of cold vegetables doused in vinegar, small wines mixed with soda-water, &c. Many a maiden of our day, with the same object in view, would not have the strength to bear his regimen.

8. *excelled:* I have heard that, despite his lameness, Lord Byron once played with Harrow's eleven against Eton at Lord's cricket grounds, and gave a good account of himself. Of his swimming nothing need here be added to popular report—he is the most famous swimmer since Leander, whose feat at the Hellespont he imitated. I cannot swim a stroke, and would be gone like Ophelia if ever by mischance I fell in; but on *top* of the water I can skate, when the same stream is in a different physical state, as well as the best.

9. *Young Roscius:* William Betty, the child actor (in truth an adolescent) whose beauty and power so enthralled our grandparents, was said to have resembled my father—tho' upon attending a performance of his in London, Ld. B. declared himself unmoved. Lord Byron no doubt comported himself well in the famous Speech Day exercises at Harrow School. It may be said that he performed all his life as *himself,* and no one could have played the part better—tho' many have tried since.

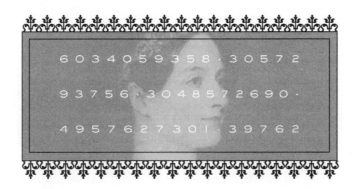

From: "Smith" <anovak@strongwomanstory.org>
To: lnovak@metrognome.net.au
Subject: No novel

Lee:

Well, bad news. There's no novel, not anymore.

It seems (why do people say that, when they have news, especially bad news? "It seems," when they mean it just is? "It seems your father is dead." "It seems you've lost." But it's in old jokes too, right? "It seems this lion went into a bar." Okay forget this) it seems that when she was dying Ada just gave up, and turned everything over to her mother. And it looks like, from a letter I turned up in the Lovelace archive, that it was then that the novel got burned. I've scanned the letter for you to read; the handwriting's hard but be patient, and see if you think it means what I think.

S

Attached: ada12.tif

> *My beloved Hen I can no longer write with pen and ink I shall use pencil your loving eyes will read what I have written tho no one else can. O my dear I have resisted so*

foolishly and for so long and now I can resist no longer nor
shd I. You say you will not believe me if you do not see the
thing burnt yourself but will you believe William. I will ask
him to be present. He too has suffer'd because of my obses-
sion and I am sorry and not for that alone. I know now it
is the right thing and you are right to ~~demand~~ *ask it of me.*
You have not read it nor shd you and there is nothing in it
that the future need know and I suppose much that it shd
not   O I am so tired and I hurt so dreadfully   My resis-
tance to all the goodness you have pressed upon me is gone
trust me   it is gone   You say that all my suffering has a
purpose and the purpose is that I may not regret the loss of
all that is a part of this life and not a part of the next. I
know not if that be the reason it has been given unto me
but O Hen I can no longer think of any other reason and I
shall finally and humbly accept yours. Only I wd think that
by now I have learned my lesson and I ought to be released

From: lnovak@metrognome.net.au
To: "Smith" <anovak@strongwomanstory.org>
Subject: RE:No novel

I think it means what you think it does: that Ada burned the manuscript of the novel because her mother wanted it burned. Hen was
what she called her mother. She and her mother and her husband
(William, named in the letter) called one another by these bird
names when they were feeling sweet. Ada as you know died of a cer-
vical cancer and apparently suffered atrociously. I can well believe
her mother told her that her suffering was all for her soul's good.
I don't know what to say. I can hope it was nothing solid really,
just a few odd pages. Though the notes of Ada's that you sent me,
if I read them right, suggest something pretty substantial. I feel
like a child has been stillborn.

Lee

———————————

From: "Smith" <anovak@strongwomanstory.org>
To: lnovak@metrognome.com
Subject: RE:Re:No novel

Lee—

It seems to me from the letter that Ada's mother never even read
the book. Right? Could she have asked Ada to burn it if she'd never
even read it? How did she know it wasn't harmless? It wasn't *hers*.
Maybe we're wrong. Ada said that her mother wouldn't believe it
was burned unless she saw it burned for herself, so she suspected
that Ada would hide it. Maybe she did.

S

———————————

From: lnovak@metrognome.net.au
To: "Smith" <anovak@strongwomanstory.org>
Subject:

S—

No we're not wrong.
You do know that Lady Byron—Ada's mother—with others, including Byron's publisher John Murray, and his friend John Cam
Hobhouse, and his friend and biographer Thomas Moore, all collaborated in burning the manuscript of Lord Byron's memoirs,
which she hadn't read—in fact only Moore had. Technically they
were the property of Augusta Leigh, the half sister; but Lady B.
bullied her into agreeing; she'd already convinced Augusta that
she was the greatest sinner who ever lived—no, second greatest,
after Byron himself. And so the men gathered in John Murray's
rooms and together they burned a book by the man they professed
to love, which only one of them had even read, supposedly for his
sake: the worst piece of literary vandalism of the century, anyway
the one I regret the most. All because Lady Byron feared that her

husband would tell his side of the story of their marriage, and she would no longer control the spin.

I'll tell you something. Ada's story contains a monster parent, but it's not her father—it's her mother. There is no comparison I know of adequate to this woman but characters out of Gothic fiction. She isn't a Romantic monster though but a Victorian one: a whited sepulchre, a soft-spoken self-controlled bombazine-clad mass of self-deception, self-righteousness, appalling mental cruelty passing under the name of religion, morality, "higher" feelings, and "pure" motives. She used her money to control people who depended on her, or who could be induced to accept her help, without ever admitting to herself she was doing so. She took dozens of people into her confidence about Byron's supposed sins and enormities, each of whom thought she, or he, was the only one to be trusted with these secrets. It's amazing the numbers of people she got to lie down in front of her and abase themselves. I'll tell you something wonderful. She was intensely interested in education— all her kind was and is—and liked to set up punitive little schools where children of the deserving poor would have the latest theories practiced on them and were expected to show constant gratitude; but she was also interested in prison reform: she took up Jeremy Bentham's Panopticon, one of the most astonishing combinations of social control and moral high-mindedness ever conceived. The Panopticon was a prison—maybe you know all this, it's become a staple of social theory—which was arranged as a round tower, in which the individual cells were in an outside ring, able to be observed continuously from a central station. Guards could see the prisoners in their cells, but because of the way the place was lit, and through a system of blinds, the prisoners couldn't see the guards; they knew they could be observed at any time, though not whether they were being observed *right now,* so they had to assume they were being observed all the time. They couldn't communicate with or see any other prisoner, but the guards could see all of them all the time. It would be, Bentham thought, all that was needed to control them. Like God: always with his eye on you, himself invisible. Or as Edmund Burke said, who hated rationalistic schemes like this, a spider in its web. God's eye, spider: you can see why Lady Byron liked the idea. It's how she ran her life: each of her prisoners in his or her separate cell, her eye on all of them. And she ran it that way in order to punish crime, or sin: her husband's, long before, unforgotten, unforgivable.

We're not wrong. Ada says she'll get William to certify the thing is burned. Almost up to the day of Ada's death—when her awful soul cruelty finally alienated even him—William was enamored of Ada's mother, and did everything he could to please her. Read *The Late Lord Byron* by Doris Langley Moore. Read it now. It's heartbreaking.

Lee

────────────

From: "Smith" <anovak@strongwomanstory.org>
To: "Thea" <thea.spann133@ggm.edu>
Subject: Wrong

T

Okay that story I told you about Byron's marriage isn't quite right. In fact it's all wrong. I got a book that Lee recommended. We're dealing with the Wicked Witch of the West here. She's so awful that you have to forgive her, nobody could be that awful who didn't have some bent in their personality from somewhere. I don't know where.

────────────

From: "Thea" <thea.spann133@ggm.edu>
To: "Smith" <anovak@strongwomanstory.org>
Subject: RE:Wrong

wrong about who   ada   byron   mom byron   all of them   who is
so awful

———————————

From: "Smith" <anovak@strongwomanstory.org>
To: "Thea" <thea.spann133@ggm.edu>
Subject: RE:Re:Wrong

Not Ada. Lady Byron, her mother. She spent her whole life
after Byron justifying herself as the righteous one. She bent and
corrupted everybody she loved (and I think she did love them
in her way) to get them on her side. She had Ada from the beginning, and did all she could to keep her ignorant of her father until the time came to let her too in on the secret of his evil ways.
What she feared more than anything was to lose Ada to him—
not physically, but emotionally. I know what you're thinking
right now, Thea, but you know it's really not so: my mom couldn't
plot against anybody or *for* anybody, not even herself, not
even me.

You know the more I learn about Ada the less I think she actually
accomplished, and the more I love her. I don't think she was a
Strong Woman. Her mother was the strong woman. She never did
very much of all the things she thought she could do, and in the
end it doesn't matter what you *want* to do or think you *can* do, it
only matters what you *do* do. And it doesn't matter what you think
about what you've done, only what it really *is*—man I know what
that's about, and you know I know it.

But I love her. It's hard not to. For her vanity and her amazing
hopes for herself, her visions of what was going to be possible in
the future, which were so clear-sighted, and right, even though
she had no way of proving them, and they were so different from
those of the real scientists around her.

And for her craziness too. And for her awful suffering, and how brave she was. She was nuts. She reminds me of you.

——————————

From: "Thea" <thea.spann133@ggm.edu>
To: "Smith" <anovak@strongwomanstory.org>
Subject: go easy
Importance: Normal

reminds you of me   why   she doesnt remind me of me   i think you are coming detached   like a balloon lost from a kids wrist you know   like i did that time in stanford   sokay   just write and tell me

t

——————————

From: "Smith" <anovak@strongwomanstory.org>
To: "Thea" <thea.spann133@ggm.edu>
Subject: RE:go easy
Importance: Normal

Actually she doesn't remind me of you or anybody like you. I don't know why I said that. Maybe she reminds me of me. When she was a little girl she invented a science called Flyology. They didn't let her have any stories or fairy tales or *poetry* at all so that her natural tendency (supposedly) for mental aberration or craziness or whatever she was supposed to have inherited from her father wouldn't develop. So instead of dreaming about that kind of stuff she dreamed about science. The Art of Flying. She studied the wings of dead birds to learn how they did it, and she set up a lab called the Flying Room, strung with ropes and pulleys and a "triangle" of some kind. She made plans and drawings and paper wings, and she wanted to build a flying horse powered by steam (she loved horses) with room inside for a driver or pilot, and she would become like a carrier pigeon, delivering and collecting her mother's endless mail. For a while she signed her letters Annabella Carrier Pigeon. Why does it make me want to cry?

I just think about you. Studying math when nobody wanted you to and you didn't care. But maybe you did care and did it anyway. Thea I love you. Right now I just want so much to put my head in the crook of your neck and cry, I wish I knew why but it doesn't matter.

Smith

———————————

From: "Thea" <thea.spann133@ggm.edu>
To: "Smith" <anovak@strongwomanstory.org>
Subject: cry

you want to put your head in the crook of where   jeez dont cry you know what happens to me then

she reminds you of you   becuz you had a father who was kept out of your life   for a good reason   and something about him couldnt be talked about   but should have been   i see that now   it should have been

okay   im here and i will be   so but what if you come all the way back and i turn out to be just me again like before   sthat going to be cool   i hope   cuz im all i got

t

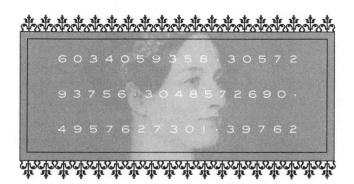

FIVE

In which all hopes are dashed,

and all love lost

HE CHOICE OF WHICH University Ali would attend to *complete his education* was made almost without thought, and this account needs pay no more attention to the progress of Ali's studies in that Athens upon the Fens than he himself did—or better say than does the *average well-born undergraduate,* for indeed Ali found an occasional delight in learning that he had not known at Ida—tho' he had there sometimes excelled in the arts of *rote memorization* and the getting of things 'by heart', a process whereby the *heart* is commonly bypassed entirely— just where such unloved and unforgotten things are stor'd ever after I profess I know not. Among his fellows at University he was not known *solely* for his odd habit of now and again looking into an

1

ancient or a modern Author—but certainly it was remarked upon in some wonderment.

In the other common course of study engaged in by the bloods, Ali was not behindhand, when once set upon a path previously unfamiliar to him. 'Tis said that a term in Prison will tend to harm a man's character, because of the Company he will commonly find himself in, and the conversation there provided, and the *subjects* touched upon; he may come out a better Criminal than he went in. The same may be said of those who attend our Universities, or at least of those who come there not already corrupt, and only ready to continue. Ali soon learned the arts of opening Bottles, and tossing away the Corks; of awaking in rooms not his own, after adventures unremembered; of being the sole support of young women residing with aged female protectors in the neighbourhood, and in want of Charity in every sense. His greatest disability in these pursuits, in particular the last-named, was a violence of feeling which would, without his willing it, become concentrated, rather than spread abroad, where it would do him little harm—he felt he could lose the world for what he now found it contained, and in his single-mindedness (the *opposite,* in a sense, of Libertinism) he ran the constant risk of *fixation,* a condition his fellows noted in awe and mockery, the Objects of it being considered.

Then he might ride out, after too great and long carousing with companions who in fact cared little for him (and those were 2 of *both* sexes), to a quiet place, a still pool of the serpentine stream that crossed the grounds—and there purge his sullied soul in cold water—and only then allow himself to think upon Susanna, far away, and of her brother, of whom he heard little—for the *pen* was by now as unfamiliar to that young Lord's hand as the sword or the gun were companionate. But a lapse came also in Susanna's communications, which wounded at first, till it was forgotten in the course of Ali's new and absorbing preoccupations—in the throes of which, thoughts of such a one as Susanna were indeed unwanted, and best kept at bay. When at length a missive in her hand was delivered to him, he felt before opening it the shock of a reproach, for his forgetfulness at the least.

'My dearest Ali,' began this letter. 'As you have shown, by so many kind words and acts, your feelings towards my brother and myself, and (I hope) towards my family as well, I write to tell you of our fortunes, and what times we have fallen upon—I hope it will not wound your *most gentle nature* to hear—tho' it is the fear thereof, I think, that has kept me thus far from writing to you. O dear—I see there is nothing but *preamble* here, and it is likely you are already searching the page for the news I wish to give. I must tell you that Corydon Hall is let, to a Banker desiring to try being a Landlord, and upon terms I do not pretend wholly to understand. My dear brother might have been able to forestall this, or to strike a better, or a *safer* bargain for our dear home than my poor mother and I could have done, but he is far from home. O my dear Friend you know so little, I see I must start farther *upstream* of these tidings if you are to see our fates whole. —To begin with him whom we both hold so much in our hearts: My brother having joined the Regiment to which all his friends and mentors urged him, had every reason to expect a posting nearby, so that he could continue in that double service—that *triple* service, I should say, of son, brother, and head of House, as well as doing his military duty—for there were several among his officers, and above them in those Offices of government concerned in Army matters—do not ask me to explicate—who knew our story, and who desired to aid us. So it fell out, for a time—but then—and I know not how, nor could he discern the reason—that former understanding vanished. His regiment having been ordered to the Peninsula, he apply'd to those Offices where he had formerly received aid, but now found all changed. He asked that he might be exempted from the general orders—that the hardship to *us* and to his young brothers might be considered—but he found no one to listen—doors once open were now shut—those who had before been kind were not at home, or otherwise engaged—and appeals fell on deaf ears. So he is gone, my dear Ali—the light and warmth of our Sun and yours, is set in the South—and yet we remaining are determined to do our Duty as he does his. And in what does *our* Duty consist?— Well—in Pleasure, it seems, now—at least what the 1500 inhabitants of hot rooms (I mean Society) deem Pleasure—I must say that it seems as laborious to me, and to cause daily as great anguish to those engaged in it, as if they dug a Ditch, or cleansed a Stable.——I mean to say, plainly, that my Mother and I have taken a small house in Bath for the season, and each day we sally forth, to see, and to *be seen*—O my dear Friend let me not dwell on the particulars of a pursuit whose purposes must be evident to you, if you but consider our condition—mine, and my *House's*—for my House is mine to preserve, as much as it is anyone's. I hope that your opinion of me may remain unaltered by what Necessity impels me to—tho' I fear it may not.—Remember only that I hold *you* in as high regard as ever I did, and will continue to do, no matter what befalls. And who knows—I am my Father's daughter—I will believe that something may *turn up* as he was wont to say, and change our case for the better.'

She closed this letter with the tenderest of compliments, and beneath these a *post-scriptum* that struck like a knife into Ali's vitals: 'I know not how it may be, nor what it portends, but the name of *Lord Sane* was more than once mentioned, in connexion with my brother's appeals, and as well in the application of our Banker to take the lease of our home. Is not this curious?'

Lord Sane! No more than Susanna could Ali know what his father's name, insinuated like the worm in the bud into the affairs of the Corydons, might mean, if indeed it meant aught of consequence: but it kept his hand from the response it should make. For many days he bethought him—began a reply, tore it up—tormented himself, castigated himself for a fool—but still could make no answer. For he had, he saw, nothing but *words*—which, having nothing behind them, were as useless as so much sand. *Take heart,* he wrote; or, *I will never abandon thee;* or, *My heart as my hand is for ever thine*—and then he would crush these helpless sentiments, which indeed made him no resistance, and toss them into the fire. After long enough, he grew desperate, and—risking *Rustication* or *expulsion*—he took horse and left the University, meaning to cross the country and offer her—what? At each station where he stopped along the road he asked himself. What had he to offer? A loyal heart and a willing hand are invaluable things—and much wanted in this world—yet there are species of trouble that they are impotent to battle. Half-way through his journey, having defeated *himself,* Ali turned back, and took the same road the other way. In his lodgings once again, he *contented* himself with a written reply—and yet he was not content. He received no further letters from Susanna, indeed so many weeks passed that he became certain there would be none, that his ineffectuality deserved none—and he was on the point of departing from the University at term's end when a further letter came from Bath.

'My dearest Ali,' Susanna's missive once again began, and a hot shame flew over him to see this salutation, so that for a moment he could read no further. 'It happens some times, does it not, that the dreadfullest griefs come when *Happiness* seems nearest, or is even upon us—and so it seems for me. I know not how I may write to you what I *must,* except to state it plainly—tho' I thought I should die immediately when it was stated so to me. Ali—my brother Corydon is dead. No sooner had he reached the Tagus, and before he could be of any service to King or country, he took a fever—the same that destroys so many of our Soldiers who enter that land— that *cursed* land—No! Let me not complain, let me be patient to endure this, or I shall surely die of it! He is gone—we will not see him more—and I am half of what I was, and a *half alone* can hardly survive. I can only hope that my own changed state—for it is soon to change—will in part bring some little forgetfulness, tho' only briefly. For this is the Happiness of which I spoke—I am to be married. And surely it *is* happiness—it is always described so—and I am assured that tho' the prospect may not fill me with delightful anticipation, yet certainly the *state* itself may satisfy, indeed *must*— there is no alternative. The gentleman to whom I have given my hand is that same gentleman who has occupied Corydon Hall these months—one whose name you may know—' And here, in the near-blindness of his tears, Ali discerned the name of one whom indeed he knew—an aged man—the *father* of a scholar in his own College, one with whom Ali had once got drunk—a widower, one wife already buried—and one whom Ali had *met in Lord Sane's company* in London upon the time when he had first been carried through that City. Rich he indeed was, though without rank or property—which Susanna would supply! With grief changing to despair, Ali read on: 'O my dearest, dearest Ali!' Susanna concluded. 'When you think of me, consider—if it be not in your heart immediately to *understand*—the grief of my poor mother, and the situation of my young brothers, without guidance, without a model upon which to mould themselves! I wish above all that you retain your memories of me as I was—as *we* were—before this Gulph opened—on whose nether side I now stand. And yet your hand, and your voice, seem even now not far but near. I am in want of your good wishes—your best thoughts—your prayers, even, if ever you make such—and your dear and constant Friendship, which I will believe I ever have—*ever*—in the Path I now shall tread!'

To this she appended only a signature, so rapid and brief as to suggest she could not have easily writ more, had she more to add; and Ali studied it with a sense of a door shutting fast, and a bar fallen. Dead! The Sun, now set, never again to rise! For a time Ali felt the dead cluster unrefusably about him, as though to claim him forever for their own—his mother—and Lady Sane—his ancestors—Lord Corydon hardly yet cold in his grave—to claim him, to drain from his veins the warm blood, and from his sinews their natural vigour—yet to withhold from him the one gift he would ask of them—their *sleep,* their blessed *ignorance*! Instead, a turmoil, a rage of consciousness seemed to fill him—he thrust the letter within his pocket, and ordered the last of his baggage put upon the coach that went the North-ward way, and within the hour was upon the road to Scotland. Yet the wheels of that conveyance seemed to turn as slowly as the chariot of Sisera, and Ali by his constant turnings and twistings in his seat, attempted to push it along the faster, that it might carry him from *himself* and all that he was and knew. Toward one goal he bent all his thought—and that lay at the journey's end, in his Father's stronghold.

When that pile appeared, at eve, it seemed not a place that any heart would chuse to rush upon—indeed, it warned him away. Its gloomy walls and far watchtower seemed to have fallen deeper into desuetude & decline even than before, and projected far abroad an air of utter desolation (I have at times wondered why so many words suggestive of sadness and neglect, falling-off and faltering, begin with the letter D. What curse fell in the beginning upon the 5 fourth letter, that it must be the one to carry so many *dread* associations?). Through the emptied halls he strode, past the shadowed walls where the brighter squares still showed that pictures had once hung there—of the frightened servants he came upon, he asked only and without preface for the whereabouts of the *Laird*—was misdirected—and at length found the man, in his billiards-room, bent over the table, which almost alone of the furnishings he had seen fit to keep.

'You have been quick upon the road,' said Lord Sane calmly, as he took his shot. 'I did not expect you for some days yet.'

'Sir,' said Ali. 'I am in receipt of certain news that—that have shocked and distressed me in the highest degree. I am led to think that you know something of these matters, though I hope you are innocent of any machinations against me, or my happiness, or that of some I hold in the highest regard.'

'A strange way to address me,' said his father without undue excitement. 'You must be more frank, Sir, and say plainly what you mean. Of what persons do you speak?'

Ali related to him those matters of which he had not for a moment ceased to think since he had heard of them—of Lord Corydon's death in Portugal, his former exemptions having been mysteriously withdrawn—and Susanna's impending marriage to one whom he could not think a guarantor of her happiness, to say nothing of the dashing of his own feelings and hopes, though these had never been spoken—and as he told of these things, he observed minutely his father's face, for some sign upon it of complicity in them.

'I am sorry to hear of your friend's demise,' said Lord Sane, as he studied his position upon the baize. 'Yet *dulce et decorum est,* of course. I have been a Soldier myself, and asked for no such exemptions as he so easily had. As to his sister, I congratulate her. A fine Match—an old rich man who will make upon her few demands, and will strive by every means to keep her *good opinion* of himself. As I remember the man, he is somewhat deaf as well—he will observe little, and hear nothing. She may do as she likes—as all the world likes.'

'Withdraw those words!' Ali cried. 'They are offensive, and shall not stand!'

His father, then busy chalking his cue, seemed to take no notice of this demand—indeed he regarded Ali as though nothing at all had been said to him. 'I recommend her example to yourself,' he then said. 'You are now deeper in debt than before—your College expenses have been far beyond any present means I have to pay them—therefore I have had to sign certain instruments in your name, with persons in the City whom I have not liked to deal with, but to whom I have, in point of fact, had recourse myself in former times. These deficits shall be added to the other costs of your Minority, which (as I have said) have not been small.'

'You have placed me in debt without my knowledge? How is that possible?'

'You have no idea, Sir, of what is *possible*. Perhaps, however, upon reflection, you may now chuse to attend to my former instructions, and look for a *wife* who may unburden you. I have lately noted the appearance upon the stage of Society of several new-fledged Birds, among them a certain Miss Delaunay—Catherine Delaunay—of whom I have heard that she is chaste, demure, common-sensical and *rich*—attend me in my Study tomorrow, and you shall learn more of her.'

'Indeed I shall not.'

His father now replaced his stick upon the rack, with slow care, and the air of a man who has at last decided to address an annoyance. 'Failing that,' he said, approaching his son, 'you may apply at the Kirk, and be given a licence to *beg,* and a blue gown to wear—there are several of this parish who do well enough in the position—perhaps you may have a talent in that way.' He had now drawn close to his son, and of a sudden, reaching inside his son's coat, took hold of his clothes in a firm grip. 'Or does your hesitation at the prospect of a *wedded life* perhaps turn on other fears—of an inadequacy of Body—if so, an examination may dispel them'—here his hands searched intimately his son's person—'Let us reassure ourselves you are *as other men*—Nay! Resist me not!'

'Have done!' cried Ali, thrusting him away. 'Have done, or I will—'

'What shall you do? *What shall you do?* Have a care, Sir! Remember—all in a moment, and in defiance of consequence, I gave thee life—all in a moment I can take it away again. "The Lord giveth, the Lord taketh away." '

'Devil!'

'Ah!' said Lord Sane. 'You know that exalted Being is said to have a knack for quoting Scripture to his own purposes. Here is another—"If thy right eye offend thee, pluck it out"—therefore challenge me not, Sir, not though you be the *apple* of mine own!'

'I warn you, provoke me not further,' Ali said, lifting his balled fist before the great Lord's face, 'or indeed I know not what I may do. I have borne more than flesh can bear, and I am no more than flesh!'

'Raise not your hand against me,' said his father. ''Twould be a sin of dreadful note—moreover, 'twould be useless—for weapons can do nothing against me—no—I see you shudder to hear it, yet 'tis true—hanging also would be inefficacious—for, you see, *I cannot die!*'

Now he had come to *loom* over the slighter figure of his son— and the fire in the grate threw up his even greater shadow upon the wall—and he cried this in a loud voice—*I cannot die!*—and *laughed* in his son's face—and went on laughing, as it were the laughter of his *cognomen* himself, at the futile resistance of Men—as Ali, amazed and furious, turned on his heel, and threw himself from the room.

It was that night, then, that Lord Sane summoned his carriage, and his Coachman, and without further intercourse with his son, betook him to a nearby Town, with what purposes he did not say. Ali would learn nothing further from him, not of his plans, nor his past actions, nor indeed of anything—for on the night of the following day, his son kept watch beneath the Moon upon the Abbey's battlements, as has been here recounted—and went abroad in the deep midnight, *fast asleep,* to find 'Satan' Porteus dead, and hanged up within his own watchtower—a clear and irrefutable contradiction to that man's awful claim to his son:—*'It is useless to hang me—I cannot die!'*

1. *Athens upon the Fens:* Lord Byron briefly attended Cambridge University, though he took no degree. There he met, among others, Mr Scrope Berdmore Davies, and Mr John Cam Hobhouse, who would be among his loyallest friends. Mr Davies will later appear in the person of Peter Piper, Esq., one of the story's droller creations, though how much like life it may be, I know not.

2. *still pool:* There is a weir of the river Cam above Grantchester that is still called 'Byron's pool'. I wonder if a guide to all these sites, from here to Constantinople, ought not to be gathered in one Almanac, not only the genuine but the supposed ones, for those who wish to make the pilgrimage conveniently. Though for all I know such a guide exists, and has escaped my notice.

3. *my family:* It appears to me a notable thing that, in the entirety of this romance, there is not a family left whole—Father, Mother, and children. Authors, of course, have the right, as they have the power, to simplify their stories, by pruning the family trees they introduce, and by a convenient fall from a horse, or a

sudden fever, to bring about what circumstance they need to advance them. Still I wonder if my father had the power to imagine a family unbroken, or other than eccentric, or incomplete.

4. *chariot of Sisera:* I know not what is here referred to, and no book of reference upon which I can easily lay my hands can tell me. It does not burnish an author's intended effect to employ *comparisons* to whose import the common reader has not a clue.

5. *the letter* D: Disgrace, degeneration, distress, decline, despair, dread; disappointment, disgust, detriment, deprivation, disability, darkness (but also day!); dirt, dearth, desolation, desuetude, doubt, and death.

In which the Reader is reliev'd

from his tenter-hooks, and

Ali from his dungeon

NOW, GENTLE PERUSER of these ungentle pages, whosoever thou might'st be (and here I extend a ghostly Hand to thee, and a spiritual Salute to thy perceiving eye—my compliments, on thy perseverance!), Ali's tale has all been told, to the moment of his Confinement, by the pitiless (and not altogether sober) Magistrate, within the dungeon of the Tolbooth that stands by the sea in the Royal and Ancient Burgh wherein the Abbey of the Sanes lay—and no doubt still lies. And surely it will not be wondered at, if Ali, lock'd up in his stone Apartment all alone, in the hours remaining of a darkness more utter than any he had known, should think it possible that, in his dream, he had truly *done* what he was charged with. Had he not slain Lord Sane a hundred times in his mind? Had he not arisen from his bed—armed himself—

found his way *asleep* to the mountain's height, before some good angel woke him? And might it not be that though in his dream he was on his way *upward* to the fatal tower, he was in actual fact *on his way down again,* having only just committed—Ah!—but no! Impossible! What—in sleep, struggle with a living man of more than normal strength, subdue, strangle, bind—hoist, like a calf in a butcher's window—no! And yet the visions raced through his brain, and the utter darkness seemed almost to stroke his face with icy fingers, and night had no end. We may say, of a dreadful hour, that it *seemed a dream;* but though we may believe we are in waking life when we dream, when awake we know—we weep, we rage to know!—that we dream not. The cold and sweating walls were real—his dead father—all too real—the Turnkey's footstep without—the farther sound of the sea on the rocks below. Oppressed with horror of the *real,* he groaned aloud, and at the sound the heavy tread without paused, and then commenced again.

At length on the meagre pallet allotted him he threw himself, and slept—but only struggled the more in dreams with his father—drew on him—slew him; *dreamed* that he awoke, and found his father before him, 'in his habit as he lived' and grinning upon him—awoke then in truth, and for a fearful time recked not where he was—in the grave—in Hell—in a ship's hold (for the sea had risen toward the dawn, and beat against the prison's base)—or nowhere—nonexistence—a blind eye only, and a beating heart. We would not, truly, live our lives again, except to regain some hour or two at the most of heightened life—but if to have those we must endure again one such night as Ali then endured, we would instead leave all our days where ever Saturn keeps them, and seek them not.

But now a clamour of some kind in the halls beyond his cell shook him from unhealthful sleep. The shackles upon him, dependent from a great staple in the wall, would not permit him quite to reach the tiny barred window in the oaken cell-door, past which he perceived the Turnkey's terrified cries—crash and clatter of a stool, or a weapon—then no more cries—a silence. Then the rattle of the great ring of keys, just at his door, and Ali knew for certain that the lock of his cell was being tried, in a manner slow and methodical, with each iron key in turn. He waited and watched: and the door was pushed open.

The dull light of the lamp in the passage beyond illuminated the shape of a man in the doorway—a man, and not yet further to be known. He entered in, his step seeming certain, and yet blind, and Ali drew back from him in wonder, for now by the small moonlight entering in at the window-slit, he perceived the man before

1   him to be a *Herculean Negro,* shirtless, in a long black and ragged surtout.

'Who are you?' Ali asked this dusky personage. 'Who has sent you?' But answer came there none—the black man was deaf, or seemed so—*blind,* too, for the great yellow eyes in his dark face look'd seemingly at nothing—and yet saw, as though by another sense. After a moment's unmoving hesitation—when he seemed to *listen* for what he knew he must find within the cell—he knelt before Ali, and, as he had into the door's lock, he began to fit in turn each of the keys of the great ring he carried into the locks of Ali's shackles, until at length the cuffs fell open.

Before Ali could demand more of his strange saviour, the great black figure turned, and out the now-yawning door he went on bare feet; then he looked back, or *turned* back at any rate, as though his sightless eyes could tell if Ali followed or no—just as the bear who (as Ali dreamt) led him to his father's corse had done—but Ali did not immediately follow. *Reason* was indeed far from him at that moment; *caution* and *prudence* he had none of; sweet *freedom* lay ahead the way the sable fellow led: and yet by some sense whose workings he could not perceive, he was at first held back—some apperception that by fleeing now he would certify to the world his guilt for the murder of Lord Sane. But then again—said this unsensed sense to him—was he not now believed guilty by the world? And if not yet by *all* the world, enough of it to hang him thoroughly? And was he friended at all? Without the least pondering— of which he was at that moment incapable—Ali knew the right answer to all these questions, and others like them; and so he rose, a fire as though banked in his bosom flaring up, and went out.

Down the drear corridor they went, he and his guide. The

Turnkey lay stunned in a corner, overcome, whether by Fear, or the force of a blow, Ali did not consider. The black's naked feet fell upon the flags with no more sound than a cat's pad; his stride was long and sure, and yet he held out his arms somewhat before him, as though to learn of obstacles in his path. The wide front doors of the Tolbooth whereat Ali had first come in stood heaved ajar, and they went out into the street, and along that street not a window of a house was lit. 'Where do you take me?' Ali whispered to his guide. 'Whose man are you?' But—without insolence, yet not turning back his look—the man went only on, down to the Harbour of the town, where the rising tide had lifted the crowd of small sail, which lay on the softly-heaving bosom of the sea asleep as kine. Unhesitating, the black man stept from the wharf into a small open boat, not waiting for Ali to precede him, and—as though remembering the use of tools he once upon a time knew well—he took the Oars, slipped them in the locks, and was already pulling as Ali climbed aboard.

Last bright stars of Morning! White thighs of Aurora, carelessly spread, created each day afresh by Apollo's gaze from beneath the world's edge! The small craft made for the Harbour's mouth, and the breeze freshened; the Charon (as he might be, and Ali care not then) shipped his oars, made sail, and took the tiller and the boom. Ali knew his part—though the rôles he and the black might have been expected to play were reversed—and he lowered the oars and rowed with a will; and it may have been only the steady labour of his hands that stilled his heart, and made him glad. In not too long a while they were able to round the point that marked the Harbour's limit, and it was not yet full day when they came in sight of a Ship at anchor in the farther cove—toward which the helmsman of their craft now guided them. And as they came near, a light winked in the forecastle, once, and then again.

Even as it became evident to Ali that the ship waited there upon his arrival, the mainsails rose to the arms, and tightened in the breeze—the anchor-chain could be heard ringing round the capstan as the anchor was weighed—and a ladder was dropt from the gunwales with a clatter, just when the small craft with Ali aboard was laid against it. There was no question what next he ought to do, and above him as he stood in the rocking boat to take the dangling ropes of the ladder, there appeared a pair of faces, each topped by a hat, and encouraging gestures were made. On that uncertain stair Ali lifted his body—his spirit arose *of itself*—and in a moment he was taken hold of by hands above, and pulled aboard. Looking down, he saw the Negro, sitting as though a carven figurehead, regarding nothing: till Ali was secure—whereupon he turned his tiller, swung round his sail, and was taken by the breeze from the ship's side, with never a backward look. Ali was of a mind to call to him, but knew not *what* to call—nor *why*—nor whether the fellow would hear. He turned instead to the two Gentlemen who had made sure his boarding, and 'Thank you,' said he, knowing not what else he might add.

'Thank us not, young sir,' said the one; and the other said, 'We have been compensated, well compensated; 'tis you ought to be thanked, for making ours a profitable *detour,* and therefore—' Here the other chimed in as at a cue—'Thankee, Sir, thankee!'

They were a tall and a short man, a long-faced and a round-faced, and to Ali's eyes they closely resembled the two Officers of the Peace who had taken him before the Law. But these fine fellows were of the Irish race—and as such it may be that they spoke, and comported themselves, as Irishmen do in the pages of Miss Edgeworth's admirable tales—or perhaps they did not—but I hope I may be forgiven if I do not attempt to reproduce that speech, and those manners, for I have not the *apostrophes* at hand properly to do the one, nor the heart to do the other.

'You are welcome, I suppose,' said Ali. 'But compensated by whom?'

'Why, by one who had the *desire* that you be accommodated,' said one of the Hibernians— 'And,' said the other, 'who had the *means* to effect it.'

'Will you tell me nothing more?' Ali asked.

'That personage of whom you inquire,' said one, 'has very definitely requested that we do not.'

Ali turned to look out over the sea—and saw the small bark of his black rescuer, drawing fast away toward a far cove, even as the

2

ship Ali stood upon made out to sea, doubling their distance apart. 'And was *he*—'

'In the same personage's employ? Indeed so, and so described to us.'

'We were instructed specially—I should say we were *warned*—that he not be taken on board. For the which I am not sorry.'

Now to Ali there seemed to be no *succeeding* question he might ask, unless it be the ship's name, or her masters'—for so his interlocutors appeared to be—or their Destination, which would now be his; but these seeming, in his circumstance, irrelevant to a high degree, he found he could ask nothing—and was only rescued from his predicament by the two Irishmen, who importuned him in chorus to come below, and refresh himself with a Potation—which he could hardly refuse to do.

'T HE SIGHT OF THAT blackamore who conveyed you to this ship has put me in mind of another such, yet of a character entirely different.' Thus spoke the Master of the *Hibernia,* his name being Patrick—and his brother Michael, the First Mate, nodded in agreement. 'The faithful Tony,' quoth Michael. 'A paragon,' said Master Patrick. 'The mildest and best of men, as all who knew him would attest.'

Ali—who had been given a glass of golden Irish whisky tinct with honey, at which he sipt with care, as it were his own alarming freedom—had now an inquiry or two to put to these mariners, but held his tongue.

'Tony,' said Master Michael, 'had, as I think, no other name. He was for years in the employ—yet more companion and mate—of the late and blessed Lord Edward Fitzgerald.' At the speaking of this name, both brothers swept the hats from their heads, bent to their drink, and then replaced their hats. 'Lord Edward—yet perhaps you know well his tale?'—here Ali shook his head—'Lord Edward, I say, was but a youth, a junior officer in his Britannic

3

Majesty's army, his Regiment being then engaged with the American partisans of Carolina, in that late war. Eager to win his meed of honour, and blood his virgin sword, he champed (as 'twere) at the bit to be in the van of every engagement. In an encounter with the forces of General Harry Lee, among the ablest of the American leaders, young Lord Edward was so severely wounded that he fainted, and was left for dead upon the battlefield. But a Negro—by name, Tony—came upon him, and found him to be something *short* of dead—carried him to his own cabin—nursed him with great diligence and skill. When the young man was sufficiently recovered to rejoin his fellows, he had no reward he could offer his saviour but a place in his service, for as long as the valiant fellow desired—which the faithful Tony, as he would be known, accepted—and ever thereafter, the Lord and the black were inseparable.'

Here Ali—perhaps it was the whisky, little of it though he had imbibed—made bold to inquire, 'Whither they were sailing, and what was their destination?' He received smiles of gentle condescension from the brothers.

'I meant not to step upon your tale,' Ali said remorsefully, 'if it be one.'

'We are merchants,' said Patrick. 'We go about buying and selling, in our poor Vessel, and live by our profits, when we have any—after we have paid our Crew—and repaired our leaks and hurts—and mended our sail. We are harmless men, and mean naught but good to you.'

'And why have you done these things? Be assured there is nothing I can do for you—would it were not so—I have nothing—I leave behind only the presupposition that I am guilty of a parricide, made a certainty by my flight.'

'Ah no, young Sir,' replied the younger brother, 'we remove you from the Law's purview, that you may, as the saying is, *live to fight another day.*'

'Not,' said his elder, 'that we suggest you are one who *fights and runs away.* Ah no.'

Ali knew that they would answer no question about who it was that had employed them on his redemption. Who had that been?

Who? No one had known of his incarceration—none save the townspeople, who were powerless to conceive, far less to effect, his escape, even if any of them had desired it. The thousand enemies of Lord Sane, one or several of whom might be supposed to have suborned his murderers, whoever they were, were not matched by a thousand friends to himself—indeed he knew of no guardians at all, since the death of Lady Sane.

Thus in all puzzlement he lifted his glass to the bland and cheerful faces of the Irish merchants, if merchants they were, and bade them continue their tale, if they liked.

'It may be wondered,' said Master Michael, closing his fingers over his stomach and taking up the thread that had been dropped, 'how one who would prove himself such a friend to Liberty, and that for *all* men, not only his own Nation, could have served in the army committed to the suppression of the Americans' just desires to determine for themselves. Well! He was a British soldier, and 'twas his nature—the *soldier's* nature—to serve, and to fight, not considering his own opinions of the rightness of his Army's cause—or, rather, keeping those opinions lock'd up in his breast, lest, by conflicting with his Duty, they may weaken his resolve, or soften his blow, and thereby endanger himself, or those under his command. A hard task at times, though a common one.

'There is no doubt his head, and his heart, turned toward the Americans—though not his Arm. He liked the people, and he thought them in the right. He despised the unending concern of the British with the minutest marks of rank and subordination—liked the Americans for having none such, and accounting no man greater or lesser merely by *name,* or *birth*—liked a land where any man, or man and woman, possessed of an axe, a gun, a pair of oxen and a willing spirit, might make a home for themselves, and furnish forth their children, to do the same—to live as they liked—frank and free—beholden to none, except as they agreed. Indeed, as soon as he could after that war ended in the victory of Washington, Lord Edward contrived to return to the Continent—to Canada, there to serve with the British Army occupying that land, but also to travel, to explore, to see for himself.

'I invite you, young Sir,' he cried, rising from his seat in urgent suasion, 'to picture the land of Canada, as 'twas then, and no doubt still is—the great rivers and mountains, never yet named or seen but by savages—the falls of Niagara—the flotillas of Canoes by which the savage Nations travel—the snows—'

'*Our* experience of snow is as nothing,' interjected his brother. 'It is as the powdered sugar on a cake. There, the snows fall in November, and heap up higher than a man's head, never melting till summer—and yet there they go, the savage hunters, walking upon the shining surface in their *snow-shoes,* and drawing behind them their *tabargans* loaded with the pelts of Beaver and Moose they have slain—and get on more easily than in the summer forest!

'Lord Edward travelled thus for many a month—slept out under those stars—made his bed of spruce—or a hole in the snow—and eat his *pemican,* of the dry'd flesh of the *moose*—often in the company of a famous Chieftain of the savages, named Joseph Brant by the English, and no other companion, save the faithful Tony.'

Now his brother had also risen, as though the sights they spoke of lay before his inspired vision. 'What man of Africa,' cried he, 'what slave of Carolina, ever beheld, or acted in, scenes as diverse and wondrous as did the faithful Tony? Chased a moose for days, till it dropt from exhaustion—stood in the thunders and sprays of Niagara—shared with his Friend and Master every hardship—and with him every triumph? No American *slave-driver* could have compelled his loyalty—much less his love—but an Irish lover of Liberty could do!'

'At the headwaters of the great river of the Mississippi,' said Master Michael, 'Lord Edward was inducted by Chief Joseph into his own sept of the tribe of the Mohawks, that of the Bear. Then he parted from that proud savage, whom he had learned to *admire* as much as to *love*—while well knowing how many white men's throats he had cut, and settlements burnt—and made his way down the river to New Orleans, whence he expected to return home. It was there that he learned, from letters long in pursuit of him, that a certain lady of Ireland, upon whom his heart had long been fixed—

'And whom he had reason to believe returned his feelings—despite the unyielding opposition of her father—a cruel man, or at least obtuse and obstructive—which had, as he believed, prevented him from contracting with her—

'The Lady, it now appeared, had, in the long time of his absence, married another—showing, it may be thought, that Lord Edward was mistaken in the causes of her reluctance toward accepting himself.

'There, then, he stood—upon the Continent's lip—with his last connexion to his native land severed by these news—and found that he had little desire to return to the Old and distant World. Rather than returning to his oppressed land, or to the Army of the oppressor, he thought to go on—for there seemed a *forever* into which he might go—to the mountains of Mexico, to South America, to the Orinoco, or the Amazon—to the bottom of the world, where the ice and snow appear again—to return never!

'And yet—a letter from his mother was also awaiting him—a lady to whom he was utterly devoted—who was indeed *worthy* of that devotion. Her desire once again to set eyes upon her beloved Son, melted his heart, and weakened his resolve—and with heavy heart, and few expectations, he began his preparations to return.

'Now see what may come, when Time and Chance wrestle with a man's will, like Jacob with that sporting Angel, to see who may be the shaper of his fate! Within a month of his returning from America, he had gone on from his mother's house, to Paris, where the Directorate had then been formed—the year, it must be noted, was seventeen ninety-two—and where the embattled Revolution faced its several enemies among the Monarchs of Europe—which did not yet include, tho' soon it would, his own nominal & befuddled King. On a certain night, at White's hotel, British subjects present in Paris foregathered who were sympathetic to the Revolution, and who wished it success; and amid the wild hopes felt that night and the oaths taken, the songs sung and the toasts made, Lord Edward, of the oldest and grandest House his native isle could boast, *renounced his title,* and in its place took that only of *citoyen, frère, camarade!*'

'That night,' his brother continued, 'at the least, I *believe* it to have been that very night, the erstwhile noble Lord attended a ball, and there he glimpsed a beautiful young woman, and his heart—that he had thought *dead*—made known it was alive after all within his bosom. The lady was the illegitimate daughter, by a man *formerly* a great Duke of France, of a Lady Writer of renown—'

'Chieftainess of that tribe of scribbling women, none other than Madame de Genlis!'

4

'He woo'd, was accepted, and within weeks was married to the lady. During those weeks he was dismissed from the British Army for the oaths he had taken at White's hotel. So there he stood—not a broken Heart—not a Bachelor—nor an English soldier—nor an Irish lord (tho' all would ever call him so still), and before him lay all things. No sooner hardly than he had brought home his Wife, he attended Parliament in Dublin, and struck out upon that path—as unknown and full of hazards as any in wild America!—that would lead to his martyrdom in the cause of his People and of Liberty, and his place eternal in the hearts of all who love them both!'

'So you may see,' said Master Michael—the storm of feeling inspired in him by this tale now somewhat blown by—'we do not know what awaits, nor what we may be called upon to chuse, when once our way divides from what it was, and we know not what it shall be.'

'Step upon a Ship's deck,' said Patrick, 'it may convey you merely from place to place—but know that it may carry you from Life to Life.'

'And now,' his brother said, 'our duties call us, and we are short-handed—so I may ask you, to give us what Assistance you can—no knowledge of the mariner's art required—but a strong Arm—and a Will likewise.'

Ali averred that he would do all he could to help the kindly pair, and was soon at work doing tasks he had never done before, involving tarry ropes, and great yards of canvas, and dizzy heights, and a *language* never heard on land, which he must learn—and sometimes when aloft above the Irish Sea, he would bethink him, how he had been himself but recently a *Lord,* or the son of one; and before that a *shepherd,* and now was neither, nor hardly yet a *mariner*—and truly he knew not, what he might yet be, nor cared. He chose not to tell his own tale to the brothers, who did not seek it of themselves, however much they studied him in smiling curiosity. They were as silent upon the subject of their own business, and Ali learned nothing of their purposes, save that they seemed solely to *take on* goods as they rounded their native Isle, and to deliver none—that they seemed to have many dealings at night—and that they avoided the greater ports and more commodious harbours, where the Royal customs-houses are maintained. Yet it was not until, with running lights extinguished, they turned the *Hibernia* out to sea, meaning (as it appeared) to round the great toe of England, and make for the Bay of Biscay, and the Western coast of France, that Ali knew certainly their name & trade.

It was still the days when Buonaparte 'bestrode the narrow world like a Colossus', and among other actions shocking to the world—as, the knocking off of Crowns, the tearing up of ancient charters of Privilege, the freeing of the imprisoned, the granting of suffrage to the despised—he had locked up the whole of Europe in his 'Continental System', which forbade any of those lands he ruled as his demesne to trade with those outside it. In response, the English government—to whom a blow against *trade* must have been felt more keenly than even one struck against *honour*, or *religion*—proceeded to ban all other Nations whatsoever from trading with the French, thus beggaring themselves, provoking the Americans to a futile war, and achieving very little. For trade nonetheless flourished—tho' no duties were levelled against it—and it had largely to be done inconveniently, at night—and investors were oft-times discouraged, when a cutter of one side or the other sent their argosies to the bottom, or to impoundment—it mattered not, for like water, Trade is neither compressible, nor destructible, and will flow *underground* if stopt above. It was withal an occupation for brave men, and cold of blood: and however mild the brothers Hannigan (or it may have been Flannigan, my notes are illegible upon this point) seemed to Ali, there was little they would stop—or *had stopt*—at, to conclude their business with a profit to themselves.

'Indeed,' said Master Michael, 'there is a wisdom in choosing

5

the right cargo to carry. We are fortunate in that, and what we bring will not be stopt, for it goes from our ships to the highest offices in the land.'

Dark was upon the face of the ocean, and a sweet breeze carried the odours of the shores of France, which lay beyond a far line of whitening breakers that could not yet be heard. Ali begged to know what this precious cargo was.

'Razors of Smithfield,' replied Michael, and clasped his hands in satisfaction behind his back. 'His Highness the Emperor may despise the English, and their soldiers and sailors, and their King and Princes, and the "nation of Shopkeepers" they rule. But he will not have his cheeks shaved with any but razors of Smithfield, the world's best, a good number of which we carry below. And corn and tar and tallow and *good white 'taters* too.'

Ali's eye was now drawn to the horizon, where a dark shape had blotted out a square of pale horizon. He asked, 'If that was not a ship, and making a beeline for us?' At which the First Mate went to the taffrail—approaching thus a few feet closer to the approaching vessel, the better to inspect it—and bent out over it to sea.

'By certain signs displayed,' said the Master, 'we are assured passage to port, so long as we are *modest,* and make no show. I tell you thrice,' he added, and held up before him crossed fingers, 'we have an Arrangement.' But now a signal-lamp was flashed from the approaching Frenchman, which made clear its intent to interfere with the *Hibernia.*

'What means this?' asked Pat.

'The devil I know,' replied his brother, 'but I shall not stop to learn. Hard about!'

'I think it may be,' said Pat, 'that the *arrangement* you boasted of just now, Brother, may be in abeyance.'

'Well, well, Pat,' said Mike, and crossed himself with great delicacy, 'perhaps you may have a part of the truth. And now that I think upon it, it may be the better part of valor to be discreet, and heave to.'

For they at that moment saw, as the cutter approached, a red flash of fire—and an instant later *heard the sound,* and a moment after that *felt the passage* across their bows, all too near their *heads,* of a ball—and the simple Truth pronounced by the Irishmen, that 'when we step upon a ship's deck, we may be carried not only from shore to shore, but from Life to Life', was to be illustrated, once again, in the story of Ali.

6

1. *Herculean Negro:* Readers who look into these notes before
    completing the story will not yet know this figure to be a man
    of the West Indies, and a victim, or beneficiary, of that infusion
    of artificial life which, in the superstition of the Caribbean lands,
    can turn a corpse into a deathless though soulless labourer.
    (*Who* has re-animated him, if that is indeed his condition, will
    eventually be revealed!) This weird belief was first brought be-
    fore English eyes in a book by Robert Southey on the history of
    Brazil, which may be the source from which Lord Byron drew
    the legend; if so, the connexion is a strange one, for Southey
    was a *bête-noire* of my father's, and his life & politics a source of
    endless inspiration for his wit and sarcasm—repaid, be it said,
    with the then Poet Laureate's fulminations and anathemata
    against *him* and all his pomps and works. All that is old; they
    are both dead; yet I remember me, how Southey once wished
    to join with the poet Coleridge to create a colony of perfect fe-
    licity upon the banks of the Susquehanna, in America: and so
    did I, when I was but a child.
        I believe that the phenomenon of the *zombi* is another aspect
    of that Hypnotic Sleep elsewhere explored and described in this

novel in such farsighted fashion: it seems to me that persons placed by clever masters or powerful Witch-doctors into that state, might appear to others to be both dead and alive.

2. *Miss Edgeworth:* Ld. B. was by his own estimate a prodigious reader of novels, and claimed at one time to have read five thousand—though Mr Hobhouse says this is impossible—that Lord Byron counted a book as read if he had but looked briefly into it. He had also little compunction in respect of exaggeration, a fault I have shared, and was punished for as a child, when the thing exaggerated was not of the approved kind—as filial piety, or religious impulses, or grief at the sufferings of others who had claim on my compassion. I can well believe that Ld. B. read widely in fiction; he had no airs, where literature was concerned, and thought none the less of his own work, that many readers delighted in it.

3. *Lord Edward Fitzgerald:* The tale here interpolated is a true one—the Irish patriot, slain in the uprising of 1798, did have such a black servant, and had these adventures in America. The tale is told in the biography of that Lord by the ubiquitous Mr Thomas Moore, who can at times seem unnervingly like a shadow cast by Lord Byron, without whom he would not exist—but this is an unfair aspersion on the name of the author of *Lallah Rookh* and many lovely songs. Nevertheless it is true that Ld. B., long before he knew of Moore, or Irish matters in any way at first hand, became enamoured of the chivalrous figure (as he perceived it) of Fitzgerald, and declared at the time of the Irish rebellion of 1798, that had he been a grown man, he would have become an *English* Lord Edward Fitzgerald. Lady Byron has granted me that tit-bit from the store of anecdotes told her by her late husband.

No doubt it was during his later long friendship with Mr Moore that Ld. B. learned the story here related. His reasons for telling this tale within his own is less clear. Perhaps it is only the vision of America which drew him to include it. I know not.

4. *Madame de Genlis:* The Comtesse de Genlis was the tutor of the children of the Duc de Chartres, and at least one of her children is now generally supposed to have been his. She is the well-known author of *Madame de Maintenon, Memoires,* &c. Like so many of his generation, Ld. B. professed to despise the 'bluestocking' lady writer, the 'crowd of scribbling women' held up so often in his time to contempt. Madame de Staël was excepted by him, and I suspect that, in this as in so much else, his easy mockery is less *felt* than merely assumed, and unexamined.

5. *Buonaparte:* This is Ld. B.'s habitual spelling. As a boy he was much taken with Napoleon, but like many of his coevals, he was finally disappointed in the apparent liberator of Europe, who became a Dictator worse than any he overthrew, and instead of removing Kings from the world, merely set their crowns upon the heads of his own incompetent relatives. Lord Byron's poems and letters are rich in allusions to this cynosure of his youthful fancy, and anyone doubting the complexity of the poet's mind, or the subtlety of his judgement, need only assemble them, and see how variously, without contradiction, Napoleon is pictured—as dream of glory, or of justice and hope; as welcome affront to the settled world; as figure of comical self-deception; and as blood-stained tyrant. I for one would trade all Byron's verse dramas for *one* on the subject of Napoleon.

6. *a ship's deck:* There was nothing he loved so much as to be on a ship, both leaving *behind* what he no longer wanted, or what no longer wanted him, and going on to what he knew not. For only that moment he could love again what he had lost, or discarded; and was not yet disappointed in what he would have. I was among the left. It was not altogether his choice, yet it was his doing. He would not deny it, if I could ask him; but I cannot, and that is his doing, too—and Death's.

· SEVEN ·

In which a famous Battle

is reported upon, tho'

not as it has been

UPON THE PLAINS OF eastern Spain—that blood-boltered land upon which, not a decade ago, the powers contested so hotly—the ancient city of Salamanca rises within its stout walls, lifting above all the dome of an ancient and much-lauded University, where long the arts of Peace were taught. Among the allied forces who came to lay siege to the city during the late war, there was a certain British Lieutenant, Brevet Staff Surgeon to a brigade of the Portuguese army. The brigade was largely officered by other Englishmen, who held their Peninsular allies somewhat in contempt—no doubt believing they had good reason—and from it the Lieutenant was ever seeking to be removed by *promotion* to a loftier sphere.

These allies, British, Spanish, and Portuguese, had, after years of discouragement and reversal, begun at last successfully to drive the French from the Iberian lands, and were now arrived at a pause before Salamanca. The French did not possess Salamanca, but held upon the farther heights three strong forts—one a Convent, whence the nuns had fled, most well *in time* too—and, from batteries rigged upon their walls, they dropt balls at will within the City. Below, the Commander of the army of Allies—not yet Duke, but already *Iron*—look'd deep-browed upon Salamanca—which was pictured, as well, on the maps his officers unrolled before him, just as it was seen by the carrion-crows patiently waiting on the hot winds above. A battle was daily expected, but none knew what the French general might do—nor what *he* thought the English general might do. Meantime in the pretty town the French shot fell in the streets, and when it fell the ladies and gentlemen fled indoors, but came out again soon enough—like birds shoo'd by a crone's handclaps from the corn—and resumed their promenading—their flirting, and their Commerce, where the two were not the same—and their amusements.

2

Our Military Surgeon (whom I think you will have already forgotten) was often among those tasting the pleasures of the town, until he was ordered away to his Regiment again, to prepare his Hospital and staff for the work ahead—the sawing-off of limbs, the sewing shut of wounds, the plucking-out of musket-balls, the closing of the eyelids of the dead—if indeed this office be commonly done by surgeons in war—I happily do not know. As yet, however, he was busiest in other matters, those that consume the greater share of every officer's store of time, which is to say the finding and claiming of the best spot to pitch a Tent, the furnishing and provisioning of the same—for this requires a constant traffic in favours, paid and received—and the assembling of comforts. Lieutenant Upward—a Welshman of the Marches, and a handsome and gentle fellow—had a fine camp-bed, from whose stead his sword was hung with picturesque negligence; he had a chest of drawers cunningly made—a spirit-lamp—and a netting against mousquitoes, a treasure above price in a clime where an ell of gauze may mark the difference between Ease and Misery, unless upon one's skin, as upon mine *own,* the beast hath no power of puncture. Lieutenant Upward had also a

Spanish lad, to assemble and prepare his suppers, and pour his wine, and see to his Uniform, and polish his Boots. This small person was of that exquisite colouration found in no other land—call it not Olive, for that is too drab—hair darker than chocolate, yet not black, and eyes the same. Even more pleasing and convenient for the Surgeon, I trow, was the fact—he supposed it to be his secret, tho' 'twas well known to his fellow-officers, and a source of mirth to them—that the *lad* was not a lad at all, but a *maid*—rather she *had been* a maid, when first she came into his service—a *señorita,* apple of the Surgeon's eye, chiefest ornament of his small estate upon the Spanish earth. This *señorita,* after many slights and neglects which her Officer was ignorant of having inflicted, and conscious of her own worth too, which she set at a different rate than he, had decided that this night she would change her breetches for petticoats, and seek her fortune elsewhere: but of this the Military Surgeon, as of so much else, had no idea at all.

That morning, however, even as dark-browed Dolores (for that was her name) brooded upon her present wrongs, and future prospects, news were brought to her Master's tent: a man was come into camp, wounded unto death—as it seemed—and in the dress of a Spanish peasant—but speaking no Spanish, indeed claiming to be a British subject, though more resembling a Moor than Dolores herself. Where—she was asked—was the Lieutenant Surgeon?

He was found beneath the shade of one of the few trees flourishing thereabouts, seated upon an empty caisson, deep in thought. When not occupied by his medical duties, or the more demanding ones attendant upon advancing his Career—or visiting the Monuments his army passed (those it was not, out of military necessity, compelled to destroy)—or attending Balls, whereat ladies of rank might be met—Lieutenant Upward liked to sit before a *view,* a pen in one hand, and his chin in the other; for he was of a literary bent, and hoped, after not too long a gestation, to birth a Romance, or an *Epic*—he cared not which.

Hastening to the regimental hospital—a place he liked not to linger in, without necessity—he found already brought there the man in Spanish smock, who had ceased by then to speak in any language, and indeed almost to breathe. His wound was not deep, but it was old, and had been made not by a ball, but by a blade. 'Carry him to my tent,' said he, 'and I shall follow after,' for well he knew that the worst of all places for a man in a medical crisis was a regimental hospital. When he had gathered up those tools and medicaments he thought necessary, and forestalled the questions of his Superior (who put in, just then, an inconvenient appearance), he proceeded to his tent, where he found the young fellow already put in his own bed, and his own Dolores pressing a cloth soaked in his own eau-de-Cologne upon his hot brow: nor was she, at the Surgeon's suggestion, fain to retire. He was about to upbraid the wench in proper form—summoning to his aid the small Anglo-Saxon vocabulary she had acquired, most of it however pretty pertinent—when the man upon his bed began to speak. And indeed it was English in which he spoke—then French, which the Lieutenant knew—and another language, unknown to either of them who bent to the chappy lips and fluttering lids of the man to hear. 'Look not upon me,' says he, in a stark whisper, and then, 'I have done thee no wrong—no—pass away, or I will—I will—!' Yet what he *would,* they learned not, for his rolling eye and tossing head now seemed filled with other visions. *'Rangez votre epée'*—so cried he, as to an opponent, and held his hand before him—*'Je ne me battrai avec vous—Non! Non!—Vous vous trompez—Vous avez mal compris!'* Whereupon he fell again into feverish incoherence, and only an application of brandy to his lips helped him to recover—with a great shudder he half-arose from his litter, and cried aloud, 'The *BEAR!'* He gazed about himself, yet seemed not to see the Lieutenant or his servant, but *others,* elsewhere—his eyes were hot, and clouded—his breast rose and fell as though he fled some horror, or was in its grasp. Then with a groan he dropt upon the bed, putting his hand to his clothes as though to search a wound—yet it was not that side upon which he had been wounded. After a day of care, however, his fever abated, and he breathed more easily—slept—and though both the Lieutenant and his Dolores (for curiosity, and something else perhaps, had kept her from decamping, as she had planned) very much desired to question him, and learn his story, yet they would not have him killed in the telling—and so held their questions, till the man himself began to speak, in more rational terms.

So the story was told, though haltingly, of Ali's journeys and adventures—his true name—the reasons for his flight—his service aboard a Smuggler's vessel—his suborning (with all the rest of the crew who were not Irish, and thus not Allies of the French) into the French Army, and his service therein as a private soldier. Indeed the story was not told so plainly—nor in such good order—for there was incident aplenty that Ali would have been glad to leave out (as every Tale-teller knows he ought) and yet was compelled by Sense and his listeners to advert to, and include (as many a Tale-teller will).

'I served unwillingly,' said Ali, and the Military Surgeon opined that there were many among the British Army who might say the same, if certain they were not overheard. 'Yet I served. Many months indeed I wore blue, and marched and countermarched, wheeled and counterwheeled, with my fellow private soldiers *en masse,* and found them to be no different from the men of any nation, give or take a Vice, or a Virtue.'

At this he look'd into the dark eyes of the *lad* beside him, whose hand he had clutched tightly, as though it were a *life-line* holding him to the Buoy of continued existence; and found his gaze returned, with interest too. 'I pray you, Sir,' said Ali, 'a little water,' and Dolores swiftly supplied the same, and tenderly held the cup to his lips.

'But, Sir,' said the Military Surgeon with some impatience, 'tell now how you came before this City, so near to the army of your own people, if such they be, and what you did then. It is inconvenient for you to be forever beginning your tale again.'

'My knowledge of the French language was noted by my first sergeants,' said Ali, 'and also of English; and when I was recommended for these skills to a higher officer, it was further observed that I was a gentleman, and well-spoken enough—for the tricks and traits that count toward this impression are ones I have learned—indeed, have been *schooled* in, and by masters!—and so I was brevetted to serve as aide to a *Chef de bataillon,* a Captain you would say,

I suppose, who was soon sent to this land by the Emperor—one who even now is commanding his battalion before this city—but no! *Even now*—Ah no! No more! Ask me no more!'—and he turned his face from them, and for a time would not speak, though his Audience impatiently fidgeted through this *Entr'acte*.

Through that day and the night, between the attentions of the Military Surgeon, and the gentler ones of Dolores, who would not be dismissed from *her* patient's side, Ali completed his tale. The Captain to whom he was attached, he related, was accompanied by a Household, consisting of his young wife, and a female companion, and the furnishings they required, including Quarters sufficient for privacy—to provide all which, said Ali, was the chief study and most constant occupation of the Captain, who had stretched his credit to the thinnest to have a Spouse at his side on campaign. Ali's duties were largely to further this business, for the which he was not much liked among the more martial, and *single,* officers; but his duties brought him often together with the Captain's wife, to answer her needs, and arrange her comforts. Not much time passed before this lady, who was as beautiful as she was proud, grew to depend upon Ali—and to expand the scope of his duties—and the intimacy of their meetings. Would he not help her to untie this—or tie up that—or read with her this book of English poems—or make her coffee, as he alone could do properly? Not all Ali's evasions—arising from respect, and Honour, and (above all) Fear—could preserve him from Madame's attentions, whose character became every day more evident, even to my untaught hero. There came a night when, for the meagrest of reasons, she summoned him to her private quarters; Ali knew—and knew that *she* knew—her husband was long at a staff-meeting. Then indeed there were no more excuses— no parcels—no Books—no draperies to be hung—nor Vermin to be routed—only *herself,* and unconditionally.

The night was warm, and scented with the orange, and the hibiscus—the Lady's cheek, hot, and coloured—the scent of her *person* the more deranging to his senses. Ali, being unused to such a siege as the Lady now laid, capitulated in a moment, hardly knowing he did so, nor upon what *terms*. Indeed she whispered, '*Non,*

non'—but the coin was counterfeit, and bought nothing—nor was meant to do—and that moment quickly came when caution is discarded—with other and more *material* obstacles—and thus he and the Lady were unmistakably *en déshabillé* when of a sudden the curtain was torn aside, and the Captain (whose approaching tread they had not heard) stood looking upon them with fury, his hand upon his sword-hilt.

'What then did she do?' asked the Military Surgeon. 'Surprized, and guilty as she was?'

'She cried out upon *me*,' said Ali, 'that I had offered her violence, and that in fear she had not resisted me, lest I make good my threats!'

'She wept?'

'She wept,' said Ali. 'Turned her face from me in horror—shame, too—all which seemed as genuine as—as her *earlier* and different feelings—for I think fear may be pretended to, and alarm—but not such loathing as she showed.'

Here he paused, in deep confusion, as though what he *thought*, he could not *say*. 'No, it is impossible,' said he then. 'No woman would conceive of such a thing—and yet I cannot shake the conviction, that she knew very well her husband would return, and *when*—and still she offered the freedom of her Quarters to me—and all else. When indeed the Captain appeared, and found me there, where she had invited me—and I saw his face suffused in rage, and his weapon drawn even as I struggled to put myself to rights—well—methought I saw a sort of *communication* fly between them, whose nature I knew not—and yet—and yet—'

He said no more upon this score, yet Lieutenant Upward, who had more experience of the world of Females, indeed of *wives,* than Ali would ever acquire, was not so baffled as he. There are, among the great variety of our fallen race, those whose motives we may catalogue, though we do not understand, and that might fill volumes, if we cared to write them down; and the Military Surgeon knew that, just as there are men who will provoke a duel for no other reason than to satisfy an obscure rage against all the living, so there are women who will provoke a *husband* to a duel, or a *murder*—with the husband's complicity, whether *spoken* or *silent*—and in circumstances that would seem to destroy, yet actually strengthens, as in a forge's heat, the bond between them—a bond which may not have been made in Heaven, nor be sanctioned there.

'He was prepared to kill me, and for all that I begged her to tell the *truth*, she only wept—and still he came upon me, myself unarmed.'

'He wore his sword?'

'Yes,' said Ali, 'the which I wondered at—not then, but later— as 'twas unusual, at evening, in camp.'

'I warrant,' said the Military Surgeon: for he thought to himself, 'This Captain and his wife played here a delicate game—the time must be carefully chosen—their prey not so easily dispatched as to show no sport, yet not so strong or quick as to end the game altogether, in a conclusion the reverse of that expected—as here happened, it seems.'

'He struck at me, and I felt the cut,' said Ali. 'My hand took up the first thing it found to strike back with—'twas a *boot*—which came unexpectedly at the Captain, and by a chance knocked the sword from his hand. I had it before he could recover it, and thus armed I - rose to face him—but he had gone for a pistol that I had not seen— he was attempting to cock it, and withdraw from me at the same time—and in my fear and his confusion I ran him through the body.'

'You slew him? And with his own weapon? An officer of the French Army? The Devil you did!'

'I am certain of it,' Ali said. 'I saw him expire upon the ground. His wife flung herself upon his bloody breast, in tears—yet she was silent, strange as it may seem, and raised no alarm. After that I saw no more—for I fled. No one challenged me—I was a common sight in that part of the camp, running errands for the Captain—and the night was dark. I was soon beyond the limits of the encampment, and amid the Camp-followers and their fires and habitations. Truly, I knew not what would become of me among them—whether I should be discovered, and returned, for reward or other reason, or shunned, or let to die—as without aid I knew I should, for my wound, which had seemed small, and was now stanched, had occasioned a grievous loss of blood.'

Again the wounded man fell upon his pillow—for he was no Italian tenor, capable of recounting a long tale while dying of his wounds—and it was evening before he could recover. When his eyes opened, and he seemed to recognize his surroundings—and the hand of Dolores upon him—then he grasped convulsively at the smock he wore, a gesture they had seen him perform often. The Military Surgeon desired to know what it was he sought for within his clothes. For a time Ali resisted his questions, which became demands, but at length he asked for a knife—cut the stitches of his coat—and drew from within its linings a handful of papers, which with some misgivings he allowed the Military Surgeon to peruse.

'Before we fought,' he said, 'and upon his return to his wife's quarters, the Captain threw upon the table a portfolio tied with tapes. I knew not its contents, but I had seen similar despatch cases, and could guess that this one contained letters and documents of relevance to the evening's conference. Before I fled that place, I gathered them up—and these are they.'

A glance proved that indeed the papers were as Ali described them, letters and minutes relating to the strategies and plans of the French general staff. Lieutenant Upward wished to know, 'Did the French command believe the Captain to be still in possession of the papers?', to which Ali replied that he could not be sure, but considered it likely that they did not know they were *no longer* in that officer's quarters, or among his effects—and that they were therefore more valuable, indeed were intelligence of very great import, if brought before the right eyes, and put to the proper uses.

'The proper uses,' mused Lieutenant Upward. 'Yes, the *proper* uses!'

For only a moment was the Military Surgeon tempted to bring these revelations to his superiors as though acquired by himself—for doubtless the bringing of them would redound to his great Credit—and perhaps even accomplish his dearest goal, the winning of a Promotion to such a height of grandeur as would permit him to leave the service altogether, and return in triumph to England. And yet upon consideration he saw it would be wrong, and dishonourable—and, despite his brooding long over the question, he could not think of a tale to explain how such papers might have come to him. He settled, therefore, for the *reflected* glory he would earn by bringing Ali and his purloined letters to the Council of Gods who were then disposing of the human fates in their hands.

Those august Commanders were quite of a mind to dismiss the documents laid before them at first—were unconvinced by Ali—look'd darkly upon him to learn whose son he was, for even in Iberia the story of his father's death and his own flight was partly known—and he had fought for the French, had he not? Whether suborned, as he *said*, or willingly—well, who could know? Nor did it matter much, for clearly in his Impressment by the French he had chosen base Dishonour over Death (as none of *them*, they were each quite sure, would do). They would know, 'How he came in the first instance to the shores of France from Scotland?', 'How he rose from a press-ganged Foot-soldier to an officer's Aide?', and other questions that Ali might have hung his head to answer, or *not* to answer, and yet his replies were so frank, and his honesty so apparent, that they were themselves abashed. Meantime the papers were put before them, and examined—and cloudily an understanding began to arise in their minds. The French Generals held no high opinion of their opponent— '*Il est évident,*' declared these Minutes, '*que les anglais pusillanimes préfèrent ramper comme des vers à travers la terre trainant leurs bagages, leurs animaux et leurs chariots plutôt que de se lever et de se battre. Une fois provoqués, ils sont susceptibles à se battre en retraite à plat ventre. C'est donc l'objectif de sa gracieuse Majesté Joseph d'Espagne ainsi que de l'Empereur, de provoquer une bataille qui reglera la question une fois pour toutes,*' &c., with many other insults and sneers at English cowardice and temporizing. In conclusion, the French sword-rattlers declared that their *pusillanime* enemy must be inveigled into battle by '*une faiblesse apparente de notre part de sorte à tenter cet ennemi, si timide soit-il!*' The General Staff passed these papers about—they humm'd—hawed—bethought themselves what great value there was in knowing with certainty what their opponent thought of them, and what he would therefore make of what he saw them do—that his prejudices might be *seemingly* confirmed, by what he saw—and that therefore he might be drawn into that worst of military errors, an unwarranted contempt for the foe. (So the books have it, from which alone I take all the little learning in the subject as I have: and this, rather than at *first-hand,* is the very *best* way to learn it—such is the considered opinion of every legless or eyeless Veteran, as of every Royal Advisor.)

It remained for them to make certain of their rear—not of the Army's, but of the Commanders' own—for it must not appear that they had formed a strategy upon the word of a turncoat and es-caped parricide, who had traded his information for succor. No! He must be one who gave his all for the triumph of his Nation—a Patriot—a *Hero* unspotted. To that end the French soldier (as he had been) and Privateer (as he would not acknowledge) and mur-derer (which he deny'd hotly) became in a moment a British sol-dier, and a junior officer, by a *field promotion* more rapid than even the Military Surgeon might have dreamed. The Surgeon, at bottom a good fellow, was almost as pleased by the advancement of his pa-tient as if it were his own, and shone himself in its reflected light.

'We will drink your health,' he said, and clapped the younger man's shoulder, 'and celebrate your advancement, and your Rehabilitation—be it altogether deserved, or no—for who among us would have his own *upward* path too closely examined? And what I foster in you today, I look to receive from you on another fortunate day.'

'Of course,' said Ali,—'That is, if all that I have provided be as it seems, and not a figment, or a delusion—as I trow I cannot en-tirely say with confidence. And now, though wine would be most welcome, for I thirst, and fain would rest, I shall mix mine with wa-ter; my head spins already, and I stumble without any drop taken.'

At this the Military Surgeon shook his head in soldierly dis-may, at the prospect that any potation whatever or *when*ever should have any 'allaying Tiber' introduced—and so gave his charge his arm, to help him on.

In the following days the French through their spyglasses ob-served the English move their baggage to the rear, as though in preparation for a retreat, and when they issued from their strong-holds and made display of force, to tempt the craven English to bat-tle, the English did nothing, but only drew away like a Maiden before an importunate Suitor, like Clarissa before Lovelace. Even when the French generals forgot their Rule-books, and spread their forces too widely upon the hills before the City, the English forbore to attack—and then the French were certain of an easy victory—until too late. The night before the battle, a war broke out in Heaven, and Jove hammered the armies below as they had planned to hammer *each other,* and some two dozen valiant Englishmen were killed by *lightning* before the enemy could do the same. Indeed it is inconvenient when foul weather spoils our plans of slaughter and mayhem, and especially inconvenient when his Iron Lordship has forbid his officers to carry umbrellas in such circumstances, as suggestive too much of the *unmanly.* But the next day dawned as clear as could be wanted, and the guns belched white smoke against blue sky, and the Cavalry officers jingled gaily as they cantered by—the common soldiers cheered them mightily, and neither wondered why.

    What would have become of Ali if his information had been wrong—or if the wrong conclusions had been drawn from it by others—or if any of a thousand untoward turns had been taken by Fate and Fortune on the way to victory—need not be thought on, for it is universally known that the French in their impatient pride fell upon the English that day at the village of Arapiles, with all the grandeur, and all the success, of a hoary Eagle fallen upon a Steam-engine. From that day to this no battle his Iron Lordship has fought has been declared more perfect, more *elegant,* as though a battle might resemble an axiom of Euclid's, or a parallelogram. 'Twas in any case a victory rapturously received by his Countrymen far away, who had had little news of this character to feast upon in those months. The papers were loud—the Opposition *silent;* his Lordship was made a Marquess, given 100000£, and, what is more than all this, the Archbishop of Canterbury (at the Regent's command) composed and offered up a Prayer of Thanksgiving to the God of Battles, calling especial Divine attention to the victorious Lord. An Extraordinary Gazette was published, in which our Ali was mentioned, and *commended,* among the many other contributors to the victory—his name upon that list was noted, in wonder and amazement, by many who knew his tale.

3

So in the bright summer, when the French Eagles and Standards were brought home, and the lights of London lit (and every *unlit* window stoned by the patriotic Mob), Ali came to England's shores and England's Capital again, but now a Hero, accompanied by the Military Surgeon—who had won, by his part in the action, his heart's desire, a post in London—and thereupon gave himself up to the King's officers, to be tried (and most likely *hanged*) for the crime he had not committed!

A PERSPICACIOUS READER (should my tale have any such) may here object, that he has nowhere heard or read of any such circumstances attendant upon the famous Battle of Salamanca as are herein described, nor of the subsequent celebrity of one of its (purported) chief Actors, nor his generous commendation by Commander and Crown, nor the particulars which produced it—to which I reply, that I have for authority the then British Consul to Spain, the admirable and Honourable John Hookham Frere, Esq., a man of proven probity, who certainly would not deign to invent a fantastical tale, nor even to embroider a plain one.   *4*

NOTES FOR THE 7TH CHAPTER

1. *the late war:*   When Byron travelled in Spain in the year 1809, the British had just begun their incursions into the Iberian peninsula; he sets this adventure later in the war, well after he himself was a visitor there. I note that he places the date of the Battle of Salamanca (1812) 'not a decade ago', which while not as specific as might be hoped, sets the writing of this part of the story some time before 1822. Late in 1821, he left Ravenna, to take up residence in Pisa, whence he would later sail to Greece. I believe the MS of this tale to have been worked on, in desultory fashion, from the time of Lord Byron's residence in Switzerland following the separation from Lady Byron, until some time during his residence in Ravenna, and to have been lost (or abstracted) during the move thence. But all this is speculation.

2. *not yet Duke:*   That Ld. B. thought it possible to publish a novel in which the Duke of Wellington figures as a character, in which he wins one of his most famous victories in part due to the informations of one who is a turncoat, and is moreover entirely imaginary, suggests to my mind that by the time these incidents were described Ld. B. had decided that the book

could *not* in this form be published, and so he was free to write what he liked, and the whole could then be consigned to the flames, or to the future—but not to the *Public,* as it then existed. This fact may also account for why, as far as I can tell from his biographers, he made no mention of its composition, even though his beginning, or continuing, or finishing, various other works, is talked of continually in his letters to his publishers and others.

3. *umbrellas:*   What I read in Napier's *Peninsular War* tells me that Ld. B. was essentially correct about the movements of the troops, the course of the fighting, the effects of the weather, and even the Umbrellas of the officers. He was proud of the correctness of his facts, I am told, and liked to get right the small details of a ship's rigging, or a foreign government's composition, or a people's dress or habits. It is not a large virtue, and he did not always exercise it. But it is one I own myself, and likewise do not use at all times as I might. I do not use it as I might.

4. *Frere:*   John Hookham Frere was indeed the British Consul in Spain at the time of the Battle of Salamanca. He had earlier held that post when Lord Byron travelled across Spain in 1809, on his way to Gibraltar to take ship for Greece. Why Ld. B. chuses to introduce this personage into his fiction at this juncture is unknown to me, as I am unaware of any further connexion between the two.

6 0 3 4 0 5 9 3 5 8 · 3 0 5 7 2

9 3 7 5 6 · 3 0 4 8 5 7 2 6 9 0 ·

4 9 5 7 6 2 7 3 0 1 · 3 9 7 6 2

From: "Smith" <anovak@strongwomanstory.org>
To: "Thea" <thea.spann133@ggm.edu>
Subject: The Childe

I never thought I'd be doing this. I'm staying up at night trying to read Byron's poetry. Georgiana happens to have a big volume of it, in this bookcase full of leather-bound books I don't think she's looked at much, if ever. I started in on his first big poem, *Childe Harold's Pilgrimage,* the one that was such a huge and instant success that he "woke up and found himself famous," or whatever it was. Well, it's pretty funny. Read this (yeah I know, but read it). It's a scene early on when Harold's traveling in Spain and goes to a bullfight:

> *Thrice sounds the clarion; lo! the signal falls,*
> *The den expands, and Expectation mute*
> *Gapes round the silent Circle's peopled walls.*
> *Bounds with one lashing spring the mighty brute,*
> *And, wildly staring, spurns, with sounding foot,*
> *The sand, nor blindly rushes on his foe:*
> *Here, there, he points his threatening front to suit*
> *His first attack, wide waving to and fro*
>   *His angry tail; red rolls his eye's dilated glow.*

Now isn't that *exactly* like those scenes in old cartoons set at bull-fights, where Bugs Bunny or Daffy Duck has to be a matador, and the door flies open and the bull comes out, with steam snorting from his nose, etc. etc.? Just like, right? The whole thing's not all like this, but every now and then these—well *cartoons* pop up. Maybe since he was writing about things people didn't know much about, it was like a vivid travelogue, and not corny. Maybe it's good. He was only 23. But I can't read much of it. My eyes drift closed. The print is very small. The page is very dark. It was a long time ago. I'm going to bed.

S

───────────

From: "Smith" <anovak@strongwomanstory.org>
To: lnovak@metrognome.net.au
Subject: Ada Notes

Lee:

I am working through the notes that Ada made for the novel. I sent you some scanned pages. They're very hard to read (esp. as digital files, maybe you gave up on them). I wonder if she was stoned part of the time. But I am trying to understand what the burned book might have been about. Here are some things I already know are (or were) supposedly in it, or important to it somehow. Albania. Greece. Scotland. Byron's house at Newstead. Thomas Moore. A zombie (!). An Irish lord named Fitzgerald, who was a real person (?). The battle of Salamanca (Spain). The Duke of Wellington. Some-body named Frere (?). None of it makes much sense to me, but it wouldn't, would it, without the book itself.

I don't know why I'm obsessing on this. She spent a long time on it, and she was dying, and I feel like I could make it worth it. But if it's gone I can't, can I.

Tell me if you learn anything from them.

S

———————————

From: "Smith" <anovak@strongwomanstory.org>
To: "Lilith" <smackay@strongwoman.org>
Subject: Process

Lilith—

I don't think it's exactly fair that you think I am not getting the job done that we decided on. I know the reports I promised you have not been what you expected to see, but I think that what's really important is that I not do anything to harm the relationship that's building here with Georgiana. She cc'd me the letter she sent you and you have to admit she's still fully engaged in the process and considering the things she said about me personally in that letter I think I am doing the right things here to keep her focused and aware of the project and the project's needs.

I understand that keeping the site moving along without me there is harder, but if you look at some of the old pages, like the Curie pages, you'll see I've been cleaning up and making the changes on your bugs list. It's not always easy to find a place to work now that I am in Georgiana's house. The room is kind of small. She talks on the phone a lot, and she likes to wander around the house while she talks. But think of the money we're saving, and I'm going to the London Museum of Science today and back to Oxford to the Lovelace papers again on Monday. And speaking of which, is there anybody in the office, is Caitlin still working, who could go look at something for me in the NY Public Library? They have a bunch of Ada stuff too.

Lilith, I really am trying to do what I can here to keep Georgiana feeling good about us and the project. We're in a process. I can't explain everything, but I have to ask you to just assume it's for the best for a while longer. Eyes on the prize.

Love

Smith

───────────────

From: "Thea" <thea.spann133@ggm.edu>
To: "Smith" <anovak@strongwomanstory.org>
Subject: math

well now you got me doing it   im staying up late looking at this stuff you sent me   its a bunch of nonsense as far as i can tell none of it makes any sense as mathematical tables

so i went and read about babbage and his stuff   and i found out babbage and ada were also interested in statistics   about which i know not a lot   so now i go to the department to see if anybody can tell me anything   i have to tell you its a little embarrassing but i dont care   i guess   anything for knowledge   ily

t

───────────────

From: "Smith" <anovak@strongwomanstory.org>
To: lnovak@metrognome.net.au>
Subject: Leeches
cc: "Thea Spann"<thea.spann133@ggm.edu>

Lee—

One thing I found out—you can find out anything on the Web, really, it almost makes research irrelevant, or no fun, except that half of what you find out is bullshit—but one thing I found out is about Dr. Merryweather's Tempest Prognosticator. That was the machine or "engine" that Ada went to see when her friend got a look at the manuscript. Maybe you thought that was some kind of joke, but there really was a Dr. Merryweather and he really did come up with a new machine for predicting sudden changes in what, the *weather,* all this is true. Here's what he did: he had discovered that leeches, you know leeches, tend to become very agitated when there is a drop in barometric pressure. So he worked up a machine made of several glass jars, each with a leech inside, and tied to each little leech there was a silver chain—why silver? I don't know—and the silver chains were attached to a bell at the top, very delicately balanced; and when the barometric pressure dropped, meaning a storm or bad weather coming, the leeches would wiggle furiously, and the silver chains would pull the bell, which would ring a warning. In the picture I found the jars were all cut-glass, and the thing looked like a big chandelier. That's all.

S

———————

From: lnovak@metrognome.net.au
To: "Smith" <anovak@strongwomanstory.org>
Subject: RE:Leeches

Ah. And did you know that her mother—Byron's wife—was addicted to leeches? She was constantly using them, applying them, being "bled." She distrusted any doctor (and she saw a lot of doctors) who questioned the utility of leeches. She applied them to her forehead and temples for headache, other parts for other pains. Leeches! How is it that the world or history can visit these tiny sweet revenges on awful people, furnishing their lives with exquisite symbols (or metonymies might be the word) too obvious for any author to dare to use, but true.

She was bulimic too: isn't that the term? Said she never ate, but actually liked to eat a lot—especially mutton—and then she'd have herself rowed a ways out to sea, and upchuck. AND she kept an "issue"—an open wound on her arm, which she somehow picked at or did something to keep from healing, to facilitate bleeding. And everyone—all her many friends, the general public, her son-in-law till (almost) the end, thought she was a paragon of virtue and self-denial.

May I ask who the Thea is you cc'd the leech machine to?

Lee

———————————

From: "Thea" <thea.spann133@ggm.edu>
To: "Smith" <anovak@strongwomanstory.org>
Subject: got it

okay   okay   i got it   i got it
youre not gonna believe me but i got it   and you didnt

we started working on it with the computer   its first of all not statistics   there is actually an algorithm that will tell you if a list of numbers is statistics   its called benfords law and it predicts the frequency of digits in statistical data   a big data set like this if it defies the predicted frequency curve its not statistics   wow huh   yeah   i ws impressed   then i started thinking   and i got it you could get it in a second if you just think about it   about ada and her dragon mom   youd have done exactly this yourself   what she did

so heres what you do   you have to find a quiet room with a door you can lock and call me like you havent done   and be sure its in the evening   like about nine   est   and we can talk a long time   and youll tell me stuff   lots of stuff   cause nitetime is the rite time and then if you are good I WILL TELL YOU THE SECRET   BE-CAUSE I GOT IT

T

————————

From: "Smith" <anovak@strongwomanstory.org>
To: "Thea" <thea.spann133@ggm.edu>
Subject: Morning After

Thea, what if it's so? What if it's really so and you're right? If she really did that, put the whole book into a code and made it look like math stuff. I keep thinking about it and laughing because it's so great, or it's so stupid, I don't know which. O Thea you amazing person.

God what a night, huh? How could I forget that nine at night where you are is 3 AM here. Oh well. Georgiana looked at me funny this morning like maybe she heard something.

But you never mind all that. You go break that code. If it is a code. You've got to break the code, and all by yourself, and in secret. And then afterward we'll be famous. YOU'll be famous. If we can get Georgiana to let us tell anybody.

S

————————

From: "Smith" <anovak@strongwomanstory.org>
To: lnovak@metrognome.net.au
Subject: News

Lee—Maybe news. Maybe the book's not gone. Maybe.

Thea is my partner. In email you can't see me choosing that word over a few others, but it's the only one I want. And she's wonderful, and she's just done something wonderful, I think and hope. Maybe. I'll let you know soon.

S

———————————

From: "Thea" <thea.spann133@ggm.edu>
To: "Smith" <anovak@strongwomanstory.org>
Subject: codes

not a code   a cipher   heres how it works   you substitute letters for other letters according to some kind of rule   one rule you can use is to start the cipher alphabet from a different letter than the plain text   the plain text starts at a and goes to z   the coded text starts at g and goes through z and on to f   get it   so the word cab comes out igh   to break a cipher like that you need to run through all the possible letters from which the code alphabet starts until one starts making sense   but then   what you do to make it harder is you change the alphabet starting letter   you do it according to some key   you take a word for instance like lordbyron   and you drop out the repeating letters and then add all the other letters after it to make a whole alphabet   so you get this

abcdefghijklmnopqrstuvwxyz
ldbyronacefghijkmpqstuvwxz

get it   then you use that alphabet   and if somebody has the key they can figure it out   but thats too simple becuz every letter in the text is represented by the same letter in the code   every b is a d   easy to break   so there are other things you do   you can make a table 26 letters square   a to z on one axis   a to z on the other and then you have 26 different alphabets starting from different letters   and you take your ldbyron key   and you use it to specify a different alphabet for each of the first 7 letters of the text   and

repeat for the next 7 when youre done   the code was called a
vigenere code   here is the square you use   the top row and the
left column are the key row and column

	A	B	C	D	E	F	G	H	I	J	K	L	M	N	O	P	Q	R	S	T	U	V	W	X	Y	Z
A	A	B	C	D	E	F	G	H	I	J	K	L	M	N	O	P	Q	R	S	T	U	V	W	X	Y	Z
B	B	C	D	E	F	G	H	I	J	K	L	M	N	O	P	Q	R	S	T	U	V	W	X	Y	Z	A
C	C	D	E	F	G	H	I	J	K	L	M	N	O	P	Q	R	S	T	U	V	W	X	Y	Z	A	B
D	D	E	F	G	H	I	J	K	L	M	N	O	P	Q	R	S	T	U	V	W	X	Y	Z	A	B	C
E	E	F	G	H	I	J	K	L	M	N	O	P	Q	R	S	T	U	V	W	X	Y	Z	A	B	C	D
F	F	G	H	I	J	K	L	M	N	O	P	Q	R	S	T	U	V	W	X	Y	Z	A	B	C	D	E
G	G	H	I	J	K	L	M	N	O	P	Q	R	S	T	U	V	W	X	Y	Z	A	B	C	D	E	F
H	H	I	J	K	L	M	N	O	P	Q	R	S	T	U	V	W	X	Y	Z	A	B	C	D	E	F	G
I	I	J	K	L	M	N	O	P	Q	R	S	T	U	V	W	X	Y	Z	A	B	C	D	E	F	G	H
J	J	K	L	M	N	O	P	Q	R	S	T	U	V	W	X	Y	Z	A	B	C	D	E	F	G	H	I
K	K	L	M	N	O	P	Q	R	S	T	U	V	W	X	Y	Z	A	B	C	D	E	F	G	H	I	J
L	L	M	N	O	P	Q	R	S	T	U	V	W	X	Y	Z	A	B	C	D	E	F	G	H	I	J	K
M	M	N	O	P	Q	R	S	T	U	V	W	X	Y	Z	A	B	C	D	E	F	G	H	I	J	K	L
N	N	O	P	Q	R	S	T	U	V	W	X	Y	Z	A	B	C	D	E	F	G	H	I	J	K	L	M
O	O	P	Q	R	S	T	U	V	W	X	Y	Z	A	B	C	D	E	F	G	H	I	J	K	L	M	N
P	P	Q	R	S	T	U	V	W	X	Y	Z	A	B	C	D	E	F	G	H	I	J	K	L	M	N	O
Q	Q	R	S	T	U	V	W	X	Y	Z	A	B	C	D	E	F	G	H	I	J	K	L	M	N	O	P
R	R	S	T	U	V	W	X	Y	Z	A	B	C	D	E	F	G	H	I	J	K	L	M	N	O	P	Q
S	S	T	U	V	W	X	Y	Z	A	B	C	D	E	F	G	H	I	J	K	L	M	N	O	P	Q	R
T	T	U	V	W	X	Y	Z	A	B	C	D	E	F	G	H	I	J	K	L	M	N	O	P	Q	R	S
U	U	V	W	X	Y	Z	A	B	C	D	E	F	G	H	I	J	K	L	M	N	O	P	Q	R	S	T
V	V	W	X	Y	Z	A	B	C	D	E	F	G	H	I	J	K	L	M	N	O	P	Q	R	S	T	U
W	W	X	Y	Z	A	B	C	D	E	F	G	H	I	J	K	L	M	N	O	P	Q	R	S	T	U	V
X	X	Y	Z	A	B	C	D	E	F	G	H	I	J	K	L	M	N	O	P	Q	R	S	T	U	V	W
Y	Y	Z	A	B	C	D	E	F	G	H	I	J	K	L	M	N	O	P	Q	R	S	T	U	V	W	X
Z	Z	A	B	C	D	E	F	G	H	I	J	K	L	M	N	O	P	Q	R	S	T	U	V	W	X	Y

so say the first word in your text is eerie   first letter is e   you
read down from the e in the top key row to the same position in the
l row   and you have the letter p   and then you do the same for
the next letter of your text   which is e again   but this time using
the next letter in ldbyron for your alphabet   so you read down
again from the e in the key row   but this time to the d alphabet
and you get h   so see if you keep using the ldbyron key   then
identical letters in the text wont be enciphered with the same letter consistently   they will be different   not every time but often
but anybody who knows the key can translate easily

get it   i do not think you do   but you know who figured out first how to break this hard code   guess   it was babbage

————————————

From: "Smith" <anovak@strongwomanstory.org>
To: "Thea" <thea.spann133@ggm.edu>
Subject: RE:codes

I do get the idea. Your letters would be easier if you would just punctuate, you know, Thea. But we've had that talk. So never mind. And btw ADA is using numbers not letters. Do you just translate? ABC = 123? If you do, then how do you know when the number for one letter ends and another begins? If you use 1 for A and 2 for B and 12 for L, how do you know 12 stands for L and not for AB? Just asking.

S

————————————

From: "Thea" <thea.spann133@ggm.edu>
To: "Smith" <anovak@strongwomanstory.org>
Subject: RE:Re:codes

man   have to invent the wheel with you here   all you do is assign a pair of numbers for every letter   and so every 2 numbers are 1 letter   its one of the giveaways   you look to see   is every line an even number   and hers are

you also make the lines an arbitrary length   broken into regular units   adas are ten digits so five letters   that way the decipherer cant tell the word lengths   and you cant look frinstance for singletons   which wd have to translate to i or a   why   you guessed it   the only 1 letter words in english   which wd give you a clue you couldnt look for two letter words either   which there are only a few of   like of and am   babbage wrote down whole dictionaries of words of different lengths   words of two letters   words of

three letters   so you cd try them all out   its called the brute force
method   you just keep trying

guess whats good at the brute force method   a computer

t

————————————

From: "Smith" <anovak@strongwomanstory.org>
To: "Thea" <thea.spann133@ggm.edu>
Subject: Babbage

Okay. I've been doing Babbage too. I think he's very strange and
wonderful, like the world's greatest nerd, god of the nerds, but
stranger even than that. He's in this somehow, he's got to be. You
know he had a portrait of J. M. Jacquard, the punch-card loom inventor, on his wall that was woven by a loom using punch cards—
it was so finely detailed that people thought it was done in oils.
Like, here's what punch cards can do.

After Ada was dead, he wrote a sort of autobiography, called *Passages from the Life of a Philosopher,* and guess what—on the title
page is a quote *from Byron,* and here it is:

> *I'm a philosopher. Confound them all—*
> *Birds, beasts, and men,—but no, not womankind.*

Is this a hint? Or am I now totally paranoid and seeing connections everywhere? He used to call Ada his fairy, and she went
along with that. His fairy friend, his fairy helper.

btw his wife's name was Georgiana. So okay, whatever. But
here's something else: Babbage knew Isambard Kingdom Brunel.
When Byron King, Lord Ockham, died—remember, he's Ada's
son who kept all this stuff in his chest—he was working at the
shipyard owned by Brunel on the Isle of Dogs, where the "Great

Eastern" was being built. So what if maybe Babbage got him the job?

Am I learning things or just going crazy?

Smith

————————————

From: "Thea" <thea.spann133@ggm.edu>
To: "Smith" <anovak@strongwomanstory.org>
Subject: RE:Babbage

whos brunel   whats great eastern   what isle of what dogs   who cares

t

————————————

From: "Smith" <anovak@strongwomanstory.org>
To: "Thea" <thea.spann133@ggm.edu>
Subject: RE:Re:Babbage

Sorry. Isambard Kingdom Brunel was the biggest Victorian engineer. He built huge things made of iron. Bridges and ships. The biggest ever up to that time. The Great Eastern was a ship, a paddle-wheel steamship, the biggest ever built. He had a factory or a works as they say at this place in London called the Isle of Dogs, I don't know why it's called that, why don't you LOOK IT UP.

Here's a link to a picture of Brunel: http://www.bbc.co.uk/history/ programmes/greatbritons/gb_brunel_isambard.shtml

Check out the cigar and the plug hat and the thumb in his waistcoat pocket. The HUGE chains hanging behind him are the chains of the "Great Eastern." It was made *for the American trade.* Oh my god. I am paranoid, I do see the signs everywhere. But what if they're there?

S

————————

From: "Thea" <thea.spann133@ggm.edu>
To: "Smith" <anovak@strongwomanstory.org>
Subject: program

you see signs and you are a nutcase but you know what they say paranoids have enemies too wont know till we know cant take long once we get it set up but i just thought once you change letters into a string of numbers then you could even run a math program to transform the string i just thot of this hm like every line cd be multiplied by a key number or could be the result of some arithmetical operation or even algebraic to keep all the lines a consistent length you wd use modulo arithmetic the modulo wd be the same as the line length wow

which might mean this really is a program meant to run on a computer like the analytical engine was gonna be like she said it would weave algebraic patterns just as a jacquard loom weaves colored threads or something right

i like this i like it a lot theres problems but im thinking thinking

————————

From: "Smith" <anovak@strongwomanstory.org>
To: "Thea" <thea.spann133@ggm.edu>
Subject: RE:program

Okay T. So what you're saying is that what she could have done was to set out this table, which if you use it right can be used to punch a series of cards, like the Jacquard loom cards? Which you can then run on the Analytical Engine (which she was sure would be built somewhere somehow at some time) and the Engine would translate the punch cards into printed papers with the writing on them. Each punch card would have enough holes for the whole alphabet plus punctuation, like punch cards for computers when we were kids, and some way to make the machine store the numbers in order in the memory. Sure. Then last instruction, each card would force the computer, I mean the Engine, to print out a number, which corresponds to a word in 01-02-03 = a-b-c cipher, or maybe a word-plus-punctuation, and print it. Okay.

And it would only take a few years to punch the 100,000 cards you would need to carry every word of the book, if it was even a medium-sized book. And she doesn't seem to have left any instructions about how the machine could read cards she specified before she knew how the machine worked. Wouldn't that be like writing software for a computer that hadn't been built?

Maybe she could have used a compressed vocabulary somehow. Is that possible? Like a way of indicating by one holepunch or one instruction that a word has "a" at position five seven and nine. I don't know what I'm talking about. Maybe she wanted the punch cards made, and when they were all set out on a Jacquard loom, they would weave this humongous piece of fabric with the book woven into it. It would have been easier to copy it letter by letter on stones and leave them on the beach for somebody to find.

S

———————————

From: "Thea" <thea.spann133@ggm.edu>
To: "Smith" <anovak@strongwomanstory.org>
Subject: RE:Re:program

you do not trust me   and you do not get it   i can see that   you
will b sorry for your mockery when i get it all right   and soon too

she didnt need to think anybody would punch all the cards   she
knew that instructions about how to punch the cards were
enuf   that the future wd get it from that   and run it on machines
that didnt exist but she knew they would someday   and they do
they do

btw   the cloth with the book woven in it would not have to be that
big   or the number of cards either   you are not reading your history   what i read says that the silk portrait of mister or monsieur
jacquard that babbage owned was made with 24000 cards   and
each card had 1000 hole positions   so there   a book is a piece of
cake   the real problem wd be knowing how to program cards to
weave letter shapes   i dont think ada did   you tell me

t

————————————

From: "Smith" <anovak@strongwomanstory.org>
To: "Thea" <thea.spann133@ggm.edu>
Subject: ILY

I can't find out that she knew how to program a jacquard loom. I
bet she couldn't. But listen I thought of something else. It's so obvious. The one page of the novel we found—it didn't end up there
by chance. Ada saved it, that one page, so we could break the code.
So we could know the code was a code. It should be the last page, so
that you could use it to break the code with. A key. But it's not the
last page, not unless the book's unfinished, which maybe it is, so
you can't just count back from the last letter and the last number.
But I'm sure that's what it is, and what she meant it for.

I cried when I got it. You are right. It's in there, she put it in
there and somehow her son carried it away with him, and she

thought someday somewhere. You. Me. Oh my god Thea. What if it's so.

S

———————————

From: "Thea" <thea.spann133@ggm.edu>
To: "Smith" <anovak@strongwomanstory.org>
Subject: RE:ILY

yes   i thot the same thing last nite   thinking of u

it seemed crazy to me   or suspicious   that she wd put the notes she made in the same trunk as the enciphered thing   and the one page like you said   because its much easier to break a cipher if you have a bunch of the text   and so as soon as you guess that the cipher is the novel   youve got all these repeating words to look for like the main guys name   or other things

but then today my codes guy explained the principle of pgp   that means pretty good privacy   when you hide something you only need to hide it enough to keep it from the people you need to for as long as you need to   like you can spell words aloud when kids are around   thats pgp until they catch on   so adas cipher was pgp because all she wanted was to keep it from her mom   and after that she wanted it to be read   she wanted us to get it   she wanted it to be easy   we were thinking of something hard   but why   it shd be easy   am i right

———————————

From: "Smith" <anovak@strongwomanstory.org>
To: "Thea" <thea.spann133@ggm.edu>
Subject:

Thea—
Of course you're right. Of course of course.
She was dying, Thea, and she did this last thing: she made this

thing, this enciphered version of the novel her mother and her husband wanted her to destroy. She said she would destroy it, and she did. Her husband saw it burn, all of it—all but one page. Then her son came to visit, poor Lord Ockham, who never wanted to be a lord, and only wanted to run away and be with ordinary people, and do ordinary work. And she gave him these things, these papers he couldn't read, and she didn't tell him what they were. Plus the one saved page. And she said to him: Take them to America with you, where there aren't any lords. Run away now and take them with you.

But Thea it isn't so yet. It isn't so until it's translated or deciphered or decoded or whatever the right word is. I took it out of the box again tonight (Georgiana was asleep, she snores amazingly for somebody so small and thin) and I looked at it, and it was almost as though I could see through it to what it was inside. But it still could be nothing too.

So what's that mean? If the code isn't hard, or shouldn't be hard. Does it mean a month, or a year, or an afternoon?

———————

From: "Thea" <thea.spann133@ggm.edu>
To: "Smith" <anovak@strongwomanstory.org>
Subject: RE:[ ]

maybe an hour or two   maybe a day   dunno

but first you have to put all the numbers in   with nobody knowing what youre up to   you think thats easy   its not   im thinking of a way   but i aint got it yet

the thing to find is the key   any guesses what she used   even if you know just the length of the keyword you can periodize   but you can do it without   what you wait for when the crunching starts is just to see some sense   a word or a few words   then you know

and babe   youll see it   soon as i do   if i do   if im not crazy   and
if i am   i hope youll forgive me

your friend

thea

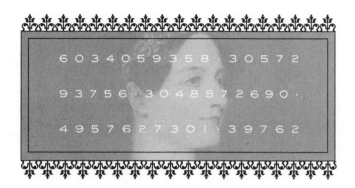

Of Fame and its consequences, and

of Law as it is practised, nowadays

 ONDON! ALI HAD once before trod her
blackened stones, and fronted the grey mobs, and avoided the
haughty equipages of the world of fashion—which had, nevertheless, *anointed* him, with the mud of their passage. Then, he had
walked and rode as in a dream, and as in a dream been taken to the
offices of Solicitors, and the inglenooks of coffeehouses, each as unreal to him as the other. Now—the father was dead who had led
him without pause or explanation along these streets, and Ali was
grown, with a world of incident already stored within him, which
even that *Pandæmonium* might not surpass in strangeness, or in horror. As has been said, the news of his rôle in the drama play'd upon
the plains before Salamanca preceded his arrival in the city, and his
progress through the streets to surrender his Person—which no

appeal of Lieutenant Upward, nor of any other officer or friend, could dissuade him from—was accompanied by a small crowd, which became a large crowd, which became a Mob—some jeering, some commending loudly, some not knowing what was afoot but giving voice nonetheless. The proceeding before the Bench was brief—the Judge, aware also of Ali's recent actions, was more inclined to permit him the extraordinary privilege of *bail,* and to accept his sureties and bonds, than the Scottish Magistrate had been. Stern was his demeanour, indeed—for the Law must regard with all gravity the murder of a Lord, whatever his character may have been (and the Judge knew the man of old)—but in not too long a time, Ali with his supporters emerged, temporarily at Liberty, to the admiring outcries of the People, as though they had had not Barabbas but the innocent Son of Man released to them.

His father's agents raised what monies they could and *must* to support him who was, no other Claimants appearing, heir apparent of the Sanes, and little though it was, it was sufficient, for few indeed were the costs that Ali was allowed to sustain. A Club offered him a Membership—then a competing club offered another—and the first offered Rooms—and another larger ones—until Ali was ensconced in a *chambre séparée* in a respectable establishment that was not Watier's or the Cocoa Tree, while his Father's former agents brooded over his situation, and his claims. Lieutenant Upward, who was his chief companion, as he knew no one else in the Capital after whom he might inquire, threw himself upon the divan there provided, and lifted a glass of the Champagne also provided, to toast his now well-connected though bemused friend.

'My Lord,' quoth he, 'you are splendidly bespoke. I warrant your wound and its discomforts have long since been assuaged by Honours and Pleasures, the best of medicines.'

'I beg that you do not address me so,' Ali said, himself remaining standing, and abstinent, as though unwilling to partake in gifts and goods he did not know how he deserved. 'I am but myself, without additions, and *shall* be till all these proceedings be resolved. Then we shall see if, instead of a Title, I have a Number, painted across my back, on a ship of Transportation.'

'Fear not,' said the Military Surgeon. 'Opinion, and the Regent, and the Generals, all are of your party; and if such are for you, who can be against you?'

Ali in some puzzlement turned away, and looked darkly, for he knew he ought to share his friend's delight, and yet found himself unable to do so, and knew not why.

Through that day and the next, the cards of men of every party, and every quality, were dropt at his club, until it amounted to a blizzard of pasteboard. Among those come to gaze upon him, as upon a fabulous monster, were a Poet, who offer'd to write an epic of his adventures, and a Methodist, who offer'd to convert him, and a young Lady, who offer'd—Ali was not sure what, for she   *1*
fainted before expressing her reasons for appearing before him. She had bribed the Porter, to be slipt in by night, in his absence—hid behind his Screen, and came forth at his return—fainted, as noted—was revived with water, and salts, and the attentions of the Military Surgeon—who argued that she might as well be entertained, once she had come round, but Ali insisted that she must be escorted out, which he did with all *tendresse* and regard, lest she, or her reputation, come to harm in that place.

He was the wonder of that nine days, which stretched to a fortnight unabated—and Ali sensed that many among those who gazed upon him, and took his hand, with 'nods and becks and wreathed smiles', saw in him something more, or *other*, than a British hero. 'I know not why I am become such an object of interest, or at least of fascination,' said Ali. 'Does every man harbour a secret wish to murder his father?'

'It is more to the point that you are a Turk,' said his friend the Lieutenant, 'and not a Christian, and yet are on the way to the House of Lords, where you may give your maiden speech upon the   *2*
beauties of the Koran, or the necessity for English girls to go veiled. Anything *contradictory* interests us, be it a mermaid or a mechanical man.'

'I am not mechanical,' said Ali, 'nor am I a Turk.' And he observed, with some bitterness, the light wave of the Military Surgeon's hand, and the airy lift of his brows, in dismissal of this tiresome objection. Just at that moment, the door was again knocked upon, and the porter announced another gentleman, and the name immediately relieved Ali's dark mood, and brought a smile to his lips—who thought he had no real Friend among the million! ' 'Tis the Honourable!' cried Ali, and hastened to bring within the gentleman who loitered somewhat bashfully upon the threshold.

'Heigh-ho, the Hero,' said the gentleman, and fell into Ali's embrace. He was a small figure, almost *miniaturised* and yet perfect in all his parts, like a piece of clockwork; his dress was of the sort called *exquisite* in that day, which meant a vast expenditure on very white linen, and an inconvenient constriction of black broadcloth about the waist and other parts. It was, to be particular, Mr Peter Piper, who had been up at the Athens-upon-the-Fens when Ali had briefly resided there, and who had had every intention, Ali had heard, of remaining there, and sitting for a Fellowship, but had not—for he had seen more scope for his talents in the Clubs and at the baize tables of the City. The gentleman who now drew back and made an ironic *leg* before Ali was a figure such as was common in the days of the *Regency* of our present Monarch, indeed some were among the dearest friends of that Prince—he privately preferred their company and conversation to that of sober counsellors, or reverend Bishops—and so did I. And why 'Honourable', the epithet by which he was known to all his intimates? The exact reasons were somewhat lost in the mists of Time—but it seemed that, once on a time, his name had appeared on a list—a subscription, or an invitation, or a register—decorated with the names of *Lord* this and *the Earl of* that, his own appearing with a simple Esq appended. Given the list to look over, he had himself added 'the Honourable' to his name, to which addition he believed he had a claim, as being the third son of a Baronet (however King-of-arms might view the matter). His contention was, that he had only desired that the list be *corrected* and not appear with errors upon it, but—as so many of our little acts of vanity or even of self-preservation reverse themselves upon us—on this petard of his own devising, Mr Peter Piper was hoist—he was for a time a general butt, and no one afterward forgot it.

'I happened,' he now said, 'to be present at the Bench, when your case was heard. No—I lie—for 'twas no accident I came there, but to view the wonder all men spoke of, and every paper lauded— or deplored, as did a few—and to see with mine own eyes if it were truly my old Companion. And lo! It was! Unchanged—unmarked, by the sorrows and hazards through which he had passed—there stood he—my Ali! And was his head down? It was not! Was his eye subdued? It was not! And with good reason too, as it soon appeared. Wise Solon who sat that day! A gentleman beside me— come to witness this extraordinary proceeding, even as I had—gave me three to one about your chances of being bailed—'twould have been higher, but something about *you* impressed even him—and I was able to collect a nice sum—yet for me the outcome was never for a moment in doubt.'

This was double or treble the words Ali had ever heard the Honourable to express without a pause, for he was in general a man who 'says less than he knows', &c., even in drink, and was known for his self-possession.

'I have brought you, in this connexion,' said he then, 'a gift beyond price, which awaits in the foyer beyond, and if he don't come bursting in as my prologue continues, I'll be swanned. He is one you would be very wise to speak to, and even wiser to attend to. No—allow me to admit him—why, here he comes, pat, like the catastrophe in the old play!'

Even before Ali could assent to an interview, the man was in the room, or *in possession* of it, for he was a large and comfortably furnished gentleman, 'round belly with good capon lined', and the sort of man who made himself at home wherever he stood.

'May I present Mr Wigmore Bland, of the Temple, Barrister,' said Mr Piper, bringing forward the man, whose slight bow and eager hand Ali took as he must—for they were not to be refused. 'I was before the Bench on another matter,' said Mr Bland, in a voice rich as plum-cake, 'which was recessed so that I might attend your Lordship's case, and its disposal.'

'You address me thus prematurely,' Ali said, 'as I have tried to tell these gentlemen.'

This animadversion Mr Bland turned aside with a wave of a hand large & pink. 'Allow me to suggest to your Lordship that your rights in the matter, and your freedom, may easily be assured. The case seems to me to present few difficulties, and I make bold to offer my services in addressing them.'

'He has saved many from conviction,' Mr Piper put in brightly, 'and many of those were completely innocent of any crime.'

There was nothing for it, then, but that Ali should invite the Barrister to enter in, and take wine, and hear the particulars of what had passed on that night in Scotland and pursuant, insofar as Ali could remember them—for it is difficult to *remember* clearly what we cannot *understand*. Mr Bland produced from within his coat a great Note-book, which he opened with the air of one about to read Gospel truths, but only proceeded to fill pages with the answers to questions he put to Ali. He knitted his brows in grave attention to Ali's answers, and nodded like a great bell tolling, and tapped his stick upon the floor in dismay at the *injustice* done to the man he regarded already as his client.

'I cannot pay your fees,' Ali made clear to him. 'If we should miscarry, and I lose my case, you will see nothing; likewise if I—if *you*—should be victorious, and I go free—for I have no incomes that are not pledged, and no properties which are not mortgaged already.'

'No more of that,' said the Barrister kindlily, 'for I ask nothing of you. Believe me, Sir, there is profit assured, beyond ready money. Yours is the most *interesting* case to come before the Bench in many moons, and will be followed eagerly in all the papers—'twill be the talk of all the Clubs, and Balls—it may excite a question in Parliament, for aught I know. And if I am successful in your defence—as I have no doubt I shall be—why, only think how many must hear of the fact, and how many with pockets deeper than your own—as innocent as yourself, and as wrongly accused—in their own eyes—will be eager to engage my services! Sir, I do not brag—nor do I rate myself at any more than my worth—for that may be easily measured, in the proportion of cases in which I have secured a verdict of *Not guilty* for gentlemen in situations like your own.'

Ali looked darkly—tho' it nothing discomfited his aspiring

champion—as he thought that he did not know, nor had ever heard tell, of any gentleman in *circumstances like his own.* Nevertheless the contract was entered upon, and to Scotland when Assizes loom'd Ali proceeded in the comfortable Coach and Four which Mr Bland's extensive practice had bestow'd upon him. The conversation therein turned in large part upon the trial to come.

'Of course I shall speak in my own defence,' said Ali.

'With permission, but you will speak nothing at all, my Lord,' quoth Lawyer Bland. 'The Prosecution of the case have no right to compel your testimony, and must prove their case without your help. You need not appear before the Jury at all. We are in a new Age, Sir, and the way to the gallows, or the ship of Transportation, is a longer one, and not so plain now as once it was, or as the Prosecutors would like it.'

'I wish the truth to be known, and the facts to come out,' Ali protested. 'I am innocent, and will declare as much.'

'Sir, the Truth is not material; as for your Innocence, I am happy to believe it, yet it too is immaterial, as far as a successful *defence* be concerned. I beg you to leave all things to me.' And with that, he turned to other matters, and pointed out to Ali the beauties of the landscape thro' which they passed, which was *picturesque* indeed, and a credit it was to Mr Bland that he admired it.

The case, when at length it came before a Jury and Judge, was attended by all the late Lord Sane's tenants and liegemen, who were about evenly divided (so it seemed to Ali, as he pass'd among them, to stand in his place in the Dock) between those who desired to see *him* hanged, and those glad to know that the old Lord had been, and incurious as to the question, by *whom.* The Officers of the Law, somehow shrunken, to Ali's view, from the minions of majesty who had taken him into custody so long ago, once again told their tale, and how they had intelligence of a high crime—this *intelligence,* as it now appeared, was a certain ragged urchin of the town, who had a Penny from a man to summon the Law, but could nothing more remember—and loud was the laughter when Mr Wigmore Bland questioned the small person, and got in reply but *'a Penny',* and *'a Mon',* and nothing more.

The dead Lord's Coachman was called, and near dead *drunk* himself he took the stand—he testified that on *the night in question* he had driven his master toward the Town, but that gentleman, having conceived a desire to rest along the way, had ordered him to halt at an Inn well known to the Coachman as a place his Lordship liked to stop, often to spend the night. The following day, the Coachman said, he was awakened by Lord Sane out of a deep sleep, the hour being about Noon (here there was some laughter in the room, which the Judge suppressed). He was ordered to drive his Lordship posthaste back to the Abbey, and yet not to enter in at the gate, but to stop at a far point, an old track across the fields, where Lord Sane swung himself down from the seat, and set off, telling his Coachman to await his return. For some hours, the Coachman said, he waited faithfully (here there was more laughter) and at dawn he returned to the Abbey, supposing his Master had found another way home—only to find the man stretched out dead upon the table in his hall, and the whole house in Uproar. No word had the dead Lord spoken to him, he averred, concerning why he chose to return, nor why he stopt short of his own Gate, nor what he intended when he set off alone.

Mr Wigmore Bland then arose, magnificent in Robe & Horsehair, and began to question the poor man sharply; and by the time he was through, the Jury might have suspected (as Mr Bland intended they should) that the Coachman himself could have done his Master to death, and if that was reasonable to think, then the Defendant's guilt was not so clear as at first it seemed. Following the Coachman, the Prosecutors brought forward the Officers and tenants of the Laird who had at first discovered Ali, weapon in hand, over the body of his father. These too Mr Bland was quick to question—to cast doubt upon what they *thought* they had seen, but perhaps had not—and when any of them averred what he knew only by *report,* the Barrister sprang to his feet, to have the words struck from the record, as being the merest *hearsay,* and according to the new rules of evidence, inadmissible—he asked that the Judge instruct the Jury to erase all such *hearsay* from their minds as though they had not heard it, whereupon the Jury looked upon one another as though the Court were mad, to ask such a thing.

It having been shown that, tho' the Accused might have been discovered standing above the dead man sword in hand, yet the man had not been slain by sword—he had been trussed and hanged, the mark of no blade upon him. The disproportionate strengths and sizes of the Father and Son being demonstrated, the Prosecutors claimed that the defendant must have had confederates—the same who later freed the Accused from prison, one being a gigantic black man obviously capable of any enormity. The Barrister ridiculed all such testimony—the Turnkey was called, and made to admit how late the hour was, how dark the place—to confess he could not swear upon Scripture that the door to Ali's cell had been well locked—and that from Childhood he had been subject to the *Nightmare* (a fact which the Barrister had been at pains to elicit from the Turnkey's neighbours before the trial began) and thus may have beheld the supposititious Negro in a Dream! At length the Judge, perhaps tiring of the matter, asked Ali to come forward, and deliver his statement, and his evidence.

'I leave that to my counsel, my Lord,' said Ali—which he had promised Mr Bland was *all* he would say, no matter how he was importuned—and it was, of all the hard things he had ever had to say, the hardest.

'Your counsel cannot speak for you,' said the Judge with weary kindness. 'You must do that yourself, if you have an account you may give to the Jury, where you was, what doing, and the like—if you have anything to observe on the evidence so far brought, you ought to do it yourself. Now, Sir, do you intend to leave your defence to your Counsel?'

'I do,' said Ali.

The Judge hereupon addressed the smiling Counsel himself. 'Will you not advise your Client to speak for himself?'

'No, my Lord, I would not advise him to say any thing.'

Thus, the only evidence against him being circumstantial, and the most telling of *that* shut up in a dark box called *Hearsay* whence it was not permitted ever to emerge, and the Prosecutors kept away from Ali like a pack of curs on a short leash by his refusal to speak, the Judge—to the regret (apparent in their fallen faces and angry scowls) of numbers of those present—must needs instruct the Jury that Ali's guilt, however likely it might seem to them, had not been proven *beyond the possibility of Doubt*—and therefore they could not convict—for such was the best London practice now, and would be followed here. Whereat Mr Wigmore Bland bow'd to Judge and Jury with a graciousness just this side of *impertinence,* and his rosy smiling face turned and shone upon Ali like the Sun.

3   *I*NNOCENT! OR, IF NOT innocent, then not proven to be guilty—a judgement only the Scots can make, and which in no way differs, in respect of the defendant's Liberty, or Property, from a judgement of innocence—tho' it may be altogether different in the eyes of some all-seeing Judge, or in the defendant's own soul. No guilt will burn, no guilt will eat at us, like the guilt that knows no object—though the sufferer be a benefactor of Mankind as great as Prometheus, still Jove's vulture will tear at him, and punish him for what he cannot say was sin! And it was as present to Ali's mind, as to every other person's who stood to observe his trial—or later read of it in every paper, Tory or Radical, where it was reported— that no one else was suspected—no party named, or even guessed at—who might have done the deed, and atrociously murdered the man—yet, 'He had surely not hanged *himself* up like a side of beef,' as one Observer noted. If *Justice* was not uppermost in the minds of those who puzzled over the case, *curiosity* surely was—and neither, it appeared, was to be satisfied.

When Ali was at last free to depart from that place, he asked one favour of his defender the Barrister—he would fain, he said, travel to his old home—his 'Scotch properties', as he said to the Man of Law, so as not to be thought *sentimental*—and, these lying not a day's distance, the Man of Law was quick to agree—for he was never reluctant to employ his fine equipage (tho' alert to the hurts it might receive upon those mean ways the Scotch call *roads* and *high-ways*). Without incident they achieved the drive that led down through the ruined Park to the Abbey gate—the way that Ali had last travelled in a different coach, in a different time—how long ago it seemed to him! He fell silent, so that even the Barrister marked his mood, and yielded to it with a composed demeanour of his own.

There were no servants now to greet him—he who was their *Laird,* by the disposition of the Court—nor did Ali expect them. And yet a long pulling of the bell and a halloo'ing brought forth at last one who opened the wicket with aged slowness: it proved to be 'Old Jock', that faithful man upon whom Ali had once leaned! Beneath the Barrister's interested gaze, Ali fell into the old man's arms, weeping in amazement—for, though he had been gone but a year, it seemed to have been *ten*—too many for flesh as old as Old Jock's to endure. Remembering himself then as host, Ali brought his guest within, and saw to his comfort, insofar as he could—that gentleman appearing a little *deflated* at the hospitality that could be provided, though he pretended not.

'It is, I perceive, an ancient line, to the name of which your rights are now secured,' said he, gazing about himself at the cold halls, and bare walls.

'It is, I am told,' said Ali. 'The ancestries of my father, and that of the late Lady Sane, are venerable. They are even connected, I believe, at a time in the past—so she said to me—I took little note of it.'

The Barrister nodded at this—his great white eyebrows rose, and he touched the knob of his stick to his lips in thoughtful interest. 'And the estates of both parents were left in a state of some confusion—profitless—entailed—mortgaged—laid under various encumbrances—not to be touched by yourself.'

'I have not inquired deeply into the matter,' said Ali. 'The Steward of this house will know more than I—indeed, I ought now to inquire of him concerning the state of my affairs—but I find I cannot—indeed, I must beg you to excuse me for a time—I declare I am unfit for company. Please regard the house as your own.'

'I shall do that,' said Mr Bland, with a smile as broad and as innocent as a babe's.

Ali meantime wandered through the Abbey, from which even the greater number of those who had formerly lived and laboured there were vanished, to other and better employment, or to the cots and fields whence they had been drawn. Whither had Factotum betaken himself? It seemed to Ali that the fellow might well have accompanied his Master to the land below—he seemed to have been but a visitor upon the Earth in any case—to serve him there in Death as he had in life. Where were those Beasts his father had liked to have by him, as *instinctual* as himself? They had died, it seemed, of grief—or fled into the Forest, there to terrify the woodcutters. There was *one,* above all, he sought in the halls and kitchens, and found not, until Old Jock at last brought him to the quiet place by the double elm where he had laid him—Warden, unfailing friend, protector, great heart! Perhaps, Old Jock averred, that heart had *broke* when Ali vanished—there was no more to say—he had been inconsolable, and refused his food, and so died. Ali kneeling by the unlettered stone that good Jock had there raised, wept freely, as he had done for no other lost to Death.

Why should he not stay on here, and live alone, with none for company but whatever ghosts might choose to walk? For him they could hold no terror now. Here he might live, and do no harm; and if he ever thought to go again into the world, then he might wish that those ghosts would rise up, and warn him again, that nothing he had done upon Earth's surface had brought good to any creature—not even to himself—therefore let him here stay!

He did not, of course—such resolves may be a necessary balm to our hearts, but we rarely cleave to them. He returned to London with Mr Bland, who occupied the time in conversation with Ali upon the condition of his Estates, and the incomes derivable therefrom, which that Man of Law thought might easily be increased. He had—he said—spent a profitable morning in conversation with the Steward and the dusty piles of account-books, papers and bills that filled the Steward's snuggery, and in that time had acquired more learning in the history of the Sanes than had ever attach'd itself to Ali. 'Place your affairs in my hands,' said he to Ali, 'and I can assure you absolutely that they shall not go *worse,* and will with a near certainty go very much better. You have not profited as you should by what is yours, and others have profited by your ignorance, and neglect—the which may result from the former Lord's own, I suspect—but never mind—a new Era may dawn for you, Sir, if you allow me to serve you.'

'My father was sure he had pressed all that he could from what he had,' Ali said, 'and that the Law was fixed as regards his situation, and was against him.'

'Ah no,' said the great man, 'ah no, my Lord—for as our Saviour said of the Sabbath, the Law is made for man, and not man for the Law; if we truly believe it to be amenable to our Purposes, when those are made entirely clear to its Guardians, then surely—though the process may take Time (indeed it is not unknown to outlive us who bring before the Law our appeals, may Heaven forbid it in your own case!)—we may have confidence in the conclusion—if we but *play our cards* astutely.'

Ali pondered these remarks, and these offers—but not *very* astutely—for he had no means to ponder *with,* so to speak, his ignorance being what it was—and after his return to London, it was not many weeks before a conclusion took form within his mind, the only he could come to.

When we place our affairs in the hands of new agents, is it not with the same trepidation as a General feels, who throws his forces against a perceived weakness of his enemy's, knowing not if he have guessed right, and ruin be as likely as victory? Or, if we know not this sensation—and few of us mere *citizens* do—then perhaps it resembles those of a man who in spite of all Uncertainties at last speaks the few necessary words to a young Lady—those few words that may never be withdrawn—not, at least, without the greatest cost, and the tearing of conjoin'd flesh. Or it may more closely resemble the *Lady's* sensations, upon accepting! But it need not resemble any thing—it is what it is—Fate personified, in the hand we take, the seal we press down, the pen & ink we wield, and our familiar name indited—appearing rather strange to us—upon papers as fraught as Sybil's leaves. It may make a man suddenly desirous of a bottle of iced Champagne, and a lobster salad, and a segar to set afire, and careless company—all which was available in profusion to a young man of such *expectations* as Ali had suddenly become.

That was a Summer wonderfully warm, the summer of the Allies, when the *stupor Mundi* had again stupefied the world, this time by *losing* his battles, and abdicating his throne, as he had before by winning them, and toppling the thrones of others: for his mind, which had seemed superior to Fortune, had proved to be not so. Very large Bourbons were then drawn through London behind horses white as cream, to be embraced (insofar as their arms could reach round) by even larger Hanovers, and congratulated on their Restoration; old Blucher roam'd the city, and his Germanic capacities and Appetites were commented upon, and also the size of his Boots, which now and again left Balls and celebrations just in advance of their owner's hoary head. Every great house in Mayfair was alight, and masquerades were the rage, with many going in Disguise, as Persons different from their true selves—and *some* of them were Masked.

At one of the Mayfair routs where Ali loitered uncomfortably—
5 being neither a Waltzer, nor an exchanger of Banter of any great skill—the Honourable pointed out to him, seated demurely at a distance from the Throng and seeming as unsuited to it as himself (yet
6 perhaps more willing to be pleased), a dark pale girl of uncommon self-possession, and no little beauty. 'She is called Catherine,' said the Honourable, upon Ali's question. 'Her family, Delaunay; she came out a season or two ago, though in respect of Gowns and Suitors and other splendours I have not seen her much shine since. She will converse—or at any rate she will *talk*—at length, and very well too, in the right company, and upon the right subjects, though often she is silent, as you see her, and the common stream of gossip and levity has little attraction for her.' Ali thought the name spoken seemed familiar, but for a moment could not remember in what circumstances he had heard it—and when he *did* remember, a cold tremor passed over him that his friend observed—and laughed to see, mistaking its source or nature—for this Miss Delaunay was the *heiress* whom his Father had, on the last night of his life, pressed upon Ali's attention! 'Allow me to ask if she would meet you,' said Mr Piper, and, before Ali could forestall him, he had slipt away amid the people passing and repassing.

Upon his return, though, the Honourable was unwontedly cast down—for his machinations upon occasions such as this were commonly successful, and this had failed. 'I offered to present the famous Lord Sane, he who was the hero of Salamanca—I spoke of your celebrity—'

'And why not my infamy? I wish you had said none of these things!'

'It matters not much,' said Mr Piper. 'She had heard of you. But she is disinclined to make your acquaintance.'

'Is she indeed?'

'Mistake not—she had no *particular* objection—no moral animadversion—nothing of that kind—she merely evinced no interest—graciously, in fact, and with a smile.'

A confused emotion then arose in Ali's breast, or brain— wherever emotions *do* arise,—for though he wanted not to be known for those *ambiguous* events which had made him famous, and sought after by so many—still, to be refused *despite* them—he knew not what to make of this—he felt challenged, or his worth called into question, though his *worth* depended not on his *celebrity,* as he was certain. 'Let us be gone,' said he shortly. 'I have had amusement enough among the *cosseted.*' And even as Mr Piper took his arm, and sought for one who might call his carriage, Ali looked back—but Catherine Delaunay was in conversation with another, and turn'd not in his direction.

NOTES FOR THE 8TH CHAPTER

1. *a young Lady:* An incident from life. Later, Lady Caroline
    Lamb would bribe her way into Ld. B.'s quarters, sometimes
    disguised as a page (see a following Chapter for an incident
    based upon this extravagant lady and her passion).

2. *your maiden speech:* Writing of London and early fame may
    have reminded Ld. B. of his own maiden speech in the House
    of Lords, a flaming denunciation of a bill calling for capital
    punishment for the crime of frame-breaking, for which
    desperate stocking-weavers in his own county of Notting-
    hamshire were at that time daily arrested. That these poor
    men's lives should have been rated at less than the price of
    a stocking-frame was barbarous indeed; but those men could
    not see the future, only the cruelty with which it cut across
    their lives. Their descendants are at work in great manufacto-
    ries today, making stockings and a thousand other goods by
    machines neither they, nor their Defender on that day, could
    have conceived—and the lowly stocking-frame is broken for
    good.

3. *not proven:* A judgement possible in Scottish courts. Would that it were possible in that Court to which Ld. B. here alludes, in which, while all the *facts* must be clear at last, the *reasons* may still remain unknowable, even to the soul brought up before that Bar, and to the Judge beyond. I shall believe that it is.

4. *Warden:* As before stated, Byron's own Newfoundland was named Boatswain. Over the dog's tomb at Newstead (which I was privileged to see) are Byron's own words:

> *To mark a Friend's remains these stones arise;*
> *I never knew but One,—and here he lies.*

Upon my remarking recently to him that I had seen this monument on my journey thence, my father's loyal friend Mr Hobhouse, Lord Broughton, told me that when Byron first composed the epitaph, he himself was *by his side* and—less than pleased at the sentiment—he suggested to Byron an emendation: 'I never knew but one—and here *I* lies.'

5. *Waltzer:* It may be supposed that Lord Byron felt himself *hors de combat* where dancing was concerned, but common suppositions concerning his abilities or disabilities in respect of his foot & leg are often wrong in fact. He wrote a satire upon the Waltz— '*Seductive Waltz—Though on thy native shore, Even Werter's self proclaim'd thee half a whore*,' &c., tho' it is ambiguous in its moral tendency, as so much of his verse both comic and serious tends to be.

6. *a dark pale girl:* My mother tells me that her initial response to Lord Byron—that she did not care to meet him, when all the world did—piqued his vanity, and his interest. I never knew if this was so, but in his depiction here Byron seems to assert something of the same concerning his hero—a curious confirmation.

In which Heads are examined,

and Souls are bared

HE HONOURABLE PETER PIPER (upon whom Ali leaned, as Dante upon his Virgil) was, it seemed, welcome not only in the Ball-rooms of great houses, but those as well where entrance was by Ticket, and a different company was to be met. He belonged, he said, to more Clubs than he could always remember, and in them he was famed for a steadiness at table that seemed also to partake of the *mechanical,* or at least the Scientific, tho' he himself averred, that in play there was none such, but only much foolishness, and a little *Arithmetic.* His game was Hazard, and once at table that pleasant gentleman was changed 'in the twinkling of an eye', though in truth not every eye could perceive it. A coolness came over his features, an attention in his person; all that had seemed frivolous and careless before, evaporated, or was shuffled invisibly off, though he lost nothing of his natural amiability. The cup went round, the bones fell upon the baize—and while others, inflamed as by fever or drink, were gripped by an excitement that turned not to weariness but only 'grew by what it fed on', *he* seemed rather a man about a nice piece of work—a glass-blower, or a clock-maker—and work it was indeed, upon which Mr Piper's income depended. Still he smiled angelically—he smiled when he won, and when he lost he played again—and ever his busy brain turned over his chances, and did its Arithmetic, while the players about him flew from Heaven to Hell in a throw, and never knew why.

'I think the gambler a happy man, whether he win or lose,' said Ali to him, as at night's end they supp'd upon broiled bones, and swallowed Champagne—for the Honourable had been this night triumphant. 'Dashed down he may be in a moment, and yet redeemed the next—his fortunes always in the balance—there is always life, which is feeling—he is never *ennuyé.*'

'Well, there is often a certain *ennui* attendant upon a long resi- *1* dence in debtor's prison,' said the Honourable, 'though I admit the *preface* may not be lacking in amusement. And are you, dear friend, *ennuyé* ? You seem at the least to be in the grip of a dissatisfaction.'

'Tell me,' Ali said then, turning aside this inquiry. 'Do you not know the gentleman just now entering? All my former acquaintance has trooped out of my memory in the last years.'

'He is known to me, and to *you,*' said the Honourable. 'He is the father of a Fellow of our former College, and his name is Enoch Whitehead.'

'Has he a wife?'

'He does.'

'Her name—is it Susanna?'

'I believe it is. She comes not often to town. Speak, my Lord—why, what ails thee?'

What ailed him he could not name—yet he looked upon the man—his hoary head, his bleared eye, his ruin, his *Nose* whereon the veins stood blackly amid the red—and he remembered Susanna, as she *was*—and could no more be! He seemed to hear again the horrid laughter of his father on that night, the last he had spoken her sweet name aloud—the night when Fortune had pitched him headlong out of doors, impotent to aid or save, not her alone but even himself—and now returned too late, too late! 'Naught,' said he, 'naught, naught but that the drink is gone, and none called for! I beg you, my friend'—and here he took Mr Piper's sleeve, and look'd upon him with an intensity that startled that mild gentleman—'keep me from yon fellow with the *white head,* and let me not hail him—I ask as a Boon—do that for me.'

'I will, 'pon my word!' said the Honourable, and lifted his hand for the waiter, with what in another might almost have seemed an air of *urgency.* Well might he pledge his word, for when summer dawn was already green upon the East, and Ali, the Honourable, and several friends whom Ali would not afterward remember were attempting to leave that Place—or it may have been a subsequent one—by means of a circular staircase, which (as the Honourable averred) must have been conceived and built before the invention of spirituous Liquors, so impossible was it to navigate in their condition—Ali espied that same gentleman he had before seen, amid his own company. The Honourable felt his young friend start in his grasp—and it was all he could do to draw him away. 'D'you see that gentleman?' they all heard Mr Whitehead inquire of his friends. 'What does he do, to glare upon me so?' 'Why, it is Lord Sane,' said another with him. And Mr Whitehead: 'I knew his father. Well, blood will out, they say'—which it was fortunate all round that Ali did *not* hear.

Yet she was near—Susanna!—she lived—not constrained in the sad vale of a former time, as Ali had before pictured her to himself. She lived, and might be met, and some intercourse with her was possible—and here Ali's imagination blenched, as it were, and looked away. 'She comes not often to town' was not the same as 'never'—never was *never,* and 'not often' was perhaps tomorrow, or the day after that. Ali found that he perused—as he had not done before—the fashionable papers, wherein the comings and goings of Society were solemnly chronicled, as though they were the catalogue of Ships at Troy, in search of her name, and the name of her *husband* (a word he did not say, even in the hearing of no-one but himself). Where ever he went that she might be expected, however faintly, to appear, he thought he saw her, in a blond head or a small foot just disappearing into a coach—and yet it was not she. The Honourable conducted him through the Gardens and the Pleasure-grounds where all were to be met by all—and there Ali was introduced to an Elephant, who abstracted his hat with its nose, and generously presented it to him again. He went as well to see *this,* and to hear *that,* and to be astonished by *t'other*—to Weeks's museum in Great Windmill Street, to see the *automata,* which included a great mechanical Tarantula (that rush'd out from its hole, and made the ladies shriek) and a number of small Persons too—amusing it was to see the Honourable, through his quizzing-glass, regard a silver mechanical Dancer as perfect and precious as might be, with graceful limbs and dark inviting eyes, whose breast seemed even to respire—and who might have made him a fine Wife—as he appeared himself to think in wistful wonderment.

2

Tho' *Susanna* was never where Ali found himself, he chanced more than once in that time to encounter Miss Catherine Delaunay, whose sparkling dark eyes and raven hair he found it easy to look upon—as though he looked upon one of the fine female creatures he had known in his earliest youth—whose mantles had not been of lace, however, and whose hair was not curled with an Iron, in the London fashion, but dress'd with the jingling gold coins of their Dowry—in London the same *figure* was exhibited more discreetly, in *gossip.* At a venue of polite entertainment—where the chastest ears were certain to receive no affront—and after further glances, and a small smile—Ali was at last granted (thro' an intermediary) an interview, which seemed an achievement unequalled, like winning the Golden Fleece, though he found the Lady herself, when at last he took a seat beside her, to be the soul of welcome & warmth. She was unafraid to speak of Intellectual and Philosophical subjects (which her sisters in art are commonly warned to avoid, for fear of startling their unlearn'd Prey), and engaged Ali upon the same.

'I have long been a student of human nature,' said she to him at supper, 'and I have arrived at certain general principles.'

'Have you indeed,' said Ali— 'And have you travelled widely, to make the observations from which you deduce your principles?'

'No, I have not,' said she gravely, 'but I have read a great deal, and now have gone about somewhat in Society, and everything I see confirms the principles I have lighted upon.'

'The principles, then, came first, the observations after.'

'I think you mock me,' she said with a gentle smile, and yet with that about her which suggested she did not well abide mocking. 'I should tell you that it is my constant habit, when I have known a person for a sufficient period, to write a Character of him or of her, so as to fix my thoughts and impressions.'

'I hope you will make an exception in my case.'

'When I come to know you well enough, I shall perhaps consider it—yet it is my *constant* habit, and I should be loath to break it. Tell me please why you would not wish it.'

'You say you wish to *fix* your impressions,' said Ali. 'I know not that I should wish anyone to *fix* her impressions of me. I know myself to be quite unfixed, and perhaps unfixable.'

'The character of anyone may be described accurately, by a careful observer.'

'And what of those parts that cannot be observed?'

'You speak,' she said, with something that was *not quite* reproach, 'of the Soul, do you not? Yet even that most private thing may be read. Why, even now a scientific practitioner has come to London from Germany—a *craniologist,* who is able, by careful palpation of the Head, to determine what qualities of the brain beneath are prominent, which deficient.'

'Is the brain then the seat of the Soul?' asked Ali. 'Is it not rather the Heart?'

'Aristotle supposed it was the liver—I hope you are not of his opinion!'

The 'Herr Doktor''s recent arrival from Germany had, indeed, created much stir among the *ton,* and his celebrity far eclipsed Ali's, which was already on the wane. Ladies and gentlemen all the day long presented themselves at the Doctor's chambers, to subject their crania to his long and sensitive fingers—some younger maidens (and some *older*) were certain they felt their deepest natures drawn forth from the chamber'd Nautilus of their skulls, to be analysed as to their Amativeness—oh, very marked!—and their Acquisitiveness—more marked still!—until they nearly swooned from excess of self-knowledge. Miss Delaunay closed her small white hands decidedly before her, and declared to Ali that she herself had been examined—and her smile showed she was sufficiently gratified by what she had been told. 'I beseech you, my Friend—for so I may call you, may I not?—that you, too, submit to the Doctor's examination—so that you may compare what *I* have discern'd of your character, to what *Science* may determine.'

'If I should,' Ali said, 'I am certain that your own discernment will be found to be the greater. I am as glass before your gaze.'

'Now you do mock me.'

'If I do not,' Ali said, and laughed, 'then I shall have to take you *seriously*—and acknowledge my faults, if not my sins—the which I should not wish any so gentle as yourself to hear of.'

At this, the lady lowered her eyes, and lifted her fan—but not before Ali saw the red upon her cheek changed for white—and then changed again.

It was not Miss Delaunay alone who urged Ali upon the *Craniologist*—everywhere he went now, he heard how altered by revelation were the lives of his acquaintances—some having, upon the Doctor's advisement, forsworn Gaming, or strong drink, or certain Company, as too *well suited* to their inclinations—for a week and a day at least. Still Ali resisted the wise man's omnipresence, his omniscience too—for a presentiment that he would learn what he did not chuse to know, was cancelled by a near certainty that he would learn nothing at all. —'But then what harm?' exclaimed the Honourable, who if he could would gladly have lifted the lid of his dear friend's temples and taken a peek within. 'Come! I have set the day, and the hour—it will occasion you no inconvenience—painless—modern—unlimited in instruction—and the cost is negligible,' at which he named a figure hardly small.

'So many pounds,' said Ali, 'for a head so little.'

'Not pounds, my Lord,' replied the Honourable, nothing discomfited. 'Guineas.'

As the two friends loitered in the ante-room of the Doctor's chambers on the appointed day, examining charts and porcelain heads whereon the areas governing all human passions were boldly marked, there came forth from the examining-room or surgery, ushered by the Doctor himself, a dark-eyed young Lord of whom all the literary world then chattered (though he too is nigh forgotten now). He touched, somewhat cautiously, the head beneath his hyacinthine curls, with an inward look, half wonder, half amusement.

4

'My Lord, you have been examined,' remarked the Honourable—who knew the man, as he knew everyone.

'Why so I have,' remarked the young Lord, 'and been told remarkable things.' Here the great Doctor beside him modestly inclined his head—which was large and lovely, seemingly carved in generous strokes from pink-veined marble. 'I am told that every quality indicated on this skull of mine has its *opposite* developed in equal force. If this good man is to be credited, good & evil will be in perpetual war within me.'

'Pray Heaven they come to a truce,' exclaimed the Honourable.

'Or the last don't come off victorious, at the least!' Here for a moment a sort of doom dimmed his Lordship's visage, but like a cloud it passed.

'Shall we *not* see you this evening then, my Lord, in your usual haunts?' asked the Honourable—'Given the Skirmishing that might there ensue, between the *good* and its opposite?'

'Ah well,' said that Lord, as with gracious nods he took his leave, 'Ah well, we shall see—oh, dear, yes, we shall see!'

Then Ali and his friend were brought within, and Ali was seated upon a stool, the better for the Doctor's examining—which examination continued long without a word spoken by the man of Science, save for a variety of hems and haws such as Ali had not before heard, and a German grunt or two, whose significance was lost upon him.

When the fingerwork was done, the great-headed Doctor sat down before Ali, and with chin in hand studied him long without speaking. 'What!' exclaimed Ali at last. 'Do you perceive that which alarms you, Doctor? Am I a divided man, like that young Lord just here?'

'*Ach, nein,*' said the great man, 'or *ja,* but in a different kind.' In the deep orbits of his eyes, the hooded pupils glittered cunningly. 'The faculties of our brains may be in conflict with one another— we may be *divided.* But there are other brains wherein the faculties are not opposed but so contradictory that we are in effect *doubled.* Most men are one, and despite their alterations from day to day, they know themselves to be one. But there are some few who may be one person in the main, but *another* at intervals—and the one may not know of the other's existence—when the one sleeps, the other wakes.'

'I do not believe that to be possible,' said Ali quickly.

'Tell me this, my Lord,' said the German. 'Has it ever happened to you, that in a dream you have walked abroad, thinking you were in one place—doing one task, or office—and awakened to find yourself in a different place, and doing what you did not intend?'

'No,' said Ali shortly. 'Never have I been subject to such illusions—I cannot conceive of them, in respect of myself.'

'The condition is rare indeed, yet not unknown. You are perhaps familiar with the history of Colonel Culpeper, an English officer.'

'Indeed I am not,' said Ali, and made to rise.

'Colonel Cheyney Culpeper one day shot a Guardsman, and   5 killed him. He shot the man's horse, as well. Yet all that time he was asleep, and being apprehended, could not remember the deed, nor account for it—he was deeply mortified—he had no ill-will toward the man he had murdered, indeed hardly knew him—and certainly none toward the beast.'

The Honourable now anxiously took Ali's arm—his friend had gone quite white, and a tremble appeared upon his lip. 'That is dreadful,' Ali whispered. 'Dreadful! I would you had not told me of it.'

'It was a hundred years and more ago,' said the Doctor calmly, and yet regarding Ali's countenance and posture closely. 'The man received a Royal pardon. He was unconscious of the crime, and therefore blameless.'

'And yet *the crime was done,*' said Ali. 'The crime was done!

Excuse me, Sir, I am in need of air. Your science is remarkable indeed, and I hope to have further conversation upon these topics—good day—good day!'

*T*HERE *WAS* THEN a doom upon him—a judgement, that no *human* Court could make—a guilt that not even *he* could prove upon himself! Ever and again Ali found himself staring in surmise upon his own hands—as though they were two enemies, inveigled somehow in among his friends, and were even then contemplating mischief he would know nothing of. His couch he forbore, till Sleep could no longer be resisted—or he measured out a dose of Oblivion, in Kendals drops, to assure his body would not *stray* when his soul slept—and indeed when he woke his limbs felt to him as though forged by a Smith, of heaviest Iron!

Now—in fear of *himself*—he sought those realms where he was sure he would *not* find Susanna, circles infernal where the Honourable drew him. One such was 'the Fancy', wherein huge fellows with heads large and hard as cannonballs battered one another to insensibility, while others admired their *style* and laid bets against the outcome. There Ali at first saw nothing but that abominable and operose *cruelty* it was ever his study to avoid—but in time he came to see it as an Art, and a source of beauty and interest, tho' carried on as it was in quarters reeking of blood, sweat, and fear, clouded with tobacco-smoke and loud with the cries of the spectators and bettors, winners and losers alike. 'I have studied the Art myself,' the Honourable informed him as they stood one day by Ring-side, 'and taken lessons with Jackson, though to be sure I always insisted he wear the muffers, so that my beauty might not be marred.'

The match that day had gone for twenty rounds without either *pugilist* failing to come 'up to scratch' again after falling, roused it may be by the profane urgings of the *phans,* who crowded so close as to be spattered occasionally with the Claret exuded by the combatants.

'Art!' cried one among the company. 'I will take Force over Art any day.'

'I,' said another, 'have seen Daniel Mendoza, the wonderful Jew, a fighter of great art and delicacy, defeat Martin the Bath Butcher in twenty rounds—or it might have been *fewer*—and by his Science throw down any number of your Bulldogs.'

'Well,' said the first devotee, '*I* saw the great Gentleman Jackson, who for *delicacy* is unexampled, pummeled almost to death, and certainly to defeat, by the beast Cribb—so *delicacy* don't always answer—nor Science neither—so say I.'

'Cribb,' whispered the Honourable to Ali, 'once reply'd to a certain Youth who asked him—myself being by—what was the best *Posture of Defence,* by saying, "Why, to keep a civil tongue in your head!"'

'I admit to you,' said the opponent of Science to his friend, 'I would not quickly challenge, nor taunt a Jew again, for he might have taken lessons from Mendoza, and make me answer for it.'

'Jackson when he beat Mendoza did it by taking hold of his *hair,* as it were Samson's, and buffeting him unmercifully. When Mendoza complained to the Umpires, he was told there was no rule against it, *"And that's a d—n shame, is it not?"'*

'Cribb too is a taker-hold of hair, and indeed there *ain't* no rule against.'

'No rule against! A fine argument! Tom Molyneaux, a Negro of America, nearly beat Cribb—Cribb won only because the Ref would not call *Time!* on him, when he was fallen, and could not come to scratch—for a half an hour by the clock!'

'I'll pummel you my self, if you say England's champion could not fairly beat America's blackamoor!' cried his friend—having no regard, seemingly, for Cribb's own advice—and it was all that friends around them could do to keep the two belligerents from demanding satisfaction then and there.

The match having been concluded, and the Honourable having collected his winnings from the Bankers, as the crowd unravelled into the darkness of eve, Ali saw at a distance one who turned to *look upon* him, from amid others who obscured his person—but

then, observing more closely, Ali saw that it was not (as he had supposed) a dark *man* in a furred coat—but a *bear*—who looked, and
held his regard. The Bear-ward too—a bent man smaller than his
Beast—sought Ali's eye as well, and then both were gone, as
though they had not been! Ali fought his way through the uncaring
crowd, which was made *pugnacious* by absorption of the exhibitions
they had witnessed—but he caught no further glimpse of the Beast,
nor of his Ward. Closely he questioned Mr Piper, who just then
took his arm—had he not seen this show, for a show it had surely
been—a catchpenny show—a mangy animal, and a beggar to make
him dance? But the Honourable and his companions had seen
nothing. Nothing! Once again he seemed to himself to be seated in
the examining room of the German Doctor, denying thrice, like Peter, that he had ever or *could* ever see that which was not there, or *do*
that which he *knew not*.

'Come, my Lord!' said his Companions, 'all pleasure here is
fled—do not stare so upon the Scene—we return to Town, do
come!' So he departed with them for the Clubs, laughing as they
laughed, tho' a cold wonder had entered his breast, that neither
Brandy nor Punch could wholly wash away. *Think when thou see'st me
again*—had not the dream of his Father's bear promised him so?—
that thy time is come, and a different journey is to go on. Foolish! Mad! Was
there but *one bear* in the Universe? And had it not been but in a
meaningless *dream* that he had been thus spoken to? He called for
further drink—and sought a place at the Table, and cards to play. A
different journey to go on! Well, so he would—he had embark'd already! Seeing, by the fever'd light in Ali's eye, his eagerness to burn
away the night, his friends, as surprized as they were amused, willingly indulged him—the cost being borne by *him*.

NOTES FOR THE 9TH CHAPTER

1. *ennui:*   Lucky is the human spirit immune to the excitements of Chance. There is no exaltation that is like the certainty that a perfect system of betting exists, at the race course or the card-table, and that it is in hand, and needs only the refinement that comes with actual play. The exaltation is itself as fixating as the result, and the *proof positive* that one's system is in fact sound would, in my own opinion, be a gratification beyond any sum of money won at Newcastle or the St-Leger. The costs to be paid for failure being, concomitantly, twice as bitter as mere money lost.

2. *Weeks's museum:*   Decades later the silver lady here described came into the possession of Charles Babbage, who would make it dance and nod, beckon and gesture, for guests who came to his house, that house so full of wonders, mechanical and intellectual. He had fallen in love with the lady when he was a little boy and she was shewn at Merlin's museum, of which Weeks's was the successor. Yet I remember that she was disassembled when he bought her, a box of parts long stored in Weeks's attic, and it was left to him (like Pygmalion) to bring her back to

life—she had never danced in public since 1803, when Merlin's closed. How then did Ld. B. see her? Or did he invent her, tho' she existed before his invention? It is quite mysterious.

3. *craniologist:* The phrenology of the last generation, which so took the imaginations of many—among them Lady Byron— seems now inadequate to the unequalled complexity of that organ, and moreover its principles are based on no particular experimental result, but only on supposition. I have my hopes, & very distinct ones too, of one day recording cerebral phenomena such that I can put them into mathematical equations; in short a law or laws for the mutual action of the molecules of the brain, equivalent to the law of gravitation for the planetary and sidereal world—a Calculus of the Nervous System. The great difficulty, which was not present to the Phrenologists, and vitiated their system, is in the design of practical experiments. I must become a most skilful practical manipulator in experimental tests & that, on materials difficult to deal with, viz., the brain, blood and nerves of animals. In time I will do all I dare say I hope & so may bequeath to future generations by application industry attention a *system* w^{ch}

Much pain this week Dependent upon my drops more than in former days All this needs to be corrected & will be if I am able But no more this night

4. *a dark-eyed young Lord:* Here Lord Byron permits himself an appearance in his own tale, and is seen cutting a rather foolish figure. He did indeed, it appears, undergo a phrenological examination by Dr Jacob Spurzheim, a famous German practitioner, who reached exactly the conclusion the fictional Lord here pronounces.

I think it is a point of the greatest importance—though it seem insignificant—that Lord Byron was one who could see himself as at times comical, and laugh at himself—at his adventures, his

ambitions, his character even—whereas Lady Byron was forever on guard as to how she would be seen, and understood, by
others. Her watchfulness seemed to her then, I am sure, to be
natural, and universal—she was likely indeed to have been
wholly unconscious of it—and so she thought that Lord Byron's
self-ridicule and exaggerated expression of his own shortcom-
ings, which were but a *line* meant to amuse, were admissions of
the gravest weaknesses and even sins. There would be no rec-
onciling such opposing natures.

5. *Colonel Cheyney Culpeper:* The tale is told in Mr Isaac Disraeli's
'Curiosities of Literature', though if Ld. B. learned it there or
elsewhere I know not   I came upon it by chance   if chance it
can be termed when a name of no importance whatever but to
oneself occurs in two unconnected places in the course of a week.

6. *'the Fancy':* The barbaric sport here described has vanished
with bear-baiting and other villainous indulgences of our
grandparents. It is reported by Moore that Ld. B. indeed took
lessons in boxing from 'Gentleman' Jackson, and proved an
able pupil. I am told by certain sporting males whom I con-
sulted that all the names herein mentioned are actual Boxers of
the time, or just before, yet here seen to be already (in Ld. B.'s
account) figures of the past—which, for him when he wrote
this, they were.

TEN

Of Shows and Pantomimes—and of

a Fate both strange & dire

RUE IT WAS THAT Mrs Enoch Whitehead came not often to town. Corydon Hall was hers, her duty and her delight, and it was a world to her— and within it, a still littler world, yet the *largest* too—a Nursery, wherein there reigned the heir of both families, and a Despot he was—though with all his Mother's beauty. There was, besides, her own Mother, still smiling but now partly absent from the world, as though she had already joined the Angels whom she had always resembled, and was closing her earthly books—and there were her Brothers, growing straight and tall and grave, so unlike yet so *like* their departed elder that Susanna sometimes knew not if she would laugh or weep to see them at the Butts, or at leap-frog.

Mr Whitehead, on the contrary, was not often at home—which, it must be said, did not much diminish his wife's liking to remain there. For a time after he became Master and Proprietor of Corydon's manors, he tried country pleasures one after another—got himself pinks, and fox-hounds; shot pheasants; planned a Park—but soon enough he forgot why he should have adopted these pursuits, and increasingly returned to the less *ambiguous* pleasures he had formerly enjoy'd—though (odd as it may seem) his conversation when in Town turned frequently upon his Estates, and the Crops grown upon them, and the Improvements he intended.

In one season, though, his wife too was eager for Town, and that was the time when new plays were opened at the Theatres. *1* How could it be that such a plain and honest heart as Susanna's could so love artifice, and the sight and sound of bewigged and rouged ladies and gentlemen speaking verse, and the undoing of tangled plots by the sword-stroke of authorial contrivance, merely to bring his 'two hours' traffic' to an end? It cannot be explained, except perhaps by a *bump* on her shapely head. Her husband, still contrariwise, got little pleasure there—he could not hear much that was said, understood but half of that, and approved less. Having brought his wife to his box, and sat through the curtain-raiser, he often slipt away, to other parts of Town, and other *scenes.* Thus Susanna sat often alone—or with a Companion half-asleep after a good dinner—and looked and listened, and criticised too, comparing this year's Greeks and Romans, Barons and Friars, Harlequins and Clowns, with last year's. And now and again she was lost—and wept—or laughed—was touched, and absent.

When thus caught up in the imaginary doings below, she would now and again lean out from her box, her white hand upon the velvet lip—and thus it was that Ali saw her, from his own seat. For so long had his eye roamed without hope over every Crowd, so often had it been tricked by the sight of those who were *not her,* that at first it (that Organ, I mean, our proudest sense, and most easily deceived) passed over her—then returned—and as it were grew *telescopic,* filled with nothing but her, as with a new Planet. As soon as he might, he left his own box and sought hers—entered one that was *not,* and withdrew with apologies—and then hit upon the right place. Parting the curtain in the greatest trepidation he had yet felt, he saw her form lit by the stage below—saw that she was *alone* save for that sleeping Argus—and he slipt in. Still for a long moment he made not his presence known—she turned not, absorbed in the sights and sounds, the waves of Laughter, the clash of Instruments, all which made his approach unnoticed. Looking upon her—she all unaware of him, her soft lips parted, her eyes sparkling in the hundred lights—he wished to stay forever, so she changed not—or contrariwise, that having drunk his fill, he might slip away, without awaking her notice at all—but he found his thirst was not to be allayed—and at last the Animal Magnetism (if such thing there be) exuded from him caused her to turn, and find him there.

'Ali!'—'Susanna!'—What more? For a moment, only confusion—then both together spoke, each with an Account to make, each eager to forgive what the other *must* consider unforgivable, and at the same time to *speak not* of it, to deny all that had occupied their thoughts so long. 'All that befell—'Twas *I—I,*' Ali insists, and before he can say *what* he was, Susanna cries low, '*No no,* the fault was *not thine*—never think so—but *I*—— All this conducted in a whisper, and yet—as a sudden *silence* may wake us, as well as a sudden sound—her Companion rouses, though she had slept like the dead through the orchestra's tootling and the roars of the crowd. Now Ali must be introduced—he is *a close friend* of Susanna's departed Brother's, and wished but to pay his respects to that dear Memory—the Lady Companion is most interested, and desires further information, which the two supply, tumbling upon each other's words. Fans are opened then, and manipulated. The show, which meantime continues upon the stage below—though they two, while looking down upon it steadily, perceive little of it—is the new Pantomime (as new as any Pantomime may be, where the same things always happen in the same way). Just now they see Dame Venus conclude the 'Transformation Scene', wherein the young lovers are turned into Harlequin and Columbine, the old jealous father into Pantaloon, and the sleepy *duenna* into Clown.

'I have been for a time abroad,' says Ali then stiffly, at which Susanna cannot help but laugh—for she knew his history, as did all the world.

'Your mother and brothers?' asks he of Susanna. He sits behind her, where he may not himself be seen by the spectators without.

'Well,' says she. 'All well.'

So they remain—their talk, when they talk, is of the kind called 'small'—yet somehow pregnant, nonetheless, with matters larger—He hopes he may call upon her—She avers that her *husband* does not often entertain—Yet she notes he has taken a House in Town—She would have him note the performances—the Clown's no Grimaldi—and in all this Ali knew not if he advanced, or retreated—nor *to* what, nor *from* what!

Now the gloomy Chords strike up, and the curtains part upon the 'Dark Scene', as the players call it—the Grave-yard, Ruins, Tombs or Cavern, wherein poor Harlequin must suffer, and be tested, before Dame Venus in her kind wisdom restores all to what it was at first—the scene of Life—the same we act in every day. But before this, and while Bats and Ghosts on wires still pester poor Harlequin, and all's still to be resolved, Susanna sighs—and says Mr Whitehead soon will arrive, as is his wont, for the final Scene—and Ali (though for a moment he does not catch her drift) takes his leave, with a mumbled Farewell, to her—and another to the sharp-eyed Friend—who (though he knows it not) will become *his* friend, as well, in the fullness of time. And then he's gone.

Though Ali had noticed it not, Susanna Whitehead had learned from him, and had remembered, his present Residence—and there, not very long at all after that night, he finds a Letter addressed in her familiar hand—as though it had been summoned by the constancy of his thought upon her, all that time 'twixt that hour and this. Her words within are brief enough—glad, though, and eager to know more of him—and they include *instructions* as to how he may reply, through an intermediary—that same Friend!—by enclosing his letter to herself within one to that person—but few can need instruction in such methods. *'Write quick and I will answer'*—and his heart lifts as lightly and foolishly as a paper kite—only to fall as quick, when the string tugs—for he knows what first he *must* write, and yet not *how:* how it was that he, tho' all unknowing, had doomed her family to wander without rudder or compass, to a comfortless harbour.

'It was I,' he wrote, 'who brought about your brother's death—make no mistake—I also who contrived it, that you should have no option but to marry one you despised—all this was my doing—for I drew you both into the web of evil in which I was caught—the web I AM—for my own selfish purposes—that I be not *alone*—you must hate me, you have no other choice, and I shall welcome that hate, as one *should,* who receives his *due.*'

'Never believe it to be so,' came back Susanna's reply as quick as thought, or at any rate as quick as posted Letter may. 'What Fate or Chance ordains, is not only foolish but *presumptuous* to claim for our own doing—it was not yours. Is it not useless to be consumed with Remorse for what no *human* effort could have prevented, nor may now make right? I fear that what you say may keep you away from me—and that is, of all the regrets I may suffer, the one I most fear today. O my dear Ali—you ask why I never sought you out—never wrote, tho' knowing you were returned—know you not how I followed the news of you—of your disappearance—your return, & fame—never say I *cared not*—yet I feared, not *you,* but *myself,* if we two met again—I must say no more—I feel like a fortress besieged, and traitors are within my walls—do not write more—O yet do *not cease* to write, and *think of me* always—as I shall think of thee—I know not how to sign—except SUSANNA.'

To this Ali replied, in a kind of fever, his pen chasing after his thought as it spun across the page, his thought chasing in turn his heart, which was tumbled along between Hope and Despair—for the one he had loved, and thought lost, was not lost, and yet *was,* absolutely. My young Hero, too gallant in all the ways a hero ought to be, had had too little experience of the world to know that the common contradiction he then found himself in had a common resolution—yet he was on the way to learning it—he had already in place the Postal System whereby his suit might be made, and all that he received in return by the same System, only instructed him further. 'I inclose as you ask a lock of my hair—I know not for what purpose you desire it—yet puzzling upon that makes me think that a lock of *yours* wd. give me great comfort. I wish that you wd. set the conditions for our intercourse, otherwise I may overstep and offend—the which I dread more than to be kept in my place—tho' I dread *that* sufficiently, for my place may be too far from you! O relieve these anxieties, Susanna! Tell me what I may ask, and what not!'

Time was, when a billet of the heart was consecrated to privacy, meant for but two other eyes, carried by winged Mercury with finger to his lips. Now every letter of any interest is copied over, as often as not by the Authoress herself (for it is that sex that has, if not the *monopoly* of that business, at least the *majority interest*), to be circulated as wanted, or deserved. The foolish *duenna* to whom Ali was to send missives intended for Susanna thought it not beyond her duties that, having opened his cover to extract the letter inside and re-cover it with her own, she should first copy it, for her own meditation.

Odd you may find it—or perhaps not—that, while for many months, amounting to a year and more, Ali and Susanna had never met, it happened *now* that hardly a week went by—nay, sometimes not a day—that they did not encounter each other, and pass some time together. It is certainly not an *Author's* contrivance that makes it so—tho' his Tale depend upon it—but an *instinctual* wisdom of the Sex, that will ever astonish the Male, who generally thinks he happens upon the object of his affections by wondrous Chance. Thus it was they *found themselves*—the English says it plainly—at Billiards, in a splendid room, looked down upon by portraits of Lords and Ladies in armour or in silks. Their conversation was of the blandest—save that, whenever the three spheres their sticks impelled collided, as Newton conceived they must—the angles of their incidence equalling the angles of their reflection—the remarks he made to her, or she to him, of Triumph or Defeat, had each a double meaning, open to no-one else. Meanwhile about them the talk was general, and scraps of this and that remark penetrated even to their ears.

'Have you not heard? Buonaparte has escaped from Elba, Paris is taken!'

'What, again? I suppose it will be an annual event—every summer, Paris is taken—well, I am sorry for it, I say.'

Said Ali to Susanna, ''Tis this *third* fellow on the table's the troublesome one! Could he but be removed, the game were soon won.'

'Is it not the essence of the game, that there he be?'

'I care not,' said Ali—'I'd gladly knock him in a corner—so these two could go their way together.' He chanced at that moment to raise his eyes, and found with a cold horror that Mr Enoch Whitehead—the very one he had spoke of, tho' *allegorically*—had without his noticing come to stand not two yards' length from them—whereupon Ali looked stricken upon Susanna.

'He hears nothing,' said Susanna softly to him, 'or little enough. You need not fear.' And with that she chalked her cue in unconcern. Ali, though, with profoundest shame, bethought him of his last Interview with his Father—which had taken place beside a billiards table!—and of that Lord's words to him concerning Mr Whitehead—how he was *deaf,* and would not notice, so the Lady might do as she liked—*as all the world likes,* said he. Shame—and horror—but not *repentance*—for Mr Whitehead's disability now entered Ali's calculations, those calculations that the master Arithmetician, Venus' child, is always about, as he must be if the world is to go round. They two play'd on, and spoke low, and the balls rolled—yet now they *counted not the hazards.*

More such *collisions* (and deflections the more painful) took place among those three social *molecules,* till Ali retreated altogether from Society to the solitude of his apartments, to read ancient Authors for wisdom—stern good sense he got there, too, till his eyelids droop'd upon the midnight—yet this is not a copy-book, and none of it shall be repeated here. On a certain gloomy morning the Post brought a letter, not from Susanna but from Miss Catherine Delaunay. It was, like the young lady herself, both precise and feeling—it adverted to their recent meetings, which seemed to have been more full of significance than Ali (whose thoughts were often elsewhere) had thought them to be. 'I am not one who can *show* what I do not *feel,*' quoth she. 'Indeed I have learned to my cost that I do not always show what I *do* feel, and may leave those whom I would most wish to know my heart, in some puzzlement—which may cause them to turn away from me—when that would be to me a very great sorrow. I remember that in our conversation I dwelt upon that Ideal Man whose qualities I have long pondered—and so I have, and I believe my picture to be perfect in all respects—but I surely meant not to assert, that only he could win my favor who matched my Ideal in *every detail*—nor *could,* perhaps, any living man! Well—dear Friend—as I hope I may *always* call you—I shall say no more, lest I say that which I do not precisely mean—a Fault against which I struggle daily!'

As these gentle sentiments—which indeed did credit to their Author—pass'd beneath Ali's view, and the many compliments too with which she closed, a thought began to form within him, or even to *hatch,* like an egg.

'Why, then, should I not wed?' thought he. 'At a stroke I should decapitate all my troubles. I would be as a ship who comes into port—I might lower my sails at last, and drop anchor. This lady seems to think me worthy of her—if I read her right—and perhaps she is right to think so—and if not, still she *thinks* so, and if I do naught to disillusion her—she may *go on* thinking so. What dreams have haunted me may pass, if I lie in a bed with one who loves me. I might not walk in sleep—if I have. Such a one, if she be kind, might make the double, *one!*'

His valet disturbed these thoughts to announce that a young gentleman was below, come to see him, who would not give his name—should he be sent up? Ali asked, 'What sort of young gentleman?'—'A Soldier,' reply'd the valet—'A young officer, insofar as his coat could be glimpsed beneath a mantle.' And Ali idly waved the fellow an assent—his mind already turning to his *dilemma* and its horns again. 'And yet—and yet,' thought he, and hugged himself, and crossed his legs, and stared into the fire, dissatisfied—'And yet—'

At the opening of the door again, he rose, and turned to greet—a ghost! For before him stood the young Lord Corydon, as he once was—in his uniform—the mantle drawn up before his mouth, but his eyes sapphire and laughing—no ghost at all, but flesh, as Ali was himself!

5

The wild fancy faded in a moment—Ali having staggered, and righted himself with a chair's back—the Soldier dropt the mantle, and Ali saw that it was not the dead lad *redivivus* but Susanna his sister. Her hair cut short in downy curls as *his* had been, her cheek as smooth as his had remained—she took a soldier's stance, and saluted Ali with a soldierly salute, yet smiling a questioning, a hesitant smile.

'Is it *his*—your dress?' Ali asked her.

'He never wore *these*—they were by mischance made too small.' She approached—but a step. 'Ali!' said she. 'I passed thro' public streets—I turned not a head—your valet knew me not, but for what I seemed to be.'

'Clothes make the man,' Ali said—and with that the young Cornet laughed in delight, and rushed to embrace him—and he refused her not. Now she was not a demure *wife* in silks and petticoats—she had left that personage in her *dressing-room,* and stood here as another—bold—frank—arms akimbo now, after releasing him, and her eye even subduing his, as she would say *How like you THAT*—and now Ali too laughed, at this Transformation Scene.

'Must you soon rejoin your *Regiment,* young Sir?' Ali asked—'Or may you stop awhile?'

'I am on *furlough,*' was Susanna's rejoinder, 'and I may do *just as I like,* as any Officer may.'

It need not be said how they occupied themselves that day, except that it was not as Soldiers—no smoking of Cheroots, or roaring at tales, or making tuns of themselves into which cavalry-punch is poured—not those pleasures. I shall relate, that Ali wept, remembering Corydon, his Friend—wept, at last, as he had not in his rage and horror before done!—And Susanna wept too—wept for the loss of what she had surely brought here to *sacrifice*—and yet might we not shed real tears at parting with our Honour, however coldly we may have contrived to be done with it? And when they had wept, they laughed again—as the *three* of them had so oft, when together they had wandered the green ways, and spoke wonderful nonsense, only for the delight of seeing the other two smile—or throw back their heads in laughter. How easy and common is Love—how quick are its delights achieved and done—how rare and lasting is lovers' laughter, the *greater* gift of the ungenerous Gods!

But now the evening is fallen—the young Soldier will be missed, if longer she linger—and yet another candle burns away before she will pull on her buff breetches again, and do up the frogs of her red coat—and still, even as her person is part-way out the door, still her fingers are extended to keep touch with his—and her *gaze,* last of all to be broken!

Thus did Ali and Susanna embark upon that unfortunate course of conduct so common in Society, and in Novels too—a course that in its perfect form is mark'd by being at once *invisible* and *patent*—for no-one would *see* evil, but all are disappointed if *hearing* of it be kept from them—and for that to be so, those who delight in *speaking* it are everywhere welcome, tho' they may be disparaged *in absentia.* If I did not so cherish these two, and wish for them all that they desired so much (nay, it must be said, so *blindly* now and then), I would face the telling of it all with some *ennui,* and might beg leave to dispense with the account—how they believed themselves secure— yet were prattled of—they two alone being ignorant of how *well known* were their comings and goings—just as the *Husband* was the only one ignorant of the comings and goings themselves. The Honourable Peter Piper indeed was loyal to his friend—*he* dismissed this loose and invidious talk, descanting on the beautiful friendship of Ali and the deceased Lord Corydon—Mrs Whitehead's desire to continue an Intercourse through which her Brother might be remembered—their mutual passion for the Stage—&c., &c.—all of which had of course an effect opposite to that intended.

In that Grand Chain of the dance called the Lancers—which is what Society in its *amours* most resembles, as the best men and the boldest women are pass'd along in a gallop from partner to partner, sometimes to find themselves at length back in the embrace of their dizzied Spouses, who have spent the dance elsewhere, and have only just come round again—it is of the greatest importance to take nothing as permanent, and to be ready upon the instant to part hands, and spin smiling away. Yet it has been noted that Ali was one given to Fixation, rather than to Variety—he saw his course as

Fate's election, and his heart was One. Where another actor on that bright stage, seeing how near to Disaster he draws, and how the rubber of Society has stretch'd as far as it may go before snapping, might indite a pretty letter, and then go abroad for a while—or agree with the object of his attention that after all the best is past, and only the Dregs remain, which might best be poured out, and an end made—or pack off his unsuitable Paramour with a gift of nicely calculated value—or any of these and others, which are all as though written in a book, a book all have read—Ali could not—he *would* not! Therefore, if the *affaire* could not be broken, then all else must be.

'Why may we not flee together? What holds us here?' So says he to Susanna, as upon a Sopha in the Library of a great house, to which they have both contrived to be invited, they sit alone to study an album, of Pictures they hardly see, showing Cities they have not visited. 'What matters it where we are, so that we are together? What matters Opinion, or what *others* may think? I tell you that there is nothing that holds *me* in this land—nothing but yourself, Susanna, and the little part of its earth, where *he* lies buried—nothing more!'

Yet at this Susanna has lifted her eyes, and now presses her hand against his lips, and stops his words even as they issue. 'Ali,' said she, 'O my dearest Ali!—But consider what you say—true it may be that *nothing* holds *you* here—but *I*—my heart is divided, my love owed to more than one!'

'Speak not of him,' Ali cries. 'He forced your hand—bought you as a slave!'

'Not *him*,' quoth Susanna. 'I mean my babes—my son, my daughter. From *them* I cannot part—I cannot.'

Long Ali gazed in that hour upon her face, in which Truth shone unmistakeably, and Pity too. He stood then, and went away, and faced the fire. 'I knew naught of a mother,' said he. 'Naught of that solicitude, that constancy—well. I am *told* it is of all things the most precious, that a man proceeds through life as though wounded, who has not known it. Yet I cannot say this of my own knowledge. I well believe that those babes of yours will forever profit by your love.'

'Be not so cold.'

'Not cold! Never cold!' He turned again to her, and knelt by her where she sat. 'Think, though, what now I must do. No—no—take not my hand! If we cannot flee, we must part, Susanna, before you are dishonoured—put away, perhaps—and perhaps lose those babes—and gain nothing by it. Do you not see?'

'You have killed me to say so. I could not say it.'

'No—not killed—not *you*. That cannot be. 'Tis not so. *You* shall live. You must—or this is all for naught.' He spoke it with certainty—as a man may who knows the ship upon whose broken deck he stands, is sinking—yet watches the ship's boat pull away, bearing all he cares for—'tis enough! For Love has her claims, and they are just, and great—yet she may not claim *all*, not to Ruin—so think the Wise, who are not to be confounded with the *timid*—but are rather those who know how little may be the mede of happiness in the normal course of any life—ask for *all*, and we are in the way of losing all.

'What then—what then?' said she.

'I shall go away,' said he—'I cannot be in the same City—no matter how large—I shall go away, and learn how I may live, though without you.'

'Where will you go? Surely not forever—say not so!'

'It matters not,' said Ali. 'Perhaps I shall embark on a long journey. I know not. I ask but this—Susanna! Avoid those places where by chance we may meet!'

'What! Must we give up all friendship—all kindness? Do not say so—I will not permit it.'

'No—that we shall not—if you desire it—and I can bear it—you shall have my *friendship*—and all else of mine you may want—always!'

So they resolved—so they vowed—so they abjured— But oh! Is there any spur to our tender feelings that is as sharp as Renunciation? We say we must part—we gaze upon each other—we feel every reason why we should *not* part, thrown as it were into relief, even by our resolution—we see the drear and empty desert of our Future, lived alone, for surely no *other* can ever—no, no, never! And we cling again, to comfort one another, in close embrace, whispering *we must part*—and part not! How long Ali and Susanna thus hung upon the wave's lip in trembling hesitation, not either could afterward say—and they would still be there, did they not hear the approach of boots, and the Library door tried—and they 'started like guilty things', and were sundered!

*W*HAT EVENTS MAY befall one who is becalmed—who is removed from Society—who bestirs himself but to dress, and to eat, and that not frequently—whose evenings in that Company which now and then draws him from his couch, is given to the consumption of waters of Lethe in such amounts that it is just as if the night had not been spent at all (save for the head-ache, and the soda-water, and the crapula, upon the morrow, whose very source is forgot)—I say, such events *may* perhaps be recorded—but were best not.

Upon a certain day no different from the others before, Ali chanced to see, from some distance, Miss Delaunay enter a coach— with as much aplomb as the thing may be done, and yet perforce granting the vision of a very little foot, and a slim ankle, to the passersby. He walked on, deep in thought—if thought it may be called—and when he regained his own quarters, he sat down and wrote the letter whose lines had run all that afternoon through his brain:

> MY DEAREST CATHERINE—I know not by what rights I may address you in this manner—if I offend I am heartily sorry for it, and at your word I shall cease any attentions you may find oppressive to yourself—believe me that to cause you pain would be the greatest pain to myself I can presently imagine—and yet I will risk all to say to you, my very dearest Friend, that your spirit and your kindness to me have so penetrated my soul that I find I may not give them up—I would find Life so much the less tolerable without them, and the prospect of being forever deprived

of them so unwelcome, that all I am able to do (indeed I desire to do no other) is to present to you my Petition, that
you accept me for your own, to serve and to love you despite every handicap under which I may labour in so doing, and my great inadequacies therein. I am well aware,
that I am not one whose History or Forebears are such as
would win the hand of one like yourself, if *they alone* were to
be counted in my favour; and there are further flaws I *have
not owned to* but shall, should you entertain in the slightest
degree this suit of mine——

——Here Ali paused, and lifted his pen from the foolscap, as
though stopping his mouth before *too much* was said. For a crowd of
misadventures bustled then into his brain, that he might enumerate,
if he would, in a bill of particulars—but he did not so. Instead he
hurried to his end—beginning to feel the wind die down that had
carried his bark so fast and far, and eager to reach the harbour of a
last Compliment and a Subscription before he should find himself
becalmed. When he had done (and his conclusions may easily be
imagined, they were not so rare nor so new as to be inconceivable),
and the letter was blotted and doubled, he dropt it upon the table,
and sat to look upon it—did not move to carry it farther—did not
move at all. At about midnight—when a tomcat, in the mews behind, announced the hour, a-calling to his love—he leapt up, put his
first letter into the Fire, and wrote another, to a different recipient:

I was wrong to think I could live without you—I shall not
live, if you instruct me not to live—I shall take that as your
intention, if you will not meet with me and prove to me
that *you do not wish it*—If you *will* meet me, I care not for the
cost—do not you either. If you will not meet me—where
and when, *you* may decide, so it be *ours alone*—then you
shall never see me more.—ALI

This missive, without Salutation, he sent immediately to the female
Accomplice whose good offices he had often before employed—a

woman to whom, be it said, he gave no more thought than he might to the Post-men who carry all the rest of the world's missives so reliably, and anonymously. He then proceeded to *wait*—which to certain natures is galling beyond expression—the minutes fall like the water-drops in that Chinese torture, which we commonly employ for comparison, though I think none of us have undergone it—*I* have not—indeed I should try to imagine *it,* by thinking 'Perhaps it is like waiting for a Letter that may mean Life, or Death, and listening to the clock tick'—but then again it may be quite unlike. No answer came—and when even Hope could see that none would come, then he found himself no longer able to bear his rooms—the streets around—the Town, the *Ton,* the *Monde*—and bethought him where he might go to hide himself, perhaps for ever—a wigwam among the red Indians, a kraal among the Hottentot! There came to him just at that moment, in the same Post that brought no answer from Susanna, a letter from Lieutenant Upward, that very Military Surgeon who once upon a time—in another land, another *Planet* seemed it then to Ali—had befriended him. The Military Surgeon had had excellent luck, it appeared, in the common matters that so bedeviled Ali—for he was married, to a good woman, and a *fruitful* one—he heartily recommended the *wedded state* to Ali, as all do who find themselves happy in that Republic, and would expand its borders till it encompass all Mankind, and Womankind. His House upon the Welsh sea-coast was blest with little Upwards, lilting in Welsh; and he wished Ali to come to him, to rejoice in his happiness. Ali wrote by return that he would be delighted to see him, and all appurtenances pertaining, and *as soon as he might* he would depart the City—whether to return ever, he knew not—though *this* he said only to that bruised and panting organ within him, his Heart. At any rate he made solemn oath— tho' he knew not to what Gods, or Powers—that he would remain forever far off from anywhere Susanna Whitehead, or her husband, or her children, or her ox, or her ass, or anything that was hers, might be met with in any wise whatsoever, until that Heart had grown so strong again as to grant assent to his returning, and ceased to swell hotly in grief even at the thought.

HE MILITARY SURGEON welcomed one who had once been his Comrade (tho' briefly) in arms, and led Ali within the Bosom of his new family—a plump Wife, as advertised, and two plump Children, all three as alike, and as likeable, as three great blushing Fruits in a Dish. The fire was lit, and a bowl of Punch in the making, and all was as warm as the Womb. Nor was Ali insensitive to the beauties, and the Delights, of such domesticity; he was at first shy amid so much hubbub and welcome, but by that eve he was more at ease than he had been since—since—and here the memory of Corydon Hall obtruded, and he turn'd away from the spillikins he would pick up, or the lead soldiers he was to command. Yet the little Son of the Upwards could smile upon him, and the Daughter tug at his sleeve, to bring him round again.

For a week and more he kept the vow he had made—that he *would not think* of Susanna—but the hours and days of that week proved remarkably elastic, stretching to fill an Eternity—and what with the well-known impossibility of forbidding one's thought to dwell upon a certain object, the very act of forbidding being itself but one more thought of the forbidden—and the sullen Sea offering him no whit of comfort, and no suggestion of a Resolution, though he flung himself into its cold embrace twice a day, all but naked, to solicit its wisdom—he approached, in a short time, to Despair. Easy and sweet it seemed to him to leap into that sea, and easy to swim out so far he could not return—sweet to sink beneath the wave, and know no more, of Susanna, of Love—yea, of Ali! Yet what commended him to the Deep, and Forgetfulness, was the same as what he could not give up, which demanded that he cling to Life, and Hope—the Paradox is a common one, which does not make it sting the less.

More than once indeed did Ali determine to carry out his stated resolve, and 'take up arms' against his own 'sea of troubles, and by opposing, end them.' He stood long on a height above the

6

roiling waves, that dashed upon the rocks where he might dash himself—*they* ever to re-form, and be flung back again, but *he* never! Or he took a Pistol, and clutched it as though it were the hand of his only friend—or he considered the long & honed Razor that might in a moment's spasm release his pulsing blood from the carotid artery that beat along his throat. But—and it will not surprise any, who have known the vagaries of a fit of Melancholy—there came a night when Ali felt almost that his raging soul might cross over by its own volition to the realm of the unhappy Dead—and of a sudden sleep seized him, and when he woke, he woke *calm,* a sea after storm—and in wonder and a little shame he found that he intended to live and not to die, and to have a Bath, and eat his Breakfast.

'As I predicted,' said the Military Surgeon gravely—for his manner had grown suitably grave, with the increase in his responsibilities, and the numbers and ailments of his Patients—'Sea air has done for you what Nature and Nature's God intended it might—why, your cheek is as bright as a girl's, and your eye as clear as—as—as anything clear. Another week or two, and you will be sleeping like an infant, and eating like one too.'

'Forgive me,' Ali said. 'The cure you propose must be cut short—I left all my business at sixes and sevens—truthfully, I did not expect to consider it further. Will you make my obeisance to your dear wife, and your delightful babes? And here, take this as a gift from myself—you see it is a fine one—made by Joe Manton himself—you see the chasing, upon the stock? Nay, nay—take it—I would have it far from me, now—I have no *use* for it, I hope!'

He had not returned to Town but a week, however, and had not chosen a new path (tho' feeling sure one lay before him, or more than one), when on a fateful afternoon—fateful he would later name it—a Visitor to his lodgings was announced.

'A Female,' said his valet, in some disapprobation, as such creatures, come a-calling alone, inevitably added to his own cares. 'She requests an *interview.*'

'Is she known to you?'

'The Lady is veiled.'

Beneath his servant's critical eye Ali stood in an agony of doubt. Susanna—should she not be sent away? Had she not sent him to his death—or well *might* have, had he had a little more *resolve*—and spake not a word to call him back? Had he not vowed— had he not sworn before his own soul—had he not promised *her* never to put her again in shame's way? Never! Never! 'Admit the Lady,' said he, and then when the cursed valet pretended he had not heard, and cupped an ear with a large and hairy hand, again— 'Admit her!'

Yet when the *female* stood upon the threshold, and lifted the heavy veil, Ali saw before him not Susanna, but Miss Catherine Delaunay. Pale she was as though she had passed through the Valley of the Shadow, yet she held herself erect and brave, and look'd steadily upon Ali.

'Miss Delaunay—Catherine,' said he, and came to greet her. 'Why, how do you do?'

'My Lord,' she said, in a voice of icy calm, one not her own, and yet a voice he was not entirely surprized to know she could deploy—it struck a strange fear, and a stranger pity, into his heart to hear it. 'I come to tell you that there have been consequences of our late meeting.'

'Consequences?' responded Ali. 'What consequences? To which meeting do you allude? Will you not be seated? Will you take tea, or a glass of wine? Your coming here is unwonted—I hope the matter is not such as to cause you great distress!'

At this word the lady seemed suddenly suffused with feeling— whether anger, or affront, or horror, could not be told, but for an instant she seemed ready to *detonate*, like a hand grenade just toss'd. Then—it was terrible to see—she drew herself together, and made herself ice again. 'Consequences,' she said again. 'If I speak not plainly enough, I shall: *I am with child.*'

There is—it is comically reliable—an attribute in Man such that, upon hearing Woman speak so, he feels himself instantly solicitous, and at the same time alarmed beyond reason—he must bring a chair, and insist she sit—await any command—speak tenderly—all this he will do, except in *one* circumstance, and that is when he suspects he is about to have a claim of Paternity brought against him, which he intends to deny—then there is no wight crueller, or less pitiful. Ali sensed a claim upon him, indeed, and one made by a person whose uprightness, and truthfulness, and probity, he would never doubt—yet it was not a claim whose *basis* he could admit—or even imagine. Therefore he only stood, between solicitude and aloofness, unable to respond. At last he spoke—'I know not,' said he, 'of what you speak.'

'Will you deny me now?' said Catherine, in a voice like a subtle knife. 'I do not believe you will—you cannot be so changed from the one I knew.'

'You must forgive me,' said Ali. 'I am innocent of all that you say—I know nothing of it.'

'Do not mock me,' she cried then piteously, and all the cold reserve she had theretofore shown slid from her as a garment undone. 'O do not! If you deny me now, I know not where I may turn—indeed there is nowhere—nowhere in this land—this *Earth*! I swear to you I shall not remain upon it—not for shame, tho' that be reason enough, but that you *deny me*—that is too terrible!' She sank then at his feet, and like a grieving child clutched at his knees in abasement. 'No!' Ali cried to her—'No! Do not do so!' He knelt to lift her from the floor—found her too shaken even with his aid to stand—and ended by sitting on the Carpet beside her, as though they were two children at a game. Ali took her face, now all wetted with her tears, into his hands, and by his look made to subdue her horrors—so shocking as coming from *such a one,* who he thought may never have wept before—surely not such a storm! 'Tell me,' said he, 'what you believe to have happened—tell me, for you have surely been deceived by *someone*—and trust that I will do all I can to aid you, and to learn the truth—more I cannot do.'

'I came to you in response to your summons,' she said, and from within her reticule she withdrew a paper—which she had not halfunfolded before Ali recognized it, tho' 'twas worn with much reading, and stained too with tears—for it was the letter he had sent to Susanna, that last desperate missive she had not answered—his answer, as he had thought, being *her silence*. Catherine now read from it—'I was wrong to think I could live without you',—'I shall not live, if you so instruct me', and 'Meet me, where and when you may decide', and the rest. A blackness swam before Ali's vision as he heard the words, and he felt the sensation of a sword cutting him in two—not *dividing,* but *doubling* him. 'Tell me it is not your hand,' said Catherine, proffering this letter. 'You shall not say so—you cannot!'

'Who brought this to you? Did it come by post? How addressed?'

'Not by post—it was given me by a messenger, who insisted he must put it in my hands—he was commanded, he said, to wait upon my answer.'

'I sent you no messenger,' said Ali—but not now as one who insists upon his Innocence, or argues his case, but as one stunned with wonder, who knows not what will resolve the contradiction he is caught in, that offers no Resolution—no more than the immovable object, that meets the irresistible force. 'What answer made you?'

She looked upon him as though he were mad. 'You know what answer!' cried she. 'You know! That I would not have harm come to you—would not have the guilt of that upon me—I know not what words I used—as wild as those you addressed to me—I wrote that I knew not where we might meet, that I knew nothing of such places, save public ones. The next evening a further communication was brought me—naught but the name of a street, and the number of a house—an hour, late—O Heaven forgive me!'

There she had gone, she related, with but a single trusted servant, to the house named—was admitted—her servant commanded to await her return. She was conducted to a darkened bed-chamber—its drapes drawn—without lamp or light—and there awaited *him,* Ali, in dread and hope!

Ali had ceased to speak—found he could as little interfere, or question her narrative, as a spectator at a play, who watches in a state of suspended excitement—scarce breathing—while the persons of the drama enact their foregone dooms:—or as our own innocent spirits may watch, from their abode within us, the fatal words we speak, the actions we take, that can never be undone.

Anon one had come into the chamber—she scarcely knew

how, or from where, as though it were a Ghost, or a Sorcerer—and lay down beside her. He spoke but her name, and yet—she said—she knew him surely for Ali—how, she could not say—as even a blind dog knows its master—as a storm-toss'd Bird the way to its nesting place—she knew! She had believed she would speak to him—tell him of the higher purposes of Life, and the infinite value placed upon every soul by its Creator and Judge—that his despair was but a temporary madness, a dream from which he would wake, and Reason and Proportion return him to himself—all this and more she had designed to say, and had spoken over to herself, as an uncertain actor his part, as she went thence, and there awaited him—but he only laid a gentle finger upon her lips—and then met them with his *own*—and 7 all was forgotten. But thrice more he spoke—*'Fide in Sane,'* he said; and again, 'Without you I am nothing.' And last—when all was 8 yielded, all surrendered—'Remember Psyche.'

All this she told over now to Ali—in disjoynted sentences, as though he knew all, and needed but a hint, a word of reminder—but he knew *naught,* and only gaped at her and goggled, like a caught Trout in a Net, till she withdrew from him, pale and in terror. 'Stare not so upon me!' she cried. 'What mean you? You cannot deny this—O that I had lit a lamp then despite your commandment—made you acknowledge yourself!' At length she flung herself heedlessly into his arms—begged that, after all that she had *given,* and he *taken,* he would never abandon her, never despise her—that he loved her, and that all which had occurred was from this source alone.

'Catherine,' said he, drawing himself from her, as far as she allowed. 'You must know that the German doctor who examined me has found it to be possible that I might suffer from a condition, as rare as strange, whereby I may, in a fit like sleep, and all unknown to my self—I mean my conscious self, this self that knows that I am here, and I am I, and you and all this are here before me—I may do things that I know not I do. I say, 'tis *possible,* it *may be*—I know not—I doubt it could be—and yet—perhaps—'

She looked upon him as he spoke, and to Ali it was as when we watch a weak & failing flame, wondering if it will die away, or grow strong and burn—he knew not if she would shrink away in horror from him, and her heart die—or rather would she rise, in fury, or in *love*—'struth! He knew nothing, who knew not if he had possess'd the girl—for, who knows not *that,* knows nothing indeed! 'Ali!' she breathed then. 'My Lord! Do you then not love me? Tell me now if what you did, you did from love—for my part I swear it was!'

There was then but a single course open to my hero—heroes being, in general part, those who have but a single way to take, and take it. Catherine Delaunay believed him to be the one who had gone to the bed where she lay, in a darkened house, in a dark street, and had got her with his child—and had done these things because he *loved* her. He had *not* done so—or what was more dreadful, perhaps *had* done so, but in a Dream, or a blindness—yet it was *he* alone, & awake, who could bear the blame, there was no other. Now if he took her up—whether he acknowledged the night, and the deed, and the child, or did not—it could *only be because he loved her*—she would refuse him else. So he said—'I indeed do love you, Catherine. I love you, and if I do not affright you—for truly I know not who I am, nor what I may do, if I have done *this*—I desire your love, too—forever—from this time forth.'

'You do love me, then!'

'I say that I do.' It was in truth all he *could* say; and—his honest heart moved to pity & awe at what she had done for him (though he had known nothing of it), which was done in response to his outcry of despair & love (though that outcry was meant for another), and in apparent possession now of what she could give but *once*—he was persuaded—he was nearly sure—he thought it certain—that indeed he did.

NOTES FOR THE 10TH CHAPTER

1. *new plays:* Lord Byron loved the Theatre, and was for a time early in his marriage a member of the committee of Drury Lane which chose new plays—though his own plays were never meant for performance—he was greatly annoyed when one of his dramas intended only for the Closet was performed in London without his permission and against his wishes. Sorry he would be, I think, that now-a-days no-one would think even to try—they are not much read, except *Manfred* and perhaps *Cain.*

2. *Argus:* The being with a hundred eyes set to watch upon Jupiter's love Io, and not the ship of Jason, which was the *Argo.* He never entirely slept, which is the jest. The reader will encounter him again in the 12th Chapter.

3. *Animal Magnetism:* The supposed fluid or property of living things (not excepting trees and flowers) that M. Mesmer and his followers claimed to control by their baths and manipulations. Like many things once thought to be fact, it persists as

fancy, a term used loosely and generally to mean sex attraction.

4. *the Authoress herself:* It has long been Lady Byron's habit, to retain copies of letters she has herself sent. Even when she has composed them in the heat of feeling, she is able coolly to transcribe them, and if *disagreement* arise as to what she said, or implied, to any correspondent, she may thus refresh her own memory. I sometimes wish that such habits of forethought were mine, and the past were not lost to me, as it sometimes is. O what a tangled web.

5. *A young officer:* Lady Caroline Lamb used often to go to my father's apartments dressed as a Page, with her hair cut short as here described. All that tale is as well known as Beatrice and Benedick, or Lara and Kaled, or I know not who, but the future (it may be hoped) will have forgotten it.

6. *two plump Children:* Ld. B.'s tale flies faster than his system of time—there could hardly be time between the battle of Salamanca and this sojourn, stated to be shortly before the battle of Waterloo, for this character to marry and generate two children. Ld. B. was (it appears) very fond of children, and happy in their company.

7. *'Fide in Sane':* The Byron family motto is *Crede Byron.* This nice pun may reflect upon the real motto it echoes, for it can mean 'Have faith in Sane', as *ours* says 'Believe in Byron', or it may mean 'Be certain, (he is, or I am) insane'. (My thanks to C.B. for the Help with Latin, of which I have none.)

8. *Psyche:* Psyche loved the God of Love, but was warned never to look upon him during his nightly visits to her. When her three sisters urged her to break his rule—for, they said, her husband may be a monster, or a demon—Psyche lit a candle to

look upon him as he slept, and found him to be a God. The hot wax dropping upon him, he woke—and all was spoiled. After many trials the God and his love end happily—tho' not all remember this conclusion—which is less memorable than the moment when everything was lost. Happy endings are all alike; disasters may be unique.

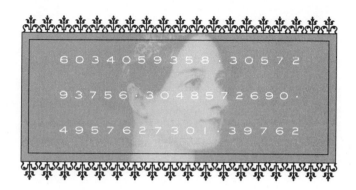

From: "Smith" <anovak@strongwomanstory.org>
To: lnovak@metrognome.net.au
Subject: No sense

Lee—

We got it and we don't know what to do next. Look at what it looks
like:

OBSER	TCHWR	OTOFT	THASB
VEBUT	APTIN	HISNO	EENFO
NONOO	ASCOT	RTHER	RTHES
NEMAY	CHMAN	NLAND	EPAST
OBSER	TLELI	SMANU	SEVEN
VESAV	TTLED	FACTU	OREIG
ETHEU	IFFER	REHEH	THERE
NFEEL	ENTFR	ASTWO	ISTHE
INGMO	OMTHA	POCKE	OLDBA
OONWH	ATWOR	TPIST	TTLEM
OSAIL	NINAL	OLSAS	ENTTH
SWITH	LTIME	WELLM	ATFAC
OUTPR	SBYHI	ADEBY	ESTOT
OGRES	SANCE	MANTO	HENOR
STHRO	STORS	NSFOR	THWHE
UGHTH	ANDNO	THISI	REONH
ECLOU	TONTH	SAYEA	ESTAN
DSAYO	ESCOT	RINTH	DSWHO
UNGLO	CHSID	EPRES	SESTO
RDWHO	EALON	ENTCE	NESHE

That's part of the first page. What Ada did was copy out the
whole manuscript, translated into numbers and enciphered. She
got sheets printed with numbered lines, fifty to a page, and then

started filling them in with her cipher numbers, four groups of ten on every line, with a dot after every two to make it look sort of mathematical. Every ten numbers stood for five letters (two numbers to a letter, if you think about it you'll see why). But instead of writing right across the page she wrote down the page in columns, until the whole page was filled, and then started another. To read it you read down a column and then down the next.

It was enciphered with a Vigenere square, which means that you keep changing the alphabet you use to substitute with. You change the alphabet according to a keyword. You know what Ada's keyword was? AMERICA. She *wanted* us to decipher it, and made it as easy as she could. All you had to do was guess what it was.

I think Ada made some mistakes in copying (three o's in moon) but Thea says the text seems to be all there. All the punctuation got stripped out though and I don't and Thea doesn't know how to put it back in or what punctuation would be right. In a way it doesn't matter and I know it doesn't; we got it, the thing. But I have a question. Would you have any interest in helping to edit this? To make some guesses about the punctuation at least, and turn it into English? Figure out where the sentences end and start? It would be a big help to me.

You don't have to. Really you don't have to, and I'm not saying that just because I want you to think I'm not being pushy but really *am* being pushy. I do mean it. I know there are other people who could do it, and you've got a life. The main reason is so that only a few people will still know about it. I'm so scared that the story will get out and Georgiana will go and burn it herself. Oh my god I wish I hadn't said that. I didn't think it, I just said it. Now I know it might be true.

S

————————————

From: lnovak@metrognome.net.au
To: "Smith" <anovak@strongwomanstory.org>
Subject: RE:No sense
Importance: Normal

My dear—yes—I can read it—how strange—I even started in and respaced this. And sat a long time before it.

I will do what I can in the time I have, and if it appears that it will take a longer time—scholarly decisions about periods and dashes aren't made in a *trice* as my own father used to say (you met him when you were one)—then I will find some other time somewhere. I can't tell you how eager I am to read it all, even in this Babel form. Did I tell you that when I first saw on the shelves of the university library here the collected volumes of his letters and journals—I was looking for the volume with the letters from Switzerland—I put my hand on a volume, and thought, *No, no, that's the last*—and suddenly a real, palpable grief came over me: The last. He's dead, he died, it can't be made better. That'll happen again, when I don't expect it. The dead we love keep on dying for us again and again, and he is one of those I love.

Lee

————————————

From: lnovak@metrognome.net.au
To: "Smith" <anovak@strongwomanstory.org>
Subject: Query

You'll not believe how I'm flying along. A story is emerging, that's a version of his own life, but as in a masquerade. It has its wild barbaric parts but also a lot of scenes set in London, the London he knew. I try not to look ahead to see where he's going, I'll just go nuts if I don't progress through it methodically—though I can tell you I've got pretty good at reading without spaces between words. You know that those spaces are recent—ancient writing didn't have them, and they don't seem to have felt the need.

I've come on one problem. There are some numbers showing up in the middle of text, often the same 3-digit numbers repeated, in places where text seems to be missing. I have no access to the originals and I wonder if there's some way to study the places in the original where these bits occur, and see what's up. Do you think you could put me in touch with your friend who did this deciphering?

Lee

———————————

From: "Smith" <anovak@strongwomanstory.org>
To: "Thea" <thea.spann133@ggm.edu>
Subject: FWD:

Thea—

Here's a letter from Lee I'm forwarding. I know this isn't easy but can you work with him on this. It might be a quick fix. Really he's okay.

PS Please when you write try to put in a few periods etc. Remember he's old and an English professor, or once was.

I've got a date to leave. I talked to Lilith. One month. I love you. (Now see once you start you have to keep on saying it, or it looks like you don't anymore. I remember this from high school. Boys worried. It was funny.)

S

———————————— .

From: "Thea" <thea.spann133@ggm.edu>
To: "Smith" <anovak@strongwomanstory.org>
Subject: him again

yike   but okay   i think i got an idea anyway   its obvious   do i at
least get to be icy cold   oh well   do my best to do my duty

btw   you know hes gone thru like four girlfriends in the last 3
years   arm candy   thats what they say   i saw it on cable   man
the stuff on cable   DISGUSTING   why didnt you warn me

t

————————————

From: lnovak@metrognome.net.au
To: "Thea" <thea.spann133@ggm.edu>
Cc: "Smith" <anovak@strongwomanstory.org>
Subject: Query

Dear Dr. Spann:

Thanks for your offer (relayed through Smith) to help clear up
these little problems. I'm faxing some of the pages where this
stuff shows up, and have underlined the places. The difficulty
is I can't compare them with the original enciphered version—
not that I'd learn much if I could. What do you think?
    Also—now that I can—I want to offer you much greater
thanks for your brilliant guess about what this thing was, and
your work in breaking the cipher. I wish there were something
I could offer in return.

Yours

Lee Novak

———————————

From: "Thea" <thea.spann133@ggm.edu>
To: lnovak@metrognome.net.au
Cc: "Smith" <anovak@strongwomanstory.org>
Subject: RE:Query

hey—

i cant tell you what it means   but the cipher shows that sometimes she uses an extra number   a 3-digit number which couldnt
signify a single letter   so the computer left it as a number   but
what about this   we talked about compression   what if shes
just using shorthand annotations for common stuff   like peoples
names   or phrases   like   i dont know what phrases   common
ones   if she had a list   like 100 means one of the characters
names   or 556 means a common phrase like THE NEXT DAY or it
might be THUS WE SEE   or anything   youd have to guess   look
at the context

hope this helps

i dont want any thanks   be nice to have this over tho

———————————

From: lnovak@metrognome.net.au
To: "Thea" <thea.spann133@ggm.edu>
Cc: "Smith" <anovak@strongwomanstory.org>
Subject: RE:Re:Query

Dear Dr. Spann:
I think that's it! She did do that. They seem to be numbered in
order, starting with the first time she thinks of compressing
them. Actually old-fashioned shorthand worked that way—
shorthand books were full of business and legal phrases you
could represent by a single stroke. She probably kept a book of

her compressions. The clue is that the first time she uses one of these she puts it after the phrase it stands for—then the next time she just substitutes. It must have saved her a lot of time not having to spell out "Albania" (101) or "his Lordship" (214) or lots of others.

I'm back in business.

Lee

───────────────

From: "Smith" <anovak@strongwomanstory.org>
To: "Thea" <thea.spann133@ggm.edu>
Subject:

Omigod you're so smart.

And see he didn't insult you or make a smarmy remark or any-thing. Maybe he *used* to be bad and now he's not.

S

───────────────

From: "Thea" <thea.spann133@ggm.edu>
To: "Smith" <anovak@strongwomanstory.org>
Subject:

yeah   ok   you go think that   but hes not coming to my wedding

t

───────────────

From: lnovak@metrognome.net.au
To: "Smith" <anovak@strongwomanstory.org>
Subject: Flying along

Your friend Thea is quite brilliant though perhaps a little spacey. Does all her email have that robot look? Never mind—I'm very grateful. I'm flying along now.

You know I actually assumed—I was a little cautious in actually asserting it—that this was probably a forgery, either from back then, or from now—probably now, the story of how it was preserved was so unlikely. But now I don't think so. I think I'd know, which is maybe pride on my part, if I heard his voice, or his *mind,* and I really think I do. I don't know how to characterize it, really—it's a comic view that also grants authority to feelings of desire, loss, and pain; it ascribes events to Fate without really believing that Fate is anything different from the awful or hilarious muddles brought about by ignorance and coincidence; he mocks, but he almost always smiles, and almost never hates. *Nil alienum humani*—he thought nothing humans could do or desire was alien to him, though he was both honorable and generous, and you can hear that too in this. I'm sure.

The punctuation question is interesting. Should I give it the punctuation I think it might have had? Or modern standard punctuation? Byron was himself a careless punctuator, and more than once in his letters asks John Murray his publisher to have a manuscript "pointed," or punctuated. Printers in those days could all punctuate. Imagine. Now hardly anybody can.

L

———————————————

From: "Smith" <anovak@strongwomanstory.org>
To: lnovak@metrognome.net.au
Subject: RE:Flying along

Not a forgery!! I'm glad you're sure, but we've got to do all the tests still, right? I know that now you can certify whether a piece is by an author by computer analysis of the vocabulary.

You make him sound so nice. I wonder if you *identify*. I mean how could you not, you couldn't have studied him so long.

————————————

From: lnovak@metrognome.net.au
To: "Smith" <anovak@strongwomanstory.org>
Subject: Identify

I don't know what you mean exactly by "identifying." Do you suppose I think he was like me, or I am like him, and that's why I'm drawn to him? It's not so. I'm not very much like him. If we were to meet, in hell or wherever, I would not say, *You know, you and I are a lot alike.* No—we're not alike, though I confess I like him. It's more that—for reasons I can't exactly state—I can apprehend him as a human person, and in that apprehension understand myself as human. I can't do that with Shelley, or Franklin Roosevelt, or Ted Williams, or Edgar Rice Burroughs, or Robert Flaherty, or most other people I've admired and loved and strained to understand. But Byron, yes. Byron's humanity is open to me, and through it I see my own—as you can with your best friends, whom you would never confuse with yourself ("identify") but whose souls are open—not to everyone, but to you.

Watch out for that computer analysis thing. It recently certified a couple of anonymous poems as by Shakespeare, even though any real reader/friend of Shakespeare could tell in an instant they weren't his.

L

————————————

From: "Smith" <anovak@strongwomanstory.org>
To: lnovak@metrognome.net.au
Subject: RE:Identify

Lee—I'm thinking of you sitting up and struggling with those weird pages—let's split the job—tell me how far you've got, and I'll figure out where I can start—heck I've got all night and all I do then is sleep. And send me pages as you finish them—I can't wait till you're all done to start reading—I almost started in on it myself till I thought, no stupid—so that's why I'm sending this letter. I don't even know why I care so much. I think of Ada encoding it all, hiding it. Enciphering I mean (that's what Thea says it is).

S

———————————

From: lnovak@metrognome.net.au
To: "Smith" <anovak@strongwomanstory.org>
Subject:

No I will not share. I want it all to myself, and I am not struggling. Your job is a different one: you have to find out what Ada did, and how she thought about it, and where this thing was for all those years, and (by the way) who the guy is who sold it to you and what's become of *him.* And you have your Strong Women still to do, right? You can't lose your job over this.

My god do you know what I sound like here? A *parent.* I seem to have just sort of blacked out for a minute, and when I came to it was all written there. I ask your forgiveness. I have no right, and no desire. On the other hand it's true, you know, and good advice . . .

I tried at first working with it as a computer file but it turns out actually to be easiest to just copy it out with pen and paper. So I will end up with a *manuscript* or what the Victorians called a Fair Copy. Weird. I am beginning to see how Ada's notes go with the text. The fact that it is coming to be out of this scrambled matrix before my eyes—and that I am doing it on your behalf as well as

his and hers—makes me feel almost as she might have, only backward, if you see what I mean—I'm sure you do.

Love

Lee

————————————

From: lnovak@metrognome.net.au
To: "Smith" <anovak@strongwomanstory.org>
Subject: 100

Hooray. I'm sending an attachment—this is a first—with nearly
100 pages of text I've reset and roughly punctuated. I'm sure that
Byron—as he did in his letters—used mostly the all-purpose
dash—which all the writers of his period did—maybe they
thought it went with their impulsive, spontaneous natures—they
were being, literally, dashing. I've gone through a few boxes
already——have to buy more—

We'll lose things in the process. Byron had his own way of capital-
izing words seemingly at random, though when I read his letters I
seem to sense why he does it when he does—for emphasis, or to
express a kind of rank the word possesses for him in the thought.
That's all gone and can't be re-created. Capitalization was going
out as Byron wrote; a hundred or even fifty years before the rule
was, capitalize all nouns, but he wouldn't want us to do that.

Lee

Attach: Byron1.wpd
————————————————

————————————

From: "Smith" <anovak@strongwomanstory.org>
To: lnovak@metrognome.net.au
Subject: RE:100

Okay. I read what you sent. Thanks. I didn't know what to expect but I don't think it was this, exactly. I haven't read all the poetry (it's tough, it's tough, I can never decide if I'm more bored or more pissed off) but shouldn't this novel we've got be, I don't know, a little more satanic? I thought there would be more sex, for one thing, with all kinds of people. Didn't he like de Sade? Sex and death? Where's all that stuff? I keep thinking the thing can't be real because it's not like what I thought it would be.

———————————

From: lnovak@metrognome.net.au
To: "Smith" <anovak@strongwomanstory.org>
Subject: Satanic

Actually I'm not surprised. There's a lot of misunderstanding here. A lot of it arose at the time, in Byron's lifetime I mean, and was doubled or tripled by later misunderstandings of those mis-understandings (and then the Annabella spin machine). There's actually not a lot of wild or violent or miscellaneous sex in Byron's poetry. Juan in *Don Juan* has relations with four or five women in the course of hundreds of pages, and *they* seduce *him.* In the Ori-ental tales (where I imagine you are fuming or nodding just now) sex is singular and intense and purified by love, as in all Romantic poetry: disappointed or misunderstood lover/heroes go off and commit nameless crimes or lead lives of nonspecific sin, but never forget their true loves. *Beppo* and *Juan* are casual about sex, adul-tery, etc., but not satanic or Sadean: the opposite of compulsive.

The confusion arises because in his time Byron was seen as shocking because he was *irreverent:* he mocked religion and the religious establishment, made fun of heaven and the after-life, sneered at the king, willingly voted in favor of hell over servi-tude, etc., etc. So he's a mocker, and then he was fabulously attractive, and women fell for him continuously—and so, QED, he must have been raping and swiving and seducing constantly.

Then there was the Separation, and all the rumors that swirled around it. Byron was deeply unhappy in his marriage—he

knew he'd made a big mistake, that he'd talked himself into believing that he loved or *could* love Annabella, and found he
couldn't, and he blamed her (I think) for the end of his relations
with his half sister—even though he'd married her in large part
for that reason, to put a stop to that affair. So he *was* cruel and
awful to her, though all we have is her account, largely, of what he
said, and what he *meant*. She found a bottle of laudanum and a
copy of de Sade's *Justine* among his things, the snoop, and that
did it for her. She told her lawyers and advisers, of whom she had
many, that she believed Byron might be insane, and if he was, then
she felt obliged to stay with him and nurse him—but they convinced her (or she pressed them to convince her) that he wasn't insane, and therefore he must be wicked, so she had to leave him. So
there were the rumors of incest around him, and rumors of madness too. One of her lawyers, a person named Henry Brougham,
spread the tale that the real reason for the separation was "too
horrid to mention," by which he meant what? I don't know, but it
certainly left the imagination free to ponder.

Then there were the stories of what he did abroad, particu-
larly in Venice, where he did have a lot of lovers, several of them
married, a lot of them pros or semipros. He gave the number as
200 at one point, but he liked to exaggerate almost everything
about himself, his faults and his successes and his excesses. I
think (this is personal observation, that is observation of myself
and my own observation of others) that men are at their horniest
and most intense about sex in their early 30s, which Byron was
then. But remember he thereupon fell in love, and became a *cavalier servente,* and was, apparently, domestic and faithful the rest
of his life—except for one last Grecian boy who never returned his
feelings.

I actually think of him not as seducer or (certainly) rapist
but more often as object of seduction. I mean Paul McCartney
and John Lennon surely had a lot of sex when young, and for
the same reasons as Byron, but you don't think of them as
satyrs. They just had a lot of girls who wanted them. And older
women. It was like that. Or even like Elvis, a kind of faintly

femmy or passive object of adoration—Elvis liked his buddies, and he liked girls too, but mostly for cuddling, it seems. I have a paperback anthology of Byron's poems here that I found in the airport bookstore—how weird what you find in those, especially in faraway airports—and the introduction, by a poet named Tom Disch, makes the suggestion that in his Oriental tales and early success and the way women (and men) felt about him, he most resembles Valentino. I think that's just right. Valentino's great ability was the way he could suggest being *overwhelmed by feeling,* erotic feeling above all, and it might make him do bad things, but the women were swept away by the feelings they seemed to cause in him, and they went along gladly. Like that.

It might be (you know I keep expecting this computer to forbid me to go on and on like this, but it's patient, don't know about the reader) that Byron was one of those men who seemed to attach all their need for warmth and comfort and physical reassurance to sex. It happens. To men who grow up without mothers, or maybe whose mothers are very intense, I don't know. It's as though all the delight we all take in contact, in hugs and touches and being held, the delight children and parents take in each other that way, all goes into sex. I think that when it does, the person (I'm speaking generally here, or objectively, you see) might be a pretty generous and unhurtful lover, just a constant and continuous one. And maybe such a person might sometimes pick some oddly assorted partners, or allow himself—or herself too, I don't know, surely the condition applies to women, it would, wouldn't it?—to be picked by some very odd or very wrong ones, or by any, or almost all.

I've never said these things to anyone. Actually I've never said them to myself. I hope you're still reading. I kind of hope. I mean I want to go on talking to you, and to hear you too. In my mind's ear.

More, more to come, more that's relevant or at least concrete.

Lee

──────────────

From: lnovak@metrognome.net.au
To: "Smith" <anovak@strongwomanstory.org>
Subject:

A couple of further notes on sex (sorry).

At least one author recently asserted that for all the scandal
and wild carryings-on, assignations and plans to run off together and the page outfits etc. etc., it might be that Byron and
Caroline Lamb never actually "consummated" as they say. She
really didn't like sex much, apparently. Said her husband had
brutalized her and turned her off for good. Wonder if she was
gay, despite B. Well I don't know, and neither finally does anybody.

   And Augusta, half sister. What Byron liked best about Augusta was that he could with her revert to a kind of childhood:
they laughed together a lot and talked and joked in a silly way that
Lady B. could never enter into. Chums. You know I think that Byron had all the prejudices about women that men of his time had,
and he died too soon to find out that he didn't believe them, and
never had.

Lee

──────────────

From: "Smith" <anovak@strongwomanstory.org>
To: lnovak@metrognome.net.au
Subject:

So do you mean he and Augusta never did anything? I mean never
had sex? It's not what I read.

S

──────────────

From: lnovak@metrognome.net.au
To: "Smith" <anovak@strongwomanstory.org>
Subject:

No. They had sex, though probably Lady Byron was wrong about how much. Augusta apparently stopped it before B. got married. Lady B. thought that one of Augusta's children was Byron's but that's unlikely—more of her fascination with his sins. Ada seems to have believed it too—convinced by, or at least agreeing with, her mother. This child (Medora Leigh) was quasi-adopted by Lady Byron when she ran away from her mother's house, and Lady B.'s attempts to use her as evidence against Byron and Augusta were matched by Medora's equally ferocious attempts to get money out of Lady B. Awful person.

It was impossible in their day not to regard what Augusta and Byron had done as a great sin—mostly a sin of *his*. Now, of course, it's impossible not to regard it as a crime, or a wrong (*abuse*) that he committed against her. Augusta, under Lady B.'s later tutelage, came to regard it as a nearly unforgivable sin herself, one that *she* had committed, though she could never go along with Lady B.'s conviction that in her degradation and vice she had deliberately destroyed the Byron marriage, which is an untenable claim anyway. I think Byron considered that he had committed a sin, but not that he had done a wrong—which made him defy the power that named it a sin—for how could something really be a sin that wasn't a wrong done to somebody? What I think is—and I want you to know that I say this in full consciousness of its unacceptability now, especially coming from me—that it probably wasn't a sin OR a crime, however unfortunate it turned out to be for everyone.

Lee

———————————

From: "Smith" <anovak@strongwomanstory.org>
To: lnovak@metrognome.net.au
Subject: My name

Did you write me a while back saying that before I was born you wanted to name me Haidée? After the pirate's daughter in *Don Juan*? Gee. I was glancing through *Don Juan*—that's the one you think is his best, right? Maybe you forgot that in the poem Haidée is killed by her father, when he finds out that she's married Juan. Or did you not care?

S

————————

From: lnovak@metrognome.net.au
To: "Smith" <anovak@strongwomanstory.org>
Subject: RE:My name

My dear—

Read it again. You misunderstood what happens at the end of that canto. Haidée dies, but not because her father kills her. She dies of what used to be called a burst blood vessel, brought on by seeing her father's henchmen wound (not kill, of course) Juan. Haidée (though she's all girl, in all the ways girls were conceived of by English men in 1820) is obviously a person Byron regards with the greatest affection. I am always moved by her death, and especially the death of her unborn child: *closed its little being without light.* Authors can feel very sorry about the characters the plot or story says they must do away with. Byron more than once says it—he even says it in this book we've got. You'll see.

But I don't want to confront you on this. Suppose I say it was a little careless and unfeeling of me to think of naming you for someone who dies young and in extremities. (A lot of saints' names have the same drawback, of course.) I was a lot younger then—not a lot older than you are now.

L

From: "Smith" <anovak@strongwomanstory.org>
To: lnovak@metrognome.net.au
Subject: RE:Re:My name

So are we supposing this or are you actually saying it?

Never mind

Anyway you're right, I'm wrong about Haidée. Reading too fast, I
guess. I get embarrassed sometimes at it—as though I'm stuck in a
locker room or somewhere with a guy, who's not a bad guy at all,
but I'm stuck and he remains a guy. I admit I did stay up late to
see what happens. I liked this:

> But words are things, and a small drop of ink,
>   Falling like dew, upon a thought, produces
> That which makes thousands, perhaps millions, think;
>   'Tis strange, the shortest letter which man uses
> Instead of speech, may form a lasting link
>   Of ages; to what straits old Time reduces
> Frail man, when paper—even a rag like this,
> Survives himself, his tomb, and all that's his.

Smith

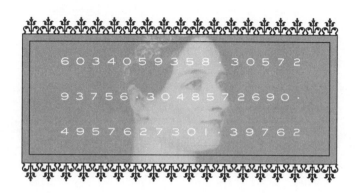

6 0 3 4 0 5 9 3 5 8 · 3 0 5 7 2

9 3 7 5 6 · 3 0 4 8 5 7 2 6 9 0 ·

4 9 5 7 6 2 7 3 0 1 · 3 9 7 6 2

In which the path is trod that

may not be retraced

W E MAY THINK THAT a great gulph is fixed between Comedy and Tragedy, yet it is but a matter of *outcome* that distinguishes them—for may not Othello have seen through the shifts and impostures of mad Iago soon enough, and set a counter-trap for *him,* as Malvolio is trapped in *12th Night,* all ending in laughter, and the villain's discomfiture? Likewise, without the machinations of the Duke, *Measure for Measure* must end in as terrible a doom as *Romeo & Juliet*— the Friar of *that* play being given to comic inventions involving letters and sleeping-draughts that might have just as well succeeded! But the Bard—however long of two minds he remains—at length decides whether his Sock or Buskin be on, and thenceforward is compell'd to declaim & brood, or to laugh and be witty. Imagine then that *we* live in a Play, one filled with such engines as *his* are—bed tricks, and counterfeits, and tyrannical fathers, and doubled lovers—shall we believe ourselves in a Tragedy, or a Comedy? Shall we jest, pun, and believe Love to be all-conquering, however rough his course may run? Or shall we talk of 'the slings and arrows of outrageous Fortune', and think ourselves but 'as flies to wanton boys'?

Thus far, as regards the fates of Ali, and Catherine, and the child to be born something too soon to them, we know not *what* we ought to think—for the Author has not finally decided—he but taps his lip with his pen's end, and contemplates the melting scene outside his window—the thermometer shows eighty degrees, Fahrenheit—anon he considers a Brandy, or perhaps a *limonata,* or a segar—and if he be unable to choose among *those,* how is he to decide if his be a Comedy of Errors, or a Tragedy of Fate—or the one, with the other's conclusion?

The wedding that, as soon as was convenient, was to join the two young people, was not to be a great or a public affair, but was instead to be conducted with but the few who must needs attend— a Parent or two upon the one hand, rather more grave than gay, and upon orphan'd Ali's side, the Honourable Peter Piper as groomsman, to hand him the Ring, and shore him up, at need. A special licence having been obtained, with the help of a Bishop in collusion with a Barrister (Mr Wigmore Bland), the ceremony took place in a suitably remote house of the Delaunays, a gaunt grey place above a rocky shore, whereon the cold sea beat uncon- soled—and yet somehow the fashionable papers in faraway Lon- don learned all its Particulars, the dress of the Bride, the fortune of the Groom, the wise words spoken by the man of Religion there attending, and would soon report these in absorbing detail. Ali for his part suffer'd on that morning the common anxieties of a man about to be a husband—but with some especial additions quite uncommon. 'You appear to have lost a dear friend,' spoke the Ho- nourable, upon seeing Ali appear in his blue coat, 'and not as though you gained today your dearest.' 'I would that we might be wedded and married in an instant,' whispered Ali, 'as people are electrified in company, by holding the same chain—I fear I shall not be suitably *transformed* else.' 'Depend upon it,' said the Honourable, whilst aiding Ali's nerveless hands to don white gloves, 'the lady shall be the agent of all needful transformation; I have seen the miracle worked a thousand times.' 'You assert this, yet have not taken the step yourself.' 'Ah well—perhaps there is no hope for me—I have found too much entertainment in the marriages of others—as the Methodist preacher admonished his hearers, on perceiving a profane merriment among them, *No hopes for them as laughs.* Shall we go in?'

So with Pledge and Ring do Pantomimes end, and lovers are returned again into their own skins, and the confusions of Venus resolved—and yet in life we know it to be no ending—only a further Transformation, into more trials for all. At eve, having signed the Parchment, and partaken of a Repast, the Bride and her Groom departed in Ali's coach for a month of Solitude—snow was upon the way, and the iron clouds hung close enough to touch. Silence too, as of a Winter's day, obtained within the Coach and between the Couple—and not only because the Bride, in an extremity of propriety (so it seemed to her Husband), had ordered her Maid into the coach with them, rather than on the seat above. What were their thoughts, who had wed so, under such circumstances? Might not silence be best, when all the thoughts we have are of what *might* have been—of what we might have done, and did not do—or *did,* and should not have done—that led to *here,* where we had not thought to be? And yet—no matter where they begun—all now lies before them, as on every morn until the last it does, and (it was indeed the thought of each, though unformed in either) they might still be happy—quite happy—as happy as if they had never wed at all.

'If we have erred,' at length said Ali—and he said it with a sound intended for a merry laugh—'I hope you will not hate me. I make promise I will not!'

'With all my heart I will love you,' said she, with a calm *certainty* that any new Husband might be reassured to hear, but which only caused Ali to retire again into silence—for he could think only how his own heart is divided, and that, for her *all,* he can not *give* all— and knows not if *he* or *she* be the cause of that.

Not soon enough did they reach that hall of the Delaunays set aside for them, where their wedded life was to commence. Faithful servants welcomed them with smiles, and had warmed the place as well as it could be warmed, and prepared a chamber for the couple, and laid a suitable supper—indeed Ali and Catherine were quite fussed over, as though they might be overcome with Joy, and unable to act—Ali whispered to her that he wondered if paper crowns were to be brought out, and a song sung in their honour—at which Catherine laughed—she *laughed,* as she had not in all the time that had pass'd with them for courtship. Yet when all the house was still, and retirement unavoidable, they could not but fall again into a silence—for they seemed each as strange to the other as two beings both in human skins could well be, notwithstanding they considered that they *knew each other* in all the senses which may apply to that word *know*—and yet (it may be stated) in fact they knew *not*—and knew not that they knew not. Indeed it was a question, whether they should share a bed—the Bride being in that condition before described, and she having had from learned female relations the strongest warning that this *delicate* condition must on no account be endanger'd—but at length, like two children afraid of the dark, they crept together within the crimson Curtains of the bed denominated *theirs,* well bundled, and—and here I must let fall a Curtain too.

3

In the midnight tho'—awakened she knows not how—Catherine finds herself alone in that bed—yet without, in the room, the Fire has been stirred, and a *shape* moves against the glow of it, which she sees through the bed-hangings—a shape that grows larger, approaching— and then the curtain is pulled roughly aside, and she gasps in horror—before her stands her Husband, in a dressing gown—glaring as in rage, yet seeming not to see—and in his hand a pistol!

'My Lord—what do you do?'—Only this could she think to say—and he, as though he had been unaware another soul was near, started, and looked on her amazed—and she knew that she had *awakened him from sleep* even at that moment—and her 'fell of hair' rose in uncanny dread.

'I heard a sound,' said he. 'I knew not what—I rose—'
'Do you know me?'
'Catherine! How should I not?'

'I beg you—think that I am with child—with *your* child—do not shock this heart, that not one but *two* suffer for it—perhaps irrevocably—I beg you have a little kindness—for your Child if not for me!'

'Calm—calm yourself,' said he, and uncock'd and laid down the pistol. 'Look—there is no danger—I was perhaps foolish to think so—I know not what it was.'

'Come back to bed, then—'tis deep in the night.'

'Yes.'

'Pray with me—'twill soothe us both.'

And so he did—or listened, at the least, to *her* prayers—and yet when he was again within the bed-clothes, his Cap on his head, and his Cheek against the Pillow—still his eyes closed not, from wonder. For in truth, he had heard no sound—he knew not *why* he had left his bed, dressed, or armed himself—only that it was for reasons appertaining to *another realm,* where he had been at other tasks—yet that was all gone—realm, tasks, self, and all—run away from him like water from a sieve—and waking he had not been able to account for himself to his wife, except to say *I heard a sound,* when there was none!

NO SOONER HAD THEIR *treaclemoon* closed, and the Lord and his Lady returned to London, than they were called upon in their new Lodgings by Lawyer Wigmore Bland. No less smiling than ever, no less delighted with himself and the world that lay about him to bustle in, he brought news that, while the prospects remained sunny for Ali's success (which would be the great Barrister's as well) in breaking the entailment of the Abbey, it now appeared that more months and years must fly away before those parchments were signed and sealed.

'I know not how it may be,' said Mr Bland—and now his face seem'd to dim, as when a scarf of palest cloud dims the Sun—'but new presentments have been delivered to the Courts involved, bringing in question your sole claim upon the lands and incomes to which, by your Title, attach to you—asserting that *other claimants* live, and that proofs of this will be forthcoming in the course of time—which assertions the Courts concerned may not ignore, however inconsiderable they prove to be.'

'What!' exclaim'd his Client. 'What other claimants? Who has made these presentments, as you name them?'

'They have been received from one John Factotum, without address given, in the name of—'

'In whose name?'

'Lord Sane's. Young Sir! Believe me that whatever frauds or impositions the fellow intends, they will not succeed—one by one they shall be answered, and spurned as worthless!'

Ali begged to know what, till then, he was to live upon, and how he might make provision for Wife & Child, and hold off his Creditors. Mr Bland averred that he might live quite long upon Air, though not forever—he admitted, that it would be a close-run thing, between Ali's case in Chancery, and his Creditors' impatience.

For Ali's Creditors had themselves acquired Counsel, not of that generous and optimistic sort that Mr Bland manifested, but—as Ali would soon have reason to perceive them—more resembling a pack of vicious curs, snarling for blood—fang'd, iron-clawed, stony-hearted! These produced, in not too long a time, a Bailiff, come to attach the young Husband's goods, and to prevent his removing them, or aught else of value upon which the said Pack might gnaw. The Bailiff posted upon Ali's door the Notice of his right to possess the house, and, like a German sprite, make mischief everywhere; he entered in at the door, despite the attempts of the valet and the cook to prevent him—he took his seat upon a chair in the Hall, and laid his ragged staff upon his lap, and put his feet apart—nor did he see fit to remove from his head a hat which he wore cock'd, as insolent as his grin. Enough in himself to drive a young man mad, who must pass by him at every egress, and upon every return to his house—to see and to *smell* him there, the Minos of his future life—yet he was not the figure that Ali most feared. *That* was the one who appear'd only in the

Glass he looked into—and *that* one he knew not how he might contend with!

'Have I in aught offended?' asked his wife, seeing him at the limits of his temper after a day's black silence. 'Tell me.'

'*You offended?*' Ali replied hotly. 'Why, think you that your offence is all that could cause a man to fall silent? *You* know what burden has been placed upon me. Do you not see it, feel it? Do you not see me struggle to lift and bear it, with all my strength? Allow me at least to show, in my actions, now and then, some *strain* in this—allow that I may be curt, and even harsh—I mean not to be so—and be patient.'

'I will do all that I can,' said she with greatest care, 'to be what *you wish* me to be.'

Such an answer—such a *calculation*—was then to Ali's soul as those chemicals we see, an acid and an alkali, seeming bland and plain, that when toss'd together immediately commence to foam and reek and overflow their vessels. He could say nothing—could not upbraid her for *patience* and *willingness*—yet he felt himself diminished, and affronted—in short, a desperate man, with no name for his desperation. Each day, with the *unspoken* yet unforgiving reproach of his Wife, couch'd in gentle remonstrance—the Bailiff sitting at the door like an Idol of stone, yet with a cold eye that missed nothing—his own sensation of being entirely in the wrong, and yet unable to act otherwise—Ali felt caught betwixt Fire and Ice, and unable to guess what he might do next—a sensation so terrifying to his soul that, casting at Catherine a look of horrid rage—which he could, with a strange Pity, observe reflected in her countenance— he would fling himself past the stolid Bailiff and out the door.

In that ill-starred house in the fullness of time was Catherine, Lady Sane, brought to bed of a Daughter, surrounded by aged and experienced female relatives—three in number, as they must be, who gather upon such occasions, to pronounce the Fate of a child, and cut the Cord that has bound it to its mother till it be sent out 'in this harsh world to draw its breath in pain'—as this infant was, with an initial *cry* that could be heard in the kitchens below and in the drawing-room where Ali paced and brooded, as all prospective fathers ought. Yet he was *not* like all other fathers, and his feelings

4

5

upon that night, or morning (for the last stars had faded, and the familiar sounds of carriages upon the street without could be heard, and the cries of early vendors, when the news came to him), were all at war within his breast. Then he went up, and at the door of the room where his wife lay, he stopt—unable for a long time to step within—seeing the strange wonder of the child in her arms, so infinitesimal, a molecule, an atom of life—the child he could not own as *his,* yet could not deny or spurn.

6

'Is it—healthy?' asked he, still outside the room.

'Ali,' spoke Catherine—she seemed as *deflated* and worn away as though God had taken flesh and blood from her to make the child—which indeed He had—and for a moment he felt a great pity—or love—that took him by surprise—so that he still might not come in. 'Ali,' whispered Catherine again. 'Will you not come to see it—will you not?' And thereupon he did.

The name they chose for her was Una: for Ali feared she would be always singular, and alone. Yet she was strong, and fat, and wailed mightily, as though for *good reason*—for her House was disordered, tho' she knew it not—and a flaw had grown between her parents that would soon be past mending.

On a certain night, having left his house to find some distraction in places where Distraction is thought to reign—with Dissipation on her right hand and Oblivion on the left—he went from Theatre to Club, from dice to cards, seeking surcease from thought, passing among the madding crowd, yet remaining an observer more than a participant.

'Waiter,' he heard one Exquisite weakly cry at the supper-table, 'bring me a Madeira negus, and a Jelly—and rub my plate with a challot.' At which a rough fellow nearby him at the table cried to the same waiter—'Waiter! Bring *me* a glass of good strong grog—and rub my arse with a Brickbat!'

A Female in fury rose at the far end of the table, and look'd Basilisk-like upon a grinning fellow who had offended her. 'You darest not say so—you *would* not, if I were a *man*! Why, I am of a mind to pull on breetches, and demand satisfaction!' 'If you do so,' says the fellow, 'I shall pull *off mine,* and see that you receive it!'

Passing from the supper-room to other precincts where other pleasures might be called for, he came upon a group of gentlemen studying a certain paper, who when they saw Ali approach, looked guiltily, and put away what they studied.

'Why, what have you there?' he asked them without preamble, yet smiling upon them. 'It seems that it may concern myself.'

'Indeed it may, my Lord,' said one of these, a fellow who acted sometimes as Banker for those at play within. 'I have an *instrument* which by rights it is not possible I may possess. I must tell you, I know the hand, and am certain it is *his*—surely it is not your Lord-ship's.'

'I know not what you mean,' Ali said, and smiled no more. 'Whose instrument? What is it to me?'

'In truth I saw not the man who made it,' said the Banker. 'A friend—better say an acquaintance—having received from a Gamester at table a cheque for his losses, and being himself in need of the ready, sold the cheque to me, at a certain discount—and here it is.'

The paper he then produced stated that the bearer was to be paid by a bank in Lombard Street a certain amount, and it was signed with a bold hand *SANE,* the paper then being folded and sealed—and on the broken seal, spread like a gout of blood, Ali saw stamped the *sign of his father's ring*—the Σ—the same sign that long ago, in the hills of Albania, had been cut into his own arm, to mark him as his father's son! 'It is his,' Ali said—and dropt the thing upon the table as though it were a missive from the Beyond, where, if the most approved Sermons fable not, his father now dwelt in uncomfortable circumstances.

'And yet observe the date—the thing was executed by him but a few days ago,' said the Banker, in a hollow tone, and making no move to pick up the paper.

'I knew the man,' said another at the table, red-cheeked with drink, and not afraid of revenants, it seemed. 'It was oft his way, so to settle a debt, upon a scrap of foolscap.'

'He is dead,' said Ali, in a tone that brooked no objection.

'Then he is up to his old tricks, despite that condition,' said the jolly fellow. 'Still at play, and still taking losses.'

'And upon what,' asked another reveller of the Banker, 'will you spend this spectre's money? Upon a long-dead mutton-chop, perhaps—or the ghosts of whores? Or upon *spirituous* liquors?'

'Ah!' said his red-faced *chum,* 'but there ain't any money to spend.'

'That is the final proof that his hand is in it,' said the Banker, an uncanny fear upon his features. 'For today *the bank have dishonoured the cheque*! How like him, eh? What say you?'

Ali drew out his own notecase, and gave the Banker a few pounds for the bad cheque, which the Banker was glad enough to part with—for more than one reason, it seemed, though his Poins and his Bardolph mock'd him for his scruples. Merely a desperate scheme—so Ali told himself—a money-cadging scheme—a trick played by a *living* rogue, and not a *dead* one. At his next opportunity Ali crushed the vile paper in his hands and gave it to the Fire—yet hearing, as it burned away, a whisper—*'I cannot die!'*

*U*SELESS IT IS TO GO to the Law, if there be no-one to Prosecute—no-one to confront—even though the no-one continues to offend! Ali on another night overhears one say that a certain Sane has won largely at Hazard—which Ali has never play'd; he learns by rumour that a tilbury very like the former Lord's was seen careening upon the Brighton road, the driver 'tooling the ribbons' and horse-whipping the turnpike-men for sport as he tore by, and vanish'd. Then, on passing through the crowded rooms of his Club in St James's Place, amid the voices lifted in *repartee* and triumph (despair too), Ali hears—it rakes his soul—the very *voice of his Father*—unmistakeable the harsh grinding of it, like shingle drawn down by a cold sea wave—and he searches through the crowd in a passion, flinging open the doors of private chambers— yet finds no-one—and so desists, feeling all eyes upon him, and his Heat turn to freezing Fear—for surely he was deluded, it was not *he*—could not be—not Sane!

At the Members' desk, he asks for pen and ink, and writes out a Note:

> TO HIM POSING AS LORD SANE—Will he be so good as to reply to the Undersigned, or give the holder Notice, where and when he may be met by one demanding Satisfaction for his impositions upon unsuspecting persons, and the false presentments he has made in a Name he does not own—the time and place being at his Pleasure.—SANE

This he doubles, and seals—addresses with the name of one not among the Living—unless *himself* be understood to be the one named—and the challenge therefore addressed to *himself.* To the wondering Clerk, he directs that the letter be given to the first claimant, and departs.

The Honourable agrees with alacrity, in the event of this challenge being taken up, to act as his Second,—the duties of which office he takes with the greatest gravity, viz., the duty to soothe and reconcile the principals if possible—the duty to consult with the seconds on the opposing part, and to agree as to a Ground, which should be free of obstacles, outside the Law's immediate purview, with a good light, &c.—the enlisting of a Surgeon—the preparations for Flight, should the encounter end in a fatality—and all other concerns small and large attendant upon an affair of Honour. But these are moot, the party offering the offence appearing not—nor did any one come forward as Second, in response to the proffered challenge.

'It is,' Mr Piper averred, 'quite irregular! I cannot imagine that good can come of it—I tremble at the issue, 'pon my soul!'

Tho' none took up the note he had deposited, Ali on a day not long after found awaiting him at his apartments a letter, whose cover bore no sign of its origins, and which contained this response:

> TO LORD SANE—the compliments of LORD SANE, who proposes that he meet you upon the Ides of this month, in the evening at about eight on the clock—not for your satisfac-

tion, for he considers that he owes you none, but for his own, and *perhaps* for your Enlightenment. The choice of weapons is of no interest to him, and is left to your preference.

To this note was affixed the name of a place of poor repute, in a desolate district, where commonly such transactions are carried on, that the Law may not interfere; and it bore no signature.

'This is worse than before!' cried the Honourable. 'It is quite impossible to fight a duel so late in the evening—with night coming on—in such a place—I think we are mocked, or illuded—I insist no answer be made, and that you not appear in the matter at all!'

'But I will,' said Ali. 'I must know, who it is that thus pursues me—if he be a *man,* or—or what indeed he is.'

'If he be a *man?*' quoth the Honourable. 'Do you expect a sprite? Or a girl?'

'I meant only, a *man of Honour,*' Ali said quietly—knowing not, indeed, just what he meant. 'I will go to this place, at this time; I should be glad of your company, but if you decline, from whatever just scruples, I shall entirely understand.'

'What! Not accompany you! Not likely!' said the Honourable. 'When who knows what devilish tricks are afoot! Do not you stir abroad without me—I should certainly take it ill, if you did.'

Upon the appointed evening, then, Ali ordered his coach, and he and Mr Peter Piper (who carried a case of Pistols, a lamp, and a portmanteau of needful things in the event of flight) were driven to the place. The time was eight on the clock, as stated; the place deserted, save for a fellow loitering there, alone, smoking a segar, a broad hat drawn low over his face. The quarter of an hour having passed and no-one else appearing, the Honourable climbed from his coach, and called to the smoker.

'Who are you, Sir?' demanded he. 'Are you he whom we have come to meet?'

'I may be—it much depends upon whom you came to meet.'

'Where is your principal?'

'He has declined to appear. He wishes now to withdraw his earlier impertinences, for the offence of which he makes apology. He hopes this will be acceptable, and declares you shall hear no word from him further.'

'You have come to tell us this?'

'I am his messenger.'

'This is irregular,' said the Honourable. 'I declare upon my word it is.'

The man made no reply, unless the sudden glow of his segar in the darkness might be one—it seemed, as he lifted his hand, that he took a glowing coal from out his mouth, and held it before him till it cooled—a trick of the light in that shadowed place—and then he turned to go. Ali then stept from the coach. 'You, Fellow!' cried he. 'I know you not, but I shall not withdraw my challenge, and you may answer it if *he* will not!'

'I!' said the fellow. 'Why, I am *no-one,* and no fit object for your Lordship's spleen.'

'I demanded satisfaction,' Ali said. 'His communication to me denied me that, most impertinently, but promised enlightenment. I desire an Explanation, of all that he has done.'

'Ah!' said the other. '*Explanations* be dear now-a-days, and may not be wanted when they can be had.' Then he tossed down upon the stones the segar he smoked, where it scattered red sparks at his feet. 'The matter is nothing to me. I have delivered my message, and have done—I bid you good-night!'

'Wait!' cried Ali, and made to follow, whereupon Mr Piper, who was somewhat encumbered by his case of Pistols, tugged Ali's sleeve, and whispered to him that 'He should not go with this fellow, for a trap may have been laid!', at which Ali removed his friend's restraining hand, and went after the man—down the dark roadway—the one ahead quick as an elf, despite a halt in his gait— to where a small fire burned in a cairn, and one or two low fellows warmed themselves. From among them at the hatted man's approach there arose a large and burly carl, who lifted a head—no, 'twas a *muzzle!*—and Ali saw the two, his Mocker and the Mocker's Beast, greet one another with every mark of friendship, as the others laughed—then, taking the chain around the bear's neck, the man went off with him into the fog—where Ali would not follow.

PON HIS ARRIVAL once again at his own house (but it was not *his,* nor were the things, the spoons and sophas, the fire-dogs and salt-cellars, his) Ali found that his wife had decided upon a visit to her family home—and was filling trunks and directing servants, with the aid of the three Ladies in black who seemed ever in attendance upon her—that is, her Mother, her childhood Governess, and one of those *ambiguous* Relations without whose gimlet eye and serpent tongue family life cannot be conducted, or adequately spoiled.

'Upon the morrow we set out,' said she, and he noted the flush upon the heights of her cheek, and the eye too bright. 'The country air will be good for Una. And for me.'

'Perhaps you are right,' said Ali coldly. 'You ought not to be in the same house with one such as I am.'

'What! Why do you speak so? I said nothing against yourself!'

'You need not *say.*' Before him, the fire was dying away in the grate—it seemed suddenly, and madly, to Ali that his own life would perish with it—Why had no-one attended to it? Had his servants fled? He grasped the poker, and turned again to face his wife. 'I say you *need not*—your feelings are plain—yet I may demand you *do* say—or else—'

'Will you kill me?' said Catherine, and clutch'd at her throat. 'I will not believe you would do me harm.'

He saw in her face an alarm that astonished him—and which then moved him to a rage beyond reason, a rage that unreasonably grew as her alarm did. 'What! Why think you I would not? Is it not bruited everywhere that I *killed my own Father*? Am I not the scion of a line of madmen and villains? Did I not in a sleep-walking state dishonour you? Why should I stint at your murder?'

'Speak not so wildly—they will hear—I beg you!'

'*They!* Why, let them hear! They have long believed—they have long said—nay, I will speak no more on the topic! Follow after your lady mother—Go where you will. Forgive me. A strange phrenzy was just now upon me—regard it not.'

'I shall not.'

'I am calm again. You are right—it were best you go into the country.'

'Yes.'

'See that you take good care of our child. Send me word of her. And of yourself.'

'I shall do so.'

'It is well—it is well!'

On the morrow, then, they were gone—a coach and a waggon—his infant daughter astonishingly furnished, like Royalty, with more necessities than Ali had before known existed—and at the coach's window he took Catherine's hand, and kissed it—how cold it was!—and stepping back gave signal to the driver. His wife retreated into the coach's seat, and into the furs in which she wrapt herself—and Ali saw her no longer—nor was he ever again to see her more!

For 'now began the tempest to his soul'—and whether he stopt at home, or went abroad—whether he meditated alone, or threw himself into Company—where'er he went, between him and Pleasure, between him and Forgetfulness, fell a Shadow, the shadow of *what* he dared not think—of his own confusion, or of horrid possibilities he would not believe the world contained. As though a beast of supernal cunning tempted him to the hunt, and left its spoor, and its trace, in every place, even let its form be glimpsed as it skipt away, Ali saw—or *thought* he saw—the Ghost that haunted him, his pursued Pursuer, in every street and house, every Crowd and corner. Vain was it for Peter Piper and others of his friends to dismiss his fears—to point out the unreasoning suspicions to which he was subject, and how he *would* put two or three trivial *mysteries* together with one or two innocent *coincidences,* and from them conceive a Plot, or a Nemesis, that was no more material than his own figure in a glass. For it is exactly this that Ali most fears—not that he is *conspired against,* but that he is *mad!* In the low society wherein he mingles, Ali begins to hear, at second and at *third* hand, rumours concerning himself—things he is said to have done, dishonour he is charged with, old tales of his Father that had been forgotten, and of his own History—none of it *all* true, and much of it all false. Who speaks so of him? Do untruths

7

sprout rankly unfathered from foul ground, like toadstools, or is there one who *sponsors* them, and *authors* those that are without basis in Fact? Who? Ali can find no single source, and fears there may be none—that all he hears, or hears *of,* comes only from his own poisoned mind! 'That he beguiled the late Lord when he was in Albania—had relations with him not now to be spoken of—convinced him to adopt him as his *son*—and always with this object in mind, his present Eminence!'—'That the Child born to his Wife was not his—that moreover it was conceived before the Wedding, against all the uses of good Society, where illicit children are properly conceived *after* marriage, not before!'—'That he forced upon his wife certain Enormities brought from the East, and unknown in this land, ruinous to her Health, and her Soul—that when she resisted these he threatened her Life—that the Child of their union was born monstrous, or deformed—that he attempted to *dispatch* it with a pillow before it had taken breath!' At last Ali fixes upon *one* whom he believes responsible for these things—not without some justice, for the fellow has indeed *passed on* the slanders, though he has invented none—a hopeless sot, the son of a sot, yet a gentleman, and loose of speech enough in company that Ali catches him out in circumstances that allow him no denial—he strikes the fellow, challenges him, crying out upon him in such insensate rage even as he button-holds him, his face so close to the young Esquire's, that spittle flies upon him.

8   The young gentleman—let his name be Brougham, I care not, or Black, or White—soon puts forth a pair of Seconds no more capable than himself, who are certain their friend has been grievously insulted—injured—besmirched—and though the Honourable, acting for Ali, this time in form proper, points the way they might go, to make the bad better, and avoid the worst, there is no help for it—Brougham-Black, Esq, and his high-mettled friends blaze on, Ali in his empty house broods and may not be spoken to, and closer draws the appointed Day. Ah! Little recks the common Reader, how it grieves an Author, when—the dictates of Fate being unalterable, once he has *decided* upon them—he must push his Hero to commit an enormity, or even a foolishness—how he longs to warn him, dissuade him, appeal to Reason or to the angel of his

better nature, even as the skirling of his pen propels the poor fel-   9
low onward!

Chill November has come upon the world—the bitter smell of
coal-burning is sharp upon the damp air—new-dropped dung
smoaks in the street—Ali stands shivering and near witless upon his
step in the dawn, not knowing why he stands there—and the Post-
man's red coat appears, he and his Bell more regular than the English
sun, and presents him with a letter from his Wife. Ali pays his penny
and reads—and finds that Catherine intends not to return to him, or
to their house, but to separate, and live apart. 'I beg that you not address me directly upon this matter—I do not trust myself to read
your letters, and I hope you will forgive me, conceiving (if you can)
how little I may resist you—but write only to my Father at this address, and make arrangements with Messrs Bland, Attorneys, who
will act on my behalf—You know my reasons, and I will not state
them—I long believed that you might be *ill* and that a disorder of the
brain (such as you have described to me) might cause you to be *unwittingly* unkind, and to behave when fever'd in your imagination as
you would not if entirely well—and if you were ill then I should be
obliged to remain with you, and I surely would. But certain information has now come to me, from sources which I think *you may guess,*
which makes me more believe you are responsible for your actions,
and your actions are such that I may no longer share your house, and
your bed,' &c., &c., all of which Ali reads over as he stands there before the house to which she will not return, and reads *unmoved,* as
though it were a Gazette concerning the doings of people he knows
not. Lastly—and as though in a different hand—or written on a different day, or a different *mood*—is appended this:—'Ali—A dark star
presided at our meeting—I feel a doom upon me that I cannot limn!
Remember—where there is sin, there may be Forgiveness—if there is
Repentance. It will be my constant prayer for you.—The child is well
and I hasten to tell you of it for I believe you are fonder of it than I   10
am, and fonder of it than you are of me.—CATHERINE.'

A carriage, just at that juncture arriving, deposits before Ali the
Honourable Mr Peter Piper, done up in fur-collar and gauntlets, all
again prepared as before. Without words Ali brings him within the

house—from which by now the plate, the valuables, the books and most of the moveables have been taken away for sale—and on the last chair before the last table he takes paper, and in the few words necessary he makes a Will, repudiating all previous ones, and leaving all that he may possess, in whatever kind, to Catherine, Lady Sane, and to her Daughter—this he sands, and turns it to the Honourable, that he may witness. 'All is accomplished,' then quoth Ali. 'I have presentiment I shall not ever return to this house. Do you keep that, and see that Mr Bland, of the Temple, receives it.'

'I shall do all you ask,' said that faithful gentleman, with all his kind heart, and nothing foolish added, of unwarranted hope, or good cheer.

'Then let us share a glass,' said Ali, 'and be off!'

So we must make our way again to the dark neighbourhood of shuttered shops and dull hoardings where men may meet without the Law's notice, there to await the election of Fate. On this occasion, however, all went according to the world's way, without *mysteries*. The light was clear—as clear as the smoky air of London, that half-unquench'd Volcano, may ever be—and the Seconds discoursed in the field, and made their measurements, and here kick'd away an inconvenient Stone, and there tossed a Straw into the air to see which way the breeze blew, and examined the case of Pistols which the Honourable had again provided, the young gent from indifference (or Dutch courage) not caring to choose, as was his right. Ali in his place felt an indifference too, that frightened him more than the prospect of a slug in his heart—it seemed he cared for nothing, that *Nothing* had swarmed up from the lock'd place where it had always dwelt within him, and cloaked him in its cloud—and if that were so, then he might upon the moment carelessly toss away his Life—which he truly wished he cared to keep—a philosophical tangle that only a *double soul* can know! Thinking on these things, he stept to the centre of the ground, where the Honourable had been elected to toss a Coin determining which gentleman should fire first. Ali now saw clearly the bloodless cheek of the boy before him—the tremble of his lip—bethought him that the man was some mother's son, some Father's hope—and he *cared not*. The Gods thereupon, noting his indifference—so like their own!—favoured him, and the shilling came down with the King's likeness facing up.

'*Lord Sane* will have the choice, if he first give fire, or receive,' said Mr Piper—whose voice fluttered like his cognomen's instrument, for fear of his friend's safety, of which Ali himself seemed so little aware. The question is indeed a nice one, which choice is the more honourable, and (on the contrary) which gives the greater Advantage, to fire or receive first—but these niceties shall not trouble us, for they did not trouble Ali, who immediately elected to receive, as this was likely to bring the quickest end to the matter—or to *himself*—the youngling being known as a competent Shot when not in drink. But Ali now standing at the prescribed distance saw his opponent tremble, his former *bravado* gone, and turn back to his seconds for their support—which they lent him very literally—taking him by the arms and turning him to face Ali again, and lift his weapon. Ah, how little they may know of the sweetness of existence, who have not stood upon this ground of Honour, and seen Life exit from their mouths in a cloud upon the cold air of dawn, and felt Life tremble about their rib-cage, where in a moment the ball or blade may pierce—*I* have not, indeed, but I can well believe it is a sure cure for *ennui*, and better than Prayer for lifting the soul to think of last things.

The young gentleman's shot went through Ali's cloak, scored his shoulder, and pass'd away without doing more hurt. The physician whom the Honourable had brought wish'd immediately to inspect the wound, but Ali refused; he stept toward the young man, and—as in a play, where the Ending is first conceived, and all the Incident that precedes is foreordained by it—he lifted his pistol— fired—but coolly now, and aiming somewhat to the left of the slight figure before him, so as to spare him—yet at the same instant the young man's courage fled him, and he shrank to his *right*, to avoid the shot he expected—which therefore struck him full in the breast!

For a moment, as all present hastened to attend to the fallen man, Ali but stood, as though become nerveless and insensitive as stone. Only when the Doctor arose, and turned away—signifying that there was naught to be done by *him*—did Ali approach, and look down at the fellow, and his sorrowing friends, who held up his head. 'You have killed me,' he whispered, seeing Ali. 'You have satisfaction!' To which Ali responded nothing—only look'd upon the man, and his white linen turn'd to ruby, and his face to grey, and then to silence—and he thought *I have done this thing, that may not be undone*—which he may well have considered beforehand, and had not. Then the Honourable drew him away, with urgings to quit the place, before the Authorities arrived, and endless trouble resulted.

'Never fear,' said the Honourable. 'You will not need to remain long abroad—I shall arrange all, and soon enough this Matter will vanish, as if of its own accord—there will be no Prosecution—you will be understood to have acted as you must, and shall be pardoned—you have my word—and shall return.'

'No,' said Ali, for he saw now where his Destiny pointed him, as we sometimes may—as those poor fellows chained up in Plato's cave may of a sudden break away from a world of Shadows, and come out into the Sun—which burns their bedimmed eyes, but with the Truth of things. 'I shall depart—but I shall not return. I have lived too long in this land, whither I never chose to come. I am *satisfied*—yes, fully satisfied—I am gorged—I am surfeited.' He grasped the hand of his friend, and that Gentleman could protest no further, seeing Ali's piercing eye, and the firm resolve therein. 'Be my agent,' said he. 'Put not yourself at risk, or at charges—I cannot bear that you should—but be my eyes, and ears—my steward—my post-office.'

'But where will you go?'

'I know not,' said Ali—'Only that I shall *not* return.'

'Then let us be gone,' said Peter Piper with the greatest firmness. 'We make for Plymouth, where passage is already purchased—here, take my arm—let me but make a Memorandum, of all the business I may do for thee—No, no, speak not yet—Mount, Sir, Mount! I shall be beside thee, wheresoever thou goest, in *thought* at the least! Now Silence, and Flight!'

So at dawn on the following day Ali found himself once again upon a ship's deck, awaiting the turning of the tide, and the sail's filling. The seas rocked impatiently, and 'fair stood the wind for France'. Ali lifted his cap to the lone figure of the Honourable upon the dock, who answered with a wave of his white handkerchief, his other hand busied with keeping his own hat upon his head. Ali remembered then, as there he stood, a tale he had heard told in the great room of the Pacha's house in Albania far away, on a night when the Pacha's fighters in their coloured head-cloths and embroidered coats were foregathered there. Long ago, the tale went, in a certain Pacha's lands, a wicked magician was abroad, doing evil and thwarting his Lord's designs. At length, by force and cunning, the Pacha captured the magician and made him prisoner in his palace. On a night when noble visitors gathered at the Pacha's divan, when the pilaff was eat and the sherbets drunk, the Pacha was of a mind to summon the prisoner, and have him perform some wonder for the amusement of the Company. The magician was brought forth, and when he had done many things that mystified and astounded the Pacha's guests, he called for a large Bowl of Water to be brought. Into this bowl he tossed a handful of Salt, and asked his auditors to look within. Did they not see the Ocean, rolling there? And they did. Look more closely, said he—do you see a harbour there, and is it not the harbour at Malta? They marvelled to see that it was. And a ship in that harbour, just setting its sails? Yes—a fine ship—a black flag—a broad deck they looked down upon. The magician then arose, and, lifting the skirts of his robe, he put his toe into the basin of water—and before the eyes of those gathered there, he vanished—only to reappear (they all witnessed it) dropt through the air and fallen upon the deck of that ship. He made a mocking obeisance to those who look'd down on him, and took the wheel—and graceful as any steed the ship turned into the wind, and was away! 'Where then did he go?' the Company demanded of the teller to know—for the tale seemed not complete—and that clever fellow said that of course *he* did not know—how could he?— but it was later said that the magician sailed to America, where he still lived, grown rich and still doing much evil.

Wonderful are the ways of the mind, for no sooner had Ali remembered this tale, that had for so long lain unnoticed in a corner of *his,* than he knew very clearly where now he would go, and with what purpose.

1. *a gaunt grey place:* My parents were married at Seaham, in Durham, which indeed is situated upon a cliff overlooking the North Sea. It is a place I love, and where I spent my earliest years. It was in the garden of that house (I remember) as I was walking with my mother, that I asked why I had no papa, as other girls had—it was a matter of curious interest to me— whereupon she sternly and in an almost threatening manner instructed me never to speak of it again. I think a sort of dread thereupon entered my mind, which I had not known before, and have never been wholly free from since—I know it turned upon my mother, though I know not its name, nor wholly its source.

2. *electrified:* It was an entertainment of our grandparents, to gather a large number of people in a circle, either holding hands or all holding to a metal chain, and a shock being ad- ministered from a Leyden jar or similar device to the first per- son, all the persons in the circle leapt at once, to the general amazement and amusement. Lady Byron says that Lord Byron had a peculiar fear of shocks, even the little ones that come

from touching hands after crossing a thick carpet, and once re-signed from a gentlemen's club because it was thus carpeted, and hand-taking a necessity.

3. *crimson Curtains:* So, apparently, were the curtains of Lord and Lady Byron's marriage-bed at Halnaby. That evil-minded man Samuel Rogers (the 'Banker Poet'), who called himself a *friend* of my father's, spread the tale that, awaking in the night and seeing the fire through the curtains, Ld. B. believed him-self in Hell, and wedded with Proserpine.

4. *an acid and an alkali . . . Fire and Ice:* I have no doubt whatever that this paragraph is not less than an exact description, with no fable added, of my father's feelings at that time—feelings he could not then own, and perhaps could not have described, till some years had passed. All his wit, that kept away grief, now put aside. Pity it summons—Pity for what he then felt—pity too that he could so honestly limn it.

5. *desperation:* Ld. B. frankly reveals, to anyone who has heard the gossip about his relations with his wife, that he was at fault, as often as he was the injured party, and *when* at fault, was guilty of the worser things (at least until Lady Byron and her agents and supporters conspired—as he saw it—to take *me* from him, and put an end to his marriage). The picture of these events that he painted in his *Memoirs* must have been carefully designed to increase his own credit, and this is *not*—how strange then that the *Memoirs* should be burned, as injurious to his later fame, and *this* should survive—if it survives!

6. *the child he could not own as his:* On some days I know not why I continue these notes. Here do I appear, it seems—or my simu-lacrum, now born to him—yet *not* to him, for he has divided himself, as the writer of novels perhaps must do, into a worser and a better half, and pitted the one against the other—and I am the child of the worser half. No heartlessness of his behav-

iour toward me *in life* seems today as cruel to me as this—that he cares not what fate, or what harm, or what disgrace, come to those who loved or knew him, when he enlists them for his tale. Sticks and stones, so the children cry, may break my bones, but *names* shall never hurt me. Ah no. He said it himself: words are things.

7. *untruths:* It was always Ld. B.'s contention that he left England because the rumours of his sins and crimes at the time of the Separation from Lady Byron made it impossible for him to live in Society, without constant affront, or embarrassment—cut by old acquaintances—whispered about—ostracized. It may be so, yet I have heard old friends of his aver, that they all knew men about whom worse was said, who lived comfortably enough, and were not despised; and Ld. B. had many defenders, who would not believe the worst of him. I know not. We make our persecutions the cause of what we would do in any case.

8. *Brougham:* Lord Byron was convinced that Mr. Henry Brougham, who acted as a legal advisor to Lady Byron at the time of the Separation, was the one who argued against reconciliation, and that he was also the source in society of all the rumours (both true and false) of what had passed between Lord and Lady Byron that occasioned the parting. Indeed he was known as *'Chronique scandaleuse'* for his willingness to bear tales, but Ld. B.'s obsession with him was perhaps unfair. (It was he of course who later defended Queen Charlotte in her trial before the House of Lords, a marital dispute of quite another order.) Byron told Thomas Moore that if ever he came back to England he would be obliged for his honour's sake to fight Henry Brougham.

9. *skirling:* This word indicates the sound of the bagpipe, shrill and continuous. I know not why Ld. B. uses it here, perhaps an error, though for what word I know not, or because he sees

the curling ribbon of a line of ink resembling a curling line of continuous sound.

10. *fonder of it than I am:*   I hear in this post-scriptum my mother's own voice   as though indeed she once wrote so to him   and he never forgot   or never relinquished the letter. I weep and know not for whom

11. *a wicked magician:*   I know not if this tale be an old one, an Albanian one, or Ld. B.'s own.

12. *America:*   I remember, reading just now this word, that I dreamt this day of a future state—not my own but a future state of the world—and this book there opened—studied—& I thought perhaps these notes too should be enumerated—as too quickly giving the key. In that future, I saw that the possessors of the text read numbers as we do letters, and equations as we do sentences. The book was clear to them at a glance. Absurd idea. I saw their fingers pass over the pages and the numbers, as the fingers of blind men pass over the raised letters of those texts made specially for them, and the numbers became words thereby to their eyes What if I have counted wrongly   all nonsense then   too late to recast it now   But what if all was wrongly encypher'd and yet when decypher'd returned a book, but a different book   unknown written by no one   absurd   what odds of a single true sentence even appearing   too high to calculate   but what book what book

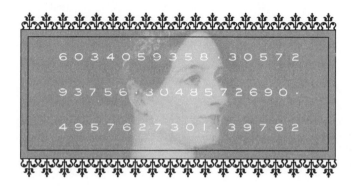

From: "Smith" <anovak@strongwomanstory.org>
To: lnovak@metrognome.net.au
Subject:

Lee—

I got the new pages. Are we still not surprised? Is this still a Gothic?

I see what Ada's notes mean now. What this meant to her, to have this. I read some pages to Georgiana (that's the lady with the orig- inals). She said What an awful shit he was. I don't think so. I don't know what I think.

S

———————————————

From: lnovak@metrognome.net.au
To: "Smith" <anovak@strongwomanstory.org>
Subject: Gothic

Well it *begins* as a Gothic—the ruined abbey in the moonlight, the somnambulation—interaction with scary animals—immurement— a family curse, or evil taint—flight in the dark. There is the mon- strous parent, huge (his great shadow thrown up on the wall comes right from another famous Gothic, but I can't remember now which one). Parricide, or apparent parricide; a mysterious pursuer, the hero's double. Thomas Medwin, a gossip and something of a fool whom Byron entertained a few times in Pisa and who thought of himself as a Byron expert ever after, says that Byron told him of a narrative he wanted to write or had written, about a man pursued by a mysterious other, who keeps interfering with his plans, seems to know all about him, seduces his beloved, etc., and when finally the hero finds him and kills him in a rage, he pulls away his cloak and discovers the pursuer to be himself—and dies in horror. So maybe Medwin got a whiff of the novel and got it cockeyed. In the usual Gothic all the apparent supernatural events turn out to have reasonable causes—they've been staged by the villain, or have been misunderstood, or are the result of an episode of epilepsy, etc. (I don't know yet about this one—Ada's notes suggest the story's going to come out nonsupernatural.) But then the story seems to lose the Gothic furniture and becomes a society novel about marriage and affairs. Combining these things is a bit odd, but we are here at the beginning of the popular novel—all these things were new in this form, and Byron's trying them all out, along with some I've never seen deployed before: his Ali is a character in a situation I think is unique.

Let me know what *you* think.

Lee

———————————

From: "Smith" <anovak@strongwomanstory.org>
To: lnovak@metrognome.net.au
Subject: Who

I don't know what to think—it's such a strange voice to me—such a combination of jaunty and formal—sort of "earthy" or whatever and highfalutin. I don't know who I'm listening to. But I wonder what's going to happen, and I guess that's the main thing, right?

And underneath always I hear my own voice asking Who is this guy speaking to me? What is he, what does he think really? And I don't know.

S

————————————

From: lnovak@metrognome.net.au
To: "Smith" <anovak@strongwomanstory.org>
Subject: RE:Who

One thing I find fascinating is that it's about an alienated boy with a monstrous father, who's never known a mother. Byron's case was the reverse—he never knew his father, and his mother always loved him and smothered him, which he hated—they had huge battles. Throughout all his writing (as far as I remember) there's nothing much about fathers and sons, much less huge threatening fathers—everyone in Byron tends to be Byron-sized. Whether he was repressing all that, and it only came out this one time, or— well leave it to Uncle Sigmund to determine. It did give me pause— like you (maybe for different reasons), I wondered who I was listening to.

It's also interesting to me that the novel turns on a failed marriage that's so like Byron's and yet motivated in completely imaginary ways—ways that spare both parties—not his fault, or hers, only the fault of this pursuing Fate, whose identity I think I can guess at. Most autobiographical novels work the other way: the causes, the resentments, the blames are all retained even though the events might be all imaginary.

Byron really believed that Annabella was entirely truthful and frank, and that it was those evil women around her that turned her against him. He always said he had no idea—beyond his admitted reckless self-indulgence, or melancholic fits, or occasional rages—why Annabella determined on a separation. Actually he had a *very* good idea of what things in his past—his sister Augusta, those boys in Greece, the Cambridge chorister—would have been impossible for Annabella to accept; what he didn't know—what accounted for his air of injured innocence—was that Annabella actually knew about them. Caroline Lamb had told her, and Augusta eventually confessed. Neither one told Byron that they had betrayed his secrets. And Annabella kept her counsel.

It wasn't like my story, police, arrest, all over the papers. Your mother not only knew, she knew everybody else knew too. And you know too, unlike Ada, who for years had only her mother's word. You do know, don't you?

———————————————

From: "Smith" <anovak@strongwomanstory.org>
To: lnovak@metrognome.net.au
Subject: Know

I know. That is I know what I read. I know the statute of limitations on child rape is fifteen years from the time the child is sixteen, and that ran out a long time ago. But there's still a bench warrant out for you for fleeing prosecution or whatever it's called, and if you come back you'll get arrested, and you don't know what will happen then, maybe nothing, maybe not nothing. And people are a lot angrier about these things than they were then even. All those boys and their priests. People want to repeal the statute of limitations, and they also want to make the repeal retroactive, but that might not be constitutional. See I've kept up. I can read the news, and I can imagine you reading the same news and thinking Oh what the hell, and logging on to Expedia and buying a ticket home. I know you have dual citizenship too, so you have a passport. I know. I've given it some thought. Over the years, as they say.

But here are the questions you have to answer:

1. When do you think he wrote the book
2. Why do you think that

3. When did he stop (I don't know how to look for hints in any papers if I can't limit it a little)

S

————————

From: lnovak@metrognome.net.au
To: "Smith" <anovak@strongwomanstory.org>
Subject: RE:Know

I want to answer your new questions, but much more I want to tell you the history of my absence from your life. I wrote letters long ago but they were sent back to me unopened (a thing Lady Byron used to do, by the way, to baffle those she couldn't control): a letter to your ten-year-old self, and one to your sixteen-year-old self (it should have come with the Javanese devil sculpture I sent that year, but it seems that wasn't given to you). For a number of years I just forgot it all, and you: that is, I rarely thought of you for long enough at a time that the thought would force a commitment to do something, say something—you'd come into my mind and I would right quick open another door for you to go back out by. I got good at that. And I had work that kept me busy and that I loved. I knew people in the industry who had kids from early marriages they never saw, kids they sometimes talked about when they were drinking at day's end—as I did—and the fact that *they* had these lost kids made it seem all right that I did, and maybe their selfishness made mine seem all right, or at least normal. They were—they *are,* some of them—monsters of egotism, great white sharks, blue whales of egotism, and mine seemed like nothing beside theirs.

The first thing that kept me away from you was the law, as you say: since I had skipped, there was no way I could see you, unless your mother had somehow decided to run with me, bringing you; but she was in fact the other thing then that kept me from you. She was so angry at me for what I'd done, or was accused of doing, and then for not staying to face the music, that the last thing she wanted was to be by my side. If I had gone to trial, it wouldn't have been one of those you see on TV, where the scumbag who has murdered the secretary he's been having an affair with shows up in court or at the microphones with his wife (dark dress, dark glasses) and kids beside him to "support" him. I neither claimed nor expected that kind of support. I would have been ashamed to take it even if it were offered. I am not good at repentance. Regret, yes: very thorough in that regard. But I have always thought that public repentance was actually closely akin to self-exculpation. I don't think myself guiltless, and see no way to get guiltless. Ada's mother would have found me a hard case.

So I missed your early years, never saw you after your fourth birthday. And even later on, when the memory faded (though not the statute of limitations) and your mother might have felt more tolerant—after all as far as she knew I'd led a blameless and even selfless life since then—she wouldn't bring you to see me, because—well, this is going to sound almost impossible to believe, but irrational feelings can run very deep, irrational loathing and distaste and revulsion at least as deep as irrational love and sympathy—because she didn't want you near me when you were reaching puberty. She didn't want to *bring* you near me. Maybe she didn't even know this. Actually though I think she did. And she got a lot of support for that distaste, a lot of theoretical support, from the feminists she associated with. Just as (okay, this is a stinger, I admit it) Lady Byron got support for her unkindness, her lack of charity, from the evangelical ladies and ministers she gathered around her. In fact I wonder if she wasn't just a little glad, or relieved, to learn you weren't likely to have much to do with my sex at all. Some of those women she knew were plenty glad, if their published writings are any guide: in their rogues' gallery I have my mug shot and number. I hope—I want to believe—they didn't make it impossible for you to ever love me, or even like me.

Well I can't write more after all. More to come.

———————————————

From: "Smith" <anovak@strongwomanstory.org>
To: lnovak@metrognome.net.au
Subject: Love

what do you think, that mom and her friends made me a lesbian?
Is that what you didn't say but thought? You know, funny thing,
but mom was the girliest girly-girl ever, except that instead of the
barbie way it was the hippie-moongoddess way. She sure didn't
hate men. Maybe you don't know. After all you didn't know either
of us all that long. I can tell you that first with Jonah and then afterward with Marc she tried *every day* to show me what a good relationship with a good man is like, how much fun it is when they
treat you right, how much fun it is to treat them right, how they
ought to be *true* and *kind* and kick every little stone and sharp object out of your way and try their best to see that no harm ever
comes to you. I am what I am because I just am. And I know what
love is, and ought to be.

—————————————

From: lnovak@metrognome.net.au
To: "Smith" <anovak@strongwomanstory.org>
Subject: RE:Love

Sorry. Email is awful. I'm not used to using it yet. The message
flies out from under your fingers as fast as thought (as B. might
have said) and then you push one button and it's mailed. If I'd had
to pull it from the typewriter, sign it, fold it, find an envelope and
a stamp, I probably wouldn't have sent it.

   I spend all that time showing that I'm not bitter—and I'm
not—and then say dumb bitter things. It's because you've come to
Europe at last, where I could actually see you and touch you, just at
a time when it's quite impossible for me to get there. Tell me why
you can't just keep going east—take some time off—see the
world—and me too. Don't come so near (well a thousand miles
nearer) and then slip away. Don't worry about the money either.

Now I've reread this and it looks okay. So here it goes. Except I see I need to add—

Love

L

———————————

From: "Smith" <anovak@strongwomanstory.org>
To: lnovak@metrognome.net.au
Subject: RE:Re:Love

I didn't love you or hate you. You weren't there. You know, half the kids I knew growing up had parents who were divorced, or not married, or not men, or whatever, it was just so usual. A lot of them never saw one parent or the other, and got stuck too much with the one they didn't like as much, the one that was "better for them." It was okay to ask somebody, So where's your dad? (Or mom, sometimes.) But if they just shrugged, or evaded, it wasn't polite to pursue: if somebody didn't know, or didn't care, then it was none of your business. And you usually weren't that interested anyway. But it was different if every now and then you saw a thing about your father on TV, and there he was. His picture anyway. And they would always bring up the CRIME, which you (I mean me) didn't really get, not when I was little, and Mom snapping off the TV and putting out some distraction, Oh let's go make a *corn doll*! Let's go read *Pippi Longstocking*! Let's go have a *bubble bath*! What I learned from that was that if I wanted to find out about you—and I did—then Mom couldn't know about it.

There were things I thought you should be there for—certain moments when I felt you ought to have been there but weren't—I can't describe what made them so, but I don't mean the big things, like graduations and birthdays, well maybe those too but other things, random times, just a picnic by the river or fireworks or even just nothing, finding a dead baby bird, watching the water

truck spray to lay the road dust, and I would say *My daddy should
be here. Why isn't Daddy here?* And I'd wonder.

S

—————————

From: lnovak@metrognome.net.au
To: "Smith" <anovak@strongwomanstory.org>
Subject: Corn doll

Alex—

That's devastating. Honestly.

I'm sorry. I haven't got further with the research today or yesterday. Tonight I went out and had some sake and ate noodles. And
then more sake. And a long bath, hot as hell. Maybe tomorrow.

Sorry.

Lee

—————————

From: "Smith" <anovak@strongwomanstory.org>
To: lnovak@metrognome.net.au
Subject: RE:Corn doll

Don't feel bad. That was basically a lie. I can't really ever remember saying *Why isn't Daddy here?* I just thought I'd tell you I did.
The fact is you were gone so completely and from so far back that
it was easy to think you *ought* to be gone. The dreams where you
came back were always disappointing, messy and wrong, sometimes even horrible. I remember one. Well never mind. You know
how you can remember certain dreams you dreamed when you
were less than ten, that are as real to you as memories? Especially
bad ones. But awake I thought you were supposed to be gone, and

if you stayed gone that was okay, because I liked things to be the way they are supposed to be. I still do.

What I don't know is—Do you ever think about that girl? I do. I think about her. I was her age when I first found out about her (I was a champ researcher, even then). I wonder what she thought.

———————————

From: lnovak@metrognome.net.au
To: "Smith" <anovak@strongwomanstory.org>
Subject: Her

Do I ever think about her? I think about her every day. I mean that. I'm given a reason to almost every day, some little consequence that leads right to it, even though it might not seem it should: some little trouble about transferring money, or renting a car—anything. And if nothing like that happens, I think of her anyway. I replay that night, and I edit it, to make it come out different. Instead of staying at that party, I leave early. Or I get drunk and fall asleep before I come upon her. *She* gets drunk and falls asleep. Her damn fool parents show up and get her out of there. I come to my senses. Lots of new endings, or beginnings.

You know I recently read the memoirs of a man who'd been an officer in the French army in some colonial war. (I often find myself reading odd things for good reasons. Like you do for your work. We're alike in that.) He wrote of how he and his company had fought a daylong battle through some North African settlement, perhaps Berber, I don't remember. His company were outnumbered and many killed, but eventually the other side broke and fell back, and left the settlement to the French. He remembered going through the smoke of the burning bazaar and the streets feeling exalted, smeared in blood, sword in his hand, alive; and at one place he pushed in through the curtains, and found a young girl, a very young girl, alone, and afraid, and (he thought) quite aware of what would now become of her in the hands of the victors; and this officer says it was her abjection, her *knowledge in innocence,* that made it impossible for him not to take her— that and the battle he'd fought; he was, he said, as though possessed by a god of battle. And I thought I understood for the first time rape in war, and the intensities of battle too. I've been close enough to battle, and all that it causes, to think I'm right.

Around the time of that party in Hollywood in 1978 I'd been lifted into an atmosphere unlike anything I'd ever known—I mean of course I knew *about* it, it was everywhere to read about, but I'd never experienced anything like it. These were people with so much self-love, so much money, so much of the world's attention and respect (not all for trivial reasons either), that they almost seemed freed from the requirement to care, or regret, or mend anything. Some of them were intensely spiritual, of course, but that only seemed to mean that they believed that everything was all right, and nothing truly bad could be done by anybody they knew personally, least of all themselves. "Bad" wasn't even a word they could use. So long as I said the right things to them, they would talk to me about moving forward my projects as though by magic. I would say to one of them that I wanted to explore the possibility of making a film in Nepal, about Buddhism and the mountains, with an all-Nepalese cast, but starring this man, one of these fabulous monsters, sprawled on a leather couch before me. And he'd say, *We can do that.* Just say it, like that.

So there was a sudden freedom from all restraint, and I don't mean just moral restraint, I mean all *physical* restraint, as though common biological limits didn't matter. A lot of drugs powered this feeling too, of course. And then it was late at night in these huge rooms with wide windows and Los Angeles—surely you've seen the pictures, you've been there yourself for all I know about you—laid out below as though you inhabited a high tower or a spaceship. And this child. And I thought: I can do anything, and no harm can come of it. That was really the thrill.

I can tell you absolutely that I didn't rape her, in the sense of forcing sex on her that she didn't invite. I wasn't even the only one who had relations with her, if that's the right word, that night and morning. She wandered everywhere in that place, like Alice, fetching up against these *scenes* as we called them then, as though they were imaginary, or unreal. Knowledge and innocence: I can see her eyes now, at once taking in what she saw and at the same time so blind to it. No, I wasn't the only one. Just the one whose wallet she took, which she was found with later, in another part of town. So I was the one who could be charged, when those impossible parents at last showed up to retrieve her. I don't know what she really thought, then or later. There's no more reason to believe what she told the police than to believe what she told me. You certainly couldn't believe both.

I didn't know I could write an email this long. It wasn't easy. I'm going to stop.

Lee

———————————————

From: "Smith" <anovak@strongwomanstory.org>
To: lnovak@metrognome.net.au
Subject: RE:Her

Lee—

Interesting story.

Are you going to be able to answer those questions?

S

———————————————

From: lnovak@metrognome.net.au
To: "Smith" <anovak@strongwomanstory.org>
Subject:

All right. No more, if not wanted. Just answers. All I have.

I think he began writing it where Ada thought, at the Villa Diodati in Switzerland, and that he continued in the subsequent months— dropped it and picked it up again later on—that's likely, for rea- sons that Ada has already perceived: its contents seem to reflect, now and then, things that were going on in his life as he wrote— first the separation (or Separation as it would come to be called everywhere, as though it were the only one, or the paradigmatic one), which had just been finalized; then Venice, and his relations with the Carbonari.

So here are the reasons:

First, the Mary Shelley challenge, which got him thinking about prose, and prose romances. Next, right then he got a visit from Matthew Gregory Lewis, "Monk" Lewis, the author of the most successful Gothic novel ever written, *The Monk*. Lewis was gay, an old chum of B.'s, who was always glad to see him; Lewis was rich, not from his royalties mostly, but from his sugar planta- tions in the West Indies, the Caribbean as we say, where he ran a large number of slaves. (Byron doesn't need to have got the idea of zombies from Southey, as Ada guesses; he could have learned it from Lewis, who surely would have been very interested in it.) Maybe because he'd been talking long with Shelley, but Byron on the occasion of this visit actually convinced Lewis to add a codicil to his will providing funds to alleviate the condition of his slaves and freeing at least some of them on his death. You can imagine the negotiations—come on, Lewis, why not free them *all*?—and Shelley and Byron actually witnessed him signing it.

So Byron was thinking about slaves and the West Indies.

Then there is the fact that just about that time, he was sent the three volumes of that novel by Caroline Lamb I wrote about be- fore. It was called *Glenarvon*, and was a huge seller. So he was reading—and we know he read it—a fictionalized account of him- self, pictured as the villainous/glamorous Lord Glenarvon, guilty of a thousand crimes, and she the innocent unspoiled Calantha. Here's what he wrote to Thomas Moore, his friend and later biog- rapher: "It seems to me that if the authoress had written the *truth*, and nothing but the truth—the whole truth—the romance would have been not only more *romantic,* but more entertaining." So maybe he thought about that, and decided he would try again with a story in prose, but turn it more in the direction of a *roman à clef* of his own, only truer to his nature as he perceived it, and the story of his adventures.

More to come.

───────────────

From: lnovak@metrognome.net.au
To: "Smith" <anovak@strongwomanstory.org>
Subject: Ghost novel

A—Okay—I keep reading—you see how hard I work for you, and on my vacation too—Anyway I've been reading Marchand, the great biog of B., and here it says—September 1816, same time & place as the Shelley/Polidori thing—that "he had begun a prose tale, a thinly veiled allegory of his marital difficulties, and when he heard that Lady Byron was ill, he cast it into the fire." !!! No note about where Marchand learned this.

So maybe he didn't cast it into the fire. Planned to. Thought he ought to. But didn't. Just an idea.

Lee

───────────────

From: lnovak@metrognome.net.au
To: "Smith" <anovak@strongwomanstory.org>
Subject: Stop

Alex—

Okay—3: When did he stop.

When he laid it down for good I can't tell, but I wonder if maybe it had something to do with his discovery of a comic epic by a poet named Frere, who wrote as "William and Robert Whistlecraft," rare instance of a double pseudonym. (You've noticed Frere gets a brief nod in the pages set in Spain, where he really was the British consul.) Frere's "epic" was a poem in *ottava rima,* the same stanza Byron would use in *Don Juan,* and like those poems it was full of jokey Ogden Nash rhymes and mockery of various pretensions. Frere actually based the style on the Venetian wits like Pulci, whom Byron had read in Italian. Byron's publisher sent Frere's thing to him, and said he thought it was remarkable and difficult; Byron said he thought it was remarkable but not difficult, and in a few days he'd written *Beppo.* (He says a few days; he always minimized how hard he worked at writing.) And that was it: *Don Juan* could be written, a poem that could include everything Byron knew and had experienced. Maybe he felt that he'd found a way to do what he had tried to do in this novel, only better, and using all his talents, and dropped the novel. Well. Wonderful as *DJ* is I find I can't read very much of it at a sitting. I wish he'd finished this— if it is unfinished—and then done another, better one, and then another. *Don Juan* is *sui generis,* and the long narrative poem was running out of steam in that period, but the novel was just getting under way. He might be read now, today, like Jane Austen. Oh well.

I don't know at what point Byron decided the story couldn't appear, but he obviously made the decision because of how frank and unmediated (as we critics say) his account of the marriage was. When he used the facts of his own life and of others' lives in *Don Juan,* he knew how to transform them—retain the truth of them but not the tale of them. It was a challenge he was very much aware of—maybe you noticed the epigraph to *DJ,* which is from Horace: *Difficile est proprie communia dicere,* it's hard to speak rightly about commonplace things—things we all share. And it is. When people thought about Byron it was the *un*common things they relished, bad or good. But he thought he was made of *domestica facta* like everybody else.

Alex, I'm tiring of email. I want more than this epistolary novel we're making together. Have you thought at all about that offer I made? It may be that by now you'd rather go in the other direction—west not east—and I'm getting word myself from various sources that I might be going to New Guinea soon, which is so far east it's almost west again. And I'm afraid too—not of *you* exactly—of the past and time and my inadequacy, maybe—but still I'm going to hope. There's got to be something more for us. It's more up to you than me, but if there's anything I can do, I think you ought to tell me.

With all my heart

Lee

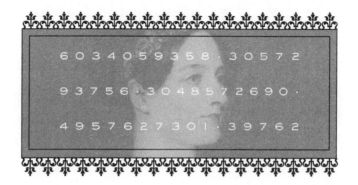

6 0 3 4 0 5 9 3 5 8 · 3 0 5 7 2

9 3 7 5 6 · 3 0 4 8 5 7 2 6 9 0 ·

4 9 5 7 6 2 7 3 0 1 · 3 9 7 6 2

TWELVE

In which the Beginning is returned

to, inasmuch as it may ever be

O N THE COAST OF EPIRUS, at the Port of Salora, the fishermen mend their nets through the afternoons, or perchance do not, and instead nap in the shadow of an upturn'd boat—smoke a pipe—make their prayers to one Divinity, or several (Allah and the Virgin at a minimum) so as to avoid the ire of any *one*. Their ancient forebears did the same, and parcelled out their sacrifices with even hand upon several Altars. One day upon these shores, beneath that dome that bluely turns above, is much like another—few are the Ships, or the folk who step ashore from ship's boats, who are strange to these fisherfolk—but on this afternoon there *is* such a boat, and bearing a stranger too—a man in the dress of a European, and yet who, when he has hailed them, speaks in the tongue of Albania (tho' haltingly) and not that of the Infidel.

The net-menders answer him, but the young man seems not to hear—he looks about himself as one who wakes from a Dream, and yet knows not if this palpable world is any the more substantial. What does he here? He intends, he says—as though for his own ears, to inform *himself*—to travel North, to the lands of the Ochridans—he is in need of a guide, and a man or two, and horses—and the fishermen direct him to a place where such may be bargained for. They see no more of him—yet but a day and an hour have gone by when a greater wonder still intrudes upon their indolence—for *another* man, likewise in the dress of Europe, also alights there upon their obscure shore—and asks certain questions, to which the fishers know the Answers—though they look upon one another in amaze, that they should—and when the man has gone, the Christians among them cross themselves, not knowing why, as though an uncanny being has passed among them.

The first of these strangers is of course our Ali—here he has come, to the peninsula of Hellas, by stages, over a half-year's time, while knowing it to be his last destination, as it is his Destiny. After departing the shores of England in consequence of his all-too-successful exploit upon the field of Honour, he landed firstly upon the shores of France, where in a cold Inn's worst room he wrote to Catherine, and to Una—for he wished his Lady to know, that he has defended himself from certain slanders, which he would not repeat to her, and what the consequence was; and his Daughter, to know that though she saw him not, his love to her was constant, and he would one day hold her in his arms, and kiss her lips again. To Mr. Piper next he sent such Authorities and Powers as he could imagine—having no Law-book by—by which the Honourable might extract from his Bankers and Agents the wherewithal for a long journey—for such he even then intended to go on, and when return, he *knew not*—if within the bounds of his mortality, 'twould be all too soon—such was his thought, as there his candle guttered, and his breath appeared before him like smoke.

From France alone on horseback he travelled across the well-named Low Countries, and almost without noticing, he found himself upon a Battle-field—mark'd by a Monument—more, mark'd by Harvest rich, still fertilized by that disintegrating bone and sinew, so generously cast about upon a day not long past. Waterloo! *I* will not memorialize thee yet again—nor that man, yet both *more* and *less* than Man, who threw all that he had gained for Mankind upon the green table of this field, to see it snatched up by his fellow Gamesters—the one Hazard he could not recoup! Ali pondered there, drawn out for an hour from the toils of his own mind to contemplate Mankind's, and he considered—'twas not Pride, nor Vanity, but only a humour of that moment—that all the difference between himself and that great man was, that he had less treasure to expend, yet not less of guilt that it was spent. *He* had not 'slain his thousands' nor yet his 'tens of thousands'—he had laid but *one* man beneath the earth by his own hand—yet *nos turba*, any one or two of us is a multitude, and all the suffering there is when blood runs like a tide is not more than the soul and nerves of one man bears—there is no *multiplication*, for we each suffer and die alone, though we thrive and grow together—ask the Indian gymnosophist how it may be—'tis so!

He left the Field behind—he crossed the Rhine—climbed the Alps—he saw the Avalanche—the mountain torrent—the Glacier— *1* but since in the midst of these scenes he remained *himself*, and lost not that Self in them, he gained little peace in what he beheld. By such removes, by horse and ship and foot, he came at length to the shores I have described him reaching, the shores of *home*, a word he knew not in any language—not as to its meaning to his heart.

He set out with his small company from Salora, and he had passed a number of days in the saddle, sleeping where he might and eating what he could acquire, and paying little attention to either, when he began to taste in the air, or see in the wisps of white cloud, or feel in the coarse earth underfoot, something that awaken'd his sleeping sense. On a certain evening he saw, as though heavenly avengers pursued him from his former dwelling-place, a long bolt of grey cloud unfurled above, and a wind as cold as any that crosses Salisbury Plain blew in his beard and clothes. He had reached the partial shelter of an old Turkish cemetery when the storm broke in unexampled fury—the rain lashed, and the thunder sounded with all the majesty and reproach with which God speaks to Job, to remind him of his *littleness,* and the Creator's might. When the tear of the lightning across the sky illumined the stones and the claws of the branches, he saw another figure, or *thought* he saw—not one of his party—a Brigand, or Robber, but that they never come singly—and on the next flash, 'twas gone!

At Jannina he paid and bade farewell to his dragoman and servants, and there put off his European dress and put on instead the garb of that land. In the wide leathern belt he thrust the sword that the Pacha had once given him, which he had carried from England, now far away and baseless as a dream. Alone he set out, and ascended from the plain into the Albanian foothills, until he came one eve to stand on the pass above the Capital of that Pacha, whom once he had served—whose sword he wore. The sun going down still gilded the minarets, and the windless air tasted of dust, and the stones of the way had not changed—but the town was not as it had been. The reign of that Pacha had ended, and where once the crowds of supplicants had gathered, to wait upon his Favour—and the Turks had strutted, in their black pelisses, bearing messages from the Sultan—the black slaves, and the caparisoned horses—all marching to the rhythm of the great Drums, and the calling of the boys from the Minaret—now there was silence, the courtyards empty, save for some few malingerers too poor or too indolent to find other employment, and a spavined nag or two in the place where 200 of the Pacha's steeds once shook their high heads, and jangled their trappings!

Not long did Ali linger there to ponder the transitory nature of earthly splendour. He changed his mount, and filled his panniers, and all alone went on, into the empurpled heights beyond the town; at night he wrapt him in his capote, and slept upon the ground, if he could not beg shelter in a Barn or Cot; went on, until—tho' he could say not by what signs he knew it, could point to no single peak or valley, no turn of the way or clutch of houses, that called out to him—he stood upon the hills of home! Yet they were not the same hills—for 'We cannot step in the same river twice'—the river is not the same river, and *we* are not what we were then. Ali look'd now in vain within him for that boy who once roamed here, who beneath this sky adventured, loved, fought, eat & slept—but he is nowhere to be found. A grown man—whose thoughts, even to his own soul, are spoke in English—looks out upon dry stones, and bare promontories—and thinks, How bleak all is!—And yet how fierce within him does he feel its claims! As he rode down to the plain, along a slope cut by a water-course and burdened with tumbled stone, he began to think to himself, 'There I walked—There I followed my flock—There I sheltered from a storm, in that high fort, so long deserted—And there—and there—' But even to his heart he will not speak a name, of the one who *there* went with him; and yet his breast was *with* that name, as a woman is with Child—and it grew.

He rode down into a grove of cedars, wherein he expected—tho' indeed he could not have *said* he expected—a fountain of good water—not a *heavy* water as the Albanians say but *light*—for they can assess the various waters they taste as nicely as a connoisseur his various Clarets. There was the fountain, in a cairn of stones—and as Ali came in sight of it, he saw also a number of people—men, on one side, and women, upon the other, and a dispute in progress. Stopping where he could observe and not himself be seen, Ali determined that the dispute concerned who had rights to draw water there, the men forbidding the women to come near, and they contesting this, loudly and *manfully* indeed, so that it seemed there could be no settling of Claims—and then there came into the grove a Youth—for his face seemed yet beardless—who bore a long gun, and a pistol too thrust into his belt. Ali observed how, at this one's approach, the women seemed cheer'd, and the men abashed—and with a brief word, and a *gesture,* the youth disposed the Case—the men (tho' with a few curt words and warlike gestures, meaning nothing) withdrew, to let the women fill their jugs. The youth stood apart, as though to watch over them—his gun he slung across his shoulders, an arm resting over either end, as an Albanian with a long gun will do.

When the women, jugs balanced upon their heads, wended up the far path and away, Ali went down to where the youth remained—and who now, his attention caught by the stranger's approach, turned to face Ali, and greet him—and Ali fell of a sudden silent.

Beauty is no respecter of sex—the *Fairer* having not the advantage, if the case be judged by some Tiresias of wide experience, and practised eye. And yet rarely are the two kinds confused—indeed, insofar as they *may* be, just so far is the Beauty lessened—on *either* part, though surely upon the Female. A nice question, certainly, but it was not the question before Ali, who knew in but a glance that the youth before him was a *maid*—and a fair one—so fair, indeed, that his mouth was stopt, and his hail died upon his lips. The Maid, nothing discomfited, and putting aside her weapon, held out to Ali her right hand in greeting, as any *man* would do to a stranger—her look, frank, her face composed, her eye with an aloof *assessment* regarding him—'twas the very look that every boy Ali had known, and every Youth with whom in the old Pacha's service he had consorted, was at pains to cultivate. And yet she too, as Ali did, fell silent as he came near to her—silent, and wondering—and that for a reason *not* like his.

'Stranger, do I know thee?' said the Maid-Man at length, and her voice was low and stricken with a surmise Ali could not guess at.

'I think you cannot,' said he, 'for though long ago I lived here, I have for many years been gone, and who I was *then* is not this man you see.'

'No—no!' quoth she— 'Not this man—nor was I this man *you* see. Tell me your name.'

'My name is Ali.'

'Why then,' she said, and sat again, as though she *must,* and could not longer stand. 'Then I will not say my own—no, I will not!'

Nor did she need to say the name *thou,* Reader, wilt have guessed a page or more ago—Ali was behind thee in perceiving, for indeed he knew not (nor ever *could* know) what sort of tale this was he figured in, as surely *thou* dost! Yet as the knowledge dawned upon him, he too sank to sit beside her—and looked upon the woman warrior—and spoke not further.

By some ancient authors it is believed—or supposed—that the Amazons of lore dwelt in these regions we now designate Albania, *3* and old Euhemerus, were he to consider the case, might guess that the tales of woman warriors arose at first, from a certain Practise common there, which indeed may go back to Hesiod, for aught I know. For among that stern people, what is not black is white, and what is not Female is Male—female being subject in every particular to male—a beast of burden at necessity, and at birth a Commodity, sold to her future husband as soon as she is weaned, at so many *paras* in payment down, the rest due upon delivery at a convenient age. (In such cold calculation were the marriages of Kings and Queens once made, and they may still be—though *affinity* was surely paramount in the considerations of Britain's Monarch.) The marriages so contracted in swaddling-clothes are not at nubile age to be repudiated—a spurned Wife, or Husband, would be a stain to honour, to be washed clean only in blood. And yet—patience, I pray, the reason for my Sermon will be made clear, even while Ali and the Maid in men's garb still look amazed upon one another—I say, it may happen that a girl, having reached the age at which she may be wed, refuses the husband chosen for her. And if she prove adamant, and courageous, and defy all duress, and all threats even to her life, then she may be excused—but only upon one condition: that having rejected the husband, and the *house,* to which she was first contracted, she solemnly vow before the Council of Elders that she will contract with no other, ever! Then—since she will ever after remain unwed, unbred, unsubjected—she may no longer be accounted a *woman* at all, and must therefore become a Man—for she cannot be nothing. Her clothes, her manner, the weapons she bears, the duties she attends to (or shirks), the horse she rides, are all as a man's—she is in all *apparent* particulars wholly a man—let whoso forgets it, beware!—for not one house but *two* are watching, jealously—and the Maiden herself is armed, as well!

Ali now of a sudden has recalled to mind this strange system of life, and remembered an old woman he knew as a child, who dwelt thus as a Nun alone and unhusbanded—and now he understands both *what* and *who* the maid before him is.

'Iman!' breathes he. ' 'Tis thou!'

She turns away, then, as though ashamed that *he* should see her thus—though when *alone,* she had stood in proud sufficiency, and gazed about the world as one in possession of it. Anon she raises her head, and looks to him—she, who was first to recognize *him,* the companion of her childhood—and she laughs—so changed is he—and he too laughs—and says that in his heart and mind she is still a Child—still as he last saw her—she too avers the same—then they must needs look long, on eyes and lips, hands, heads, and all, which are the eyes, lips, hands, &c., of the one each knew, and of *another,* whom they know *not,* at the same time—and they cannot speak, or speak but cannot *say.* At last with a soft and hesitant gesture—a gesture from which all the *man* is gone away—Iman pushes up Ali's loose sleeve, to show the old mark upon his arm that she remembers being made. And when she has seen it, she turns back her own sleeve, and there upon her arm is the same mark—self-made, more roughly drawn, as though half-remembered—but the same. Then all the years that have divided them dissolve as though they had not passed, and they two are as they were, *one soul* that passes between two beings, without let or hindrance! And yet when Ali moves to take the hand that once he would not *relinquish* but at need, she draws away from him, as from danger.

'Tell me,' Ali beseeches. 'Does our old Grandsire live? Tell me what befell you, that you are as I see you. Was there no one to protect you?'

'He is dead,' she replies. 'Dead long ago—I will show you the place where he lies. He never ceased to grieve for your absence. Until he died I was permitted to live alone and serve him, but thereupon the Elders contracted a marriage for me—an old Widower eager for a Handmaid—and I refused.'

She had when taken to the Widower's *han* refused his advances—fought him like the tyger Ali knew her to be—and as soon as opportunity presented itself, fled into the Desert alone—not caring if she died. Captured again by people of her own, *she* fought them, too, with fierce resolve—swore that if they returned her to her proposed *fiancé* she would flee again, or slit his throat as he slept, or do such things—what they were she knew not, but they would be 'the terror of the earth'. They bound her in straps of hide to keep her from running away, and she bit through the bonds, and so escaped again—was caught again—and thereupon, though without sponsor or ally, she demanded to be allowed to take the vow of Chastity that one such as herself was permitted by their laws.

'Did you so hate that old man, as to give up all to quit his claim on you?' Ali asked—and she answered, 'She had not hated him—nor any man—did not hate—no, 'twas not that,' and she cast all down her eyes, and tugg'd her hood forward, that he might not see her face.

Then had she never loved? Had all those years, the Spring of her own life, been spent in nun-like renunciation? Had no Youth, of all those fine young men who guard the flocks, and ride for the Pacha, or hunt the Boar, caused her to regret what she had done, what choice she had made? 'Why, what *choice*?' said she then. 'Little choice had I—to live a life with one I did not love, or to die. I chose not to die—'tis all—and thus—' —Here she lifted her head, and he saw she smiled, and her eyes were amused—'Thus it is *I* who ride, I who hunt, I who speak in council. Is not this much? Is it more than love? Tell me.'

'Little enough I know of love,' responded he—'except its cost—I know not what it may be traded for. Iman! Now I have found thee—and thou me—I see thou art lost to me as surely as if I had never returned from that curséd land where I was taken!'

Iman made no answer—she stood then, and summoned him too to rise. A great tenderness suffused her features, and a great sadness the eyes that gazed upon him—orbs that were unchanged, of all that belonged to her. 'Come,' said she. 'I will take you to our Council, and my *fellows* will make you welcome—for you were thought to be dead, and you are returned. Ask no more!'

Silent they were, those stern Herdsmen, at the Prodigal's return, when Ali made himself known to them—most expressed no delight—nor disapproval neither—one, tho' unsmiling, took his hand—another wondered at his mount, and baggage, what it might contain, and asked to see his sword, mark of the old Pacha's favor—but another turn'd away and refused his Salute, for the same reason, that Ali had been (last this fellow heard) a soldier of that Pacha who had despoiled their clan. He tried to describe to them his adventures among the Infidels, but they could little understand him—they laughed, as at a joke, or an extravagance—or grew bored by the Impossibility they perceived—and so he left off. Nevertheless his place among them was not disputed—he found shelter, and (when his soft hands had toughened) would find work to do too.

With Iman indeed 'twas otherwise—with her he opened, as it were, a book long closed and clasped, the time of his earliest youth—some pages he had forgotten, or misremembered—some he still had *by heart*. In a dim vale they lay together as they had once lain, to listen to the sleepy noontide—and remembering what he had then *felt,* yet had then no name for, Ali experienced the breaking-open within him of old sealed springs of purest serene. Now indeed he knew a name—knew whither his feelings *then* had tended—and so did Iman too—yet they were kept as chaste *now* by her vows, as they had been then by childish Ignorance—still as delighted, but now not satisfied. Her hand slipt into his—and as soon withdrew—her eye fell from his—yet her smile remained—and he sighed, and stirred—and anon they must depart from those solitudes—they *must,* and they know it.

When it appeared (as soon it did) that all Ali cared for was to be near Iman—and that *she* had changed—and cared for naught but to wake him in the morning, and ride with him at noon, and laugh with him at night—then the tempers of those clansmen darkened. The story of how he and she had been *as one* when they were but *kids* was remembered—at Fountain and Fire-side they were watched as suspiciously, and as closely, as any two Youths in silks and broadcloth are, who conspire together at a Ball or a Masquerade in London or in Bath—*more,* for the consequences were the more fatal, the punishment being *singular,* and each man an appointed Executioner, hand upon his weapon even as a smile is upon his lips. In the nations called Civilized, only those transgressions that involve two who are *truly* of one Sex, no matter how dressed or appurtenanced, are at risk of a hanging—*there,* the Law is otherwise. Nor in that well-trod and naked land were there those hundred convenient *spots* where a man and his leman might avoid the judging Eye—wherever she and he sat down, and spake their hearts, within an hour by the Sun would appear one as though by chance, to pass by in seeming indifference, yet note every particular of their suspicious retirement. Unbearable did it soon become to them—who were a world to each other, and yet could not shake the world from them!

'Then I will be gone,' Ali declared to her at last. 'I bring nothing but danger to you here. Better far that we be parted—as before we were!—than that I should bring death upon you.'

'Then be gone!' cried Iman, starting up. 'Now when thou hast found me, leave me! Yet know that that, too, is death to me!'

'And to *me*—yet do not die—be what you were—let me go, and forgive me!'

'Dost thou fear death? I do not!' And here she drew forth the Pistol at her waist—prepared (Ali had little doubt) to make an end of him, and then herself—an *absolutist,* like all her people! Yet she allowed him to take the weapon from her gently—and in his arms like a girl she wept.

'Iman,' spoke he then. 'If you will brave death—then seize *life*—it demands as much Courage—yet the reward is more than night & the Pyre—if it be had.'

'What thou wilt dare, I will dare,' cried she, and her dark eyes were alight as a tyger's, all resolve, all courage. 'Never doubt me!'

'Never did I,' said he, 'and never shall. Now attend!'

So matters stood when Ali made it known publicly that he wished to address the clan's general Council of Elders, who passed on all matters of importance, and settled all questions. His petition was not answered immediately, but, after some doubtful Consideration, was admitted—and, when still further time had passed to allow for the gathering of some far-flung personages of rank, the Council was duly called. A proper Solemnity soon obtained, and when a pipe had been smoked in thoughtful silence, Ali was invited to speak. He began by paying the company such high compliments as he could retrieve in his first tongue, and then gave to their Excellencies his humble apologies, that he had not sooner come before them,

to make obeisance—a sentiment they received with grave demeanour, as befitting their dignities. Next he proposed to them a
feast, in honour of himself—here there was some laughter at his presumption—or rather in honour of his returning to his home and people, never more to roam (and here his eye, as it were passing over all
to *include* all, struck upon Iman, whose look remain'd solemn). All
things, said he, would be furnished, and the Cost would all be his—
which won much approval—and the proposal was thereupon consented to, man by man. Nodding and smiling were general at the
conclusion, and a propitious day was fixed, tho' indeed all days in
that season were alike; and the pipes lit again; and to signal Unanim-
ity, a few guns were discharged at the cloudless blue.

It is commonly thought that our vices differ from the Mussulman's—in that he foregoes strong drink, and favours a pipe,
and Pathic, where we like a bottle, and a Wench—but 'tis only true
in part. In the realms of the Sultan and the Faith are many lands and
peoples—and though in these Albanian parts drink is not often seen,
the men call themselves the greatest swillers of all the Prophet's followers, and can gape and swallow better than any—the only limit
being the *bottom of the tun*. It was not long—yet it took a search—till
Ali found enough skins of wine and jars of *rakia,* as they name their
potent Brandy, to furnish forth the Celebration he conceived. It was
to be *al fresco* of necessity, for there was no interior large enough for
the clan's men to foregather, and indoors is less convenient than out
when guns are to be fired, and powder wasted with the proper extravagance. All were invited, of those not *in blood* with one another,
or at least willing to vow to shoot only *upwards* for these few hours—
all the *men,* I mean, which of course included the man Iman.

'Do not *you* drink—only seem to,' Ali said privily and as though
in passing to Iman. 'Nor shall I. Be ready upon my signal.' To
which Iman made no reply—no more than a Warrior might, to a
Companion, not *needing* to reply to that which necessity ordains,
and is agree'd to without words—and never had she seemed more
a man to him, than in her composure and courage then—he smiled
in secret, to know otherwise, and to think how strangely the world
is arranged.

At sunset the celebration began—a great fire was lit, and the Elders led to seats of dignity (tho' they were but carpets thrown over stone) and the Musicians set a-wailing in that music unimaginable till heard, and unforgettable ever after. A whole kid stuffed with Raisins and Rice had been turned upon the spit since noon, and now was parted, and the pieces eat with eager hands on plates of Flat-bread—and the Drink was broke out, and the skins passed and re-passed. The effect of those was instantaneous, and joy was unconfined—voices lifted in Song, if so it may be named—weapons discharged, and reloaded—and discharged again. As night darkened and the sparks of the fire soar'd into the black above to die, the dancing commenced—as the *moralizing* does in a Quaker meeting—when the Spirit moved one to begin, and then another. The supple boys the first, who in a snaking line proceeded thro' the company, with languorous gesture and a demeanour at once proud and smouldering—*interpretation* being impossible—and as the pipe and tambour quicken'd so did they, and others then leapt up to join.

4

Through all this, Iman by removes withdrew, tho' arousing no question—laughing with the rest, and lifting a Cup never emptied—to the outskirts of the gay circle—as she (though a *man*) by custom ought, lest some insult be offered her under Bacchus' influence. There she noted where stood Ali's swift horse—its panniers readied, its saddle on—as well as the best of the mounts the visitors had arrived on, the best being none too fine.

Now the drink flows as water in that land does *not*—all freely and overmuch—now the deepest guzzlers totter and sway—some old ones already wrapt in Oblivion—but others, in thrall to the laughing demon in wine, dance in abandon. The youths whirl with the speeding music, and some lift their shirts even to the brown paps, to show a *danse du ventre*. One grey-headed bright-eyed fellow, his beard flecked with foam, is so inflamed as to advance with felonious intent upon them, but confused as to which he would seize—they avoid this satyr with laughter, let him fall to his knees. Soon those not whirling are spewing or sleeping; and even the dancers themselves begin to fall like ninepins—and in the uproar that follows, which draws all eyes, Ali makes his sign to Iman.

In silence they slip separately from the throng—no one takes notice—they draw away their horses—till they are beyond the circle of light the fading fire makes, where they take hands for a breath's duration, mount, and in a moment they are gone—silent— vanished, as ghosts vanish upon the sound of the morning-bell!

*T*HUS THE TALE is ended—love and daring in two souls conjoin'd, and two swift horses, and all's told. Where they may go—how live—how love, against the world's conspiring— how grow old, and still be as they *were*—none of that is, as a usual rule, to be recounted. Yet if this tale is to be *like life*—which, I have hoped, it may a little be—tho' perhaps more filled with interesting Incident, and less dimmed by doubts, and rankling wants unmet, hours of Boredom, &c., &c.—then in *one* way at least it might—and that's to come to *no* end, for that is the way of Life, to begin (or continue) one tale, even as another runs out—even as wave follows wave, and wave returns on wave.

Therefore observe now upon the heights of the bare knobs that look down upon the Sea, where a man of no ordinary shape leads a weary mount—now and again he stops, alert to sounds that are not those of the unpeopled hills—eagle's shriek, or wind's moan—but he hears none, and so goes on. He knows well for whom he seeks, for he has followed their progress, though unknown to them—he lately fell behind, that he might not himself be discovered, and now has lost his way—yet sure he is that somewhere nearby, in a Cave of these heights, they whom he follows have taken refuge—as would he, he thinks, were he in their case. And now as he rounds the sharp flank of a vasty yellow slab of stone he *sees* what he was sure he *heard:* a horse, as weary as his own, at a dark cave's mouth: and there, in the hot shade of that same slab, out of view, he sits him down—as though he there kept a Guard over them—or waited to catch them as they emerged—it could not be known which— and, silent and still though he sits, he cannot *hear* them within.

What say they, then, those weary ones, who have fled so far, and still know themselves to be in danger—who lie near each other on the Cave's cool floor, and take each other's hands? Why does she weep, now, after riding so many miles with him, matching him hardship for hardship, without complaint?

'I cannot tell thee why,' she whispers to him, in answer to his plea. 'Ask me no more.'

'Is it the wrong we have done? I say we have done none.'

'We have not done wrong—no, we have not.'

'Do you wish, now, I had *not* returned—that all things might now be as they *were*—that I had not come to disturb all?'

Iman answered nothing to this, but arose from her place beside him, to sit at a distance from him—she lowered her eyes, and from the grey earth took up a handful of dust—that dust such as we all name our first Ancestor, and our own last State—and let it pass through her fingers unregarded. 'I cannot tell,' said she, 'if the greatest grief to me, was that you were reft from me when we were children—or if a greater grief would have been to have you stay by me.'

'Why say you so? Did I not do all I could that you might be *mine* when we were of age? When I was taken by the Pacha's horseman I heard you cry out—I know my own heart cried—therefore why say you so?'

'My Ali,' said she, and lifted her eyes again, all pity and trepidation. 'There is a thing you know not—one fatal thing—that I came to know as I lived on there alone—one thing you might have come to know too, by thought, if you had bent your thought that way—a thing that was long buried, but that I pluckt out, and then could not put away from me again.'

'Tell me,' Ali said, though her eyes warned him that it were better he did not.

'Know you, my dearest, onliest, how we two came to these lands, and this people?'

'For myself,' Ali said, 'I know *to-day*. I did not then. I know that my father was an Englishman, who ravish'd the wife of a Bey of this clan, and sired myself. My mother was slain by the Bey, and I sent away.'

' 'Tis just so,' said Iman. 'And I too along with thee, to go whither thou went, and live where thou lived'st. Ali! That poor woman, thy mother, had not one only child! I was her daughter, as you were her son!'

The dark of that cave is relieved by but a single light, Sun that through an aperture of stone in the deep backward casts a narrow Beam, which over the hours has crossed the rough walls, and now looks directly upon the two, two unmoving and apart—and it may be that what she has told him, he knew—for that aged Herdsman had long ago so said to him—and though he had refused to understand, perhaps in truth he *had*—and what he knows *now,* he had always known.

'Tell me which is the greater sin,' Ali said. 'That you break your vow of Chastity, and lie with a man—or that you lie with your own brother?'

'Both are fatal. Do the one, what matters the other?'

'Then come to me—as you fled *with* me.'

'We shall lie in Eblis, then, if anywhere.'

'If it be with you, I care not.'

'Nor I!'

Love may claim much—it may not with perfect right claim *all*—so this Tale of mine hath firmly asserted, and supplied good examples thereof—and here the last. No love such as they were ready to lose all the world for can the world allow—for that which was perforce commanded to Adam's children was forbid ever after to *theirs*—never ask why, for it is inscribed upon the fabric of Earth and Sky and the substance of our mortality, as the Ten were upon Stone—so it is—and so it must ever be; and the Fates (in the form of men, and women too, armed with pens as with swords, and guns as with Law-books) will not rest, till any *instance* be erased, as if it had not been. *Vide:* Toward that cave, from whose precincts that odd Watcher (before noted) has slipt away, there now proceed over the hills certain other men, mounted men, well-armed, fired by Outrage and Indignation and the spirit of Vengeance, who have, unresting, pursued the fading trail of the sinners, and now make close approach. Only their firing of weapons into the air, to alert one another to their whereabouts, reveals them to the two within the cave—for the pursuers knew not how close they were—and Ali and Iman mount, two upon one horse, for the horse that Iman took for hers at the first was abandoned in the flight, unable to proceed. They had intended to make for the Coast, and thence to that port where first Ali set foot on his return—but their Pursuers are several, and the pursued are driven before them, away from their destination, though Seaward still. He urging that steed—she with arms about him, cheek upon his shoulder—a day and a night, with but little rest—and they have eluded Pursuit! The Fates are after all not *omnipotent*—or perhaps now and then they change their minds— and think to let one caught soul go—as an Angler might, who *need* not, but *may*—for it more gratifies him, and flatters his Power, to *give* life, as well as take it.

So the Sea is in sight, though no human settlement near, and wide and blue as it is, it is both escape and final obstacle. And— though I have just asserted otherwise—there is in fact *one* strong fellow of their clan who has *not* fallen behind, given up and turned back—who all unnoticed has come closer—tireless—silent as a cat—and as Ali and Iman stand there upon the shore, clinging bewildered and outwearied each to other, he creeps through the grasses toward them.

'Ali,'—so speaks she, hanging upon his shoulder—and the word, as she would have chosen, could she chuse, was her last: for that single cursèd man of infinite Righteousness has now stood up, but a few yards off, and has put the brace of his Mousquet in the sand, and taken his aim—Ali sees not, till all at once he feels his beloved give way within his arms, as though struck a fearsome blow by some invisible foe—and only *then* does he hear the shot, sound following after sight. As an arch may instantly tumble at the removal of its keystone—a watchtower at the harbour's side slide all at once beneath the water that has undermined it—a flock of doves turn in mid-air all at the same moment, to descend—so Ali in that instant knew that every hope, a lifetime's worth, all the store Heaven had reserved or ever would reserve for him, was *gone*—indeed, had never been but a snare! He let fall the lifeless girl—unable to support her—laid her as gently as he could upon the earth—and sees, upon the dune, her Slayer now preparing another shot, as coolly as may be—for his work's unfinished! Ali steps toward him, arms open and empty, and awaits the shot meant for himself—impatient for it—and indeed the fellow has now readied himself,—but now instead of firing he *turns,* for he has heard a sound from behind him, below the dune's height. What is it he sees? He lifts his gun, and turns it away from Ali, and toward that lone Spy we have before *observed*—yet did not *understand.* It is he! His horse climbing with great persistence the shifting sand, he has nearly reached the bemused Gunman, and he has a long Pistol in his hand, which without a moment's hesitation he discharges fully in the other's face, propelling him feet over head down the slope—dead!

All this Ali has observed unmoving—unmoving, he watches the horseman pick his way down to the beach toward him—and sees something of the *familiar* in his shape—which is not as other men's—but is a shape that Ali knows, that has haunted his imaginings—unless this be only a further Apparition, despite the *actuality* of the dead Albanian display'd upon the sand, and the snorting of the near-spent steed. All this arising within him, as water or oil comes to seethe, Ali at last draws from his belt his sword—and, as the mounted man approaches, he rushes to him, drags him from the horse's back, throws him with superhuman strength upon the shingle, and lays the edge of his sword upon the Stranger's throat— no stranger to him now.

'Why, what do you do?' says that one calmly enough—and the voice is the voice Ali has expected. 'Have I not slain your enemy, and am I to be repaid thus?'

'Upon thy life, tell me now who thou art, and why thou hast pursued me over half the world!'

'Tell me you know not,' said the one beneath his sword. 'Deny me if you are able.'

'I know you not,' said Ali, 'but as the Shadow that I cannot avoid, who dogs my steps, who hates me, who seeks my ruin, who has now saved my life—when *that* is the greatest harm he may do me! I say *I know you not!*'

'I am Lord Sane,' said the other.

'Do not dare to mock me,' cried Ali. 'I saw him dead. You are not he.'

'Not he—but his heir.'

'How! His heir! What claim have you? Prove it and you shall have all! Think you I care for the name?'

'Put up your sword. You do not desire my death. I tell you I am Lord Sane: *For I am his son, your brother, and the elder.*'

At this, he knew not how or why, a conviction broke upon Ali's mind, that the man told naught but the Truth—that he looked into the eyes of his brother. Still he moved not, nor relented—the edge of his blade still against the other's throat.

'Release me,' said that one—his *brother*. 'There are sad obsequies to make now. I will aid you in them, if you will have my aid. When those are done, you shall have my tale. It is one you may profit from—and if not—then kill me after—as Scheherezade was destin'd to be killed—though my tale's no fable.'

Ali in despair arose—he threw his sword upon the sands. True, true it was—he desired not this stranger's death. If the man was mad, or inhabited by an evil spirit, or if he spoke the truth—Ali cared not—he cared for nothing save for the figure lying upon the rocks, her heedless limbs uncradled, her face still and pale whence the light had fled. From his own limbs the strength drained, and he fell upon his knees beside her, and laid himself across her stiffening breast. The knot tied within his spirit, tied by his father in the beginning of his days of life, seemed likely now to strangle him, deprive him of breath, so that—and it was all he desired—his starved and desiccated heart should *break* at last.

'Look,' said his foe, or friend—'see here, upon this Strand, the dry limbs of fallen trees, and the ribs of some stove vessel—the harsh Thorn-bush—let us pile them together, for a Pyre. Is this not the manner of your people?'

Ali spoke not in return, and yet he rose. 'Come,' said the other, 'while day is still light, and word of what has passed here has not reached the places of men. Put your sharp sword to this use—bring down yon thorn-bush, throw it upon the pile!'

So he did—yet still without a word spoken. The two laboured through the day, until they had built a place for Iman to lie; Ali wrapt her in her man's capote, and then in his own too, even her face and hands, for he would not look upon them consumed by flame. Around her bier they threw the grey and twisted Drift-wood plentiful there, and the thorns that Ali cut. Side by side they laboured, until the mass was tall, so that the fire would be high, and quick. Then the other produced from his pack a tinder-box, and in a short time produced a blaze of sea-grass and twigs, which Ali would not permit him to thrust within the pyre—that duty he did, with a loud cry, that was all the mourning that he would make for her—and indeed his heart *had* broken, and he knew it not, for he was neither slain, nor blinded, nor relieved: but thus it is with hearts, despite the Poets' claims—they will go on beating in our breasts, and burst not with our Griefs, and yet still lie broken within us, never to be healed.

From eve to midnight they stood or knelt upon the sand. The towering blaze was seen from a village nearby, and a few brave souls came by night to see what was the matter, and why there was a fire by the sea—but having seen, and seen the two still figures there, withdrew in fear and awe, with signs against the Evil One. At need the two piled the fire high again, until the inferno at its centre had done all it must, and there was but Ash, wherein the ruddy embers shimmered in heat, trembling with what seemed *life,* and was not. When the night was at an end and all was black, all consumed, all spent, the two mourners—celebrants—attendants—howsoever they may be named who have performed such ceremonies, and done such labours—turned from the remains, and faced the Sea, over which the Sun would rise—if it would—and they shared what bread and drink they had.

'Then tell me,' Ali said, 'all that you have to tell, as you promised. There is no *better* use for this day, I think. And when you have done, I shall part from you, I hope forever.'

'Agreed,' said the other; and so he began the tale that the following Chapter will recount.

NOTES TO THE 12TH CHAPTER

I know not now if I may be spared even to complete these
notes   I cannot look back   All this month I have done little
but lie upon my back, and when that provided no relief, I have
haunted my house and roamed the halls and stairs, seeking I
know not what by way of succor. My old friend Opium has not
been as faithful as once he was, and I am afraid to make too
great demands upon him. There is so much left to do   when I
close my eyes I see letters & numbers, as when retiring after a
long evening of cards one sees only cards   pips   faces   meaningless   I want the sea   sleep   begin again upon the morrow

1. *Alps:* It was not two years after my father's death that I was
    taken abroad by my mother's constant companions, three
    ladies whom it was my pleasure to term 'the Furies', for the in-
    tensity of their attention to me, and the incessant care with
    which they watched over me, and reported to my mother any
    sign of *ancestral* weakness, or moral incontinence. I was then
    eleven years old. We travelled first to Switzerland, to the lake
    my father always called Lake Leman in the old-fashioned way,
    on whose shores he had lived after the separation from his

wife—though I did not know that, I knew nothing, hardly knew then that he had lived and died. Now I look back to see myself, collecting stones and botanizing upon those shores— for it was from childhood my delight to know things, and learn how the world and its parts are made—and I know that I was near where he walked, and it is almost as though time doubles, and I am where he *once* was, and yet we are together.

There is a Villa, quite near where we were then residing (myself and the Furies), and it is the place where Ld. B. and the Shelleys once gathered, after Ld. B. had left England. I may even have seen this place as I later wandered nearby, and yet not known it. In that house, if we may believe Mrs Shelley in the Preface to her romance *Frankenstein, or the Modern Prometheus,* the three friends each began a tale in prose. Byron's was believed to have been abandoned. I cannot know if this present tale be that one. Perhaps the Future, if it possess this tale (as I hope to make certain it shall), may adduce evidence to show it is the same he started then, and hid away. So much was hidden, and yet what is *hidden* is not destroyed, while what is *patent* may be.

2. *The reign of that Pacha:* Ali Pasha, for whom this 'Pacha' is meant, was assassinated by a Turkish agent in 1822. That Byron does not allude to this, suggests it had not yet taken place when these pages were written.

3. *Amazons:* The Amazons of legend are placed by most authors in Scythia. Euhemerus was the Greek who taught that the stories of Gods and divine beings arose merely from exaggerated reports of the doings of heroic kings and warriors in a long-ago time. I know not if Byron's account here of the practices of the Albanians be factual, or his own invention; his companion upon his Albanian journey (which was brief, for all that he later made of it) was the present Lord Broughton, who has not responded as yet to my request for information upon this point.

4. *unconfined:* 'On with the dance! Let joy be unconfined'—*Childe Harold's Pilgrimage*

5. *Adam's children:* The same theme is adumbrated at length in Ld. B.'s drama *Cain,* wherein Cain's beloved wife is also his sister. The sister in the present tale is more correctly a *half-sister,* as was Ld. B.'s only sibling, Mrs Augusta Leigh. He chose to give to the sister-wife in *Cain* the name Adah. Augusta   Adah   Ada Augusta ada adust

6. *his starved and desiccated heart:* 'The withered heart that would not break'—*Lara*

7. *a Pyre:* It is astonishing to me that, though by all evidences I am able to assemble these pages were written before Lord Byron's residence in Pisa and Leghorn, and therefore before the death by drowning of Shelley, yet here is the pyre set up by the water, the beloved figure consumed, &c., all so much as it *would be* that a thrill as of the uncanny passed through me to read it. Here is what Ld. B. wrote to Mr Moore of that day in Lerici when the bodies of Shelley and his friend Williams were burned: 'You can have no idea what an extraordinary effect such a funeral pile has, on a desolate shore, with mountains in the back-ground and the sea before, and the singular appearance the salt and frankincense gave to the flame.' And yet *he did* have an idea beforehand, and an exact one. It is said that Shelley was glimpsed walking in the woods near his house in Leghorn, but when his friends hailed him, he would not turn, and vanished away; and on that day, in fact, he was upon the sea, and drowned. What then *is* Time? Is its course but one way? Or is it like a swift stream, that rolls some things along faster & some slower, leaves, sticks and stones, which may change places, and pass each other by, collide, and combine, even as all are borne along? I sometimes think that we lead many lives between birth and dying, and only one, or perhaps

two, are ever known to us consciously; the others pass in paral-
lel, invisible, or they run backward while the one we busy ourselves with runs forward. There is no expressing this in words;
only in dreams or in the power of certain stimulants is it possible to experience them—that state where two things can, after
all, occupy the same space.

Wherein a Tale is told,

yet not ended

HAT NAME I was given by my mother and father, or what name had been chosen for me, I know not,' Ali's interlocutor began. 'My father bestowed none upon me; I was not christened. I had come before my time from my mother's womb, and ill-finished, an "unlicked bear cub that carries no impression like the dam". My father believed—indeed he hoped—that I should not live to see the Sun set on my first day. He considered it best that I not be fed, and be let to pass quickly—as the more *merciful* way—and he supposed that it would be done as he decreed. My mother, however, hid me away, with the connivance of her servants, and though I did not flourish, I did not die. Nameless—unformed—rejected—given suck in secret—a pale worm not quite of this world: so was my coming hither.

1

'When some week or two had passed, the Lord my father discovered the subterfuge, and, judging me still unfit for Life, in a rage took me from my mother's Breast, consigned me to a Nurse chosen from the household, and sent me with her to a distant cot amid people from whom she had sprung. Privily upon her going away he gave her a purse of Money, and told her he would be glad of news that I had *succumbed*—which he was certain I should do—by one means or another.'

'I cannot conceive how you came to know this tale,' said Ali.

'I did not, till I was grown,' said the other, 'for that good woman, who took my father's silver, was not able to do what she had been paid to do. Instead she found among her people a couple whose new-born had but a week before died of a fever, and who agreed, for the same fee, to foster me—whereupon she sent word to my father the news that he desired to hear.

'I grew, then, among simple cotters, who knew only that I had come from the Laird's house—yet not *who* I was. I was called by the only name I have ever borne, which is Æ̃ngus—a wanderer's name, in Scots legend a lad born to a King and fostered in another's house—tho' I learned not if those who bestowed the name upon me recked that. There were reasons enough why a *bairn* should thus be outcast. I grew, I say—never straight nor very strong—and though the people who raised me as their own were kind, I thought of little but how I might escape the land of my birth, where I was feared as a *changeling*, and mocked as a cripple—or worse than that—for among those people Religion was not the mild affair of Glasgow and Moral Sentiment, but of the old fierce prophets of the moss-hags. A deformity of Body, as they perceived it, showed clearly the disfavour of God—or, just as likely, the favour of the Devil, for they were not done burning witches in that country. There was talk that I was possess'd of the Evil Eye, and some spoke of making an incision in my forehead, in the form of a Cross, to prevent the effects—and, if the eye is the window of the Soul, as not only poets aver, then well might mine have projected an evil from within, that 'twere best good folk avoid! My kind fosterers, seeing clearly enough that neither in my person nor in my mind was I destined to be a prop to them in their age, at length permitted me to depart; and when I had reached the age of sixteen, and resolved upon a career at Sea, they put into my hands the very purse of silver that had come with me in my basket from my father.'

'Kind people indeed!'

'It was but mine own,' said Ængus with a shrug, 'with much more too, that I was likely—indeed, as it seemed, certain—never to enjoy. On the day I struck out for the coast and the harbour, that nurse who had at first taken me from my father's house stopt me along the road, and there gave me—along with her blessing—the account of my coming-to-be which I have told you. Then I knew two things—that I was the heir of the Sanes, and of my mother's lands, including that upon which I stood; and that my father had desired, and conspired in, my death. I vowed that however far I went, I would return to have vengeance upon him, and to see the ruin of his house.'

'Which was your *own.*'

'What was mine was nothing. What was not taken from me I threw away and look'd not back. I had—I *have*—nothing but the power to act *as I will*—even to act against myself.'

'So it was said of *him,*' said Ali. 'So I saw it in him, myself.'

'I am his son.'

'And so am I.'

Ængus looked down upon Ali then, and a smile—a terrible smile, a sneer of triumph—cross'd his features. 'Then I will hold the mirror up to thee, my brother,' said he, 'and do thou look—look well!—and tell me what thou seest.'

'Nay,' said Ali, nothing abashed, and returning that gaze. 'If thou wert nothing, so was I: what I am, I have made. It may be the same with thee. Continue with your tale. Did you go to sea?'

'I did,' said Ængus. 'When a man has an object in view such as I then had—when his every thought is of an act he *will* perform, and measures he *will* take—it may so concentrate his mind as to make his daily labour, howsoever tedious or arduous, of no consequence— and he may make no *objection* to it—strangely, it may make him singularly attentive to such Tasks as fall to him, for each has its Reason, and its end in view, no matter how far off. Thus may an avenger re-semble a Saint, in the execution of his daily duty, his thoughts fixed upon a *future state*. In this mood I became a Sailor, despite the dis-abilities under which I laboured—I did twice the work another man would do, and did it more conscientiously. I learned, quickly enough, the heedless *courage* (if so it is to be named) which a man needs below decks, not to be ground underfoot by stronger and better-friended men—you must make them know you will not stop at cutting their throats, if they abuse you, though it mean your own execution.

'Thus it was that upon the Seas I became educated—not only in the nautical trades but in Commerce as well. I devoted myself to learning the most lucrative branches of it, which are Smuggling, and the Slave-trade—the two not then having become one. I rose to be Master of my own ship, and turned to the buying and selling of men, upon which I profited much, and rarely disappointed my Investors—tho' once an intire *cargo* was lost to a fever, and had to be thrown overboard, to my great cost. When the Slave-trade was banned, the traffic in them became more operose, subject to the whims not only of Chance, but of Law, and soon I lost my taste for it. With my fortune, I bought sugar lands in the West Indies, and be-came a Planter, employing many slaves in the business—the aboli-tion of *commerce* in them having no impact upon the *owning* of them, nor the *working* of them to the limits of their appalling endurance, nor even their Increase, tho' by natural means, rather than buying and selling. I drove mine, indeed. More than one I saw put to death—their lives, as their Liberty, being entirely in my hands, no magistrate needed to be summoned. Had I not been willing to take such measures as needed, I should not have lived long among them, but would have been murdered in my bed—or revolted against by my own Overseers, and stript of my *property*—for that sort took every advantage of their *employers'* weakness, as of the weaknesses of the folk they oversaw. I drove my slaves—I flogged them—I worked them. Yet I laboured with them too, and sweat beside them, often as near-naked as they in the heat of those regions. After a year and more I had a fine house, and they mean cabins; I had Pistols in my belt, and they welts upon their backs. After three years, despite my youth, I was a man of wealth—and yet no sooner had I accumulated Money to a degree I deemed sufficient, than I was done with *Sweetness*—whose true bitterness the tea-drinkers of England do not think upon, and perhaps cannot conceive. At that time, observing that the uprisings in Santo Domingo had—at least for a brilliant moment—succeeded, and having grown conscious of their own base servitude, and desperate enough of Life to throw it off, the blacks of the Islands I inhabited had determined upon revolt. There were leaders among them as astute as Marlborough, as ruthless as Caligula—and with a more noble aim, *Liberty,* than either. I called to me those of my *own* whom I knew to be allied with the Rebels, and offered them Manumission, which they rightly scorn'd. I thereupon congratulated them, and that night, with a Treasure in specie and a small crew of those who insisted against all good sense on remaining loyal to my person, I sailed away. I left behind my house, an amount of gold in Spanish dollars, the keys to my strong-room—wherein was kept not only a supply of arms but several nine-pound Japan tins of Powder,—and a list of the names of those whom they would do well to make the first targets of their insurrection.'

'You fomented revolution against your own neighbours?' Ali exclaimed. 'When you knew what the result would be?'

'*What* did I know?' said Ængus. 'I knew that the Judges, Officers, overseers, and planters whom their Revolution intended to shoot were quite deserving of it, myself first among them. Whether the revolted Negroes themselves, who (as I hear) now sit in the seats of Power, and decorate their uniforms in Gold, and have their portraits painted, have *already* earned a hanging, or *are yet to do*—that I cannot tell. 'Tis no matter; I shall not return thither. I sailed into the rising sun, toward my *Homeland,* now with the means to effect my vengeance, which was all that I had sought in my business dealings. I know not how a heart may become so singular, as though a coal were to keep its fire forever, and neither consume itself nor grow cold—yet so mine then seemed to me—it does not now. I disposed of my ship upon the Irish coast, and the crew I gave their freedom, with papers attesting, signed and sealed, with the understanding that they would return to whichever land they now considered Home, and speak not a word of me, or my comings and goings—to which they willingly consented. Now without hindrance I went to and fro upon the land, and walked up and down in it—a purse-ful of gold being a fine Cloak of Invisibility, if used as such—and learned much about the fortunes of my House, and its shameful decline in the keeping of my Father, and the fate of my Mother—dead, dead before my hand could touch hers, before I could ask her blessing, or offer my forgiveness! I learned, moreover, of *you,* my Brother, and of your usurpation.'

Ali at this might have bridled, and challenged the stoop'd and bitter figure who related the tale—but somehow upon the man's features he saw that which stilled him—a kind of carelessness of heavy usages that made them seem light, or unmeant—yet still able to sting. Usurpation! Would he had never heard the tongue in which the word existed, nor seen the lands he had *usurped*! 'How came you,' he asked, 'to learn of these things—of me—without raising questions concerning yourself?'

'I made myself known to one of the household,' said Ængus. 'Rashly, it may be, yet (for a reason I know not), I now believed my plan could not fail, that the Stars had sealed it, or that the Angels— no, not they!—had written it in the Book of what's to be, and it could not now be erased. 'Twas an old serving-man, who had waited upon my Grandfather, and for aught I know upon *his* father too—a hoary-headed ancient—a heart of oak—'

'Old Jock!' breathed Ali. 'He knew of you?'

'By certain signs he begged to see, he had proof of who I was,' said Ængus, 'as Ulysses' nurse knew him. I asked for his silence, which he readily gave, and was my spy within the house in that week when I laid my plans. Indeed, he aided them—for he supposed I had returned to claim but my rightful place there in the House—to supplant, that is, *yourself*—the which I permitted him to believe. I see in your face that this shocks you—for by his own words he professed to love you—I know he *did*—yet such men are bound most by their ancient loyalty—their hearts, and their *backs,* will break before those chains are broken. Your sudden return to the Abbey was an

inconvenience, as it fell just upon the time when I had determined
the deed might best be done. Still I continued as I had planned. Old
Jock it was, who on that night, set out astride an old galloway after
Lord Sane in his carriage; and finding him next day becalmed, as it
were, at an Inn of ill-repute upon the South-ward road, told him
that a Stranger had appeared at the Abbey, who desired some private conversation with him—the subject being his *legitimate son,* and
a *Fortune*—which conversation the said stranger would not hold in
any public place, nor under the Lord's roof. I believe that if any but
that good old man had told Lord Sane of these things, he would not
have agreed to come that night to the old watchtower. But so it fell
out, and so he came. And there within was I.'

'And there you intended to murder him?' Ali here exclaimed.
'Was such from the outset your intention? Did you consider yourself able? Did you not tremble, at the enormity—nor even at the
difficulty? He was one not easily to be conquered.'

'I had no fear of *that.* My *own* strength—which is greater than
those who oppose me often suspect—would not, I thought, be sufficient to the accomplishing of *all* my purpose. But I had brought
with me, from those Islands where I had formerly reigned, a power
that the land of my birth reck'd not of. For, among those people
suborned from their native Forests, and brought in chains to the
New World to labour in unaccustom'd servitude, there is yet
preserved an ancient Science of life & death, a *practique* known only   3
to the wisest among them (who may *seem* the lowliest) and passed
on by them to their epigones, in whispers, and under close vows of
secrecy, not to be broken on pain of death—or *worse.* In short, there
is a means known to these priests, or doctors, by which one apparently dead—to all our senses cold, without breath or motion—may
be preserved from Corruption, so that—though he be no longer
conscious, of himself or the world—he may go on serving the Master
who so animated him—or rather his *flesh.* Such a one, though he
seem alive, is *not*—he feels nothing, knows nothing. Yet he responds
to commands unquestioningly—feels no pain, no fear—is tireless,
ceaseless, insensate, horribly strong—and unable to be slain, for he
is dead already!'

'Can this be so?' Ali breathed in horror.

'*Can* it be? It is said that the Army that overthrew the soldiers of Buonaparte on Santo Domingo were composed of such. Of the truth of that I know nothing—but you yourself know it to be possible—for it was a being of this kind that, at my command, took you from your prison cell, and carried you to the ship of the Irish brothers, whereby you made your escape.'

'My God!' said Ali. 'Dreadful! And was it he also—*he*—who in the watchtower—'

'I desired,' said Ængus, 'to have some conversation with the Lord; so much was the truth. I wished in the first place to *enlighten* him—what he had been, and *done,* and what I—and how it stood between us now—*his* life in the balance, and not mine. *This* was what I had so long meditated upon—the dawning of *knowledge* in him—knowledge of his Evil, that it would not go unpunished—of his Design, that it had not succeeded—that *one* at least of his many victims had not been crushed, and that Justice would be done upon him.'

Here Ængus paused a moment in his tale, and look'd out to sea; he seemed to smile, as he remembered—a mocking smile, though it could be only *himself* that he mocked. 'You see,' said he, 'this is the flaw in the practise of revenge—which is little noticed by mankind, so few *obtaining* their revenge, among all those who *dream* of it—that the soul of our enemy is better defended than his life, and even our sure and certain power to take the latter, will not always prise open the former. So it was with him. He denied all at first—towered in Rage that I should insult him thus—laughed, then, at my Insolence, and my supposed lies, which he said *no-one would believe.* He accused me of designs upon his *own* fortune, of having concocted a scheme such as he might himself have conceived, and he called it a bad one, with no chance of success. When he became convinced that indeed I meant to call him to account, and would not be deflected—that I should stand in the offices of Judge, Jury, and Executioner—that the Pistols I had in my hands were primed and had their object in view—still no light of remorse lit his features—no more than were he a man-eating Tyger whom I had trapped, and must destroy—only a cunning, to see what chance he had still to escape. Thus he suddenly changed—he admitted the wrongs he had done to me—and to his Wife; express'd his gladness that I had survived; promised me a seat by his right hand, all by-gones to be by-gones, he and I to join together in the restoration of the House—yourself to be cast out.'

'Villain!'

'He said that, in his anguish at *my* death, by mischance as he claimed, he had set out to wander the Earth—that the years had been cruel to him—in a duel he had lost at a sword-stroke all further power of generation—that only then, and in desperation, had he sought *you* out, poor substitute for the true son he had lost—myself.'

'Villain! *Damned* villain!'

'You were but a straw he clutched at,' said Ængus. 'I have no doubt he would have slain me, or given me over to the Law, if I had for a moment acceded to any of his evasions. No—he truly admitted *nothing* but what was to his advantage—sought that alone—and (I have fought enough men to the death in my time to see it) there was in him a readiness to spring upon me, if he could—to catch me in a moment of inattention—to die fighting at the least—indeed, every species of animal Vigour—but of shame and remorse, no hint! But at last my creature entered the watchtower, summoned by my call—he had waited in the darkness beyond, unmoving as a stone, all this while—and then upon my father's face I saw the dawning of a certainty of *defeat*—yet it was not the same as if such an emotion were to enter your mind, and features, or mine:—No! Rather it was a sudden *rise*, a readiness superb and calm, as though a vast success were his at last. He smiled.'

'I can see it!' said Ali. For indeed he had seen his father thus, and it would never depart from his memory.

'Then began the final act. You know the old saw, that *revenge* is a dish best served *cold*—yet it seemed to me that now, when 'twas grown cold, I had no taste for it—I forgot, almost, why I had given my life to it, or why I thought it would heal me—to *warm* me, for it was *I* in truth was cold!'

'Did you not think then to forebear—not forgive, perhaps—but consider your Object possess'd—or impossible to have?'

'No! That he resisted was fuel to me—that he fought to the last was all that pressed me to my task! *I did what I had come to do*—I only failed to understand that to defeat and destroy him, I had myself *become him*—as cold, as heartless. I live now with him in me always—not only as a father lives in a son—but in a more dreadful sense.'

'He had no mark upon him, that I saw,' said Ali. 'No wound from pistol nor from sword.'

4   'Ah! He was strangled, like Antæus,' said Ængus. ''Twas not I did this, nor I who suspended the corse—yet it *was* I. And I *alone* it was who took from his finger the seal-ring, with his sign upon it.'

'I saw that not,' Ali said, in wonderment. 'That his ring was gone from his hand! And what then became of your Negro?'

'What care you?'

'He saved me from prison—and worse. I would know his fate.'

'I gave him the *quietus* soon afterward. It was all he would have wished for, if he could have wished for aught. Ask not for further *facts*. I know not what possessed you, that you went up the way to that Tower, on that night of all nights.'

5

'Nor do I,' said Ali—and yet across his shoulders then there moved a great Shudder—not started by the cold sea-wind, nor by any wind of the *world's* quarters. 'Tell me now,' he said then, 'why you conceived it in your interest—if so you did—to rescue me, after I was discovered in the Tower, and charged with the crime *you* had committed. Your every object was then achieved—your enemy dead—his only heir (besides yourself) taken by the Law on a presumption of murder, against which he could scarcely defend himself—'

''Twas none of my doing.'

'Yet it fell out so—just as you might have desired it!'

'Chance is the great God of this world. Some times he may smile upon us, for no reason.'

'And thereupon, at great risk to yourself, you contrived to free me, and—as I suppose—to consign me to the Smugglers, whose ship—am I not right?—was the very one you had sailed from America, and sold to them!'

'They were indeed associates of mine, of old; there were obligations, upon both sides.'

'But why?' cried Ali in bafflement. 'Why do this, for one you thought your enemy?'

'Would it have been just, or honourable in me, to let you hang? You do not suppose I should offer myself in your place—that would be honour too nice, I think, and it did not tempt me.'

'No! But why after freeing me, did you then pursue me—torment me—seek to destroy me, to divide me from what I held dear—*drive me mad*? What gain for you, what—'

'Demand me nothing,' said Ængus, arising from his seat on the sand, in a voice so like *another's* in its cold timbre that Ali fell silent. 'What I have done, I have done. You know something—not *all*—of what Injuries I have done you. You know nothing of what I have done on your behalf—nor shall you.'

'And what gain had you in it?'

'Amusement. Life must be occupied. I am my father's son. Go down to Hell and inquire of him why he did as he did in life—his reply shall serve for me as well. Ask me no more.'

'Twice you have saved my life,' Ali said, 'and to no purpose, for it is of no use to me, and I want not the remainder.'

'We are brothers in that, at the least,' said Ængus, who now wrapt himself in his Mantle, and turned to the horse that cropped the sea-grass nearby. 'Let us be gone, for day is full, and pursuit may now discover us.'

'Tell me but this,' Ali said, 'and then we shall part. Are you the father of my child?'

'If your bride came to your Marriage-bed untouch'd by you,' said Ængus even as he mounted, 'and—which I should suppose—she never before knew any man but the one who summoned her to that *rendez-vous,* then I am indeed he."

'You diverted to *her* a letter meant for another.'

'Your letter! Your chosen go-between was a foolish woman, and easily suborned. When she showed me the letter, I promised to deliver it myself—and *so I did*.'

'Then I have no daughter?'

'She was *yours* in more respects than she was mine. All our line terminates in that child. Would you had been more careful to protect her. And now, Brother, farewell!'

'Begone,' said Ali. 'I will never see thee more.'

'Say not so,' Ængus said—but the wind snatched his words away.

NOTES FOR THE 13TH CHAPTER

1. *unlicked bear cub:* Spoken by the vengeful hunchbacked Duke
    of Gloucester in the Third Part of Shake-speare's *Henry VI.* The
    reference is to the old tale that bear cubs are born as formless
    lumps, and 'licked into shape' by their mothers. How Byron's
    character, who has lived wholly in a Lowland cot, upon the sea,
    and in the most degrading of trades, has come to collect vari-
    ous sayings out of Shake-speare, is unanswered in the text—
    presumably the *appositeness* of the quote makes up for its
    unlikelihood.

2. *old fierce prophets:* Ld. B. throughout his life contested against
    the Religion of the Northern Calvinists he had at first been
    raised in; he proved over and over to himself the absurdity of
    their doctrines, and in his acts shewed his disregard for their
    strictures. Yet no number of repetitions could expunge from his
    heart the claims made upon him in his earliest youth. To those
    not engaged in it, such a struggle may seem a painful waste of
    mental energy. He wrestled with a Jehovah he did not believe in;
    better to have let Him pass, like the cruel gods of the Assyrians,

with whom (as it seems to me) He was at first born. I for one will not contest. Goodness and mercy shall follow me all the days of my life: if not that, then nothing.

3. *Science of life & death:* See the Note at the first appearance of the *zombi* in the 5th Chapter. Here it may be of interest to note that (as far as I am aware) there are no supernatural or ghostly occurrences in the works of Lord Byron. Those dramas such as *Manfred* and *Cain* which may seem to contradict this statement may be, indeed ought to be, viewed as philosophical rather than supernatural. Of tales that picture realistically our common life or historical experience, into which are intruded ghosts, prophecies, revenants, angels, &c., &c., there are I believe none. This *zombi* is the supposed product of a mysterious and yet natural science, whose likelihood may be questioned, but which is not cast beyond the bounds of Nature.

4. *Antæus:* As a child I saw in an album a print of the picture by Pollaiuolo, of Hercules strangling the giant Antæus, whom he has lifted off the ground, grasping him about the breast to squeeze out his breath. It is a terrifying image, and seemed to stop my own breath to look upon it. It must be this that Ld. B. would have us picture here.

5. *if he could have wished for aught:* How strange to think of beings able to do and to suffer, yet not be conscious that they do— a kind of doom—yet a relief too it may be. The *zombi,* the clock-work dancer, the somnambulist. To do what one must, and yet not to feel the pain of it, or know anything of it at all.

Vision thereupon after opium, that the natural world is all a clockwork, and I had discovered it to be so—the songs of birds and the motion of leaves in the wind, even the fall of dew, all the blind result of gears and springs—break open any thing and you find within monstrously tiny gears and gears within gears. Babbage nearby saying 'Gears as small as grains of sand'.—Feelings of revulsion, how much mistaken this must be, yet in the dream 'twas so—disgusting—as when an ant's nest is broken open. No no—the mechanisms are not tiny but *infinitesimal,* and living—a different order of being, as will be one day discovered.

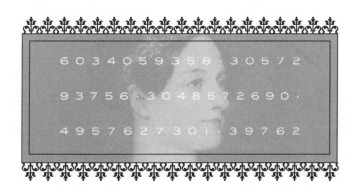

Ashfield

April 15, 2002

My darling,

So sweet to hear your voice! I'm sorry I get flustered talking at such long distances—I don't think I've ever got used to it—and then I could faintly hear myself echoed there, like I said, as though I could hear my words shooting off from some coastal station—I just couldn't talk long. Of course I got the pretty card—it's on the fridge.

So well. I'm astonished. I don't know if I'm more astonished that you went and found him (not so hard, I guess, though *I* wouldn't have known how) or because of the reason you needed to. The story's amazing—about the book, or manuscript. I hope some good, I mean *lots* of good, will come of it for you, though just *what* good might come I don't know. What good from finding Lee, I don't know either. I remember so well his being caught up in Byron— well maybe that sounds a little, what's the British word, a little *twee. Involved with* is more plain and maybe truer too, because he was then already (I thought) in the process of becoming not involved with him any longer.

Why does it surprise me that you went and looked for him? It certainly shouldn't. I mean it's natural enough, inevitable even; what's surprising is how long it took, given how little interest you ever showed—it came to seem natural that you didn't care. You know I always meant to explain it to you, as much as I could, when it was time; it was all lying there, waiting to be taken up, and I knew I'd have to someday, when you needed me to—to explain it, and explain *him*, if I could, and what I did at that time, and didn't do. I thought I'd recognize the right time when it came. I thought I was good at that, seeing when a moment is right, and since I never did—well this isn't coming out right, I sound like a dope or a flake, and I don't really think I am, do you? Anyway then we were living on River Island and you got sick of me, of me and of chopping wood and pumping water and cleaning lamp chimneys and having no phone and no friends. You know I loved River Island—I'd say "with all my heart" but that couldn't have been so, because you weren't there and I wanted you to be, and I felt your restlessness like a great sorrow. God so long ago now. Then came the long time when we were apart, when you were at school and then in NY. Anyway (again! "Anyway" always gets you from here to there) when at last I went back to the story—me, for myself—when Jonah was first getting ill—then suddenly it all seemed to have become unimportant, without my having ever noticed that it had, or *when* it had. It almost seems not to exist, now, so much else has happened. It's a little like laying away some antique linens because you can't use them now, and then opening the box years later and finding they're all rust-spotted and moldered and you don't care about antique linens anymore anyway. You know we were only together four years. Five. But ask me what you need to know, Alex, and I'll answer.

Yes it's true he wanted to name you Haidée, and I vetoed it. But to be fair, I wanted to name you Owlet. What a beautiful name, it hurts or warms my heart even now to think of it, like a child I loved and never had. He vetoed that. So I named you after my grandmother, and he didn't say no.

Alex, I love you. You know that. I hope you and Thea can come back this summer, the place will be so beautiful, we've got a lot done since you last saw it. We could talk, all you want. I'm sorry.

Mom

PS I don't mind your giving him the address here, I bet a thousand to one he won't use it. But I don't need his email address. I still don't use email. Marc tells me I'd love the Internet, that as soon as I figured it out I'd never leave it, and I said yes, that's just why I won't use it.

————————————

From: lnovak@metrognome.net.au
To: "Smith" <anovak@strongwomanstory.org>
Subject: Fin

Here is the last of it. I finished last night, well early this morning, copying my own handwritten version into the computer for you. You will see where the single page that Ada rescued goes now. I think I am going blind; the glow of this eye-book is so godlike and piercing that staring for hours into it vanquishes my regard (as B. might say) and maybe permanently. It's okay. Thank you beyond words for saving this. And thank Thea for me, if she'll take my thanks.

I remember when I was nine or ten and I read *Kidnapped* by myself. I had to decode every page, and look things up and then still not understand, and ask my dad for the meanings of words, so that reading was like an agon or a battle, and I finished it, and I won, and so did the book. When I copied out the last words of this I stopped and sat without moving for about fifteen minutes. I felt like I had slain the dragon, or been slain, or both.

About the title. It puzzles Ada that this should be the title, and she even wonders if its presence at the top of the first page is an error, or if it is there for some other reason than to title what follows; she says it seems to be in different ink from the page it heads, but of course we can't check that. Whether it was written on that page first or later or last, I think it *must* be the title he chose, and the fact that its relevance is clear only at the end is deliberate. I think of Stendhal (who loved to brag about his very brief encounter with Byron). Stendhal called his greatest novel *The Charterhouse of Parma,* even though the Charterhouse—a convent where the hero ends up—doesn't appear and isn't mentioned till the last chapter. The title is the ending. So is the title of this.

Lee

——————————

From: "Lilith" <smackay@strongwomanstory.org>
To: "Smith" <anovak@strongwomanstory.org>
Subject: Problem??

Sweetie—
Is there some kind of problem? I get no emails anymore from you and now I have a weird query from Georgiana saying that "development" on the site may have to be put off for a while until YOU can once again give all your attention to the "original mission." She is so careful to say that she loves you and admires you and loves the site etc. etc. and nothing has changed but what the hell is all this? We are trying to decode this email like it was some kind of secret message we can't understand. Can you give us any help with this?

Love

Lilith

——————————

From: "Smith" <anovak@strongwomanstory.org>
To: "Thea" <thea.spann133@ggm.edu>
Subject: Mad woman

GEORGIANA DOESN'T CARE ABOUT THE NOVEL. She's not interested. She doesn't even want to read it. She's heartbroken that the
papers turned out not to be a computer program, or a new math
theory, or something. She says the world has ENOUGH BYRON
AND NOT ENOUGH ADA. Can you believe that? She thinks we
should stop trying to transcribe it and edit it and get back to
WHAT'S REALLY IMPORTANT. She doesn't see how important it
is that Ada did this: how important it is for knowing about Ada.
Her father: that's important. She thought it was. *She was dying
and this is what she spent her last year doing.* That's not important?

Lilith is freaked. She thinks Georgiana's going to refuse to fund
the site, and that it's my fault because I've drifted off. What if I get
fired? I have to call her and start to explain.

I might have to seduce Georgiana. I won't stop. I can't.

S

———————

From: lnovak@metrognome.net.au
To: "Smith" <anovak@strongwomanstory.org>
Subject: Letter, and request

I thought you would like to see this letter I've come upon, from
Byron to his publisher John Murray. This was written four years
after he left England for good. A student at the Library scanned
it for me, a thing I'm so far incapable of, and here I insert a part
of it:

Dear Sir/—This day and this hour (one on the Clock) my
daughter is six years old. I wonder when I shall see her
again or if ever I shall see her at all.——I have remarked a
curious coincidence which almost looks like a fatality.——
My *mother*—my *wife*—my *daughter*—my *half sister*—my
natural daughter (at least as far as I am concerned) and
myself are all *only children*.—My father by his marriage
with Lady Conyers (an only child) had only my sister—and
by his marriage with another only child—an only child
again. Lady Byron as you know was one also,—and so is
my daughter &c.——Is not this rather odd—such a compli-
cation of only children? By the way—Send me my daughter
Ada's miniature,—I have only the print—which gives little
or no idea of her complexion.—I heard the other day from
an English voyager—that her temper is said to be extremely violent.—Is it so?—It is not unlikely considering
her parentage.—My temper is what it is—as you may
perhaps divine—and my Lady's was a nice little sullen
nucleus of concentrated Savageness to mould my daughter upon,—to say nothing of her two Grandmothers—both
of whom to my knowledge were as pretty specimens of
the female Spirit—as you might wish to see on a
Summer's day.

I was surprised, frankly—that he thought so often of her that he
could calculate the hour and day of her birth, and note it. A
coincidence—or maybe a *fatality* as Lord Byron calls it—is that I
came upon this letter just as I was transcribing pages about the
fictional child Una's immurement with an evil trio of elderly female relations.

But this reminds me—the latest picture I have of you is now some
fifteen years old (your mother stopped sending them at a certain
point, maybe she just thought it was unimportant, that the con-
nection was so long broken). Can you send me another? I'm sure

you could do it digitally, and it wouldn't be any trouble: not like having a miniature painted. I'd be grateful.

Lee

————————————

From: "Smith" <anovak@strongwomanstory.org>
To: lnovak@metrognome.net.au
Subject: RE:Letter, and request

How about this. I'll send you a picture (I have to get one from home, or have one taken; I don't really like pictures of myself, but I'll make an exception) if you will do something—something *more*—for me. Not just for me, though. For all of us (all of us now, and all of us then).

I need you to write a letter to someone for me. It's the person who is now in possession of the original manuscript of the notes and the enciphered pages. I won't tell you her name because it would freak her out if I did. You send me the letter, and I will forward it to her AND to the woman I work with at Strong Woman Story, who is also very keyed up and stressed out about this mystery which she actually knows nothing about. I need you to write a letter that is very gentle and very authoritative. I want you to say that this find (which you know about only from me) is among the most important literary discoveries, whatever, etc. etc. You need to sound like what you were, a professor of Byron studies or whatever it was, and also like yourself, major filmmaker person and human rights advocate. All of that. You have to convince her. You have to *seduce* her, or God that's not right, you have to *win her over* with male authority and *gravitas,* isn't that the right word? I hate asking this for a lot of reasons. But I'm asking.

S

————————————

From: lnovak@metrognome.net.au
To: "Smith" <anovak@strongwomanstory.org>
Subject: Gravitas

And what about what I also am, international fugitive from justice and statutory rapist?

I'll do anything you ask. Just be sure you know what—or rather whom—you're asking.

Lee

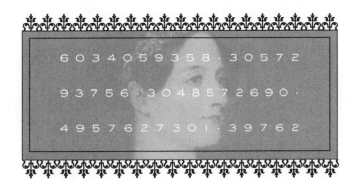

In which all are older,

and some are wiser

L ABUNTUR ANNI— and after several have slipt away, a strange Equipage is to be seen unloaded from a ship at Calais, observed in some anxiety by a small Gentleman on the dock, who peers through a quizzing-glass at its progress. It is a day in May, that one glorious day in May upon which all romances begin, and some true stories too—this present one falling somewhat flatly between the two—& the day, whether in May or November, fine or foul, is of no relevance whatever, and is only brought in to induce a sense of pleasant expectation, that the tale is commencing—or rather *re*-commencing—as it should. The small gentleman is none other than our acquaintance the Honourable Peter Piper, Esq—less honourable upon this evening, it must sadly be said, than when last we had conversation with him—and the carriage, which now rests safely upon the dock, and is being readied once again to take to the roads, is his—though little else may be. His Crest is graved upon the panels of the doors, and his man (newly engaged) is to take the reins, as soon as suitable beasts are acquired with which to draw it.

Indeed it is a delightful piece of the Coach-builders' art—a small yet commodious *lit de repos,* or *dormeuse,* more reminiscent of than truly resembling the famous coach of Buonaparte's, found abandoned at Genappe when *that* small gentleman found he had no further immediate use for it. There is space within for a couch, that may be made up for sleeping; for a stove (and its chimney), a bookcase and books, for Mr Piper will not be without his Ovid, his Montaigne, and his *Rambler,* among others. There are plates, cups and tumblers cunningly stowed, a spirit lamp or two, and any number of containers, drawers, hooks, straps and boxes for the holding of any thing that a traveller who intends not only to progress in the carriage but to *inhabit* it may conceivably find useful.

How has Mr Piper come into possession of such a conveyance? The story will long be current in those purviews where he was *once* welcome—it will be told with admiration by some, and contempt by others—how the Honourable, after a long night's play, and an astonishing run of *luck,* abetted (as in his case it always was) by his skill in Calculation, found that the young gentleman with whom he had played—who had just come into his Majority, and a fortune— was ruined. The boy collapsed upon a sopha in misery, said he was a beggar, moreover that he was on the point of marriage, which now would be capsized. When the tale was told, the Honourable— for he was *not* of clockwork, but had a heart—gave him back (yet somewhat to his own surprise) all that he had lost, upon the boy's promise never to play again. But he kept this very carriage or *dormeuse,* which the young man had toss'd at the last moment into the pot. Mr Piper was later heard to say, 'When I travel in it, I shall sleep the better, for having acted rightly.'

Now, however, those same Gods who before had smiled upon him have withdrawn their favour. As all know who live by play, Fortune is like that bridge into Paradise that the Mussulman imagines, narrow as a famish'd spider's thread, sharp as a sword's edge, that moreover crosses over Eblis, so that many a one is tumbled thence into the fires—observing which must discourage those who follow. The Honourable had always before him the example of those who had not crossed over, and tho' he had got well along the way, by exercising the greatest care, and the right Humility, yet in the end he fell. It was a matter of a thousand—it may have been two—or ten—borrowed from one to pay another—in consideration of which, and just ahead of a man with a Warrant of Attorney, he embarked upon foreign travels. He intends to go about, and insofar as possible to live, in his *dormeuse,* and spare Expense; his man will be driver, and valet, and cook his *maccaroni* on the stove, which he will sauce from a collection of sauce-bottles carefully chosen—and down below, as the coach rolls on, he can just hear the companionable clinking together of a couple of dozens of bottles of Clos Vougeot, &c., and a very com-forting sound it is. To Paris he will not go, not when the Bourbons rule there again—for he is something of a *radical,* and there is a bust of the fallen Emperor himself amid the coach's furnishings, obscured by a tin of tooth-powder. He is for Brussels, and the Low Countries, Germany, Venice—as yet he knows not—he will follow his horses. Upon a night, camped like a Gypsy's caravan in a field by the pub-lic highway, he is tucked up in his bed, night-cap on his head, with a tumbler of Brandy by, and writing, by the light of his lamp, a let-ter to an absent friend—to tell him of his changed Circumstances, and give him news (as he has done faithfully these several years) of all those whom once they knew, of ill fame and good, in the City and the Nation whose dust he too has now shaken from his feet.

'MY DEAR ALI—'—thus he begins—'You will observe from the Post-marks upon this letter that I have left my native Isle and gone a-jaunting in other lands. I expect that the next letter you have from me will carry the marks of still a different place. In answering—should you chuse to fling outward from your *promontory* or Fastness one of the brief scrawls, so dear to me, with which you have favoured me in the past—you must address it to *Poste restante, Bruxelles*—for there, in a month's time, I know I shall be—though whither thereafter, I as yet know not. I now must tell you, dear Friend, that my circumstances

are not as you would wish them to be—as I know you ever wish me
well—and yet they could be far worse, as I am not clapt up in Prison,
nor pierced through by the Sword of an angered Debtee—if we may
call the man whom a Debtor owes by that name. No, but I have fled
in shame, I must now tell you, yet with ambitions to recoup my fortunes, and bring myself once more to a position whereby I may restore to those gentlemen whose Trust I have (temporarily) abused, all
that I owe them—though I see as yet no way to do so, as I have made
a firm purpose of amendment in regard to Gaming, and have no
other way to earn money.

'Yet enough of these unfortunate and lowering events—I hardly
need burden you with *details* which would strike you as depressingly
familiar, an old tale oft repeated, 'vexing the dull ear of a drowsy man',
&c.—I shall instead supply you with your budget of news, tho' it
shall also be but *variations on an old theme*. There is hardly a Divorce
stirring this season—though many in embryo—in the form of marriages. The Summer being mild, the blood of the strong was not so
heated as it hath been in other seasons you & I have known. This
year I intervened in but a single fatal controversy—I mediated between a Life Guard and a passionate Clergyman—who was as hot
and haughty as any Irish Gamester or Cornet of horse. The woman
in question had but to speak *two words* (which in no degree would
have compromised herself) to end it—but she was cold and heartless, and a horrid sort of delight was in her countenance the time
I observed it. I managed a reconciliation at last between the two
enragés—to her great disappointment.—Our great friend Mrs Cytherea
Darling has fallen upon hard times—her life is in 'the sere, the yellow leaf', which looks poorly upon one engaged in Pleasure, tho' the
lady seemed as spirited as ever when last Winter she took a certain
Duke to Law, to resolve a breach-of-promise case, in which she felt
herself poorly used by some who had every reason to smoothe her
way in the world (as she saw it)—she would have won, too, except
for a late *ambuscade* fired by the other side, in the form of some Letters which I am afraid revealed Mrs Darling herself to have been
two-hearted in the matter. The Counsel for the triumphant Defendant is known to you & me—a certain Mr Bland—skill'd as ever in

parry & thrust. Mrs Darling has taken to the Continent herself, and now resides alone, and has covered her Mirrors.

'My dear Friend, I fear that I regale you with these light matters, which can mean but little to you in your Desert, that I might postpone telling you of things more nearly concerning yourself. A doom has fallen upon Lady Sane that even those who never wholly warmed to her—despite her many admirable qualities—will be sorry for: she has, dear Ali, *gone mad,* whether from grief at your absence, so long continued, or from the combined weight of many troubles, or from a Fairy-stroke such as none could suspect, and none avoid—I know not. I know only that she has been removed from the bosom of her family, to a house in a more salubrious climate, where she is subject to the leech, and the cup, and other remedies, attended by physicians and spiritual doctors both—or rather she *was* so attended—Science having since confessed itself baffled, they have withdrawn, and I understand she is now much alone, with companions or keepers, and occupies herself solely with prayers, and with Mathematical Puzzles, of which she never tires.

'Upon learning of these news, in the depths of the Winter just passed, I made inquiries, which gave me some certainty that your Daughter had been remanded to another property of that family, who are so well provided with forbidding and unlovely Residences from which to chuse. More investigation still discovered the place, and lo! it was that very House, so tall, so grey, upon the high seacliff, where in an inauspicious December I colluded, dear Friend, in the greatest error you had 'til then made, and the greatest you are likely to have made since—if you are indeed still on life. Providing myself with the necessities for a journey thence—a Bearskin rug, a silver flask of the best Armagnac, a brace of pistols, and a hat of Beaver—I went to call upon that house, that I might learn something to transmit to you—but oh! how dark and cold it seemed to me—like the tower where a parentless Princess is lock'd up alone— tho' she is *not* alone, but well accompanied, by three Women, old Beldames reminiscent of those three who in the tale pass a single Eye among them—by which Eye the child is ever watched, and warded. As your friend and ally I was of course forbid the house—

4

5

6

the Door was but briefly opened after my long employment of the Knocker, and it was shut again upon my inquiring nose, before my foot could be got between it and the Jamb; yet I caught one glimpse of your daughter. She stood at the top of the stair, in the light of a window there by the landing—if it was not a ghost, or an angel, that I perceived—her raven uncut hair as though set afire by the light, and her white dress like alabaster—in her hand a thing I thought to be a dead Cat but now suppose must have been a poppet or Doll she cherish'd—and her face all still, as one who looks out from the gates of Avernus upon the living world beyond, not remembering, quite, how things go on there, and who the creatures are that may be seen. Then a dark Sleave appeared from above, and a clawlike Hand was put upon her shoulder, and the Door shut at the same moment—and that is all I may report.

'Dear friend! She is supposed the spawn of Madness and Infidelity, and to bear (as received Opinion holds) your own dark Blood and its evil tendencies, whatsoever those may be; and I fear me that she will never be let out, but will grow a pale hothouse bloom in that place. I know not what recourse you have, save that you return thence, and make appeals, and even sorties, and *take* what is *yours* to cherish, & protect. I am sure that our Mr Bland will act for you—tho' forces may be arrayed strongly upon t'other side. Well! I shall say no more of this—you would have thought it ungentle of me to have withheld what I *know*—but to insist upon that which *cannot be helped* (if indeed it cannot)—Heaven forfend!—So let me pass to other topics—or none—for I feel the arms of Morpheus about me. My man upon the box keeps a short Gun loaded by him, for fear of Foreigners, and will not retire—I feel as well watch'd as Io was by hundred-eyed Argus—I trust that by dawn his fears will have passed—and then we are off again.—Heigh-ho for the wandering life! I shall write again when I have more to write of—and I remain, Sir, with all humble and obedient duty, your Lordship's servant and Friend, PETER PIPER.'

Much time had passed, and many miles been rolled over by the wheels of the *dormeuse,* when the Honourable found at a Swiss Poste Restante, along with other communications that he put aside (for it looked like courage would be needed, to inspect them), a brief Note, without mark or return: '*Thank you for your great kindness and your friendship to me. I shall never set foot upon that land again.*—ALI.' To which the Honourable could return only a Sigh, and a shrug.

After further peregrinations, punctuated by stays at Inns when the limitations of his *dormeuse* as a home grew irksome, the Honourable came down into Italy—of which Rubicon-crossing he was made sharply aware, by the painted Ceilings of the stone buildings where he stay'd, and the noisome Necessaries he there endured, and the threat of Robbers upon the highway, a species of person absent from the well-metalled roads of Switzerland—his driver now bore *two* guns, primed, upon his box, and the Honourable a pistol of his own—yet they were not challenged, and reached Milan—then followed their noses across the Lombard plain to Gorgonzola—Brescia—Verona—how sweetly the names trip from the tongue!—until at Mestre he must *disembark* from his domicile, which could not cross the water, and make for the Island City, where he had always pictured himself arriving—tho' never in the dark of Night in a pouring Rain!

Soon the sun shone, as softly it does there upon the Adriatic, and soon Mr Piper had learned enough of *la Serenissima* to continue his correspondence (so perfunctory upon the other part) with his chiefest Correspondent, and one letter ran as follows:

—'MY DEAR ALI, I am pleased with this City above all others I have seen, and may perhaps cease my roaming here—tho' I have once fallen into a Canal, which has led to a Cold, and might have been in any case Fatal, since I have not your skills in the natatorial science—it is apparently as common an accident here as stumbling into the Gutter in London, with the difference that in this city the streets are made of Water. For this reason also I have retired my beloved *dormeuse,* and packed it up, and taken a *piano nobile* in a house not too large and not too damp. I am everywhere informed that Society has fallen away from what it was in the great days—but travel has taught me this, that whenever we enter any society, we will be told that its great days are past, and it is not what it was. Still, there are but two *conversazioni* worth attending, and but four

Coffee-houses open all the night, where once there were a dozen of the first rank.

'In the mornings I attend to my Italian (tho' the language spoken here by the generality is quite a different thing, methinks, and must be learned as well) and in the evenings I attend a *conversazione* where English may be heard, as well as the best of the Native tongue—I confess I love the sound of it, like Latin gone rosaceous and soft as butter—I think I am being *seduced* when I am but greeted, or harangued. It is said of this City that she spent a thousand years gathering in the wealth of the world, and will now spend the next hundred or so in *spending* it, on Pleasure—there is a maddened quality about the pursuit, that makes one giddy, and unable to avoid joining in.'

Later he continued in this wise:—

'I learn much of Venice, and Venetians. In love they have no *morals*—at the which I profess myself shocked—but they have very strict *codes*—which supply their place, and which evoke the most grievous of *social* punishments when broken, viz., banishment, ostracism, and even the threat of a Duel, though they are by and large a peaceful people, and prefer Pleasure to Honour except in the extremest of cases. Their code has its heroes, too, and heroines—I have heard of, and had pointed out to me, a Lady now somewhat elderly, who never had but a single *lover* (her husband not figuring in the story) and who, when the lover died, remained faithful to his Memory as well, and never took another—an example of selflessness and fidelity that seemed to mark the Lady's features with a certain air of *sanctity*.

'I have also attended two executions, and a circumcision—two heads and a foreskin cut off—the ceremonies were all very moving. But these marvels were nothing, to my mind, in comparison to an encounter I must now describe to you, which involves the strange manners of Venetians in love, and also nearly touches yourself.

'Often I had heard tales of one, an Englishman (tho' as it will appear he is not *wholly* one) who had so adopted the ways of Venice, that he had become the official lover of a noble Venetian lady—the young wife of an old husband—and conformed himself to the many

and strict rules that governed his position. There was some wonderment at this, though no ridicule—these matters are taken with
what passes among the Venetians with the greatest seriousness. At
length the man was pointed out to me, at a rout—though he being
in Domino, I could learn little of him, except that he seemed somehow out of human shape—I mean *bent,* as by disease or accident.
The Lady upon whom he waited was as dark-eyed, and red-lipped,
and graceful, as she ought to be—or more. And what devotion he
display'd—what care to meet her every wish! He receives from her
her fan—delivers to her her shawl—bears her a *limonata*—opens the
window by which she sits—closes it again for fear of miasma—sits
by her, but a little *lower,* to hear her conversation, upon whatever
Subject—and when she has been delighted enough, he hastens to
call her Gondola! (It was in the execution of this task that I noticed
how he *halted* slightly as he walked, yet the flaw diminished not a   7
sort of dignity which he brought even to these slight occupations.)
He passed by me as he escorted his *Amorosa* to the stair, and looked
upon me with the most piercing—I would say *unsettling*—interest,
which I trust I well supported, returning him a courtesy.

'He must have inquired thereupon concerning me, for some
time after there came to my lodgings in the Frezzeria—a neighbourhood near St Mark's—a letter from him, borne by a pretty lad
in livery, who delivered it with the most amusing gravity, as if it had
ambassadorial status, and there awaited my reply, as he had been instructed. The letter was brief—it invited me to call upon the writer
at his own residence, at a certain day and time, whereupon I would
hear matter of interest to myself—but the hand, strangely, I seemed
to know, as though I had seen it not *often,* but upon an occasion that
might burn it into my mind. Intrigued I was—you know that an *unknown* is an interesting thing to me, and I find it hard to refuse one,
though it cost me! In short I returned a note as brief as his own,
agreeing to his request, and watched his messenger bear it away.

'At the approach of the appointed hour, then, I called for my
cloak and gondola (two nice Mrs Radcliffe words for you) and   8
glided off upon the water to his *palazzo.* The day was one such as
I have come to know and to delight in, when the Sun and Sea

combine in such a way as to cause the silver-gilt city to seem imaginary, the illusion of a sorcerer, or that hallucination the French call *le mirage,* in which a lake of water and its trees and caravanserai hover upon the desert sands, only to vanish when approached—*this* does not so vanish, but it tickles the fancy that it might, and gives a *careless* quality to all of life that proceeds here.

'I was welcomed at the stair of the *palazzo* by the liveried boy, and taken up to the first storey. There I found the man, somewhat diminish'd in stature when out of his black draperies and wearing an ordinary dressing-gown. He welcomed me with a brusque gesture, as he was intent upon a task with a yard of lace that I could not interpret, 'til he spoke. "There is," says he, as though we was come together just for the purpose of discussing this, "a right and a wrong way to double a Lady's shawl, and all my fellows seem to have got the knack, and I have not."

'I asked him whom he meant by his *fellows,* and he answered, those who like him had taken the *rôle* of *Cavalier servente* to a Lady. It is a guild, said he, with the sternest of rules; the *Cavalier servente* may act toward his *Servite* in some ways, but not in others; may wait upon her, but not refuse her commands, saving those that may injure his Honour—which is *not* injured by his shawl-folding, parasol-bearing, &c., &c. Nor is the position one lightly to be taken up—an *amicizia* is supposed to continue for many years, and those cancelling their Contracts prematurely are perfidious, and despised. If a vacancy should conveniently appear, the *amicizia* may be rounded off by a *sposizia,* and all end happily. I cannot tell you, my Lord, how ill all this contrivance seemed to sit upon the one before me—who now, having cast aside his shawl-folding and summoned Refreshment, offered me a chair by the brazier—he was almost a standing reproach to the delicacies of social intercourse, and of the taking of them *gravitate* all the more—for he hath a saturnine eye almost hard to meet, yet a tolerant smile often upon his features, as one who finds the ways of Earth a puzzle, which he will tolerate for a time. Now as we sat he came to his business, and with it my amazement grew—for he asked, without much preface, if *I knew of your whereabouts!* He had, he said, tried diligently to find them out, and had failed—when, upon seeing me at the Masquerade upon the earlier occasion, he remembered me as having once had a connexion with you.

' "I think he has leaned upon you in the past," said he to me. "Indeed he named you as his Second upon a certain occasion, when he issued a challenge to a Ghost."

'I assented that I had so acted—I forbore to say, dear Friend, that I had *also* seconded you upon another occasion, when one you challenged was *made* a ghost, tho' there was something about the man that encouraged a grisly levity—I cannot explain it, but 'twas so. Now I knew the man for sure—*this was he* who had pretended to appear for him who would not come, who spoke to us with such impertinence then—who now called himself openly by *your* name, even as he had secretly then!

' "I have request to make to you, then," continued he, nothing abashed. "I would have you send to him for me a confidential letter." I replied that I would do so, but that I was also prepared to give to him the address I superscribe upon my own letters. This he waved away, and indeed made it clear to me that he wished me only to *include,* with a letter of my own, a missive he would supply to me. Further, he asked me to keep all this entirely in confidence— that I had received anything from him, that I had sent it to you, *and* that the conversation we were then engaged upon had ever occurred. Well! This seemed to me to infringe upon mine own Honour, as being less than frank—but—I cannot say how—I sensed that it was vital that I do so—vital to *him,* and perhaps to *yourself.* To be brief, my dear Friend, I enclose herewith the letter in his hand, delivered to me *sealed,* and by a seal you know, which you may have by now already broken—let me but add, that the one who gave it me (forgive me if I do not refer to him by that *name* and *title* he himself uses, to which I do not understand his claim) was definite in saying, that if you should receive it with the seal *broken,* you must ignore it wholly, and all that it says, or requests. I take it to be a summons, and an urgent one, tho' I am ignorant of what the matter is. Moreover, and to end—he asked me to salute you, on his behalf, with this name: *Brother.*'

NOTES FOR THE 14TH CHAPTER

1. *lit de repos:* Byron when he left England in the spring of 1816 travelled in a specially built coach modelled in every obtainable particular upon the coach that Napoleon abandoned at Genappe in his flight after his defeat in Russia. It was not small and convenient, as is the one here described, but huge, and black, and subject to mechanical failures, and was soon given up.

2. *the young gentleman:* Lord Broughton (John Cam Hobhouse) tells me that this story, widely told about Mr S. B. Davies, is quite true, that Mr Davies enjoyed travelling in the coach from Cambridge, where he had a fellowship, to London, where he pursued his avocation, which was gambling. Mr Charles Babbage had a coach like it, with which he travelled the Continent. It was of his own design, and steady enough to transport delicate scientific instruments. He named it a Dormobile. I believe that fanciers of such hybrid coaches commonly convene in summer, to examine one another's recreative vehicles, and celebrate their vagrant manner of life.

3. *Fortune:* S. B. Davies did indeed finally lose large sums of money—Lord Broughton suggests it may have been in the tens of thousands of pounds—despite his skill and nerve in play. He also borrowed sums of money from his friends, which were unpaid when he fled to the Continent. It is, apparently, the only instance of Mr Davies acting dishonourably in a field of human activity where dishonourable, indeed dishonest, actions are frequent—a field which yet depends on the majority keeping its promises, and paying its debts at least a great part of the time— else the race-courses, gaming-tables, betting-shops and bookmakers of the world would vanish into air.

4. *gone mad:* How convenient and perhaps even delightful it must be, to be able to visit upon one's enemies (or their shadows) disasters that might give even the Gods somewhat more trouble to deliver, than a few pen scratches. I hear his laughter, almost, and—almost—I shudder at it.

5. *Mathematical Puzzles:* It was a commonplace of Lord Byron's scornful satire (*vide* Donna Inez in *Don Juan*) that my mother was of a coldly mathematical cast of mind, abstract and calculating, and devoted to Number. In fact that lady has little true conception of any general or higher Mathematics, and pretends to none; the only reason that Lord Byron credits her with such is that his own conception was not even as great.

6. *a single Eye:* In the story of Perseus and Andromeda. They were not evil—they were afraid—of everything. I was kept in ignorance of their fears *for me,* that I would be snatched away— but of course children (though when we become parents, we forget) may know, or perceive, more than their guardians suppose. I divined that I was, or might be, the object of my distant father's plans, and I well remember the thrill of terror and anticipation—a *mixed* feeling to say the least—when at the passage of a coach, or a late knock upon the door, I could

convince myself that the long-awaited abduction was at hand
Even now

7. *how he halted:* Mr Moore relates in his *Memoirs* that Mrs Mer-
cer Elphinstone told him Lord Byron chose Venice for his residence, because, as nobody walks there, his limitations in this
would not be so remarkable.

8. *Mrs Radcliffe:* Her Italian romances were read by one and all
in Ld. B.'s youth, *The Castle of Otranto, The Italian,* &c. Two stand
upon my own shelves in this Study, which I had in youth. I
have stared at their spines so long I feel that I must once have
opened them, but I cannot be sure, and have no strength now
to determine.

9. *Cavalier servente:* Some of Ld. B.'s most amusing letters describe his taking this employment in respect to the Lady who
became his last attachment, Countess Teresa Guiccioli, now the
Marquise de Boissy. The Countess as she then was came to
London in 1835, during the summer of my own wedding. It
was of course impossible for me to meet her, but Mr Babbage
did, at Gore House; Dr Lardiner, whom I heard lecture on the
Difference Engine, and Mr Edward Bulwer, now my friend,
both called upon her there, and from them I later learned of the
pathetic incident, whereby the Countess decided to see me married; somehow she supposed the wedding was to take place at
St George's church in Hanover Square, and there she waited in
expectation for some time on the appointed day. My wedding,
however, was solemnized in the drawing-room of a private
house some miles away. This had required a special licence—as
my Mother's wedding at Seaham also had. My private wedding
was at my Mother's insistence, her *command,* to which we (my
husband and I) assented   strange

It just now occurs to me that *here is another path* by which the MS
of Lord Byron's novel could have reached the Italian patriots in

London, who were all known to Mr Babbage—the Marquise's brother was a patriot, and a firebrand, who accompanied my Father to Greece and was with him when he died—she might be thought likely to have possessed it—with reason enough to say nothing of it—for the Marquise's memoir of my father presents him as an Angel upon whose reputation no stain or shadow is allowed to fall

if I should predecease the Lady, strike this out

FIFTEEN

In which Lucifer and his brother

perhaps agree at last

NOT A MONTH has passed since the Honourable Peter Piper's last Venetian letter received its many stamps and marks and was consigned to the Italian post as to the winds (for it too bloweth as it listeth) when a lone figure stands beside the Grand Canal, new arrived—his clothes long, his surtout black as the domino the Venetian masquers love, which draws the eye more surely than all the rainbow hues of gown and cape around it. His hair long and undressed, tumbled as the dark sea-weed—his cheek shadowed, unattended this day by barber or razor—and across that cheek a livid scar from bone to mouth's corner, like a tale named but untold. Another such tale stands in his dark deep eye, which surveys without judgement and yet without delight the throngs in their riot of colour & song. Beside him, yet a step behind, a slighter figure, in the white dress of the desert peoples of Libya—the carnival-goers but glance at him, supposing him a Reveller like themselves, but he (tho' years younger than his master) possesses himself in the same calm and stillness of spirit.

Can the one in black be Ali, this blot upon the Venetian sun, thus marked, thus fellowed? My readers (if ever this Tale is to have any—and of those, any who have, with its Author, reached this time, and place) will perhaps ask What adventures, in what climes, tempered that eager and over-charged soul, and forged this calm regard? But such readers will ask in vain—for 'twould lengthen the tale by as much again were all *those* tales to be also told within it—and so shall be left to imagine them—for see, here now comes out, from the Palazzo at hand, to greet his new-arrived Guest, a bent and misshapen man, in a coat of blue silk and a waistcoat of rich brocade—his brother, Ængus.

'I know not,' said he to Ali, 'if I may offer my hand to you. I would not have it refused.'

'We are the Sanes,' said Ali. 'The family despised you, as I hated it—at least its head, while he lived—yet it is all the House I now may own, or ever shall, and he the only Father—mine as he was yours.'

'He loved you, at the least.'

'He loved no one—not even *himself*—himself the least, even.'

'I must yield to your greater experience,' said Ængus, and for a time the two but looked upon one another, as though to discern if they would smile at last, or keep between them, as a naked sword, all that had gone before.

'There is a tale told,' said Ali then, 'among the nomads of the desert, with whom I have lived, who have their own conception of Religion, that strangely mixes Christianity and Mahomet's teachings. They say that in the beginning God had two sons, and not one—one was He who would be called Jesus, and the other Lucifer. In the beginning it was *they* who fell out, and did battle—after which Lucifer left Heaven with his angels, and Jesus stay'd at home. Then, when Jesus in His human incarnation fasted in the desert for forty days—they will gladly show you the very place, for they know it well—Lucifer came to struggle with Him again, as they had done in the beginning. Lucifer challenged his brother to renounce their tyrant Father, and join with *him,* whereupon the mastery of the Earth should be His, and Lucifer would retire to his own abode. Jesus knows it for a bad bargain, and proclaims his continued allegiance to the Father in Heaven, and His plan for Man. Lucifer thereupon leaves Him there, upon that rock—and before he takes flight to the infernal regions, his last words to his divine Brother are, *He always favoured you.*'

'A pretty tale,' said Ængus. 'Nay—it touches strangely upon the matter I have summoned to broach to you. But you will be weary with travel. Come within, wash and refresh yourself. Nothing of these matters till then—and you will perhaps consent, then, to go over to the Lido, and ride?'

1   'I am told there are no horses in Venice—save those of brass, over the Cathedral.'

'And mine. Come! May I make provision for your man?'—He meant the one in white, who stood behind Ali, and had neither moved nor spoken.

'He is unwilling to leave my side,' Ali responded. 'If you have no objection, he will stand by my chair.' At this a look pass'd between the two, master and man, if such they were—a look that Ængus observed—though, in truth, borne on that look were emotions he knew little of—feelings of tender regard, and of trust, and love. 'I have none,' said he briefly, and turned his ill-shaped form to mount his steps.

As they supt, Ali had occasion to allude to the single—and *singular*—thing he knew of his half-brother's Venetian existence, that he had contracted a *liaison* with a certain Lady, and waited upon her in the common form—a form, as Ali averred, of servitude.

'So it is,' said Ængus in reply. 'The *Cavalier* must consent to be a *servente* as well. I at first explained to my Lady, that as to the Cavaliership I was quite of accord, but that the Servitude did not suit me at all—I was overruled, however—she refused absolutely to be shamed in Society by any apparent carelessness of her feelings—I would say of her *moral sense*—and so I assented.' He lifted his mocking eyes to Ali, and though the *object* of their mocking seemed the same as ever—*himself*—yet a shadow, or a light, of compassion had entered there, perhaps for the same object. 'Comical I may seem to you,' he said then—'Comical indeed may such a life as I lead truly *be*—Still it has moments hard enough to bear with laughter. The Lady falls ill, and is thought to be in a desperate state—her *Cavalier,* tho' as it happens he has been for a time banished for some peccadillo, is summoned to her side—with her Husband's agreement—to share with him the anxieties and cares of the time—she has demanded it, tho' it must occasion the lover's taking liberties with her in *the Husband's presence,* or near enough, that would elsewhere and at other times occasion a Duel, but which by the Code the husband must regard as innocent. On the other hand, is the *Cavalier* in the wrong then to insist she refuse her Husband's lawful attentions, and permit them solely to *himself*—that dear family friend—from whom, by the bye, the husband (and his relations) feels justified in demanding now and then a *service,* or a *loan*? It is justified—it is proper—yet it is comical too—and it is hard.'

He spoke, it seemed to Ali, neither to amuse, nor to complain, but as a Philosopher—and yet still with something *un*spoken. When their collation was past, he waxed impatient, that they should depart—desired Ali to come with him unaccompanied—the which Ali refused, stating that his man knew no English, and that if they conversed in that language, he would learn nothing of it. Ængus at that assented, but made speed to summon his gondola.

'A floating coffin,' said Ali of this peculiar conveyance. 'I would not of choice employ it. As confined as a prison-car—with the added danger of being drowned.'

'Still, the life of the City could not proceed without them,' said his brother. 'You see how cleverly it is fitted out—curtains that draw shut—&c.—and a gentler motion than any hackney-coach—besides which the Gondoliers are the ones who carry messages everywhere, and are *tombs of silence,* else their business in tips would end. But here we are upon the farther shore.'

⸻

RUE IT IS THAT I am as you see me,' Ængus said, when at length three fine mounts of those that the Venetian kept were brought for them, and they had set out along that long shore—behind at a little distance, the companion of Ali following, like a shadow not dark, but bright. 'The occupations, the delights, the *frets,* and the satin waistcoats—all are mine, I own. And yet I am another as well. Tell me now: Have you heard of those here who have drawn together in Societies, vowed to oppose the Austrian, and expel him from all the Italian lands?'

'Even in my solitude,' Ali said smiling, 'I have.'

2   'Some call themselves *Carbonari,* or *charcoal-burners,* for reasons too obscure to elucidate; other ones go by the name of *Mericani,* or Americans, which makes their convictions clearer.'

'And are you of their number? I would not think you would be—I did not think you loved those who are oppressed—nor have I heard you express any sentiments, in favor of Democracy. Yet I remember what you told me, of the African slaves of your West Indian isle, and how you favoured their revolt.'

'Mistake me not,' said Ængus. 'I despise the *canaille,* and have no illusions concerning their behaviour, once established in the seats of power, or the halls of Justice. No—I do nothing on their behalf—I am not for them—indeed, I am *for* no-one, I am only *against.*'

'It seems a dreadful thing, and a melancholy.'

'It ought to matter not at all to you. I am a dog that bites, and does not bark—such a dog has its uses. I know not what others may *build.* I shall not be there.'

'What chance have they—have *you*—to accomplish that which they intend?'

'I know not for certain,' said Ali. 'There are 10,000 in Romagna alone. I myself could whistle a dozen lads—nay, a hundred—to my back at need. The *fratelli* are everywhere—they hire assassins—an Austrian officer was shot at my very door or nearly—a couple of slugs in him—and though I had him brought within, and a doctor called, I could not save him.'

'I wonder that you should have tried.'

'I think, Brother,' said Ængus, 'that—unless I am much mistaken in you—in fact you do *not* wonder.'

For a time he would say no more, and they rode on—it was Ali who took up the thread of thought again.

'Yet your duties in Society, and in matters of the heart, must often take you from these heavier things.'

'It is,' said Ængus, 'rather the reverse. Without my rôle in Society, I would soon have been stopt from giving any help to the party of Liberty, and would now be clapt up in Prison, a thing to be avoided at all costs in this Republic.'

'I begin to see,' Ali averred. 'Your *servitude* is not all it seems.'

'For a long time the circumstance has been of the greatest value to me. There are many who delight in gossiping of me—the Scotch cripple—*il zoppo*—who toils after his mistress so diligently—so like a Monkey. See, see, they say to one another, what Venus makes even such a one do, and how he dances to her tune! That is quite enough to fill their heads—they would never make further guesses concerning me. A man who would do as I have done, would never do *otherwise*—one Character per man—*two* would be a solecism.'

'So you hide yourself, and your doings, away—in the plainest of plain sight.'

'So I have done—till now. Now the disguise begins to tatter. Indeed, the very *perfection* of it is to be the means of my undoing. I am very near to very great trouble, my brother.'

'I have awaited the broaching of this matter. Now I see it come near.'

Here Ængus stopt, and dismounted, inviting his Brother to do likewise; when he had done so, Ængus came close, tho' still he look'd away, as a man might who wishes to impart a thing privily, and wonders if he might be overheard. 'My Lady's husband is a man of some parts,' quoth he then, 'and has himself not always been what he now seems. (You may be sure that I know all that may be known about the man.) He has seen some fifty Summers, and the surviving of them has made him cunning. In that unsettled time when Buonaparte's armies and officers vanished from the land like a cloud, and those of Austria returned to replace them, he took the side of a revolutionary mob—thinking it better to put himself at their head, than to have them cut off *his*. After that uprising was crushed, and the Austrian authorities restored, he returned to his former contempt for the people, and conformed himself willingly to the new Rulers. His earlier association with the patriotic movement, however, had established connexions that he thought it prudent never to give up—and through them he has drawn ever closer to my secret—indeed he is now almost certainly in possession of it—and only refrains from informing the Austrians of it, until he have disguised his own Hand in the matter, and is able to unmask me without unmasking himself. It will be at any moment now. I am prepared to leave upon the hour, if need be, and vanish with no more trace than those enemies of the State under the Doges, who, once denounced and tried in secret, were never heard of again. Yet I cannot—till I have replaced myself, and quickly, with one wholly unknown, and undiscoverable—a man whose name appears on no List, and is on the tongue of no Informer—a man who is willing *and able* to do the work I have been engaged with.'

'So it is for this that you have drawn me hither,' said Ali, with a smile—a sort of smile that could not have crossed his lips in times gone by—a smile of the Sanes, yet not, for his soul is still untainted by that dark stain. 'You will ask of me, that I be this one.'

'I know no other that I may so ask. I cannot say, still, why I have thought to do it.' Here he bent, and from the sand picked up a round smooth stone, of blackest hue, and stroked it in his fingers as though it were precious. 'Have I guessed wrongly?'

'I have no reason to consent.'

'Have you never felt those stirrings of anger, or resentment, at the powerful and the cruel, or inspiration in thinking of their overthrow? I should have thought you would. I should, if I were you.

3 Do you know the tale of Jacques-Armand? He was a peasant boy, forcibly adopted from his parents by Queen Marie Antoinette, who took a fancy to him. Yet despite her caresses, and the fine clothes

and rich foods he was given, he wept continually and was inconsolable. When the Revolution came, Jacques-Armand became the
most ruthless Jacobin of all, and beheader *extraordinaire* in the
Terror.'

'I cannot see how this tale applies to me.'

'That you cannot, seems to make plain that it does not.'

'What do you offer, should I be willing? What do I gain?'

'I offer nothing.'

'Nothing will come of nothing.'

'Yet I think something may. I have hopes that, though I have
nothing to offer, still the challenge may interest, and the hope in-
spire. I say it *may*. Understand that I am aware how unlikely is this
gambit of mine to succeed. You may judge how desperate is the
case, by my willingness to try it.'

When Ali made no response, Ængus continued thus: 'You have
heard of the Societies of Italy. It may be that you have heard of similar brotherhoods, in other lands.'

'I cannot say so. Perhaps they know better than the Italians,
how to keep their secrets *secret*.'

'I shall now tell you of something I have sworn upon my life to
tell to no-one but him who shall be numbered among us. So much
do I trust your silence.'

'Have a care. You know not what beliefs I hold, nor what alle-
giances I have sworn. How do you know I am not, myself, an agent
of that Empire against whom you contest? Or of some ally of it? Or
a seller of information, and of *men*?'

'I know, Brother, because no man could be more transparent
than yourself—you ever were—it maddened me, that you were so,
and naught I could do, would *darken* or *cloud* you. Listen to me now,
and I shall tell you of a thing known to few. Over the wide world—
at least that part of it, from our own Isle even to the throne of the
Czar, where the spirit of Liberty is not killed—there has been built
a Society whose members are united by a singular purpose, or but
a few, and who are vowed to aid all others who are so dedicated,
whatever their Nation. In short they intend to see the end of Kings,
and hereditary Lords—and all Churches and Courts, whose Virtue

and Justice consist solely in serving Kings and Lords—indeed all those borne on the backs of the peoples of the world as a burdened Ass bears his load. If it take a Century—and they believe it will take no such number of years—there will in the end be none, and so (it is held) all peoples will be free of *unnecessary* sufferings: for there are sufferings enough everywhere that none among the living can avoid.'

'Can this be true?'

'It is true. In each country where they are established, they are known by a name of their own, but universally they bear but *one*—would you hear it?'

'You seem intent that I should.'

'They are called Lucifers.'

Ali laughed to hear this, and his laughter both alarmed and delighted his Brother by him—who thought he had not heard the man laugh before—certainly not at the curious ways of the world, and the doings of that great God without a Religion, *Circumstance,* who delights to bring about such jokes as this one, having in his keeping some for each of us—who in homage to him may well laugh, or weep!

'I thought,' Ali then said, 'that the former Emperor of the French was dedicated to this same work—to sweep away the old Oppressors—break open the Prisons—unburden men, and women too—free slaves—and Jews. Yet he stands now upon a rock in the middle of the sea, and all the old Perukes have come back in.'

'Indeed. All those young firebrands, who burned to free their Nations and Peoples from tyranny, joined perforce with their toppled Kings and Nobles, to rout Napoleon and his pasteboard Monarchies—even those who had at first adored the man. Now they have seen through that trick—and they will forge a Liberty from within, not one imposed from without—a *German* liberty, different from a *Hungarian,* a *Greek,* a *Venetian*—Liberty, and self-government, to each his own!'

'I own it is a dream I too have dreamt. Yet is it *but* a dream?'

'They may change the world,' quoth his Brother—'Indeed I am certain they will—tho' for the better or the *worse* I am not so vain as

to assert. I have read in the Italian press that the two greatest examples of Vanity the present world affords are Buonaparte, and an   *4*
English poet. Think how *flattered* the old Emperor on his sea-rock
should be, were he to hear of the comparison—as only *he* had
power to hurt—the other only to *limn.*'

'I know not if I should make a success of revolution,' Ali
said then in seeming thoughtfulness. 'I am not cold-blooded—or
hot-blooded—enough. The plain humanity of the man before me,
be he the soldier of a king—or a King—or the Pope himself—if he
be not personally an enemy of mine, I am likely to think him a
good enough fellow to *live,* at the least. And I will approve a brave
and honourable man, whichever side he stand upon.'

'It is creditable to you,' said his brother, without much conviction. 'But let it not dissuade you, if you lean to this. My own case is
the reverse of yours—the Company and the contemplation of any
lot of my fellow Humans always becomes for me, and soon enough,
a perfect *ipecacuanha.* Yet I have worked long on their behalf, and
somewhat prospered in the trade, as well.'

Ali was thoughtful then again, and clasped his hands behind
him and lowered his head—glanced with careful eye to where his
companion in white waited motionless upon his horse, like the
Statue of a Ghost. Then he said: 'A man who took upon himself
these tasks—would he not risk all, even those he loved? Such a one
ought not to be burdened with parent, or wife or *child*—lest his
ruin, which seems likely enough, should be theirs.'

'I think it to be so.'

'I am not thus burdened.' This Ali said, yet without
complacency—as his Brother saw.

'Do you dare then to do these things?'

'How can I know what I dare? When I have done what I shall
do, then should you know what I have dared—or failed to dare.'

'Well said,' quoth Æ ngus. 'It is all that I would ask.'

'Your Lady—I assume she knows but little of this—'

'Nothing. Knowledge even in the slightest would endanger
both of us. I confess to you—no matter that my object is clear, and
the means likewise—I am pained that I must leave her thus—

vanish upon the instant—and she never to know where—well—it troubles me, though I know not what name I may give to this troubling. She has been loyal to me, as I to her—and believe me, there are not so many who would look long with favour on such as myself.'

'And where will you go? Into what land, to what shore?'

'That I know not, so it be far enough. I am a marked man, and once marked, I may not be *unmarked*—for you see, I am what I am—no police spy, no enforcer of the Laws, no border guardian, could mistake me—and *their* network is as wide, as far-flung, as well-informed, as our own. Where I go must be far, if they are not to follow—a place their Power reaches not.'

'To the Antipodes, then. Or China.'

'I say I care not—somewhere this side of Hades—that is all.'

'Very well,' then said Ali with sudden force. 'I will accept your proposal—I will remain here—I will execute what Duties I am called upon to perform, to the best of my abilities, if you will instruct me in them—'

'Aha!' cried Ængus, and clapt his hands. 'Splendid fellow you are!'

'But with this condition—that you likewise take up a piece of work—a dangerous one as well, though not to Life, perhaps, or Limb—yet doubtful of success—and also secret. One which by my *pledge* duly made I ought to do, but which perhaps by *rights* belongs to you.'

Ængus knitted his brows in question at this, and he demanded to know of what Ali spoke. For answer, Ali returned a question— 'Tell me,' he asked his brother, 'do you ever give thought to your Daughter?'

At the word, Ængus looked sharply away, as though stricken— but only for a moment. 'Of what daughter do you speak?' said he then, coldly enough.

'You have but one, to my knowledge,' said Ali.

'I may have several,' responded Ængus. 'There is hardly a *slave-driver* of the West Indies who may not own to a dark-skinn'd pup, or to many.'

'You know of whom I speak.'

'Then I know not if I *have,* or only *had,*' said Ængus, and he flung into the quiet wave the stone he had before picked up. 'She may well be dead—only think how much a child must pass through 5 to grow even to a few hands high—convulsions—fevers—black vomit—diarrhœa—cough—consumption—galloping this and foudroyant that—not one in six achieves it—why should I suppose she would?'

'I assure you that she lives,' said Ali.

'Is she,' asked Ængus, and his eye still avoided his brother's, 'well-formed? I mean to ask—'

'She was perfect,' said Ali, 'and I hear that she remains so.' 6

'Well then,' said Ængus, and again—'Well then'—not as if in answer, or assent, but as though he answered a question from within himself—and deep within.

'Let us,' Ali said, 'mount again, and I will tell you of this Condition I mean to make, and how you may meet it—if you chuse.'

'Then let us ride together,' his brother said; and they mounted, and together rode along that strand. Rosy grew the snow-clad tips of the far Alps as the Sun declined—the prints of their horses' hooves dotted the sand along the hush'd sea—and long the Brothers spoke, of many things.

NOTES FOR THE 15TH CHAPTER

1. *no horses:* Lord Byron's horses were famous in Venice, where indeed they are rare, and quite useless. He stabled them upon the Lido, the great strand that faces the Adriatic, and rode them almost daily when he lived there. Certainly he loved riding, as he did swimming, for on horseback he was anyone's equal.

2. *Carbonari:* Lord Byron was himself inducted into this society, and attended its meetings; in his house he stored their weapons, and a deal of Mantons' powder too, that he bought for them. He always regarded the Italian conspirators with a cold eye, and understood well their disabilities—their Latin impulsiveness, &c.—yet he espoused their cause, and never wavered. One among them though   one among them.

3. *Jacques-Armand:* I find the tale is told in the *Memoires sur la vie privée de Marie-Antoinette,* by Mme Campan (1822). I know not if Ld. B. found it there.

4. *an English poet:* Such a note did appear in an Italian newspaper, making an association that Lord Byron might have aspired to,

but on a basis that, hardly creditable to him, must have amused him a good deal. To receive the right notice for the wrong reason—the vanity of human wishes.

5. *may well be dead:* Lord Byron had, as is well known, a daughter by Claire Clairmont, a half-sister of Mary Shelley's, whom he named Allegra. She died at the age of five of a fever, in the convent to which Ld. B. had remanded her for her education. I know not, and there is no way to tell, if this tale was written to this point before her death. Ld. B. had taken the child in the first instance from the Shelleys, who had lost more than one child to various illnesses; perhaps he believed she would surely die in *their* company. He loved her, indulged her, and found her uncontrollable, vain, disputatious—a child. Yet his giving her over to the nuns was not to rid himself of her so much as to ready her for the only life he could imagine for her: an Italian life, marriage to an Italian, for which he had already supplied a dowry before she—   What if it had been me   That child   my sister   but a year and a month younger than myself   he loved her and he could not or he would not keep her   he talked of taking her with him to America   What if by some means he had contrived to take me from England, and on his journeys?? I think of this or once thought, and often too   Would *I* then have died, in an Italian convent—been sent home as she was in a small coffin—buried as he requested in the church at Harrow   the Rector refusing to have her in the Church or to have a Monument put up on the church wall, so she is somewhere unmark'd in the churchyard   He wrote for her *I shall go to her, but she shall not return to me*   no it is not I who lies in Harrow church-yard without a name to mark the place

6. *perfect:* It is said he thus asked after *me,* and asked the nurse to lift my clothes to see my legs and feet   from this may have come the untrue tale   I know it to be untrue   that when my mother was brought to bed & I was delivered of her

he came to the door of the room   drunk   and asked *Is it dead? Is it dead, then?* He did not do so   my mother will not say he did   He asked if I were *perfect*   It was natural to ask— for *he* was not.———

great pain today   mother's Bible by

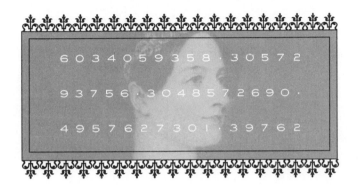

From: lnovak@metrognome.net.au
To: "Smith" <anovak@strongwomanstory.org>
Subject: RE:Gravitas

[My dear—How's this—the Salutation is part of the gravitas:]

Dear Alexandra:

I am extremely grateful to you for having entrusted me with the news of your astonishing discovery of a heretofore unknown prose fiction by Lord Byron. The discovery, when it can at last be made public, will alter our picture of Byron, his work, and above all his relations with his wife and his daughter. I can think of few discoveries of comparable importance related to writers of the period. When I completed my doctoral dissertation on Byron at the University of Chicago, he was in as deep eclipse as it is possible for a major poet to be, and yet his life, and his career, have never ceased to intrigue and excite commentators, biographers, and the reading public—even while his written work has become less and less familiar. During my tenure at two universities (you've asked me for a CV, and I am faxing it under separate cover) I of course worked to make students and others aware of his worth—the list of my papers, studies, monographs, and addresses are evidence of that. It seemed important then to rescue Byron from his legend, and thus I wrote studies with titles like "How Byronic was Byron?" and "Saving Byron from his Friends." Even that enterprise now seems somewhat recondite to me, and perhaps convinced few. I myself turned away from Byron, and the university, to pursue other interests and imperatives—for the past twenty years I have worked on a series of film projects designed to bring the calamities, struggles, and daily lives of people in many "remote" places in the world (not remote to those who live there, or those who want something from them) to the attention of that world I myself spring from. (I am proud of these films, and glad of the awards they have garnered, though there is no scientific way of measuring their real impact—any more than there was a way to measure Byron's influence on the course of Greek independence.)

Now, when even to me Byron sometimes seems part of the unreclaimable past, the world has discovered new reasons to be interested in him. There is his complex sexuality, which it is now permissible to ponder and inquire into without evasion or moral horror (or other bias)—he doesn't need exculpation, or championing, at least on those grounds. But above all there is his daughter, and the way the world has gone in the last decades, which has made her seem a kind of prophet, someone who, clearly if not in detail, saw the future. Ada really did see what few others saw in her day—really, *no* others—that machines of the future would compute, manipulate symbols, write music, store data, and perform activities that it was assumed in her lifetime only human minds could do.

She saw herself as doing more than that, however: she saw herself as in pursuit of a new kind of science altogether, a science that would bridge molecular and atomic physics and human mentality, a science in which investigators were their own laboratories, as poets are their own smithies, where they forge new realities from their selves. From the beginning her high-minded (and vengeful, and wary) mother had kept her from poetry and anything that smacked of the imaginative, the self-regarding, the emotional—the Byronic. What Ada came to know—what her mother couldn't have imagined—is that science is a realm of passion and dream as great as poetry. She saw herself, in other words, as the continuer of her father's personal experiments with the possibilities of life, liberty, and the pursuit of happiness—only in different terms, terms that his time could not conceive, and that she herself could not fully articulate. She believed there could be a molecular science of mind, a cosmology of thought, a true science beyond mere self-examination and reflection, indeed a science that without reductionism would transform self-examination itself—and that those computing machines would be a necessary component of it, both as tools and as subjects. Well, she was right—*is* right. The neuroscience of our day, which is impossible without the digital tools she envisioned, is doing exactly the work she wanted to do— and coming to conclusions, or envisionings, that she would have understood. (The phrenology she was devoted to, which came to seem inadequate to her, was an early attempt to found a science of the mind on the physiology of the brain.) In fact it's hard *not* to think that, in her recovery, rescuing, enciphering, and annotating of her father's work (a very uncharacteristic piece of it, by the way) she was consciously furthering that work, by a self-experiment in memory and heredity. She was apparently, if your research is correct, at work on it nearly till the day she died.

So the interest of what you've found isn't only for us aged Byromaniacs, if there really are any unreconstructed ones left. The interest is in the light (and warmth) it sheds on Ada—not on what she did do, of which the rather inconclusive records exist, but what she *was*, and *might have been*—which is more important to us, who live in the world she longed to glimpse—and did glimpse.

Yours

Lee

[So do you think that's what's needed? Less? More? I can spin it differently if you want. You may not think so, reading this note, but I actually believe every word of it—L]

───────────

From: "Smith" <anovak@strongwomanstory.org>
To: lnovak@metrognome.net.au
Subject: Thanks

Good. Thanks. Really thanks.
I believe it too, every word.
I'm just going to add this: "It would not only be a loss to literary history, or Byron studies, if this work didn't see the light. Above all it would be a loss to our knowledge of Ada, for whom the sources are so much slighter than for Byron. She collaborated in this work [piece? story? project?] with her dead father, and both are illuminated by what they did, but Ada especially."

Okay? It's not as pisselegant as yours. I never learned to do that. Or did it just come naturally to you?

You'll get a picture soon.

S

───────────

Ashfield
April 25, 2002

My darling Alex,

Well, the spring has come at last here, the tulips are out now and the orioles have returned to make a nest (or refurbish the old one) in the quince bush. Their orange against the scarlet of the quince blossoms is so intense it almost clashes—though I guess no colors in nature can clash really.

You know I was only afraid for you: not afraid that *he'd* hurt you, though he might believe I thought that. I was afraid that sorrow would hurt you. Sorrow for yourself, and for him too, and for the damage he *suffered,* as much as the damage he did—and for that poor child on that night above all. Sorrow, that could kill you it seemed, like a late frost can kill things just starting so hopefully. I know that's wrong. Marc and I watched a butterfly coming from its cocoon the other day—my God this is so strangely corny I can't believe it's so—and butterflies come out, you know, all wet and folded up like a stuffed grape leaf, and then start to unfold. It takes such a long time, and it looks so difficult—the poor little thing was just panting, or so it looked—and straining to set these sails. I wanted to help, and tug them open for it, and Marc said—I suppose he'd know—that if you do that, and the butterfly doesn't do it for itself, then it can't fly: it's the process of stretching and airing and waving and panting and drying out that activates the muscles, or whatever passes for muscles in butterflies. Only then it can fly.

I know all that, and I knew it then; I wanted you to fly, and with your own wings, and I knew how little I could help. I just wanted to keep sorrow away, until you had to face it. I knew you had to. I just wanted you to be stronger first. People say that troubles and grief can make you strong, but I don't believe it—I think that love and happiness make you strong, they feed you and wrap your soul in healthy tissue, in *love-fat,* so you can stand things, and abide the cold. Of course I know now it might have been really me who needed to get stronger. And from your loving me, I did. I hope you'll forgive me.

Love
Mom

———————————————

From: "Smith" <anovak@strongwomanstory.org>
To: "Thea" <thea.spann133@ggm.edu>
Subject: Hey you

My dearest dear:

Faxed you my flight schedule, or shed-jewel as they say here. Virgin Air (!) Omigod I can't wait.

You know what I thought today: that if Ada had lived now, or even a little later than she did, she might have been allowed to see her father. If *he* hadn't been so badly treated by doctors in Greece he might have lived, at least a few more years, and she might have just packed up and gone abroad to find him. If if if. I wish I were a real historian because they don't think if if if.

I want to find a letter from him, to someone, someone who was near him when he died, that says *Take these pages and give them to my daughter*. He wanted to tell her that he would have come for her if he could have, and taken her away with him to somewhere they couldn't follow. But I think he just lost them. *She* had to be the one, the one who did the work of finding and saving the book. It was nothing but a letter meant for her, and she was the one who was supposed to get it, and then in the end she did get it. That's what I have to say when I write about this, that she was the one.

It's like Babbage's miracles. Did you read about this? Babbage used to invite people to his house to see the Difference Engine work. He would set all the wheels to zero, and then turn the handle, and one wheel would go to 2. Then turn the handle and it goes to 4. Then 6. And everybody gets it—the rule is, "add 2." At 8, the wheel turns to 0 and the next wheel turns to 1, and you get 10. He'd go on and on maybe a hundred turns. Then suddenly the number jumps not by two but by a huge number, like 100. Everybody reacts—a break! An oddity at least! Babbage explains, no— he instructed the machine in advance to do that—after a certain number of turns to advance by 100 instead of by 2. In other words the break was built in from the beginning—it was a rule and not a break. That's what Babbage said divine miracles were—they were natural rules too, but just rules we didn't know about till they were manifested. See I think that too.

The miracle of Ada is not that she saved the novel. The miracle is the love she didn't know about, that would make her do that: love coming at the hundredth iteration, a sudden advance, programmed from her childhood maybe, but only just then showing up in her life, when she was at Newstead Abbey, and at the tomb where her father was, and his father too.

The book's in digital form now, Word Perfect format, haha, and I can deal with it anywhere. Georgiana's not mad anymore. She told me she wrote Lee *a card* thanking him for his advice and encouragement. I knew it. She probably sprayed it with perfume, or scent, they say here. Lilith is still pissed tho.

See you and the Honda at JFK. I can't say what I think in my heart.

Smith

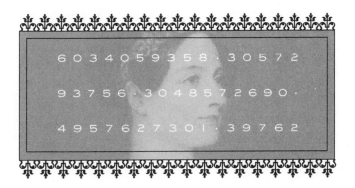

SIXTEEN

Wherein all is ended,

tho' not concluded

FROM LONDON IN ENGLAND there came to Venice on the Adriatic a letter addressed to *The Honourable* Peter Piper, and enclosed within that letter another letter, which the Honourable was charged to transmit—by other means than the well-watched Post—to its intended recipient, who, upon receipt, opened and read as follows:

MY BROTHER,—When we two parted, my question to you was, Why you should trust me, that I would do what you asked, and why you thought that I could do a better thing for that child, than her present Guardians? For in myself I saw naught, that would cause me to think I was capable of it—of the *deed,* I had no doubt, but of the rest, not at all.

I shall tell you all that has occurred, and you may judge for yourself as to whether your trust in me was well placed. Alas—unless you fail, and are hanged in some public square—I shall never learn as much of *thee.*

To my tale.—My visit to the Temple chambers of Mr Wigmore Bland, bearing the papers you were good enough to supply me with—the power of Attorney, and the rest—produced upon the inert mass of our affairs the right Leavening. The Estates of the Sanes are dissolved for ever, or soon enough shall be—and we shall be Landless—tho' richer in Cash than we have been these several years—the disposition of which shall be as we agreed, provision being made for all Servants, Tenants, cats and dogs too that your tender heart desired to see pensioned. Thus shriven, I set out for the house of the imprisoned child—Mr Bland was well-furnished with details upon the matter of her confinement, which he deplored most fittingly—indeed, he became almost *melancholy*—for a moment—before recovering himself. From him I learned that Lady Sane—as your lawful wedded Wife is still styled—has not recovered her Wits, though she has been treated by a succession of doctors of every persuasion, who fasten upon her, and her Cheque-book, with all the tenacity of the Leech they employ so freely; Mr Bland was certain that *one* at least, and in all likelihood several, were not Doctors at all, except perhaps once in Pantomime.

Upon my arrival in the neighbourhood of that house where Una was confined, I soon learned that I would not be called upon to free the child from those who held her prisoner, if so they did—for even as I came to the house, the talk upon the roads and in the Village was of how she had *freed herself.* You may not know—I think, indeed, that you know nothing at all of her—that like her father's *brother,* she is subject to Sleep-walking. I know not if this condition had made itself known before, or if the Guardians, set at her gates like a three-headed Cerberus, knew of it, but perhaps they did not—for the locks on all their doors were upon the *inside,* to keep intruders out, but easily un-done from within—and so out she went, upon the middle of the Night, and set out upon the Highway, like the Piper's son, over the hill and far away. In the morning, her absence having been discovered, a Hue and Cry was raised, but she having been gone many Hours, and observed by none as she walked unconscious among them—a sleeper awake, among the sleeping-unawake!—the worst was sus-pected. Weirs were to be dredged, and Rivers watched; hay-stacks were poked into, and woods beaten—to no avail. You may imagine that in this search I made not my-self conspicuous—you have evidence yourself, of a quality I have, or a Talent I may employ, of being, when I choose, *invisible,* or at least unnoticed, despite all that is distinctive about me.

For my part—it is my natural bent—I considered acci-dent or mischance less likely to have been her fate than Evil—I think that those who sleep-walk are commonly able to avoid falling into ponds or stepping off from cliffs—but a Child alone at midnight in her nightdress is a temptation to *some*—and a green county in England is as likely to show one or two such as any spot on Earth.

Shall I keep you upon tenter-hooks, dear Brother, as to how this tale continues, or concludes—or have you gone already to the last page, and seen the outcome, as a maiden with a French romance will do, to learn that the lovers live 'happily ever after'? The events of the succeeding weeks are perhaps worth the ink & paper to recount, but I shall not expend them—I have not the time, for the Thames is on the turn, and the tide is about to go out, carrying the nation's Trade (and some of its Populace) to far corners. A cool calculation, made at the Inn of the town where the Child had lost herself, gave me odds of an hundred to one about finding her—lower, of finding her before her Rela-tions did—lower still, of finding her unhurt. Nevertheless I did so, and that because—as it fell out—a fellow who was as cool a calculator as *myself* was the first who chanced upon her that night. In the widening circle of my investigations, I learned that in the next town a Gentleman, thereabouts unknown, had got on the London coach with his sleeping child in his arms—a dark-headed child—and thence I myself hastened.

You may know that in that City, in company with a certain Friend of long standing—anciently a companion of our Father's—I enjoy'd a brief career in the show business, and found that as to *mobility,* and freedom of seeing and hearing—which last will include *over*hearing, eavesdropping, and related Arts—it has no equal. For sure a Hunchback with a Bear may seem quite remarkable—but in fact he is invisible to most—because *expected*—no more regarded than the paving-stones, or window-sashes, or any thing ordinary—and such a one may stand about by the hour, and collect intelligence—along with a few coppers—which are not to be despised neither. Moreover, among the Brotherhood of show-men much may be learned of the former lives of those now appearing upon the larger stage of Life—they acknowledge their old friends the Countess who once danced at Drury Lane, the fashionable Preacher who lately told fortunes in Green Park, the rich Landlord whose fortune began in a House of indifferent reputation. From the gossip at inns and fair-booths, I learned much concerning the former history of one who now in Mayfair drawing-rooms was making a great stir—a Mesmeric Doctor who had cured many young ladies of maladies that *some* of them had not even known they were afflicted with, until the Doctor examined them—his Magnets, Coppers, jars, fluids, and Ætheric Engines had effected miracles. He is not the first or last who have made a success in such enterprises, but those who talked of him to me, who knew how far the Doctor had *risen,* were admiring. What caused me to inquire further was, 'twas said he was accompanied by a

Child, who was the centre of his experiments—a Child whom he could, with but a pass of his hand, or the use of a bit of magnetised Nickel, put *deep asleep,* yet remaining alert and upright, able to follow commands, and—what is far more—to *speak* upon question, and to tell others present something of the Name and Nature of their diseases, and *un*eases.—What Science now purports to do, has been done in past centuries by Saints and Priestesses, who spake truths in trances—but no—the Doctor's lectures claim'd a new revelation, drawn out of Mesmer, Puységur, Combe, & Spurzheim—his young Pythoness was subject to no old-fashioned Delphic transports, but methods never granted Man before. Well! I know not, nor ever will, aught of such things—tell me that all has changed forever, and there are truly new things under the Sun—despite Solomon's obser-vation—and that soon enough a Steam-engine will conduct man to the Moon—I am happy to suppose it—yet may not change my behaviour—nor invest my Money.

No—my interest was aroused in the Mesmerist, for other reasons—and soon enough I learned more:—that the child was not the Doctor's own, nor related to him in any way—that he had come upon her in circumstances dark, but not beyond imagining—that he had from the prompt-ings of Charity rescued her from these, and only *after* had discovered her to possess talents & powers of a remarkable sort. You may believe that, by that time, I possessed an An-thology of gossip, report, thief-taker's tales, &c., none of which satisfied me—had been to see a small Body brought out of the Thames by hook—and an unfortunate child coffin'd in a low dwelling in Southwark—neither of them she. Yet this tale started in my mind a certainty, I know not why, and in not too long a time I had found the supposed Doctor's residence, and a way of effecting entrance that raised no alarm—many are the small skills in force, fraud, uttering, and lock-picking I have acquired in my travels, to my shame. The house seemed empty—and as a Spy within

1

2

the enemy's camp, I opened doors without a sound—until one opened onto a sitting-room, and there upon a tuffet sat a girl-child, in a dress of white, a paper daisy-chain in her lap—alone. And thereupon I opened wide the door, and entered in.

Why did I suppose she would not flee, or raise the alarm? I know not, but in the event I was right. The child kept to her seat with a strange stillness to see me approach—not the frozen stillness of a Deer who thinks itself stalked—tho' watchful indeed—no, 'twas a reserve not childlike, nor mature neither, but (as it may be) *angelic,* if we think of angels as beings we cannot alarm or grieve. It would not be the last time her regard has struck me thus. 'Who are you?' quoth she, to which I at first would not give answer, but asked her of her daisy-chain, and her Doll, which sat propped before her. I cannot say she resembles me—she may, and I perceive it not in such a form—purged, as it were, of all that I see in my Glass—into which I have looked but rarely in the best of times. I know she is dark, like you—how she comes by her colour I know not, unless it is because her *mother* was not fair. Willing she was to have a conversation with me on topics of interest to her, without further inquiry as to who I was that should speak to her here; but at length—her Patience tried—she linked her hands, and struck them most definitely into her lap, and let me know that 'no-one was to come into this room but persons of the household', and I must tell her at once who I was.

'I am your father,' I said.

This took a long moment in passing through to her mind, though she seemed not astonished to find it arriving there. 'Then,' said she to me, 'you are a Mahometan.'

'Indeed I am not,' said I. 'I think it need not be true of your father—if so you meant it.'

'My father is a sort of Turk,' she said, 'and Turks are Mahometans.'

As there was no disputing her syllogism, I made no reply for some time, and she herself continued. 'I am a Mahometan,' says she. 'Why, how so?' says I. 'I am half Mahometan anyway,' says she, 'and *all* Mahometan because I say so. I have read about Mahometans and it is nothing at all to be one, but to say Allah and not God, and that is all.' So she asserted—as near as I can now recount her argument, which struck me as subtle indeed. 'However,' she continued then, 'I have told no-one, as they would not like it at all if they knew.'

'I dare say.'

'I did not know my father was like you,' she said.

Here was a new subject, and one I was prepared to treat. I asked if I alarmed her, and I had reasons to hand—even a Gift, a rich one too, to produce at need—to show her she ought not to be; but she averred she was not alarmed. And then I must ask her the question that lingered in my mind—why she was not surprised that I should have come before her here, at long last. And she said to me, 'She had that very morning beseeched Allah, as she did every morning, to bring me to her.'

3

Do you laugh? I swear that I did not—for I bethought me of those many mornings when she had prayed, and had *not* been answered. Now that I had come—however little I was whom she had expected, or *desired*—I must by some means persuade her that she must flee her present situation, and go on in *my company*—a fellow of no seeming promise. Though her regard was indeed cool, and she did not embrace me—nor would I have expected she should—still I sensed the possibility of a *Pact* between us, if I but played my own part right. And, Brother, I falter'd! I have, you may believe, a clear consciousness of my own nature—of the Crimes and Passions that are entangled in it—yet never before had I felt what I then felt, which was *unworthy*—as though my taking her hand, or winning her Favour, would stain her with that History, of which she was herself entirely innocent—the only thing I have ever touch'd, that *was* or *might remain* so! She gazed upon me—so that I forgot the enticements and suchlike that I had thought to put before her—lies, and pretences, that I thought necessary—and wished only to ask her Forgiveness—though for *what,* if not for her plain existence, of which I was the Author, I by no means knew!

By an act of will I became *myself* again—if indeed that is who this black fellow is—but too late—for just as I had made it clear to the child that I wished her to come away with me—that I would bring her straightaway again to those who loved and cared for her—and that the Doctor in whose keeping she now was, was an evil Fairy King, from whom she must with my aid escape—of a sudden the Door flew open, and the man himself whom I had just done characterizing, stood upon the threshold! I knew him by report, and also by the great authority that radiated from him—from his electrified white hair, his glittering Spectacles, and the largest hands I have ever seen on a *gentleman,* if indeed he was such. I rose to face him, prepared to tell him a Tale he might believe, or—failing that—to knock him down, when of a sudden Una too rose, and interposed herself between us.

'See, Doctor dearest,' cries she, in all innocence, 'here is my Father, come to take me away with him!'

You may imagine the good Doctor's response to this observation. Approaching me as a Boxer might a slighter but an unknown opponent, he held his great hands apart and at the ready, and turned with care to face me. 'Who are you, and what do you do in this house?' he asked of me, in a voice low and yet unmistakable in its Command.

'It is as the child has said,' I replied, as ready as he for a contest. 'I am her father; she will come away with me.'

'To prison?' he said, with a viperish hatred. 'It is where *you* are bound. You are in Trespass, Sir, upon my property.'

'Stand aside,' I said. 'We will be gone.'

Then a change came over his features, as though he quickly changed one mask for another, and he held out a hand to Una—'Come close, Child,' whispered he. 'He shall not harm thee. Come, come and stand by me.' With a strange reluctance, and yet with eyes fixed upon his, she did so—and when she had approached near enough, he moved his hands about her head, all the while gazing into her eyes, as though piercing into her Soul with an awl! In a breath, she had grown entirely still—her eyes lost their light, tho' they closed not—her arms lifted somewhat from her sides, but will-lessly, as though she floated in water. Now and *only* now, Brother, did fear come upon me—for you know I have seen such things done, and *worse*—I have myself directed the Will-less—and here stood one able to steal a Soul, it seemed, and make it his!

Yet I was not without weapons—crude tho' they were—and produced a decidedly *un*spiritual Pistol from within my clothes, and cock'd the hammer. At that the Magician—for such he was—back'd away. I demanded he release Una's spirit—reverse the charm he had placed upon her—but he only back'd further from me—out the door and to the Passage beyond. 'Touch her not, on your life,' said he to me. 'If *you* wake her she will die upon the instant. Kill me, and she will never wake. The house is raised. You have no escape!' With that he turned, and fled along the hall, crying *Help, help!* in a loud voice, and I heard voices and hollas from below.

There we were then, my Brother, she and I—she frozen in a Dream, and I unwilling and unable to desert her. I admit my powers had come to an end, and I knew not whither to turn. What happened in the next moment was, of all things I might have projected—were I able to project anything—the last. For no sooner had the Doctor turned and run away than the pixie beside me awoke—no, not so, for she had never been asleep!—she *ceased her play,* became in less than an instant a human child again, and with a mighty motion slammed shut the Door—which upon our side had its key in the lock—the which she turned, took out, and held up to me in triumph! Then without ado she went to the window of the room, and flung up the sash—it happened that we were upon the second storey—and only then did she speak to me. 'Can you climb well?' she asked me.

'Like a monkey,' said I.

'I too,' said she, 'tho' *they* mayn't know it.' She and I look'd then together out the window—where thick Vines clung to the ancient stone, and sharp Cornices extended a foothold, as from a rocky cliff—and a Trellis of climbing flowers afforded a ladder. 'I shall go first,' said my fellow Conspirator, 'and you follow after.'—'Nay,' said I, 'for if I go first, and I fall, *you* will fall on *me*—which is better than the other choice.' At this she nodded solemnly, seeing my reasoning, and I climbed out the window, upon the strong branches, a Romeo in reverse, and took her small body in my arms to help her out. There will be much I may forget, of all that I have done in all the years of my life—much that, if Providence be kind, I *shall* forget—but not that, that she leapt so bravely from the place of her confinement into my arms—*my arms!*—that never held such a Prize before—indeed, never before a prize at all!

The questions *you* may now ask—whether she *ever* truly sleep-walked and sleep-spoke at the Doctor's command, or only play'd the Part—how she had come to learn to *prophesy* as she did, if she did—how the Doctor had found her at the first, and how carried her off—to none of these have I an answer as yet, for we only fled as fast as we could without arousing undue attention, to the Docks, where at Wapping I had Confederates, at work finding us passage away, with all necessary for a journey in *one* direction only. Through all this—flight with a strange man, the prospect of a Sea-journey, forsaking all she had known, the vanishing of my promises to take her home—she was as cool as any *desperado,* with the *noblesse* of a fairy queen. When I myself took note of my pledge to return her to her Relations, she dismissed the idea—they were the *last* people in whose care she desired to be—we Mahometans ought to *stick together*—so she imply'd.

So there she sleeps, in her berth upon Thames' bosom—all her inheritance (to date) kept in a leathern Satchel, beneath my feet—for servants a *Bear,* and a Nurse I thought to engage, whom we may put ashore with the pilot's boat at Greenwich, as Una thinks her superfluous. For me, my 'occupation's gone'—I must learn another, suited to the lands to which I go. I cannot liberate a World, or free from bondage a People—these *ambitions* I here renounce, and my title to them I pass to you—they are all the bequest I make you. But do not fear—we are Friends now, and so nothing can harm you. 4

Where may you seek us, should you ever desire to? When I was a Seaman, and had conversation with men of all lands, I knew a German pilot who, if not in *Drink,* was a *raconteur* in his own tongue—whereby I learn'd a word or two—and it seem'd to me a fine thing, that he would name the Indies, toward which we sail'd, by the term *Abendland,* which is Evening Land—there where the Sun goes at end of 5 day—yet it was not Poetic in him, but meant only the plain West we name in our tongue. We shall proceed, then, to the Evening Land—the last remnant of our house—myself— the Bear, grown hoary (tho' you mayn't have known it, your black Bear can grow grey, even as his Ward)—and *she*—the daughter of a Cripple and a Madwoman, and yet herself as sound and as *sane* as a gold dollar. *She* I was able to liberate, and carry to freedom—whatever Freedom may mean—*self-government* is to be a part of it—of *that* I have evidence already. She is the heiress of the Sanes—the only there will ever be—tho' she dwell where her Nobility means nothing, and will mean nothing to her, nor to her own Descendants—if she have any—the which I intend to assure her she *may*—if so she chuse. Already I know that what *I* chuse for her, and what *direction* I give, will not be as law to her, however I may regard the matter—and this too is the legacy of the Sanes, is it not? And one that, unlike her *Title,* she may pass on to the latest generation—may they profit by it.

We are bound first for Charleston Bay, and whither thence? I am sorry I shall not be able to view General Washington, who lies asleep now with the world's true heroes—'Washington was killed in a duel with Burke,' I once heard one say at a *conversazione* in Venice, and could not think what, in the name of folly, the fellow meant by saying it—until I remembered *Burr,* who slew Hamilton and not the greater man—no matter—I am myself just as ignorant of that country in many ways, an ignorance I *delight in,* for I have done with the world I am *not* ignorant of. Perhaps we shall go down the Mississippi, as Lord Edward Fitzgerald did—the only *pure* hero I have ever known, or known of—and like him look even farther, past the gulph of Mexico, to Darien, the Brazils, the Orinoco—I know not.

And so farewell. I am not so foolish as to think America is a *Physician,* or a *Priest*—I know that all diseases are not cured there, nor all sins forgiven. And yet on this morning I feel as one who has nightlong in a dream struggled with an enemy, and has waked at last, to find his arms are empty.—ÆNGUS

———————————

There was no more. Ali, who had read this missive as he stood upon the great stone bridge over the river named ——, in the ancient city of ——, Capital of the nation of ——, now tore and cast it upon the waves, and chin in hand he watched the remnants float a time, and then sink away.—You see that I do not name the place, for it may be that this Manuscript of the tale of his adventures will come to light, in not too long a time, and therefore to reveal these things would endanger my Hero—engaged upon the work he has

been given—which, if it was at first to *tear down,* in his own conception no longer was—he had hopes, tho' they were *only* hopes, that
by his actions the Lucifers might one day contrive to unbind
Prometheus—their old *foregoer*—the Brother of that cloven-hooved
naysayer, their Namesake—and bring a new, and a better, Dispen-
sation, tho' it take a hundred years. Not he—not Una—but perhaps *her* child, and a child of *mine own* child, might live to look upon
that world. Such is my hope—you may open my heart, and see it
graven there, if you would, the only thing *not vain* that there remains.

But I have drawn my pen across that foolish paragraph—or   6
certainly soon shall—signifying that it must form no part of the
tale, nor see printer's ink. Yet 'tis just as foolish to suppose that *any*
of this tale, of Ængus and Ali, of Iman and Susanna, Catherine and
Una, will ever be set in type, or fall beneath the gaze of readers.
Whatever Poets say of outlasting 'marble and the gilded monuments of Princes', it is all but paper, and has its enemies—the sea,
fire, chance, malice, and I know not what. These pages may be lost,
or may survive only to furnish a Grocer the means of wrapping a
parcel—as we read that the MS of Richardson's *Pamela* was used, to
wrap up a rasher of Bacon for a Gypsy later proved to be a mur-
deress. Well—'twould be enough—Solomon promises no more to
all our efforts. Yet if thus these sheets must be used, kind Grocer, let
it not be for greasy bacon—wrap Eve's red apple in them, or a   7
golden plum, or any sweet fruit, and put it into a young Maid's
hands!

NOTES FOR THE LAST CHAPTER

1. *Mesmer, Puységur, Combe, & Spurzheim:*   This miscellanæum is as
    random as a quack Doctor's ought to be. Anton Mesmer is of
    course the developer of the now-exploded theory of Animal
    Magnetism; Armand Puységur his follower; George Combe,
    the modern developer of Phrenology; Johann Casper
    Spurzheim, the phrenological doctor who examined my father
    (see above, what Chapter I know not, I cannot seek it now).

2. *a Steam-engine:*   Captain Trelawney says that Ld. B. was indeed
    once solicited to invest in a flying-machine with a steam-engine,
    and did not. Even now such a thing may not be possible. I
    thought once when a child

3. *beseeched Allah:*   I missed his love, and more, his governance—
    but not only for myself—the love and governance he could
    have given to his wife, if he had chosen. They smashed some-
    thing that would surely have broken by itself soon or late. And
    yet that thing was mine, too, and not theirs alone—they had
    not all rights in it

4. *Friends:* Lord Byron had a curious superstition, that if he had quarrelled with anyone he cared for, that person was in danger somehow, or in harm's way, till the quarrel was made up, and they were friends again.

5. *Evening Land:* There is always a West into which the heroes of the older age may go. Just beneath this word, in the small dictionary that I have, is another, *Abentreuer,* which means generally an Adventure, but is more exactly or loosely a journey West. Where dawn comes, of course, as everywhere. No end to the West till those who journey thence come round again at the last.

6. *drawn my pen across:* The paragraph is not struck out, nor of course was meant to be—though whether it will see ink another age will know.

A strange thought now occurs. Might it not have been the case, that this MS was not taken from Ld. B. nor lost or misplaced by him—but was *bestowed* by him upon one whom he had reason to believe would preserve it—and its message of Liberty. Could he have guessed that it might thus come to England that his daughter being *his* daughter might grow up to love liberty as he had wd befriend those Italians in London and thus acquire that which he had attempted thus to transmit to her no no I rave here why did he not send to me his thoughts a letter to tell me there wd have been a way never now I wd give all this tale for it

7. *apple:* The pages have not met so mean a fate as that yet they have indeed their 'enemies'—they will not themselves survive to be found. Some of the sheets must have been infused with salts of copper, or other fulminates, in their manufacture—they burned blue and green Lights are said to burn low and blue when ghosts are by. The words turned white

upon a black page then gone. I would not watch all.　One sheet only I have saved—William could not refuse me one at least to keep

I had a last thing to say to all who read this　I cannot say it.
Finis

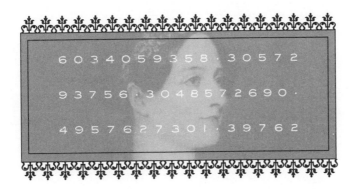

6 0 3 4 0 5 9 3 5 8 · 3 0 5 7 2

9 3 7 5 6 · 3 0 4 8 5 7 2 6 9 0 ·

4 9 5 7 6 2 7 3 0 1 · 3 9 7 6 2

From: "Smith" <anovak@strongwomanstory.org>
To: lnovak@metrognome.net.au
Subject: Oscar etc.

Lee:

Congrats about the Oscar nomination for the East Timor film. Are you going to take a chance on coming to the US in case you get it? I'll buy you lunch if you come by way of Boston, and I promise not to lure you into a trap.

S

PS The book's due out in six months—a little more maybe. Would you have any interest in writing an introduction?

From: lnovak@metrognome.net.au
To: "Smith" <anovak@strongwomanstory.org>
Subject: RE:Oscar etc.

No, not coming. It's a long shot to say the least. And my tuxedo no longer fits. And no I will not write an introduction to the published book; my credentials are a little old, Alexandra, by now, and anyway wouldn't it look a little funny? And no, I don't know anyone you might ask—that is to say, I know some names, but they are all from a long time ago, and I don't even know which are alive and which are dead. Harold Bloom? A wise man; I met him once or twice . . . I see that lately there have been a couple of what seem to me rather invidious new biographies of Byron by women, who have some very definite ideas about what Byron was up to; it would be nice (anyway *I* think it would be nice) to have this piece of his introduced by someone who likes him. But never mind all of that anyway: the only person who can, or must, or ought to, write any kind of introduction is you. Ada's written hers; it's your turn.

I'm going back to East Timor in another couple of weeks. There are people there who need to know the news about how the film has been received—it counts as security for them, or at least I hope it does—the whole world is watching, at least on Oscar night, except the doc awards are when people get up and go for beer.

Then the new project—I'm going to New Guinea for some months. It's a place I've been reading about and talking to people about for years, and some money has come through at last. I have bad dreams about it, too, or at least unsettling ones. Anyway I'll be way out of touch, probably, for some months, though I guess now there's nowhere on earth that's out of touch. If I can find a phone I can send a letter. Probably. I'll be back in Tokyo again then for the editing and postproduction as they call it, which is going to take longer than the shooting. I don't know what your plans are. I'm just letting you know. Now that I've caught you in the Web (or wasn't it rather you who caught me?) I will sit down beside you, and hope I don't frighten you away.

I love you, Alexandra, even more than I knew. I don't—I wouldn't dare—hold you to the standard that Byron set, that you must love me for my crimes if you are to love me for myself; I hold you to no standard. I wish only that I could sign this differently, with a title—an honorific—not just a name. But I know I haven't earned that, and probably never will; and so I am—

Yours ever

Lee

PS: I note that there's a Byron conference being held in Kyoto—beautiful city—in the spring of 2004. Good place for a launch?

———————

From: "Smith" <anovak@strongwomanstory.org>
To: "Thea" <thea.spann133@ggm.edu>
Subject: FWD:Congratulations

Thea—
Look what I got in the old in-box this morning. When I tried to reply, I got the Mailer Daemon: No such address at AOL. He's not on the Web either, but we already knew that, and we also knew that it's not his name anyway.

> *From: "RoonyJ" <roonyjwelch@aol.com>*
> *To: "Smith" <anovak@strongwomanstory.org>*
> *Subject: Congratulations*

> *Ms. Novak—*

> *I see by the noise in the press and the literary sites that a lost novel of Byron's, or part of one, is to see print soon. I wanted to congratulate you, and tell you how pleased I am, that you and your associates (?) discovered the secret of* The Evening Land *and Ada's devotion. It is indeed a remarkable tale. I am also thrilled and not a little awestruck that you have, apparently, overcome any doubts you might (must?) have felt as to the authenticity of the book, its provenance, etc. I only assume you have gone through the rigmarole of having the paper carbon-dated and the ink chemically analyzed etc. so that doubters may be confounded. The* lingering *doubts—e.g., how easy it would be to fill pages of old printed forms (found by chance, say, and blank) with numbers (so much easier to forge than a*

whole cursive handwriting)—these will be overcome by the overwhelming "internal evidence" that the work is by Byron, and that it is the work that Ada destroyed—I mean, did not destroy. And as no one in any case has any reason to forge a document that is then practically given away, no real questions can afterward remain.

I am of course mad with eagerness to read the whole in your transcription. From what I hear, or read, about its contents, it would seem that the book does put the old Cloven Hoof in a new and flattering, or at least not hellish, light. I couldn't be more pleased. I have always believed that when I reach Paradise—and I am sure of my election, Ms. Novak, as I am of his—I will be able to prove to myself that he was the man I even now know him to have been— a flawed and inconsistent but ultimately a great-natured and good and endlessly, wisely entertaining man. And I shall sit on my cloud or my flowery mead, and listen to his talk, and be very, very happy. Until then (not, it would ap- pear, too long a time from now) I will have The Evening Land.

Yours

"Roony J. Welch"

Wow, huh? I felt this rush of shit to the heart at first to read this, but now—I don't know. Not anymore.

Smith

────────────

From: "Thea" <thea.spann133@ggm.edu>
To: "Smith" <anovak@strongwomanstory.org>
Subject: RE:FWD:Congratulations

wow   this is the guy who started it all   sinister   very   makes
you wonder   what if   yeah its sort of like ada   when she was
wondering if she enciphered it all wrong   wrong numbers but
then got a book anyway   this book   that wd be a coincidence that
wd make anything babbage programmed into his engine look like
nothing

well i am deciding we are good here   mr welch can go back to
hell   or where he came from

babe   heres whats important

ily

lol

and btw whats for dinner

t

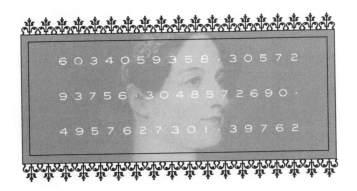

INTRODUCTION

Alexandra Novak

In the winter of 2002, I was invited to London to research the lives and work of a number of British women of science, including Mary Somerville and her younger friend Ada Lovelace, for an online virtual museum of women of science (www .strongwomanstory.org). In the course of that research I was privileged to make, or to be part of making, a number of discoveries. Some were of no interest to anybody but me, but one is of very general interest, and it is here presented as fully as possible—which is perhaps not as fully as it might be in future. The story that follows must, in other words, remain tentative, and the reader is asked to suspend disbelief for the present, as a novel or a romance asks us to do, and only attend.

Ada Augusta King, Countess of Lovelace, Lord Byron's only legitimate child, traveled to Nottinghamshire in September of 1850 to visit the ancestral seat of the Byrons, Newstead Abbey—which Lord Byron had sold years before, and which was then in the possession of a Colonel Wildman, an old schoolmate of Byron's. Returning south, Lady Lovelace and her husband went to the races at Doncaster: they were both, as it was then said, devotees of the turf. Ada backed Voltigeur, which won an upset over the favorite, Flying

Dutchman. The win didn't come close to canceling Ada's racing debts, which she kept secret from her husband. In May of 1851, the Crystal Palace exhibition opened in London; in August of that year, Ada was told that the illness she had been for some time suffering from was serious, indeed fatal—it was cancer of the cervix, for which there was then no treatment. Sometime in that autumn (Ada was careless in dating her letters) she mentioned to her mother, Lady Byron, that she was at work on "certain productions" involving music and mathematics. In November of 1852, after much suffering, she died of cancer; she was then thirty-six years old (her father died in the same year of his life). Between the date of her visit to Newstead Abbey and her death she acquired, transcribed, annotated, enciphered, and destroyed—at her mother's request or order—the manuscript of the only extensive piece of prose fiction ever written by her father.

The story of the rediscovery of Ada's enciphered manuscript after 150 years, its acquisition by the Hon. Miss Georgiana Poole-Hatton, its deciphering and authentication, is told in as great detail as is presently possible in the Textual History and Description which follows this Introduction. Of course it is still possible that what is presented here as the work of Lord Byron, annotated by Ada Lovelace, is not that at all. It might be that Ada herself wrote the novel as well as the notes; that someone else wrote the novel and sold it to her (or to those who then sold it to her) as Byron's; that both the novel and the annotations are forgeries, dating from sometime between Byron's or Ada's time and now. All that can have been done to eliminate these possibilities has been done. Tests indicate (though they can't prove) that the ink and paper date from before the middle of the nineteenth century; internal evidence in the novel does not point toward a date later than Byron's death, nor a date later than Ada's in the notes. The handwriting in the notes is demonstrably Ada's, though it differs in certain ways from other writings of around the same period, perhaps because of her hurry, or because of the effects of the drugs she was taking almost continuously in ever larger amounts. For reasons explained in the Textual History, it is not possible at this time to trace the physical

provenance of the manuscripts or the trunk in which they were al-
legedly found. For the moment each reader must decide for herself
whether she is indeed in contact with these two persons, the poet
and his daughter, and hearing their voices in these writings. I think
I do hear them; I can't imagine that they could be anything but
what they seem to be.

If the novel is what it purports to be, then where was it before
Ada got it, and who acquired it for her? In her own introduction to
the manuscript of the novel (pages 46–62 of the present book), Ada
states that she arranged to see the man who had the manuscript, an
Italian who had acquired it from another who had acquired (or perhaps stolen) it in Italy, when she visited the Crystal Palace. I thought
at first that the man who accompanied Ada on that visit must have
been Charles Babbage; it was just the kind of thing that Babbage was
forever doing for her. He did show her around the site of the Great
Exhibition as it was being constructed; but Babbage had had a public controversy with the planners and been entirely excluded from
all the planning for the Crystal Palace exhibition; his famed Difference Engine wasn't displayed there. It seemed unlikely that he
would have been eager to go there with her. So who was the go-
between, who negotiated with the Italians, who then later went to
get the manuscript? It seemed impossible to know, until I came upon
an undated note from Ada to Fortunato Prandi, who was one of
those in the émigré Italian circle she and Babbage knew—something
between a radical activist, a spy, and an agent, maybe a double one.
Here is the note, which is in the Carl H. Pforzheimer Collection at
the New York Public Library.

> *Dear Prandi. I have a more* important *service to ask of you, which
> only you can perform . . . I can* in writing *explain nothing but that
> you must* come to me at 6 o'clock*, and be prepared to be at my
> disposal till midnight. You must be* nicely *yet not* too showily
> dressed. You may have occasion for both activity & presence of mind.
> Nothing but* urgent *necessity would induce me thus to apply to
> you;—but you may be the means of* salvation. *I will not sign. I am
> the lady you went with to hear* Jenny Lind. *I expect you at 6.—*

"A more important service" implies a previous service, which might have been the visit to the Crystal Palace and the glimpse of the man with the gold earring; the present service would then be the actual acquisition of the MS. This is all merely speculative. It certainly seems that something conspiratorial was afoot, but in those years Ada worked up a lot of plots and entanglements. There is much further exploring to do among the Italians in London, and in Ada's papers, and in Babbage's too. There are for instance the several mentions in the Babbage/Ada correspondence of a "book," not further described, that must be passed back and forth between the two of them at intervals, with care taken over its delivery, etc. When I found these I wondered if I had actually caught Byron's novel in transit, so to speak. A recent biographer of Ada* suggests that the "book" may rather have been the betting book Ada was keeping: she had become consumed by horse racing, and ended by selling her family jewels to pay her gambling debts—and then re-selling them again after they had been redeemed by her baffled and compassionate husband. (So the story has always run: and yet now we have to wonder if those family jewels weren't also the source of the money Ada needed to buy *The Evening Land* from its posses-sors.) In any case the mentions of this book predate the opening of the Crystal Palace and therefore the period in which the book of Byron's was acquired.

What is certain is that it was from Babbage that Ada learned about codes, ciphers, and enciphering. The cipher Ada used for en-ciphering Lord Byron's novel is a variant of the Vigenère cipher, a cipher known since the sixteenth century, which a contemporary of Babbage's rediscovered without knowing it had long been used though never cracked. When Babbage pointed this out to him, he challenged Babbage to solve a text he encoded with it. Babbage was able to break the cipher, but he never published his solution. He also designed a wheel, like a circular slide rule, that made it easier to set up a cipher and then read off the substituted letters; maybe Ada had one, and used it for *The Evening Land*. Babbage looms over,

---

*Benjamin Woolley, *The Bride of Science* (1999).

or lingers behind, the story of Ada like a stage manager or trickster, or like one of the busy mechanical people he loved to show off, whose motives are unreadable, maybe nonexistent, and whose powers are unguessable. In the end (of the story, or of our ability to understand it) he merely bows, and draws his curtain.

Ada, as noted, was very lax about dating her letters, and there are no dates given in her annotations of Byron's manuscript, and none on the single note to Francisco Prandi. But it seems to be just before the manuscript came into her possession that Ada's relations with her mother took a new turn. Her biographers trace this change to her visit to Newstead Abbey, her father's former estate, which somehow awakened her feelings for her father and her Byron ancestors. "I have had a resurrection," she wrote a little incautiously to her mother. "I do love the venerable old place & all my *wicked forefathers*!" It's hard to know what would have happened to this manuscript if Ada had discovered it earlier—if she had found no reason in her own heart to protect it. Clearly her mother (like Snow White's) wouldn't have allowed it to exist within her kingdom.

But she did preserve it. Whether she perceived that her mother would eventually find it, either among her papers when she died or as she worked over it to make a fair copy; or if she only set about enciphering it after Lady Byron discovered it, and before she agreed to destroy it, can't be known. The labor of recasting the whole fifty-thousand-plus words of the manuscript into her cipher was so huge that it must have taken her months. My sense is that it wasn't long after Lady Byron discovered its existence that it was given up to be burned, and that Ada knew it would be, and by that time she was ready, with a pile of "mathematical and musical work" in her desk that no one would inquire about.

In that month she summoned her husband to her, and made him promise that she would be buried beside her father in the Byron family vault at Hucknall Torkard church, where she had seen and touched his casket on her journey to Nottingham in 1850. It had been her secret that she had decided even then to be buried there. She chose an epitaph too, that she told her husband she wanted put on her own casket. It was from the Bible, in which she had evinced so little interest during most of her life. It comes from the Epistle of James: *You have condemned, you have killed the righteous man; he does not resist you.* The first meaning of this remarkable choice is so obvious—she believed her father (whose remains would be lying next to her own) was a righteous man, unjustly condemned and exiled by the society around him—that it seems we discover its second meaning for ourselves: that Ada, though herself dying, would no longer resist those who condemned her. She ceased altogether to resist her mother; she wrote out, at her mother's instruction, pledges of affection for her mother's friends, including those she had called the Furies, who had so willingly constrained and punished her when she was a child. She agreed that her mother should have control over all her papers. She confessed her "errors," and confessed them again. She jettisoned her life.

At some time in these months—the note describing it has no date—she wrote to her mother to say that the manuscript of her father's novel had been burned. (A transcription of this letter can be found in the Appendix.) I can find no documentary evidence of Ada's informing her that the manuscript existed, or that she had acquired it, but the papers of the Lovelace family are so extensive that it might still turn up, not having been understood for what it is. I have found no document in her mother's hand expressing a desire, or an order, that the MS be burned. But it certainly was her wish, if Ada is to be believed.

So all was done. She had surrendered to her mother as to death. And yet still she didn't die: throughout that autumn she lingered, unwilling or unable to go. Meanwhile her mother prayed with her, and discussed her "errors" with her (she wrote to her Christian correspondents how gratifying it was that Ada saw them and confessed them): these no doubt included her gambling, her pawning of the family jewels, and her single adultery, but it's likely they also included all the irreligious and skeptical things she'd *thought.* She lived in a kind of twilight, scribbling notes only her mother could read, terrified that she would be buried alive, asking over and over who stood at the door, who stood at the end of the bed, when no one was there. Charles Dickens really did come to visit her, at her request (they had been friends for years) and read to her from *Dombey & Son,* the scene where little Paul Dombey, dying, sees a vision of his mother come to stand at the end of his bed. When Babbage came to visit her, Lady Byron turned him away.

In October Ada's son Byron, now Viscount Ockham, whom she had above all wanted near her, had been sent away by Lady Byron, because in what Lady Byron called "this state of suspense" he might "receive injurious impressions." Now he was brought back, for one last visit before returning to his naval duties and his ship at Plymouth. It was decided—by Lady Byron—that the boy should not bid a final farewell to his mother, as she would not be able to bear it; he only went to the door of her room, and looked inside a last time. It's uncertain whether she knew he was there.

But Ockham didn't return to his ship. He packed his midshipman's uniform in a carpetbag, and sent it home to his father. Then he disappeared. Lord Lovelace, distraught, called the police and hired a detective. This is the description of Ockham he ran in the London *Times,* with an offer of a reward for the boy's discovery:

> *nearly 17 years of age, 5 foot 6 inches high, broad-shouldered, well-knit active frame, slouching seaman-like gait, sunburnt complexion, dark expressive eyes and eyebrows, thick black wavy hair, hands long and slightly tattooed with a red cross and other small black marks . . .*

This description, including those dark, expressive eyes that somehow seem to have come from his grandfather and namesake, was circulated at the principal ports of embarkation for America—Bristol and Liverpool—as though Lord Lovelace had reason to think his son would be found there, and he was—at an inn in Liverpool, where he was living with "common Sailors" and trying to get a passage to America. He didn't resist the detective who found him, and came home again.

This much of Ockham's story has been known for some time. Some of Lady Byron's connections and relatives found it shockingly hard-hearted of young Byron to cause this grief to his family at just this moment. What has not before been known was that at some time during his stay there—possibly when he guessed he would be caught—he put into a Liverpool bank vault the chest containing his seaman's papers, some letters and other personal mementos, and the enciphered novel and the notes for it which his mother had committed to him. How clear it must have been to her—for she had her moments of clarity, those awful and pitiless and wondrous moments that do light up final illnesses, as anyone who has witnessed one knows—that he would try his best to preserve it. Did she want *him* to escape, as well? What was it she told him—to go straight from her house and her room, where she lay dying, away from everything, and to America?

He never did. He was put back into the Navy. He eventually won a discharge, or deserted, it's unclear what happened. After more unhappy years—at home under Lady Byron's care, then under the direction of the famed Victorian schoolmaster Thomas Arnold—he ran away again, and this time wasn't pursued; he worked as a coal miner and then as a laborer in a shipyard, living under the name of Jack Okey. He died in 1862 of consumption, aged twenty-six. The dead can't learn or change, but the one thing I would like Lord Byron to hear, the story I would most like to get a letter from him about, is the strange and sad story of his grandson, who wanted not to be a lord.

What follows then, I believe, is the result of a triple honoring. I want to say, of a triple love—the love of a father for his daughter, a daughter for her father, a son for his mother—but I can't see into hearts long dead, and one of those involved left no record at all.

IN JUNE 1816, IN Switzerland, as he began the novel he would at some point call *The Evening Land,* Byron completed canto 3 of *Childe Harold's Pilgrimage.* In the last stanzas he spoke directly to his faraway daughter—while knowing of course that his wife, and the whole reading world, were listening in. "The child of love, though born in bitterness," he calls her. "Yet, though dull Hate as duty should be taught / I know that thou wilt love me . . ." Perhaps he did know this; certainly he seemed to know he would never see her again:

> *I see thee not,—I hear thee not,—but none*
> *Can be so wrapt in thee; thou art the friend*
> *To whom the shadows of far years extend:*
> *Albeit my brow thou never should'st behold,*
> *My voice shall with thy future visions blend,*
> *And reach into thy heart,—when mine is cold,—*
> *A token and a tone, even from thy father's mould.*

And so it did; his voice did reach into her heart. Lord Byron also never got to America, nor did he ever return to England; Ada never went abroad to see him—as she might have today, if her father could have been properly treated for his illnesses, if her mother had not retained a lifelong horror of her husband, if the world then had been more like the world now, if things weren't as they are and were. But his voice reached into her heart, as it would have done, I believe, whether or not she had ever found the novel that here follows.

ACKNOWLEDGMENTS TO ALL those scholars and investigators who helped to authenticate and account for the manuscript of *The Evening Land* may be found following the Textual History. I would myself like to express here my own debt to two people for their help to me in solving the puzzle of *The Evening Land* and its fate: Dr. Lee Novak, for his editing of the deciphered manuscript, for his annotations of Ada's annotations, but much more for his many insights and his encouragement; and Dr. Thea Spann, whose cunning and constancy were both indispensable, and whom I can't find words to thank.

Kyoto
June 10, 2003

THE AUTHOR WOULD LIKE to acknowledge those who aided him in the foregoing piece of impertinence, among whom are Ralph Vicinanza, Jennifer Brehl, L.S.B., Ted Chiang for thoughts about codes, Mary Irwin for French perhaps more correct than Byron's, Benjamin Woolley for *The Bride of Science* (his biography of Ada, Countess of Lovelace), Doron Suede for *The Difference Engine,* and above all Paul Fry for his meticulous and sympathetic reading. The great dead need no acknowledgment from me.